Praise for Airborn

'Kenneth Oppel's *Airborn* . . . a terrific, rollicking adventure set in a Victorian world traversed by airships . . . Matt is a lovely hero – fearless, smart, irreverent, sunny and agile as the young Indiana Jones . . . *Airborn* bounces along, filled with irresistible optimism and a zest that makes you hope for a sequel.' *The Times*

'This is gripping stuff.' *The Bookseller*

'Brilliantly done . . . *Airborn*'s contained world is totally absorbing, cleverly plotted, a terrific read.' *The Irish Times*

'A tightly plotted, fast-paced adventure with engaging and humorous characters.' *Times Educational Supplement*

'*Airborn* is a satisfying rip-roaring adventure . . . Oppel writes with clarity and passion, particularly in his descriptions of the natural world and the world in the sky, and the plot fairly zips along, but there is also a reflective quality to his writing, and he is not afraid to tackle the issue of death . . . If you liked *Mortal Engines* and Harry Potter, this is for you!' *BooktrustedNews*

'In crisp, precise prose that gracefully conveys a wealth of detail, Oppel imagines an alternate past where zeppelins crowd the skies . . . The author's inviting new world will stoke readers' imaginations.' *Publishers Weekly*

Also by Kenneth Oppel:

Silverwing
Sunwing
Firewing
Dead Water Zone

and coming soon, the sequel to *Airborn*:

Skybreaker

AIRBORN

KENNETH OPPEL

Hodder
Children's
Books

A division of Hodder Headline Limited

A Catalogue record for this book is available from the British Library

ISBN 0 340 87856 8

Typeset in Bembo by Avon DataSet Ltd,
Bidford-on-Avon, Warwickshire

Printed and bound in Great Britain by
Clays Ltd, St Ives PLC, Bungay, Suffolk

The paper and board used in this paperback by Hodder Children's Books
are natural recyclable products made from wood grown in sustainable
forests. The manufacturing processes conform to the environmental
regulations of the country of origin.

Hodder Children's Books
a division of Hodder Headline Limited
338 Euston Road
London NW1 3BH

To Philippa, Sophia and Nathaniel

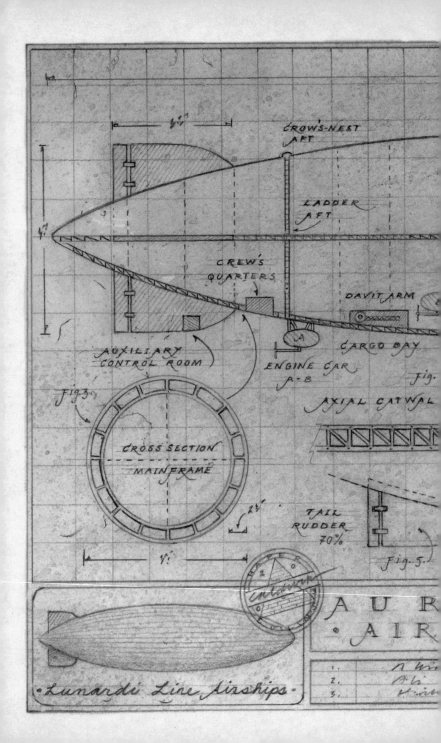

CROW'S-NEST
AFT

LADDER
AFT

CREW'S
QUARTERS

DAVIT ARM

AUXILIARY
CONTROL ROOM

ENGINE CAR
A-B

CARGO BAY

Fig.

Fig 3

CROSS SECTION

MAINFRAME

AXIAL CATWAL

23"

V"

TAIL
RUDDER
70%

Fig. 5.

A U R

A I R

·Lunardi Line Airships·

1.	A li
2.	B li
3.	li

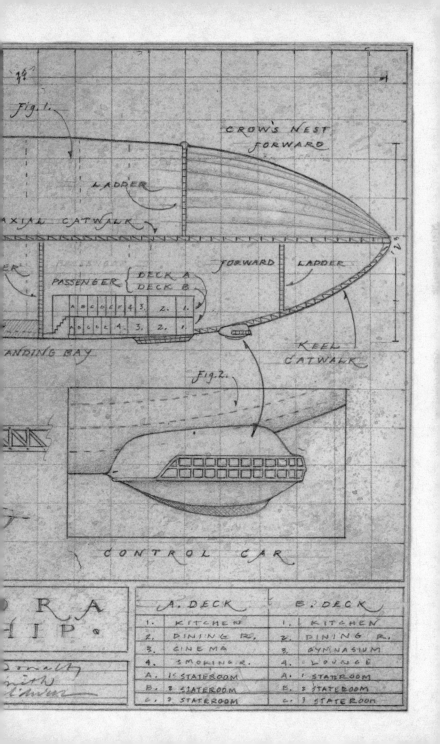

Fig. 1.

CROW'S NEST
FORWARD

LADDER

AXIAL CATWALK

PASSENGER { DECK A
             DECK B

FORWARD   LADDER

| A | B | C | D | E | F | 4 | 3. | 2. | 1. |
| A | B | C | D | E | F | 4. | 3. | 2. | 1. |

ANDING BAY

KEEL
CATWALK

Fig. 2.

CONTROL   CAR

	A. DECK	B. DECK
1.	KITCHEN	1. KITCHEN
2.	DINING R.	2. DINING R.
3.	CINEMA	3. GYMNASIUM
4.	SMOKING R.	4. LOUNGE
A.	1ˢᵗ STATEROOM	A. 1 STATEROOM
B.	2 ᶜ STATEROOM	B. 2 STATEROOM
C.	3 STATEROOM	C. 3 STATEROOM

R A
H I P.

1

SHIP'S EYES

Sailing towards dawn, and I was perched atop the crow's-nest, being the ship's eyes. We were two nights out of Sydney and there'd been no weather to speak of so far. I was keeping watch on a dark stack of nimbus off to the north-west, but we were leaving it far behind, and it looked to be smooth going all the way back to Lionsgate City. Like riding a cloud.

The sky pulsed with stars. Some people say it makes them lonesome when they stare up at the night sky. I can't imagine why. There's no shortage of company. By now there's not a constellation I can't name. Orion. Lupus. Serpens. Hercules. Draco. My father taught me all their stories. So when I look up I see a galaxy of adventures and heroes and villains, all jostling together and trying to outdo each other, and I sometimes want to tell them to hush up and not distract me with their chatter. I've glimpsed all the stars ever discovered by astronomers, and plenty that haven't been. There're the planets to look at too, depending on the time of year. Venus. Mercury, Mars. And don't forget Old Man

Moon. I know every crease and pockmark on that face of his.

My watch was almost at an end, and I was looking forward to climbing into my bunk, sliding under warm blankets and into a deep sleep. Even though it was only September, and we were crossing the equator, it was still cool at night up in the crow's-nest, parting the winds at 120 kilometres an hour. I was grateful for my fleece-lined coat.

Spyglass to my face, I slowly swept the heavens. Here at the *Aurora*'s summit, shielded by a glass observation dome, I had a three-sixty view of the sky around and above the ship. The lookout's job was to watch for weather changes, and also for other ships, especially anything suspicious. Over the Pacificus, you didn't see much traffic, though earlier I'd caught the distant flicker of a steamer, ploughing the waves towards the Orient. But boats were no concern of ours.

We sailed 300 metres above them.

The smell of fresh-baked bread wafted up to me. Far below, in the ship's kitchens, they were taking out their first loaves and rolls and cinnamon buns and croissants and Danishes. I inhaled deeply. A better smell than this I couldn't imagine, and my stomach gave a hungry twist. In a few minutes, Mr Riddihoff would be climbing the ladder to take the watch, and I could swing past the kitchen and see if the ship's baker was willing to part with a bun or two. He almost always was.

A shooting star slit the sky. That made one hundred and six I'd seen this season; I'd been keeping track. Baz and I had a little contest going, and I was in the lead by twelve stars.

Then I saw it.

Or didn't see it. Because at first, all I noticed was a blackness where stars should have been. I raised my spyglass again, and with the help of the moon, caught a glimpse.

It was a hot-air balloon, hanging there in the night sky.

Its running lights weren't on, which was odd. The balloon was higher than us by about thirty metres, and drifting off our starboard bow. The burner came on suddenly, jetting blue flame to heat the air in the balloon's envelope for a few seconds. But I couldn't see anyone at the controls. They must have been set on a clockwork timer. Nobody was moving around in the gondola. It was deep and wide, big enough for a kind of sleeping cabin on one side, and plenty of storage underneath. I couldn't ever recall seeing a balloon this far out. I lifted the speaking tube to my mouth.

'Crow's-nest reporting.'

I waited a moment as my voice hurtled down through the tube, fifty metres to the control car suspended from the *Aurora*'s belly.

'Go ahead, Mr Cruse.'

It was Captain Walken on watch tonight, and I was glad, for I much preferred him to the other officers.

Some of them just called me 'Cruse' or 'boy', figuring I wasn't worth a mister on account of my age. But never the captain. To him I was always Mr Cruse, and it got so that I'd almost started to think of myself as a mister. Whenever I was back home in Lionsgate City on shore leave, and my mother or sisters called me Matt, my own name sounded strange to me for the first few days.

'Hot-air balloon at one o'clock, maybe a kilometre off, thirty metres up.'

'Thank you, Mr Cruse.' There was a pause, and I knew the captain would be looking out the enormous wraparound windows of the control car. Because it was set well back from the bow, its view of anything high overhead was limited. That's why there was always a watch posted in the forward crow's-nest. The *Aurora* needed a set of eyes up top.

'Yes, I see it now. Well spotted, Mr Cruse. Can you make out its markings? We'll train the light on it.'

Mounted at the front of the control car was a powerful spotlight, and now its beam cut a blazing swath through the night, and struck the balloon. It was in a sorry state, withered and puckered. It was either leaking, or maybe the burner wasn't working properly.

'The *Endurance*,' I read into the speaking tube.

She looked like she'd endured a bit too much. Maybe a storm had punctured her envelope or bashed her about some.

And still no sign of the pilot in the gondola.

Along the length of the speaking tube I heard tinny murmurings from the control car as the captain conferred with the bridge officers.

'It's not on the flight plan,' I heard Mr Torbay, the navigator, saying.

Every airship has to register its flight plan before departing. If this vessel wasn't on the plan it was either a rogue, or it had drifted off course for some reason.

'Any sign of the pilot yet, Mr Cruse?' asked the captain.

'No, sir.'

'We'll try to raise him on the wireless.'

I waited. The balloon was not really moving as the wind was so light. We were rapidly gaining. There was something eerie about it, just hanging there like a dead thing, all dark and listless in the sky. After a few moments, the captain's voice sounded over the speaking tube.

'We can't raise anyone on the *Endurance*, Mr Cruse. No signs of life?'

'None, sir.'

I felt the slightest heaviness in my heels and knew that we were climbing, the *Aurora* angling gently heavenwards to meet the *Endurance*. I lost sight of the gondola, and after a moment, could only see the balloon's very top as the captain took us closer. Through the crow's-nest platform I felt the ship's pulse slow, as the propellers cut back. When you've been aloft a long time you can almost predict the ship's every movement through your own skin and sinew, like you're joined together.

I heard the Captain shouting out of the control car window through a bull horn, '*Endurance*, this is the *Aurora*. Please respond,' again and again.

If the pilot had been asleep, this should have roused him, but after a minute with no response, the captain gave up. Through the speaking tube I overheard him talking to his rudder man.

'Come around, Mr Kahlo, we'll bring her as close as we can and try to take the gondola on board. Likely someone's injured or abandoned ship – either way the *Endurance* is in distress. We can't leave her drifting like flotsam through the sky lanes.'

Bring it on board? Now that would be a feat. A mid-air rescue would surely be tricky. But it was Skyways Law to help another vessel in distress.

I heard footsteps coming up the ladder. My watch was over and I was being relieved by Pieter Riddihoff, a third officer who was still junior enough to be expected to do crow's-nest duty.

'Cruse.'

'Mr Riddihoff.'

I filled him in on the balloon and handed over the spyglass. 'She's at three o'clock now,' I pointed. 'You can just see her top. We're coming about.'

'Pretty odd business, being over the Pacificus in nothing but a bag of hot air.'

I just shook my head. It seemed madness to be at the

mercy of the winds like that, with no means of propulsion. I hoped no one on board was hurt.

Down the ladder I went, through the webwork of alumiron beams and bracing wires that gave the *Aurora* her rigid shape. On either side of me hung the walls of one of the enormous gas cells that kept us aloft. Their fabric, a miraculous substance called goldbeater's skin, glistened and rustled ever so slightly as I passed, like something alive and breathing. Perfuming the air was the faintest fragrance of ripe mangoes – the smell of the hydrium gas inside the cells.

I dropped down on to the keel catwalk. The main thoroughfare, it ran the entire length of the ship, from the control car, the officer quarters and the luxurious passenger decks near the bow, all the way back to the cargo bays and crew quarters in the stern. Normally after my watch, I'd head back to my cabin for sleep. But I had no intention of doing so right now. I was too excited. I felt the ship turning, and knew we were coming about to try to pick up the balloon.

Mr Kahlo and two machinists were walking smartly aft towards the cargo bay, and I fell into step behind them. I wanted to see this. Besides, they might need an extra hand. The bay was stacked high with wooden crates and steamer trunks and oversized baggage, but a narrow path ran like a canyon through it all and finally opened out into a large clear area near the loading doors in the ship's hull.

There were already a number of sailmakers on the

scene, plus the first officer, Paul Rideau, talking on the ship's phone, no doubt with the captain. He caught a glimpse of me and didn't look entirely pleased. Mr Rideau was a fine pilot, so everyone said, but he wasn't a favourite with the crew, like Captain Walken. He had a long pale face and watery blue eyes and a reddish nose that made him sound plugged up, and he always looked like he was on the verge of an annoyed little sigh. You got the feeling Mr Rideau didn't much care for the crew – especially a cabin boy like me.

'Aren't you off watch, Cruse?' he asked me, knowing I was.

'Yes, sir, but requesting permission to remain, and assist if needed.'

He sighed. 'Very well, but get a harness on, and stay well back. We'll be opening the bay doors in a moment.'

Everyone else was already suited up. From a row of hooks on the wall, I took down a leather harness, and stepped into it. It fitted snugly around my legs and chest, with a long line that clipped on to a mooring ring on the wall. At a nod from Mr Rideau, two crewmen manned the bay doors. Instinctively, I spread my legs apart for balance. Once those doors were opened, the wind – even though it was a gentle one – would come galloping in and knock us about.

With a hiss, the two doors pulled in and rolled flush along the ship's hull. The wind, the drone of the engines and the pungent smell of the tropical sea poured into the bay. Below, starlight painted the ocean silver. We were closing on the balloon, the gondola hanging level with the cargo bay doors. Our engines' sounds deepened as they slowed even further.

Mr Rideau kept talking into the phone, eyes fixed on the balloon, keeping the captain abreast of our position – and the captain would in turn be instructing his helmsmen, and telegraphing instructions to the machinists in our four engine cars. He wanted to bring the *Aurora* in as close as possible without fouling the balloon's rigging in our propellers. It was lucky it was so calm, or this surely would have been impossible.

Mr Rideau hung up the phone and, with a bull horn raised to his mouth, tried to hail the balloon.

'*Endurance*, please respond. This is the airship *Aurora*. Please respond, *Endurance*!'

Nothing. Probably some of our own passengers were awake now. Most wouldn't have noticed the ship slowing and turning, but even through the soundproofed walls and windows of their cabins and staterooms, that bull horn would yank a few from their sleep.

'Damn nuisance,' Mr Rideau muttered. 'Mr Kahlo, Mr Chen. Grappling hooks.'

The two men took hold of their heaving lines, each tipped with a four-pronged grapple. The engines had all but stopped, and the *Aurora* slid slowly alongside the balloon. The gondola was directly opposite us, a good fifteen metres distant, I'd say.

'Heave!' Mr Rideau cried out, and the men, their legs wide, twisted from the waist and let fly. Their lines coiled out into the night, and both grapples hooked the rim of the gondola and held fast.

'Pull her in. Be quick about it.'

Mr Rideau always had a way of sounding sharpish. Captain Walken would have said something like, 'Let's see if we can pull her in, gentlemen. When you're ready.' He said please and thank you, always, even though he didn't need to. Orders were orders, but when they came with a please you felt a lot better following them.

The men looped their lines to the winches and started cranking. One arm hooked around a strut, Mr Rideau leaned out and gazed from side to side, checking to make sure the balloon wasn't about to get snarled up in the propellers. Then he glanced up at the balloon itself.

'Leave off!' he shouted. 'This is as close as it gets.'

I moved nearer the bay doors and saw that the balloon and the *Aurora* were very close to touching at their widest points. No one wanted a collision, even with something as soft as a balloon, for you never knew if there was something sharp that would snag or tear. Problem was, even though the balloon and the *Aurora* were almost touching at their curves, the gondola was still a good ten metres away and –

Sinking.

I hadn't noticed it at first, but now it was obvious. It wasn't the *Aurora* climbing, it was the balloon falling.

Despite the occasional flare of its automated burner, it was sinking slowly but surely, and the sea would have her if we didn't do anything.

'Keep her snug!' Mr Rideau barked at the men, and they locked their winches, trying to keep the gondola from falling further. Now that it was a little below us, I could see inside.

The pilot was sprawled on the gondola's floor.

'Look!' I cried.

Still the gondola was sinking, dropping away on us, and its big balloon coming lower with it, its fat girth falling ever closer to our propellers.

Just then Captain Walken strode in. He was the kind of man everyone felt safer being around. Just looking at him made you feel better. If he'd been wearing a velvet robe and crown, he'd be the very image of a great king; if he were in a doctor's jacket, you'd trust your life to him. But I preferred him in his blue captain's jacket with the four gold stripes on the sleeve and his cap encircled with thick gold cord. His beard and moustache were trim and he had steady, kind eyes. He was approaching sixty, with a full head of grey curly hair, and wide in the shoulders. He wasn't a particularly big man or even tall, but when he walked into the room you could almost sense everyone exhaling in relief, and thinking: There now, things will work out just fine.

The captain needed only to glance at the situation.

'Mr Rideau, would you please return to the control

car and assume my watch. I'll take over here, thank you.'

'Yes, sir,' said Mr Rideau, but I could tell he didn't much like that.

'Ready the davit, please, gentlemen,' Captain Walken said.

Centred before the bay doors was a davit, a small crane with an extendable arm that swung out and raised and lowered cargo when we were docked. The crew sprang to it.

'Let's see if she'll reach,' the captain said. 'Swing her out, please.'

Breathless, I watched, wondering if it would be long enough. I knew what the captain had in mind.

I kept looking down at the man on the gondola floor. He was deathly white in the flare of the *Aurora*'s spotlight. But then he stirred slightly, and his hand twitched.

The davit's arm slowly swung all the way out, as far as it would go.

It was still at least two metres shy of the gondola.

'Pity,' said the captain calmly. 'Bring her back in, please, gentlemen.'

I looked down and saw the water close below us. The captain had vented a little hydrium to keep us level with the balloon, but now we had gone as low as we safely could. Any nearer was foolhardy, for you never knew when a sudden gust or rogue front might clutch the ship and thrust her down into the drink.

'Well, gentlemen, we've not much time,' the captain said. 'The situation is simple, and our course of action clear. Someone's going to need to hook themselves to the end of the davit and swing across to the gondola. It's the only way to get to her before she goes down.'

He looked across at Mr Kahlo and Mr Chen, and the machinists and sailmakers, their faces grey in the starlight, none relishing the idea of careening out over the ocean.

I held my breath, hoping.

The captain stared straight at me and smiled.

'Mr Cruse, I look at you, and of all the men, you're the one who shows not the slightest hint of fear. Am I right?'

'Yes, sir. I have no fear of heights.'

'I know it, Mr Cruse.' And he did, for I'd served aboard his ship for over two years, and he'd seen the ease with which I moved about the *Aurora*, inside and out.

'Sir,' said Mr Chen, 'the lad shouldn't be the one. Let me go.'

And all at once the other crewmen were vigorously offering themselves for the job.

'Very good, gentlemen,' said the captain, 'but I think Mr Cruse really is the best suited. If you're still willing, Mr Cruse?'

'Yes, sir.'

'We'll not tell your mother about this. Agreed?'

I smiled and gave a nod.

'Is your harness snug?'

'It is, sir.' I was glowing with pride, and hoped the others wouldn't see the flush of my cheeks. The captain came and checked my harness himself, his strong hands testing the straps and buckles.

'Be careful, lad,' he told me quietly, and then stepped back. 'All right, Mr Cruse, hook yourself up to the davit and we'll swing you over.'

He said it as if he were proposing a stroll up to A-Deck to take in the view. He hadn't chosen me just because he thought I was least fearful. Any of the other crew would have done it. But I was light too, the lightest here by twenty-five kilos. The captain was afraid the gondola might be too flimsy to carry her own weight once she was hooked and reeled in, and he didn't want anything heavy added to her. Above all, he needed someone light. But I was still honoured he trusted me with the job.

The davit's cable ended with a deep hook and on to this hook I shackled the ends of my two safety lines. They winched me up a little so it was like sitting on a swing. Up close the davit's arm seemed a frail enough bit of metal to hang your life upon, but I knew she could carry fifty of me.

'I know you'll not falter,' the captain told me. 'Here. You'll need this to cut the balloon's flight lines.' He passed me up his knife. I slid it through a buckle of my harness. 'If you're ready, we'll send you over.'

'Ready, sir.'

With that the crew swung the davit's arm out. The

deck of the cargo bay gave way to the ocean's silvered surface, dark and supple as a snake's skin. The arm swung to its farthest point and stopped. The gondola was still out of reach, its rim about two metres below me now. Inside, the man shifted again and I thought he moaned, but that might have been the wind, or the creak of the cable unwinding, or maybe some whalesong out to sea.

'Lower me some, please!' I called over my shoulder.

Looking back at the ship did give me a moment's pause. It wasn't fear, more interest really. Just the oddness of it. I'd never seen the *Aurora* from this angle, me dangling mid-air, the crewmen standing on the lip of the deck, staring down at me through the open cargo bay doors.

They paid out more cable, until I was at the same level as the gondola, not two metres away.

I felt no fear. If someone had put an ear to my heart he'd find it beating no faster than it had in the crow's-nest. It was no bravery on my part, simply a fact of nature, for I was born in the air, and so it seemed the most natural place in the world to me. I was slim as a sapling, and light on my feet. The crew all joked I had seagull bones, hollow in the centre to allow for easy flight. To swing across this little gap, 120 metres aloft, was no more to me than skipping a crack in the pavement. Because deep in my heart I felt that if I were ever to fall, the air would support me, hold me aloft, just as surely as it did a bird with spread wings.

There was a bit of a breeze building now, twirling me some at the end of the cable. I grabbed both my safety lines and started pumping my legs, a youngster on a playground swing. Back and forth, back and forth. At the forward end of my arc, when I looked down, I figured I was almost over the rim of the gondola. Just a little more. Back I went, legs folded tight.

Then: that moment when you're almost motionless, just hanging there for a split second before you start swinging forward again.

'Let run the line!' I shouted. I kicked forwards, body flat, legs shooting out and felt myself drop suddenly – and keep dropping. I sat up quickly as the cable payed out and I was slanting down towards the gondola fast but –

Falling short.

I flung myself forward, stretching, and just hooked my forearms over the gondola's lip. My body slammed into the side, scratching my face against the wicker and knocking all the breath out of me. It took a moment to suck some air into me. My arms sang with pain. I heard the crew above in the *Aurora*, cheering me. I heaved myself up, scrabbling with my feet for purchase, and then crashed over into the gondola.

Beside the man.

But there was not time to tend to him. I stood, grabbed hold of the davit's hook and unshackled my two safety lines. Then I cast about for somewhere secure to attach the hook – it had to be something strong, for it would be bearing the gondola's entire weight once I cut the balloon free. Above my head was a metal frame that supported the burners. The frame had four metal struts that were welded to the gondola's iron rim. It all seemed a little rickety, but it would have to be good enough; I saw nothing better. I curled the hook around the burner frame, as close to its centre as I could manage.

'Reel her in!' I bellowed up at the *Aurora*. I saw the line quickly swing up and become taut. The hook grabbed. The gondola shuddered. A long, nasty squeal came from the burner frame. I didn't like the sound of that at all. I stared, breath stoppered in my throat, at those four bits of metal that tethered the burner frame to the gondola. They were never supposed to support the gondola's entire weight. That's what the balloon was meant to do.

But now the balloon was coming down, slowly collapsing towards the gondola – and the burner. The whole lot might go up in flames, with me and the pilot caught beneath.

Flight lines. Flight lines.

I'd never sailed a balloon, and the rigging was unfamiliar to me.

There were eight lines holding the balloon to the gondola, two stretching up from each corner.

'Take care, Mr Cruse!' I heard the captain shout down at me.

I glanced overhead. Despite being hooked to the davit, the gondola was dragging the great balloon ever closer to the *Aurora*'s hull and engines. In a few minutes they'd collide. I had to be quicker.

The knife glinted in the starlight as I sawed away at the first flight line. It was thick braid, and my heart sank when I began, but the captain's sharp knife bit deep and kept going. Snap went that first line, and the gondola didn't even shift. I did the line opposite, not wanting the gondola to start hanging crooked.

The balloon was sagging now almost to the burner. I didn't have time to fuss about looking for the gas valve to shut it down, but I was sorely afraid of a fire.

The third and fourth lines went.

At my feet, the man moaned again and his arm twitched and knocked against my boot.

I slashed through the fifth line.

I looked up and saw the balloon slowly billowing down towards me, all but blotting out my view of the *Aurora*. It was awfully close to the engine cars and their propellers.

The sixth line went, and now there were but two lines tethering the balloon to the gondola, attached to opposite corners.

Suddenly the burner came on, triggered by its clockwork timer, and a geyser of blue hot flame leapt up and scorched the fabric of the balloon. It caught immediately, spreading high. I checked the davit hook, for once I cut these last two lines, the only thing holding us would be that hook and the *Aurora*'s crane.

My wrist throbbed as I began slashing through the seventh line. With a mighty crack the frayed rope snapped high into the air and the entire gondola slewed over. The unconscious pilot slid towards me and crumpled up against the low side. Without the crane's cable holding us, we would have been tipped out into the sea. I hauled myself to the high side and the last light flight line. The smell of burning fabric was terrible, though luckily the smoke and flames were mostly dancing up away from me. But the weight of the blazing balloon was oozing down over the frame now, starting to engulf the gondola.

Frantically I slashed at the last flight line. Something burning hit my shoulder and I struck it off, and then I saw with a panic that a bit of the wicker was alight. I'd deal with it later. That last flight line needed cutting.

Furiously I attacked it with my knife, severed it, then grabbed hold of the gondola's side as it jerked violently down. The metal burner frame shrieked with stress as it took the full weight. Suspended only on the davit's hook, the gondola swung out from underneath the blazing balloon, and just in time. Aflame, it seeped quickly downwards, cut lines trailing, undulating like a giant jellyfish intent on the ocean's bottom. I held my breath as it fell past the gondola.

Fire crackled in the wicker, and I grabbed a blanket from the floor and smothered the flames. There was a sharp tug from the cable, and we were being reeled in, rocking. I made sure the fire was out, and then knelt down beside the man. I felt bad he'd been jostled about so roughly.

Gently I turned him over on to his back and put a blanket beneath his head. He looked to be in his sixties. Through the whiskers, his face had a sharpened look to it, all cheekbones and nose. Lips scabbed over by wind and lack of water. A handsome gentleman. I didn't really know what else to do so I just held his hand and said, 'There now, we're almost aboard, and Doc Halliday will take a look at you and get you all sorted out.' For a moment it looked like his eyes might open, but then he just frowned and shook his head a little, and his lips parted and mumbled silently for a bit.

Scattered on the floor were all manner of things. Empty water bottles, and unopened cans of food. An astrolabe, dividers and a compass, and rolled-up charts. From overhead came a terrible shriek and I looked up to see one of the burner frame's metal struts rip loose from the gondola's rim. We were too heavy. I stared in horror, watching as the frame began twisting from the stress of her load.

'Hurry!' I bellowed up at the *Aurora*. We were getting reeled up fast, but not fast enough, for with a mighty jerk, a second strut ripped clean out. The entire gondola started to slowly keel over as the remaining struts weakened.

We were level with the cargo bay now but still needed

to be swung inside, and the gondola was slewing over, about to dump us into the drink. The metal frame was groaning and shrieking. I grabbed hold of the gondola's side with one hand, and the man's wrist with the other, knowing I had not the strength to hold us both in if the gondola tried to tip us out.

I looked up and saw the hook screeching along the burner frame, sparking, about to come off the ripped metal strut and we would surely fall –

With a violent bump, we set down on to the deck of the cargo bay. Inside.

I heard the captain's voice. 'Bay doors closed, please! Mr Kahlo, call the bridge and tell them to take her back to 200 metres.'

And then everyone was at the side, looking over into the gondola. Doc Halliday was climbing in, and I stepped back to make room for him. A hand clapped me on the shoulder and I turned to see Captain Walken smiling at me.

'Good work, Mr Cruse. Very good work, indeed.'

I felt terribly thirsty all of a sudden, and tired all the way through my bones, and then remembered that I'd been on duty for over sixteen hours, and normally would have been in my bunk asleep. Instead, I'd been swinging across the sky. I started to climb out, but my knees went wobbly, and Captain Walken and Mr Chen grabbed me under the arms and swung me to the deck.

'You're a brave man, Matt Cruse,' Mr Chen said.

'No, sir. Just light.'

'Lighter than air, that's our Mr Cruse,' said one of the sailmakers. 'Cloud hopping next, it'll be!'

Hands tousling my hair, clapping me on the back, voices saying, 'Well done' and me trying not to smile, but smiling and laughing anyway, because it felt so good to know I'd brought the gondola in, saved the pilot, and impressed everyone. All these men who had known my father. They would have called him Mr Cruse, too.

Doc Halliday and another crewman were lifting the pilot out of the gondola to a waiting stretcher.

'Is he going to be all right?' I asked the doctor.

'I don't know yet,' was all Doc Halliday answered, and his face looked so grave that I felt a queer squeeze in my stomach. The wicker gondola looked odd and out of place in our cargo bay.

'Get some sleep, Mr Cruse,' the captain said to me.

I nodded, but didn't want to go. I watched them take the pilot away on the stretcher. I wondered who he was. I wanted to go through the gondola and find out what had gone wrong.

'Sleep first, Mr Cruse,' said the captain. 'Your father would be very proud of you.'

I blinked away the hot tingle behind my eyes. 'Thank you, sir.'

My legs wobbled as I left the cargo bay and trudged aft along the keel catwalk to the crew quarters. Lighter than air, but I felt heavy as lead. I opened the door to my cabin, caught a glimpse of the clock. Five thirty-nine. I shrugged off my shirt and trousers and climbed into my bunk. And, as so often happened when I slept aloft, I drifted free of my body, and glided alongside the *Aurora*, and my father came and joined me, and we flew.

In the afternoon I was off duty, so I went to the infirmary to see how the balloon pilot was making out.

'Not good, Matt,' Doc Halliday told me. 'He's got pneumonia, and I believe he had a seizure of the heart several days ago. He's terribly dehydrated.'

'He'll live, though?'

The doctor lifted his eyebrows and his lips compressed into a sad little smile. 'I think not, Matt. Even if he were back on shore, his heart and lungs are so damaged there's not much to be done.'

'Who is he?'

'Benjamin Molloy. According to the ship's papers he was trying to make a solo circumnavigation.'

You heard such things from time to time. Some fellow trying to float round the world in a hot-air balloon. No one had managed it yet. They always got grounded or were never heard from again. I didn't know if this Mr Molloy was brave or just plain foolhardy, but I couldn't help but admire his daring.

'May I see him, please?'

Doc Halliday hesitated, then nodded. 'He's asleep, mind. Don't wake him.'

The infirmary was off the main dispensary and examination room, just two beds divided by a curtain. The other bed was empty. I pulled up the chair and sat down beside Mr Molloy. He was propped up with pillows and his breathing was raspy. It was strange the way I felt about him: connected was the only word I could conjure up. I'd spotted his balloon out there in the night sky, and I'd swung on to his gondola and found him lying crumpled on the deck, looking so broken and helpless. Maybe it was also because he looked a little like an older version of my father – but that might just have been imaginings on my part.

I put my hand on top of his. It was scalding with fever, ridged with sinew and bone, and my own hand felt icy against his. He shifted, and I took my hand away, afraid I'd disturbed him. His eyes opened. They were all milky, and he stared through me like he was focused on something else. Like he was already leaving.

He coughed a bit, and I held a glass of water to his mouth, but he didn't seem to want it, or maybe couldn't swallow. A little spilled down his chin and on to his bedsheets.

'Sorry, sir,' I said, mopping him with a cloth.

When I finished I looked back at him, and his eyes were intent now.

'Did you see them?' he asked me, his voice scratchy.

'Who?' I wondered if he was thinking clearly.

'Sailing. All around,' he said. It took him a long time

24

to get the words out, swallowing and giving little coughs between words. 'Probably always. Been there. Only no one's. Ever. Seen them.'

He tried to get up, pushing with his elbows like he had somewhere pretty important to go, but he didn't have the strength, and he sank back down. He turned to me again, swallowed.

'But you. Must've seen them.'

It seemed important to him so I lied.

'Yes,' I said. 'I saw them too.'

'Good,' he said, and that seemed to calm him down some. 'Beautiful creatures,' he said, smiling. 'They were. Beautiful.'

'Yes,' I said.

He coughed again, and I wondered if I should call for Doc Halliday.

'I'll get the doctor for you, sir.'

His hot hand was on my arm. 'Kate. Would've loved them,' he said. 'Don't you. Think?'

'I think so,' I said.

He was looking at me very kindly, and I felt ashamed of my lying, and then it was as if he saw through me, and it was terrible to see the way his face changed, disgust pouring into his eyes.

'You never. Saw them.'

His words were all gaspy now, and it started him coughing again, his whole body jerking. I looked around in a worry, and Doc Halliday was coming, telling me it was best I left.

I went away, feeling terrible. Maybe if I'd talked to him differently he wouldn't have got so riled up. Maybe if I'd said things better.

An hour or so later Doc Halliday found me in the kitchen, polishing the silver for dinner, and told me Benjamin Molloy had just died. I was surprised at how wet my eyes got; I didn't really know him at all.

Doc Halliday squeezed my arm.

'You mustn't take it to heart, Matt Cruse. He was a very sick man.'

I nodded. I just wished he hadn't been so vexed at me when he died. I told the doctor what he'd said to me. Doc Halliday smiled kindly.

'The dying often say strange things. It's got nothing to do with you.'

But that night, on my watch, Benjamin Molloy's words sounded over and over in my head, and I wondered what it was he'd seen. Or thought he'd seen. Something winged in the sky by the sounds of it. Beautiful creatures. Maybe he'd caught sight of some albatross, or some other great seafaring bird, though certainly it was a rare thing so deep over the ocean.

Well, there was no shortage of fanciful stories about winged things. Angels and dragons, sky kelpies and cloud sphinxes. They always turned out be something else: a glare off the water, shadows in mist, a mirage projected by a tired sailor's bleary eyes. But that night, I had to admit, I kept a sharp lookout as I swept the horizons and hopscotched over my constellations. I saw nothing out of the ordinary, none of Benjamin Molloy's beautiful creatures. But I wish I had. I liked to think there was no end of things aloft in the sky, unseen by us.

ONE YEAR LATER

2

UP SHIP!

Pull up the gangways! Close the hatches! The cargo was all loaded and tied down in the holds; the last of the passengers were on board. There was a cry of 'Up ship!' from the control car, and the two hundred-strong ground crew cast off the mooring lines, and with a great splash we were dumping water ballast, and the men and women on the airfield sent up a cheer and we were rising now, the passengers swinging caps and handkerchiefs from the open windows, and the people down below waving back, and we were rising, the field already far below us, and the spires of Lionsgate City spreading out to the north, and we were rising into the dawn sky, sure and smooth as an angel.

I'd just finished a week's shore leave. My first few nights at home, my mother had made a terrible fuss of me, cooking and baking my favourite things. We had all stayed up late, talking, until Sylvia and Isabel were sent off to bed, complaining loudly, for they had school the next morning. My little sisters had grown since I'd last seen them, shooting up like silver maples. They'd showered me with kisses when I gave them their presents. I always brought them things when I came home, since I most often missed their birthdays, and sometimes Christmas too. Isabel got a didgeridoo from Australia, because she was musical, and loved instruments of all sorts, and here was one she'd never heard of. For Sylvia, who fancied herself a lady of high fashion now she was pushing twelve, I brought home a beautiful tortoiseshell hairband I'd seen in the Grand Bazaar in Marrakesh. And for my mother, I'd bought, same as last time, a bottle of the Iberian perfume she loved so much. It was the scent my father had always brought home for her. My mother would never buy it for herself; she said it was a luxury we could not afford, but my father used to tell her everyone, no matter how poor, deserved at least one luxury. She had worn that scent as long as I could remember, and it was as much a part of her as her supple seamstress hands, or her large, slightly mournful eyes.

I was always glad to come back home, but I never slept well on the ground. After a few days the small apartment would start to feel like a prison. My mother's exhaustion and silent worry filled up the cramped rooms until I was afraid I'd suffocate. Worst of all, I would start missing my father so badly it was like a clenched fist behind my breastbone.

I never dreamed of him when I was landlocked, only when I was aboard the *Aurora*.

Aloft was the only place I could feel close to him, the only place I didn't feel all broken. But I was too guilty to tell this to my mother.

Now, airborne once more, I filled my lungs and felt some of the heaviness pass out of my chest and shoulders. There were few good things about being on the ground, and the best was getting to take off again. Nothing grander than feeling the strength and grace of the *Aurora*'s bone and muscle and sinew as she angled up ever so slightly and left the earth below.

Out the windows were dozens of other airships, some newly airborne like us, pointing towards all corners of the globe. There was the passenger liner *Titania*, bound for Paris, and over there, *The Arctic Star*, headed over the top of the world with scheduled stops in Yellowknife, Godthab, Sankt-Peterburg and Arkhangel. Landing below us I glimpsed the regal *Orient Express*, just arrived from Constantinople. Queued high in the sky were air freighters from the Far East, their silver skins blazing with the rising sun's light, awaiting orders from the harbour master before they made their final approaches.

All the world met here, and there was nowhere you couldn't go once aloft.

We ourselves were bound for the other side of the world, Sydney, Australia, a five-day journey across the Pacificus. The past twenty-four hours had passed in a blur, for the entire crew was busy tending to the ship, refuelling and reprovisioning her. Overnight we'd topped up our gas cells with hydrium, pumped water into our ballast and drinking tanks.

And the food! What we took on was quite something – and I should know for I, Matt Cruse, helped lug it all on board: 730 kilos of potatoes, 3200 eggs, 450 kilos of butter and cheese. All in all we loaded up close to 5,500 kilos of food for the voyage, and when you've seen it spread out in the loading bay, and hefted it up on your shoulders, you wouldn't think an entire nation could eat so much food.

Now here was the amazing thing. With all her provisions and cargo and gear and passengers and crew, the *Aurora* weighed over 900,000 kilos. She was a giant to be sure, 270 metres from stem to stem, 14 storeys high. But fill her up with hydrium, it was like she weighed nothing at all. This morning, all it took was two men, one at the bow, one at the stern, to carry her out of the hangar and across the airfield to the mooring mast.

Easy as that.

First time I saw it, I could barely believe my eyes, for it seemed to defy every law of nature. And then all the *Aurora* had to do was dump a few hundred kilos of water and she was lighter than air.

There's fancy math to explain all this of course. It had to do with hydrium being the lightest gas in the world. Much lighter than helium and even lighter than hydrogen. But when you saw the *Aurora*, and saw her floating and rising, you forgot all about the math and just stared.

Up ship!

No time for gawking out windows now. I was cabin boy, and there were 120 passengers on board and all of them needed settling. I was busy showing them to their cabins and staterooms, explaining how the sinks and toilets and showers worked, opening trunks and telling about meals and show times for our onboard cinema, and piano recitals in the A–Deck starboard lounge and –

'When do we set off?' one lady asked me inside her cabin.

'Ma'am,' I said, 'we set off twenty minutes ago.'

She turned to the window, amazed. 'But I felt nothing!'

'That's right, ma'am. She's like riding a cloud.'

And then it was breakfast time, and everyone needed feeding.

Breakfast!

A maelstrom of noise and activity in the galley, all the electric elements blazing and the ranges like kilns, and platters of fresh bread and rolls and cinnamon buns. Sausages and bacon sputtering in the pans, Portobello mushrooms and tomatoes simmering under the grill. And the eggs! Not in a henhouse would you see more eggs than in our kitchen at breakfast time. Eggs served up any way you could want: poached, scrambled, over easy, eggs Benedict, omelettes.

If I hadn't already eaten a rib-busting breakfast at four thirty this morning, the smell and sight of all this food would have had me running around like a mad dog, cramming my mouth.

Chef Vlad and his cooks and kitchen help had been up for hours cutting peppers and tomatoes and mushrooms for the omelette fillings, and making dough, for everything we served on board was fresh. Not like some of these cost-cutting liners you had now, where you practically had to bring your own provisions on board if you didn't want to starve halfway over the ocean.

The main kitchen was on A-Deck, and the bakery directly below it on B-Deck. The fresh rolls and croissants came up piping hot in the dumb waiter, almost faster than we could serve them. Baz and Kristof were on duty with me in the first-class dining room. We'd worked together long enough so that you might have thought we were auditioning for the ballet. We swirled about one another as the ship sailed on and the passengers ate and clinked glasses and ordered more Morning Glories at table nine and laughed at the sheer delight of having a meal 180 metres in the air.

Serving in the dining room was hardly my favourite part of being a cabin boy. But this morning, I smiled and served and 'Yes, ma'amed' and 'No, sired' with the best of them, and I believe I even had an extra spring in my step – for I had high hopes that this was to be my last voyage as cabin boy.

There were rumours that Tom Bear, our assistant sailmaker, would be signing on with another ship at the end of this journey. Last year, after we'd rescued that hot-air balloon, Captain Walken had told me I deserved a promotion, and as soon as there was a suitable position vacant, he would put me in it.

If Tom Bear was indeed leaving ship, then the next time the *Aurora* weighed anchor, I would be assistant sailmaker.

Sailmaker!

This was my great chance.

If I could become assistant sailmaker, then maybe one day I could become head sailmaker, then rudder man, watch officer – and one day, just maybe, captain of a ship like the *Aurora*.

But this was getting ahead of myself.

Soon I might be assistant sailmaker.

This morning, however, I was still cabin boy, and table two was wanting more pancakes and I had better go fetch them now. They were eating so furiously their forks were sparking against their knives and you'd think they were eating their last meal, instead of sitting down to the first of many delicious meals aboard a luxury airship. And if some of them were expecting a tilty meal, with their plates and forks slewing across the table, they were mistaken. The *Aurora*, especially with Captain Walken at the helm, sailed without a bump or roll. You could stand a fountain pen on its end atop your table, and it would not fall once during the entire meal.

'They're eating like starved apes,' Baz muttered as he swished past me with more food.

'Haven't they had enough yet?' he wondered a minute later when we passed again.

'Keep your hands well clear of their forks,' he warned me as we pirouetted round one another at the dumb waiter. 'I was nearly stabbed clean through. They'll be eating the cutlery soon!'

'And us if we're not quick enough,' I added, and Baz guffawed, and coughed to cover it up.

I was in a fine mood. The spires of Lionsgate Bridge were visible beyond the windows, the dawn's light seeping over their peaks and making the lions' golden manes gleam. It would be an hour before we were over open sea, but my heart was already beating for that moment when I saw the endless horizon and I felt like anything was possible: the whole world unfurling before you.

'Look at that!' cried one of the passengers, pointing out the window.

I glanced over. An ornithopter was passing on the starboard side, its beating wings ablur as it banked sharply to cut across our bow. Now this was a cheeky thing to do and I couldn't help shaking my head in disgust. What was the pilot about, darting in front of us like that? Ornithopters were ungainly looking contraptions, with their flapping feathered wings, and airshipmen tended to look down on them as a foolish business, like all heavier-than-air craft. Mosquitoes, we called them, on account of their puny size and the noisy whine of their engines.

The ornithopter buzzed round again, and this time I spotted two passengers behind the pilot, all kitted out with their goggles and leather caps. Again they cut across our bow.

'What're they up to?' I mumbled to Baz as he headed towards the kitchen with an armful of dirty plates.

'Taking pictures, maybe.'

Sometimes you got photographers wanting photographs of the big luxury airships as they came in and out of harbour, and they'd hire ornithopters to take them up for a good shot. But I hadn't seen anyone holding a camera.

I wanted to find out what was going on, and since breakfast was winding down, I thought this would be a good time to take coffee and cinnamon rolls to the bridge.

'Cover for me?' I asked Baz. 'I want to find out what's what.'

He nodded, curious as I was. Anyway, Baz was used to me disappearing to the control car, even when I was off duty. I loved watching the officers fly the ship, and there was an awful lot to learn. I strolled down to B-Deck and stopped off at the bakery to load up a tray. With the tray balanced in one hand, I hurried down the gangway to the keel catwalk and walked briskly towards the bow. There was a square hatchway in the floor with a ladder that led down into the control car. I took the rungs one-handed, and didn't spill a single drop of coffee.

The ladder brought me down into the radio room, at the rear of the control car. Its walls were covered with all manner of machinery, transmitters and receivers and lighted gauges and dials. I placed a steaming mug of coffee beside the wireless officer, Luc Bayard, who was pressing his earpiece against his head and scowling and scribbling a message on to his pad.

'Clarify please, Nimbus 638. You are requesting a landing?'

I put an almond croissant down beside the coffee, taking my time. Bayard glanced up at me and shook his head, making a loony roll of his eyes.

'For what purpose, Nimbus 638?' He scrawled a message on to his pad but before I could read it he stood up, speaking into his headset before pulling it off. 'Stand by please, Nimbus 638.'

'Excuse me, Matt,' he said, walking forward into the navigation room. It was a small room, with a chart cabinet against one wall, and a broad table against the other, where all manner of maps and instruments were spread out. Mr Torbay was taking a reading from one of the compasses, and Mr Grantham was leaning over the table, marking lines and notations as he updated our position on the chart. I quickly put down rolls and mugs of coffee, and hurried after Mr Bayard as he made his way forward to the bridge. I didn't want to miss anything. A landing, Mr Bayard had said. I could only assume he was talking with the pesky ornithopter buzzing around us.

Through the final hatchway and I was suddenly in the bridge. It took up the entire front half of the control car, a huge glass cage with two-storey windows giving a panoramic view of sky, land and sea. I'd been here many times before, and it never failed to make my skin tingle. There was the rudder man at his wheel, and the elevator man at his. There was the gas control board and the ballast board and the engine room telegraph – I knew all the instruments and what they did, and imagined I could use them if given the chance. The bridge was a crowded place, and I stood well back, not wanting to get in the way. I started putting coffee down for the helmsmen and watch officers, taking my time and listening.

'What's the news, Mr Bayard?' Captain Walken asked, turning to the wireless officer.

'He's requested a landing, sir.'

'What on earth for?' the captain demanded.

'He says he's got one of our passengers. Two actually. A young lady and her chaperone. They missed the boarding.'

'Who?' The captain looked at the note Mr Bayard handed him.

I watched the captain, wondering what he would say next. I'd never heard of such a request. If a passenger missed the ship, he was out of luck, simple as that. He had to wait for another vessel. But the captain just sniffed and gave a smile.

'Well, they must want passage badly enough, eh?' he

said. His cheerfulness surprised me, since the landing would put us at least half an hour behind schedule. The captain was a punctual man, and prided himself on his timely arrivals and departures.

'Prepare to head up, Mr Wexler. We'll keep our present altitude, thank you, Mr Kahlo. Mr Bayard, please tell the pilot he can make his approach when we've put our head to the wind. Then wire the harbour master and tell them we'll be altering course to allow an aerial docking. The breeze is light; if he's a pilot worth his salt he should be able to make a landing first try.'

The captain caught sight of me and winked. 'We've taken more difficult things on board, haven't we, Mr Cruse?'

'Yes, sir,' I said with a grin.

'Thank you for the refreshments, Mr Cruse. Your timing is uncanny, as always. But perhaps you should go to the landing bay and attend to our latecomers when they board.'

'Of course, sir,' I said, delighted. Only once before had I seen an aerial landing, and it was no mean feat. I passed out the last of the coffees and pastries and left as the *Aurora* began her slow, graceful turn. I stopped at the bakery, dropped off the tray, then hurried aft.

The landing bay was forward of the cargo holds, very near the ship's midsection. Mostly it was used for extra storage, and there were plenty of crates and cases arranged around the walls. But the centre of the bay was always kept clear in case we needed to allow for an aerial landing. When I arrived, the crew were just opening the bay doors in the floor. With alarming speed the doors split apart and each long half rolled back flush with the ship's underbelly. Air galloped in. We could see the ship's lower tail fin, and straight down to the Gulf Islands and the water, blue as lapis lazuli, and cut by the white furrows of boats headed for Lionsgate Harbour.

Mr Riddihoff pulled a lever, and with a clanking whirr, the docking trapeze began to lower from an overhead track in the bay's ceiling. The metal trapeze dangled through the hatchway into open air. The ornithopter pilot would have to make his approach directly beneath the airship's belly, cut speed so that he was almost in a stall, and hook his overhead landing gear over the docking trapeze at just the right moment.

'Must be pretty important passengers,' said Mr Riddihoff, 'for the captain to be going through all this hullabaloo.'

I looked down at the trapeze. It was a tiny place to hook a plane to. I hoped the pilot was experienced, but these harbour flyers were daredevils and used to more outlandish tricks than this.

The ornithopter's drone grew louder. Crouching, I could just see it, behind the *Aurora*'s tail fins, coming in. It seemed to be hardly moving, wings scarcely beating now, and I thought he would make it first try. But when the ornithopter was only feet away from the docking trapeze, it shuddered and dipped and I heard shrieks of alarm from the passengers as the ornithopter dropped away and banked sharply.

'Bit of a gust there,' said Riddihoff calmly.

'Bad luck,' I said. 'Look, he's coming round again.'

I had to admit, that ornithopter was a nimble thing, and seeing this one manoeuvre so smartly did impress me.

'Hope he gets it this time round,' said Mr Riddihoff. 'I've not had my breakfast.'

'I suggest the eggs Florentine,' I told him.

'Good, were they?'

'Terrific. Here we go.'

Here came the ornithopter again, skimming the *Aurora*'s belly, straight as a Canada goose towards the loading bay. His hook slipped over the trapeze and locked with a loud, satisfying *clack*, and I heard the engine cut out, and the wings stilled instantly. The *Aurora* didn't even tremble with the sudden extra weight.

'Hooked!' Riddihoff sang out, pulling levers. The trapeze slowly lifted the dangling ornithopter through the hatchway and then carried her along its track to set her down on the floor of the landing bay. A woman in the rear seat was trying to stand, and pulling at her leather hood and sounding off as if she'd suffered a great calamity.

'Outrageous!' she was saying. 'Dangerous and foolhardy like I've never seen!'

And now the poor pilot was turning about in his seat and trying in vain to explain.

'I'm very sorry, Miss Simpkins, but I have no authority over the winds. A small gust buffeted me just as we were coming in that first time. It's not unusual, Miss, to make more than one pass with an aerial landing.'

Miss Simpkins made a humph sound and gazed haughtily around the loading bay. She was no more than thirty, and a striking woman with fierce features, but right now she looked a total fright. Her hair was all frazzled and looked like it had just exploded from her head. Her eye make-up was smeared by tears and wind, and there were deep red rings around both her eyes from the goggles. She appeared altogether crazed. I was pushing the boarding stairs towards the ornithopter, but not quickly enough for her liking.

'Hurry along, boy, help me out of here! This thing's not fit for use as a kite!'

Now this was rich behaviour, I thought, all this barking and whingeing, when she should be apologizing for setting us behind schedule with her late arrival.

'Welcome aboard the *Aurora*, ma'am,' I said, stepping up to give her a hand.

'And you are?'

'Matt Cruse, ma'am, cabin boy.'

'Attend to Miss de Vries now.'

I turned to the passenger in the middle seat. A girl it was, my age probably, no more than fifteen. She pulled off her cap and smoothed her long mahogany hair. She looked a little windblown, her face pale, but there was a happy blaze in her eyes. I knew instantly it hadn't been her shrieking as the ornithopter came in to land. She looked thoroughly revved up.

I offered her my hand, and she stepped out on to the boarding stairs.

'Thank you, Mr Cruse,' she said.

'This is Miss Kate de Vries,' said the woman, still trying to claw her hair down. 'And I am Marjorie Simpkins, her chaperone. Escort us to our rooms now.'

'Very good,' I said. 'I'll just attend to your baggage.'

Kate de Vries, I noticed, was looking all around, out the open bay doors to the sea below, up to the girders and beams and gas cells and catwalks that criss-crossed overhead like the work of some giant mechanical spider. Taking it all in. Miss Simpkins meanwhile fussed and fluttered about, telling me to be careful with the luggage and the hat bags and for heaven's sake don't thump things around so. She was always pattering her hands against Kate de Vries' back, trying to move her this way and that, as though she knew where it was best for her to stand. Kate de Vries seemed used to ignoring her.

I took the passenger list from my pocket, and saw that the grand stateroom was in fact reserved under the name of de Vries. Rich then, this Kate de Vries. I couldn't help feeling sorry for her though, shackled to a chaperone and one like Miss Simpkins at that!

They had so much luggage I wondered if they were doing a planetary tour. It was too much to carry, so I loaded it on to the freight conveyor belt and sent it on its way forward to the passenger quarters. I'd pick it up when we got there.

'Shall I take you to your stateroom, then?' I asked, making sure to direct the question to Kate de Vries.

'Thank you, yes, that would be very kind,' she said.

'I'll be telegraphing your superiors as soon as I can!' Miss Simpkins hollered at the ornithopter pilot.

'Thank you very much,' Kate de Vries called up to the pilot with a smile and wave. 'It was a *thrilling* flight!'

'Any time, Miss,' the pilot said, grinning. He had not even removed his leather hood and goggles. 'I'll be on my way while the wind holds.'

He started the engine, and I heard its loud insect drone. The trapeze lifted his ship up and carried it back towards the open hatchway. The wings fluttered ever so gently, in anticipation.

'Actually, I'd like to see this, Marjorie,' said Kate de Vries, stopping to watch. Her tone of voice made it clear this was not a request. Miss Simpkins sighed loudly and stared heavenwards. I was pleased about this, since I'd wanted to see the take-off myself. I was liking this Kate de Vries more and more.

Mr Riddihoff worked his controls and lowered the ornithopter down through the hatchway.

The pilot gave him the thumbs up, and pulled a lever in the cockpit. His docking hook snapped off the trapeze. The ornithopter dropped, quite dramatically I must say, straight down towards the waves, wings flapping desperately. It seemed its plunge would never stop, but then, impossibly slowly, it inched forward through the air, and peeled off to the port, climbing. I realized I'd been holding my breath.

I looked over to Kate de Vries, tilted forward, peering intently out the hatchway, and saw her exhale.

'That was something,' she said with complete satisfaction, and then grinned. Grin doesn't really do it justice. It seemed to take charge of her whole face, and you had to smile back.

'It was, Miss,' I said.

'Come along, then,' said Miss Simpkins impatiently, hands fluttering. I led them out of the landing bay and escorted them along the keel catwalk towards the passenger decks. Miss Simpkins was most impractically shod in heels, and they kept getting stuck in the grilled metal floor so that she jerked and lurched and sighed and snorted all the way.

'What kind of corridor is this!' she complained.

'Passengers usually don't traverse it, Miss,' I said. 'It's on account of your late arrival that you see this part of the ship at all.'

Now Kate de Vries, on the other hand, was sensibly wearing flat-soled shoes and ambled along, oblivious to her chaperone's convulsions. She gazed all about her as though planning on drafting a blueprint when she got half a chance.

'Is it your first time aboard an airship, Miss?' I asked her.

'It is, yes,' she said.

'If you're interested there will be a tour later this morning.'

'I'd like that very much.' She turned to Miss Simpkins, whose shoe had come off and was stuck in the metal grille. She was bent down tugging at it, violently.

'Allow me, Miss,' I said. I handed it back to her.

I caught the girl's eye and swear it had a glint of mischief in it, and I had to freeze my face so not to share her smile.

'Some flat-soled shoes would be more comfortable if you wish to join us on the tour later,' I suggested.

'I can't imagine anything I'd less like to do,' muttered the bony chaperone.

'Perhaps someone can push you along in a wheelchair,' the girl said amiably.

'That won't be necessary, thank you very much, Kate.'

Kate. The name suited her. Quick and to the point.

We reached the passenger quarters, and I led them up the grand staircase to A-Deck where the first-class passengers stayed. The swirling banister was all walnut, though hollow in the centre to save on weight, and at the top of the red-carpeted steps was a magnificent Michaelangelico fresco. The fresco was enough to quiet the bony chaperone down for a few seconds, and her heels didn't fall off, which made her even more cheerful.

People had finished off their breakfasts now and were strolling about, yawning and stretching and groaning contentedly, weighing about five kilos more apiece. Down the central corridor we went and right at the end was the Topkapi stateroom. The luggage trolley was already waiting outside the door, ferried up by stewards while Miss Simpkins had been lurching about on her high heels.

I unlocked the door for them and led them inside. Quite a palace it was, furnished with sofas and wing-backed armchairs and side tables and coffee tables and footstools; vases of fresh flowers bloomed all over the place, making it smell like the botanical gardens of Florence. The outside wall was one panoramic window, burgundy velvet curtains tied back so all you saw was cirrus clouds scalloping the sky, and the blue of the sparkling Pacificus and off to the left the hazy shores of North America melting into the horizon.

And this was just the sitting room. Miss de Vries looked around as if enchanted. The stateroom was named after a sultan's palace in Constantinople, and it deserved its name. I myself always liked having a gander when we were in harbour. In particular I liked slipping off my shoes and scrunching my bare toes against that plush burgundy carpet.

I showed them their adjoining bedrooms, both with

four-poster beds with lace canopies, and the bathroom with the famous bathtub. It was the only one on shipboard, water being such a heavy commodity. Everyone else just got showers.

'If there's anything you need, ladies, just pull the cord,' I showed them the braided tassel draped from its wall socket, 'and someone will come right up to assist you. And you also have a message tube here.' I told them about the elaborate network of vacuum tubes that carried messages throughout the ship. 'Just put your note in the canister here and slip it into the tube and you can send it to housekeeping, the lounge, the kitchen, or the chief steward's station, just by pressing one of these buttons.'

'How ingenious,' said Kate de Vries. Her eyes took on a look of mischief again. 'Marjorie, wouldn't one of these be useful at home? Just to keep track of one another.'

'Frightfully. We've missed breakfast, I suppose,' said Miss Simpkins tragically.

'Not a problem. I'm happy to order some to be brought to your room.'

'I'm starving!' said Kate de Vries.

'Yes, a scrape with death can give one quite an appetite,' her chaperone said tartly, and she set about placing her breakfast order. Which indeed was rather sizeable.

Kate de Vries walked to the window and stayed there, gazing out hungrily. Her face was most intent and solemn, as though she expected something to materialize amongst the clouds or from the fabric of the sky itself.

3

KATE

I was in the kitchen, preparing the breakfast trolley for the Topkapi stateroom, when Mr Lisbon, the chief steward, came to tell me the captain wished to speak with me. Anticipation tingled through my hands and feet, for I had an inkling of what this would be about. So too did Mr Lisbon, whose eyes had a kindly look to them.

'I know this can be no disciplinary matter, Mr Cruse,' he said, and straightened the collar of my jacket before giving a quick nod of approval at my appearance. 'I'll have Baz deliver the breakfast trolley for you.'

I went forward along the keel catwalk, towards the captain's cabin, towards my future. I felt in my pocket for my compass. My father had given it to me for my tenth birthday, and I carried it with me always. It was a handsome thing, a smooth lozenge of brass and glass, with a hinged lid. On the back were engraved the words, 'From one sailmaker to another'. When I still lived at home I would set it on my pillow and watch the needle

53

find north and then draw a line to wherever my father was. If he were over Mongolia I would travel to the west, if he were crossing the Atlanticus I would go east; if he were traversing Antarctica my thoughts would sail to the south to be with him as he glided over the great polar ice caps. After he'd died three years ago, I avoided looking at it, for no point of the compass could bring me to him now.

My fingers grazed the cool brass, felt the markings of my father's inscription. Sailmaker. My step quickened. This was the moment I'd been waiting for. I faltered. What if the captain meant to quiz me right now? The sailmaker's job was a serious one. It was up to him and his fellows to keep the ship aloft, to check the hydrium gas cells and make sure they were all properly inflated, to check the shafts and vents. To survey the taut outer skin of the entire ship, every inch of it, inside and out, on land and aloft, to make sure the *Aurora* was in top sailing trim. I calmed my breathing. I hoped I would have quick answers to any questions the captain might fire at me; hoped I would not stumble over my words like a ninny.

At the captain's door, I knocked lightly.

'Enter.'

His cabin was small but comfortable with a single bed, a desk, two leather armchairs studded with brass bolts. He had a private washroom and instead of the usual portholes he had a large bow window. Sunlight bathed the room, warming the wood of his bookshelves and the desk behind which he was sitting. He gestured me to an armchair.

'Mr Cruse. Be seated, please.'

I remembered the first time I'd met him. My father was on shore leave, and the *Aurora* was in harbour, and he'd taken me on board to show me around. The whole tour I'd felt weak with excitement. It was the first time I'd been aboard my father's ship. I was six. In the control car, Captain Walken had been talking with one of the engineers, but he greeted my father warmly, and I'd felt such pride, to think my father worked with so important a man. Then the captain had looked down at me. 'Will you fly one day, Mr Cruse?' he'd asked with a smile. For a moment I could not speak. Then I forced out a single word. 'Yes,' I said, more loudly and boldly than I'd intended. Captain Walken chuckled, raised an eyebrow at my father and said, 'I believe he will.'

I was looking at the captain's face now, searching for signs of the happy news he was to deliver. But he was so professional he appeared no different than he did on the bridge. He began to speak, then broke off with a little grunt of irritation, looking out the window. It was most unlike him to falter, and instantly I knew I would not be getting good news today.

'This is a vexing business, Mr Cruse,' he said. 'You had my promise, and nothing angers me more than being made a liar. We are indeed to have a new junior sailmaker aboard the *Aurora*, but it is not to be you.'

I said nothing, but my mind was churning, trying to think of what grievous thing I'd done to anger the captain.

'Rest easy, Matt,' he said gently, 'you've done nothing wrong. Your service to this vessel has always been exemplary. This is not my choice. I've been forced to take on Otto Lunardi's son as junior sailmaker.'

I recognized the name, of course. Otto Lunardi was the magnate who owned the *Aurora* and a vast fleet of over forty other airships.

'I voiced my objection,' the captain said, 'but Lunardi ignored it. Seems he's decided his boy is not fit for the business of managing his empire, and so he's been exiled aboard my ship. It was quite beyond my control. I hope you understand.'

'Of course, sir.'

'Nothing would give me greater pleasure than seeing you stand before me right now, bearing the sailmaker's insignia.'

I thought of the gold-stamped wheel the sailmakers wore on their collars; I had coveted that insignia for so long now. I nodded at the captain. 'Thank you, sir. For all you've done on my behalf.'

'I've done nothing you don't deserve,' he said impatiently. 'It's all changed since I started out. Forty years ago, if you didn't have money – and my family had none – you began as cabin boy. I did it, just like you. But then you could rise by dint of hard work and honesty and skill. Now there is the Airship Academy – and getting in takes not just skill, but money, or connections or both. And they think they can train people in musty classrooms. And to be sure, they can teach them certain things. But not character. Not hard work, and not the mettle it takes to sail a ship aloft across continents and oceans. Lunardi and the other owners like Academy training. It comes with letterhead, and fancy seals and certificates, and that makes them feel they're getting their money's worth! Makes them feel they can sleep easy! Fair enough, the Lunardi boy has his basic certificate from the Academy, indeed he does. But I doubt he's ever spent an hour aboard an airship in a gale. Rest assured, Matt, there will be some remedy for this. My guess is the Lunardi boy will flee as soon as we reach Sydney Harbour.'

'He's on board now, sir?'

'Yes, as a trainee.' He looked me in the eyes for a moment, then sighed. 'You know I am always happy to arrange a transfer for you to another vessel where they have need of a sailmaker. I would be sorry to lose you, but would recommend you with the heartiest of praise. Any vessel would be lucky to have you.'

'Thank you, sir, but I'm happy here.'

And I was. This ship, the *Aurora*, was more home to me than the little apartment in Lionsgate City. Over the past three years, I'd spent scarcely any time on land. My life was aloft now. I did not want to leave Baz or Captain Walken, or my bunk with its porthole that gave me a bigger view of the world than any landlocked window.

My heart purred to the vibrations of the *Aurora*'s engines. There were other fine ships, I knew, and some perhaps even grander than the *Aurora*. But only she could fuel my dreams.

'I understand.' The captain came around the desk and clapped a hand upon my shoulder. 'This was your father's ship.'

'Yes, sir.'

'Take heart, lad. A man with your courage and skill will not go unrewarded. There has not been one moment I've regretted taking you on as cabin boy. I will not break my word to you twice.'

'Thank you, Captain.' I did not want to be childish and show my disappointment so I stood and left quickly.

Outside in the corridor, my eyes smarted with shame. A cocky young fool I'd been, assuming I'd be junior sailmaker. Me with no Academy training, and no wealth to help advance me. Of course I'd be pushed aside by the likes of Otto Lunardi's boy. I felt no anger with the captain. He was an honourable man and had always done his best for me. But in my guts I already felt a hard, hot loathing for Lunardi's son.

A thief he was. Taking what had been mine. If I were to steal from him, take so much as his uniform and cap, I'd be dragged before a judge and thrown into gaol. But he had done just that to me, and worse. He'd stolen my life. That position was mine. And there was nothing I could do to get it back. Who knew when there would be another position open for me? Might be years. Might be never. If the captain retired or changed ships, I would have no champion to forward my cause. And without that, my chances were slim of ever advancing beyond cabin boy.

There was no shame in the position, I wasn't so proud as to think it beneath me. But it was not what I wanted. What I wanted, with the intensity of all my dreams, was one day to fly the *Aurora*. To make her part the winds over the Mongolian steppes, soar over Antarctica and weather the storms of Terra Nova. What I wanted was to take her airborne and keep her there for ever.

Anyone interested in the ship's tour was supposed to meet at the grand piano in the starboard lounge at half past ten. When I arrived, there was only one person waiting. Kate de Vries.

'Is the tour still on?' she asked. 'Since I seem to be the only one?'

I glanced around at the passengers reclining in their chaise longues, some reading newspapers and magazines, others asleep with the sun on their faces, too full of breakfast to stir. Maybe they'd travelled so often they'd taken the tour before. Most likely the great lumps had no curiosity about the amazing ship that carried their lazy carcasses across the world.

'Yes,' I said, 'of course I'll be offering the tour. Is Miss Simpkins—'

'She's out cold,' said Kate with a small smile. 'Right

after breakfast she said she had a splitting headache and needed to lie down.'

'Very good then.' I was not at all disappointed to be without her bony chaperone.

We waited a couple more minutes, but when no one else arrived, we set off, just the two of us. I can't say my heart was in it this morning, after my conversation with the captain. Usually I liked nothing better than showing off my ship, but right now I felt like I had ball-bearings in my stomach.

As always, I started with the A-Deck. The *Aurora* was running with the sun, leaving behind the coast of North America and heading out over the Pacificus. In a couple of hours we'd lose sight of land altogether.

Light poured in the lounge's windows as we strolled through the writing and reading room with its wicker furniture and ivy growing up trellises, and little desks with blotters and inkwells and *Aurora* stationery. Past that was the first-class reception room where groups of people could gather at tables and order drinks and coffee before and after meals. The dining-room was being re-set for lunch, stewards clattering silverware and crystal as they arranged the place settings. All the dishware was emblazoned with the insignia of the Lunardi airship line. Baz gave me a wink as I passed.

I'd given the tour a hundred times, and the words streamed out automatically today: a smattering of history, technical details, and airship lore. Kate de Vries was a most appreciative audience, I must say. You could tell by her eyes and the angle of her chin that she was listening to every word.

'What a grand ship this is,' Kate said, and I liked her all the more.

I took her into the gymnasium with its exercise camels and rowing machines and a variety of other scarifying apparatus meant to strengthen one's muscles. I can't say it was used much. Most people were more interested in the eating, drinking and smoking aspects of the ship. But here this morning were a couple of young men, dressed in their striped exercise kit, doing sit-ups and knee bends and grunting manly encouragements to one another as they pulled levers at various machines.

Farther along we came to the cinema. A small affair it was, to be sure, but not many airships had one. It seated fifty only, but we'd managed to procure a print of the Lumière triplets' latest epic, *Gilgamesh*. I gestured to Kate to stick her head past the velvet curtain across the doorway. Ghostly light flickered over her face as she watched.

'I shall have to ask Miss Simpkins to accompany me to that later,' she said. 'It seems very exciting.'

At the end of A-Deck was the smoking room. I opened the padded leather door and winced against the pall of cigar fumes.

'Would you care to step inside?' I asked.

'No, thank you,' she said.

'There are some very fine Depressionist paintings on display.'

'I can live without those,' she said.

I didn't blame her. Despite the vigorous fans pumping the smoke outside, the room was unbearable. As for the paintings, I always felt they were a bit gloomy myself, with all their dingy scenes and singed colours. Perfect, in fact, for the room in which they hung.

I led her down the grand staircase to B-Deck. The lounges and reception rooms were much the same as the upper floor, though not quite as large or lavish. I showed her the bakery and pointed out the chief steward's cabin, as well as the crew's and officers' mess. And after that, I took the ring of ship's keys from my pocket and unlocked the access door that led to the rest of the ship. For me this was the most interesting part of the tour, when you left the passenger quarters behind and got to see the real bone and sinew of the *Aurora*. Most people didn't feel the same though. They were always glad to get back to the comfy armchairs and the drinks trolley.

I led Kate along the keel catwalk, heading aft. Of course she'd come this way earlier this morning, but she wanted to take it all in again, and have me explain everything. Her enthusiasm rekindled my own and I pointed out the countless tanks of ballast and drinking water and Aruba fuel that were secured on either side of the catwalk, and the endless bundles of wires and cables and tubing that ran all throughout the *Aurora* like veins and arteries.

Kate stopped and stared up at the giant gas cells, the bottoms of which hung shimmering not seven metres above our heads.

'They're beautiful,' she exclaimed in delight. 'What are they made of?'

'It's called goldbeater's skin.'

'What a wonderful name.'

'It's membrane from cows' intestines, actually. Specially treated to make it impermeable to gas.'

This didn't seem to revolt her in the slightest. 'It must have taken a great many cows,' she commented solemnly. 'How many gas cells are there?'

'Twenty.'

'They really are huge.' She sniffed. 'Is that mangoes?'

'You've got a good nose, Miss. That's the hydrium itself. You can always smell it very faintly, but if it gets any stronger, you know there's a leak somewhere. In the control car, there's a special board that tells you the pressure of all the gas cells. But the sailmakers' noses are even more sensitive. They patrol the corridors and shafts twenty-four hours a day to make sure every square foot of sail is shipshape. Look.'

I pointed up through the web of support beams and bracing wires.

'That's the axial catwalk up there, do you see it? It runs directly overhead the keel catwalk, right through the ship's centre, from her nose all the way back to her tail. The gas cells hang past it on both sides, like walls. It's a bit like walking along a tunnel up there.'

Twenty metres above us, through the metal mesh of the catwalk floor, you could see the small silhouettes of a couple of sailmakers. I wondered if one of them was Lunardi's boy, up there, learning his duties.

'And higher still?' Kate wanted to know.

'The gas cells go all the way up to the top, and there are vents to the outside, in case we need to lose some hydrium.'

'Why would you do that?' she asked, head tilted inquisitively.

'Well, either to lose some altitude, or because we're beyond pressure height.'

'What's that?'

'Pressure height? Oh, the higher we get, the lower the outside air pressure, so beyond a certain height, the hydrium is at a higher pressure than the air.'

'Ah, so the hydrium would expand,' said Kate understanding.

'Yes, and rupture the gas cells, so we sometimes have to vent some.'

'And the outside of the ship, what's it made of?'

'Fabric, stretched tight across the alumiron skeleton.'

'Fabric? That's all?'

'Cotton actually. But it's been specially treated so it's waterproof and fireproof too.'

'That's reassuring, I suppose. And where does that go?' she asked, pointing at a companion ladder.

'The axial catwalk,' I told her. 'There're three ladders that go up. And from there, you've got ladders to the crow's-nests, one fore, one aft.'

'Really?' she said, intrigued. 'What a view that must be.'

'Especially on a clear night, with the stars and all.'

'You must know all their names by now.'

I laughed. 'Maybe so.'

'Can we go up?'

'Afraid not, Miss. It's crew only up there.'

'Oh.' She seemed to sag a little. I wished I could have said yes.

'Are those the engines?' she asked, as the sound of propellers became louder.

I nodded. 'You probably saw them when you boarded. There's two on either side. I'll show you.' I turned off the keel catwalk, down a lateral passageway that ended at a hatch in the ship's hull. The hatch was open, a rectangle of blue sky and sea. We came closer, and looked out at the forward port engine car, a large metal pod suspended outside the ship by struts and wires. From the open back of the car whirled an enormous propeller. Like the other three that powered the *Aurora*, this car was about eight metres long, and three high. A ladder led down to it from the *Aurora*'s hatchway. It had railings, but no protective cage around it.

'Very noisy!' Kate shouted at me.

'Imagine working inside,' I hollered. 'The machinists have special leather helmets to block the sound.'

I'd been inside several times, and it was not a job I ever coveted. It was cold, deafening, boring work, doing watch by the props. I could have told Kate more about the engines themselves, and how they ran on Aruba fuel, and what horsepower they were and how many r.p.m. they were capable of, but I thought that might bore her.

'It looks like it could just snap off,' Kate remarked, as we walked away from the noise of the engine car, back to the keel catwalk.

'The engine cars are welded on,' I said with a shrug, 'as much a part of the *Aurora* as what we're standing on.'

'I won't think about that too much,' she said. 'It doesn't bother you at all, does it! You seem born to this.'

'You're right there,' I said. 'I was born on an airship.'

I'd never been so familiar with a passenger before; I suppose it was because she was so young.

'You weren't,' she said, delighted. 'You're pulling my leg!'

'I'm not,' I said proudly. 'My parents came over from Europe during the Great Immigration. Not on a ship like this, mind you. A freighter it was, all of us crammed in one atop another. My mother was pregnant, but I wasn't due for another month so they thought it safe. But I came early, halfway over the Atlanticus.'

'Your poor mother,' Kate said. 'Was she all right?'

'She was, lucky for her. And I was, too. One of the other passengers was a midwife, and another a medical student, and together they managed things. Tiny I was, light as a feather.'

'And you've been aloft ever since?' she said, those dark eyes on me, as if I was telling the most fabulous story from a fairy-tale book.

'Well, only the last three years really. But I grew up hearing all about it from my father. When we got to North America it was hard for him to find work. We went all the way across the country till we landed in Lionsgate City, and he got a job there with the Lunardi line, started out on one of their cargo ships.'

'Oh,' she said. 'But he must've been away a great deal.'

'He was. But he wrote to us, and on shore leave he would be home with us. And the stories he'd tell!'

'Like what?' she asked.

I took a breath. 'He went everywhere. Saw all the wonders of the world, it seemed. All I could think about when he came home was how much I wished I could go away with him.'

'He must've been a good storyteller.'

'A grand one.'

'My parents weren't much for stories,' Kate said. 'I got all mine from books. And my grandfather. He told me stories when I was little, made-up ones when I was young, and then real ones when I got older. He was a traveller too.'

'Your parents aren't?'

'No. They gave me this trip as a birthday present. But they were both busy, so they sent Miss Simpkins along with me. Aren't I lucky?' she said brightly.

'She seems very dedicated.'

'Yes, she'll make a dictator a fine wife one day.'

I laughed.

'Mercifully, she does sleep a lot. The whole thing's ridiculous anyway. Not that I needed a chaperone! What could happen to me on an airship? And I'm only in Sydney for two weeks before I come back home.'

She didn't sound altogether happy about these arrangements. We were making our way slowly back towards the ship's bow and the passenger quarters. Neither of us seemed in any hurry for the tour to end.

'Tell me,' Kate asked, 'at what altitude does the *Aurora* sail?'

'Varies, Miss. Right now we're cruising at 200 metres.'

'And will we keep to that for the entire crossing?'

'If the winds hold. We might climb higher if the currents are more favourable elsewhere.'

'How high?'

'As much as 1200 metres. But the captain likes to fly so the passengers have a view.'

How attentive her eyes were, taking this all in. It was rare I had such a keen listener, and I found it almost disconcerting.

'And our speed?'

'One hundred and twenty kilometres an hour when I last checked.'

She nodded absently, as if pulling open drawers in her mind, searching for something.

'Does the ship always follow the same route to Sydney? More or less?'

I nodded. 'We'd shift only for the winds or storm fronts.'

I was wondering perhaps if all these questions were brought on by fear of flying. I couldn't quite believe that someone like her, with all her money, had never been on an airship before. Some people never do get used to their feet leaving earth.

'You needn't worry, Miss,' I said. 'The *Aurora*'s as fine a ship as sails the skies. We've circled the globe a thousand times without mishap.'

'Oh,' she said, 'no, I'm not worried. Just curious. But the ship's course is essentially the same?'

'Well, it varies quite a lot, actually.' I liked to pore over the navigator's maps during a crossing, and sometimes our course might resemble a series of zigzags as we rode the winds of high and low pressure systems, and skirted storm fronts.

She nodded thoughtfully.

'Is there something particular you're anxious to see, Miss?' I said. I thought maybe she wanted to catch a glimpse of some volcanic island, or maybe pods of whales.

She looked at the floor as she spoke. 'Were you aboard the *Aurora* last year, about this time, when she rescued a damaged balloon?'

I stared at her, feeling unsettled, like it was about to thunder.

'I spotted it on my watch.'

She touched my hand with hers, and it was so cold a shiver went through me.

'You were the first to see it? From the crow's-nest?'

So I told her, and I must admit, I enjoyed telling her, feeling the thrill of it all over again as I explained how we came alongside and tried to winch the gondola in with the davit. How I had to swing across and hook it to the frame and cut the flight lines.

'You were the one who jumped aboard?'

I nodded.

'The cabin boy?'

I bristled a bit. 'The captain asked me, so I did it. He knew I could do it.'

'You're very brave, Mr Matt Cruse.'

I felt my face warm. 'Not brave, Miss. It was no hardship for me. I have no fear of heights.'

'In the report, they just said it was "a crew member". They didn't give your name.'

'You read about me in the newspaper?'

'No,' she said, 'in the Sky Guard report.'

She paused long enough for me to wonder why on earth she would be getting special reports from the Sky Guard.

'The man in the balloon,' she said, 'was my grandfather.'

'Oh.' I now understood that feeling of thunder in my bones, like a weather change coming. Somehow I'd had a premonition of this, just the way her face was when she started asking about it. And I felt a bit of a dolt now, enjoying telling the story like it was

70

a moving picture, wanting to impress her with my aerial stunts.

'I'm very sorry, Miss.'

'Thank you,' she said. 'For helping him.'

'I wished we'd found him sooner.'

'They said it was a heart attack.'

'That's what Doc Halliday thought. When I first saw him he was unconscious, fallen on the floor of the gondola.' I hesitated, not knowing how much she wanted to hear, but she nodded. 'Anyway, we got him inside and took him to the infirmary and the doctor tended to him. He woke up for a bit.'

'Did he speak to you?'

'Yes, but he seemed confused.'

'What did he say?'

'Well, I guess he thought he'd seen something.' I heard the old man's voice in my head, as I always did when I went back to it. Which was often. On my watch, gazing at the sky, I'd remember his words, the intensity in his eyes. 'He asked me if I'd seen them too.'

She didn't seem surprised by any of this, as if she was expecting it. 'And what did you tell him?'

'I lied and said yes. I didn't even know what he was talking abut. Some kind of winged creature, I gather. He said they were beautiful. Then he said' – I shivered a little bit, finally understanding now – 'He said, "Kate would have loved this".'

She nodded. Water spilled from her eyes.

'You're his Kate,' I said foolishly.

'What else?' she said, wiping her face.

'It seemed to calm him down a bit, me saying I'd seen them too. But then he just sort of looked at me hard, like he knew I was lying. And he told me so. And that started him coughing again. I guess it wasn't long after that he died. After that the captain took care of things, contacted all the proper authorities and so forth.'

'Thank you,' she said. 'For telling me.'

She looked drained, and I felt wrung out too, as if I'd swung across the air to board the sinking balloon all over again. We had reached the end of the keel catwalk, and I opened the door to the passenger quarters and led her inside to B-Deck.

At the base of the grand staircase, I asked her, 'Do you know what it was your grandfather was talking about?'

She nodded. 'That's why I'm here. To see what he saw.'

4

HOT CHOCOLATE FOR TWO

Kate could tell me nothing more, for Miss Simpkins was teetering down the grand staircase in her high heels, looking like she'd just been electrocuted.

'Kate, you gave me the worst fright!'

Kate rolled her eyes at me before turning to face her chaperone.

'I'm sorry, Marjorie, but you were sound asleep and I didn't have the heart to wake you. I thought I'd just go on the tour by myself.'

Miss Simpkins looked at Kate, then me.

'This is the tour? Just you and . . . him.'

She said *him* like I was something oozing from the bottom of a trash can.

'That's right, Marjorie. He *is* the tour guide, after all.'

'Well, I can only say it's most inappropriate. Most inappropriate indeed. Your parents will not be pleased to hear of it.'

'You're quite right,' Kate said. 'They'll be most distressed that their trusted chaperone fell asleep and left their little baby girl helpless.' She tilted up her chin ever so slightly as she said this, and her nostrils narrowed disdainfully. I'd never seen anything quite like it. Plenty of times I'd seen people flare their nostrils when they were angry; Mr Lisbon did it all the time when he and Chef Vlad were arguing. But Miss de Vries somehow made her nostrils smaller, so they were almost little slits. It was really something, the effect it had on Miss Simpkins. The chaperone hemmed a bit and patted her hair, taking little sips of air. I hoped I never got a look like that from Miss de Vries.

I was busting out with questions, but there seemed no chance of continuing the conversation with the chaperone hovering around. So I thought it best to take my leave.

'Thank you so much,' Kate told me. 'I do hope we get a chance to talk some more.'

I smiled at her, and set off towards the crew quarters. As I neared my cabin, I felt an unaccustomed tiredness descend on me like cold drizzle. Probably just the bad news I'd received earlier. Normally I would've gone to the control car and asked if I might watch and take notes. But right now I didn't have the heart. Baz was sitting on the edge of the bottom bunk, kicking off his shoes and socks, whistling. He was just getting off duty too.

'Morning,' he said. 'You look shattered, mate.'

'I'll tell you all about it later.' I climbed up to the top bunk and fell asleep the moment my cheek touched the pillow.

* * *

My alarm clock clattered me out of sleep. Seven p.m. Baz was already up, ironing his shirt. We both had lounge duty from eight till midnight, serving tea and coffee and cognac and whatever else the first-class passengers might desire.

For a moment I just lay there. I loved my cabin, small though it was. On my bunk was the eiderdown quilt my mother had made for me. Stuck with putty to the wall near my pillow were some pictures from home: one of my father in his sailmaker's uniform, another of my mother and Isabel and Sylvia on the balcony of their little apartment in Lionsgate City. I always thought of it as their apartment, not mine, because I was aloft so much now. Three years ago, after my father died, we'd needed money badly, times being what they were, and I was lucky the *Aurora* had offered me a job as cabin boy. It was Captain Walken I had to thank for that.

My mother had not wanted me to take the position, not after what happened to my father. I'd never seen her so upset. I'd tried to hide how much I wanted the job, but she knew anyway. All my life I'd wanted to fly. What she didn't know was that I wanted to fly away from her, too. I wanted to fly to my father, and I couldn't do that, landlocked in the small apartment with its low ceilings and grey views of rainy city streets. My father had spent so little time here. This was not the place I could be near him.

Built into the headboard of the bunk was a little shelf where I had my library. Crew weren't allowed many books aboard, as they were just extra ballast, so I only had a few. I'd chosen the eight my father had kept with him aboard the *Aurora*. How I loved having them here, their leather-bound spines and tooled titles like friends waiting for my return. Sometimes I just liked taking them down and holding them between my hands, even if I was too tired to read. I was lucky to have them.

With my cheek on the pillow, I could see straight out of my porthole. Sky and cloud and if I pressed my nose to the glass I saw the aft engine car, its propeller awhirl, and the water of the Pacificus below. I squinted at the clear sky.

There was something flying out there.

No, it was just a trick, a little crease of shadow on the cloud's underside. But for a moment it had looked like something large and winged. I wondered if this was what Kate's grandfather had seen. Cloud mirages. I wanted to know more and wondered how I'd get a chance to talk to Kate again, without her appalling chaperone.

'You want me to do yours?' Baz asked when I swung myself out of bed. I thanked him and handed over my white serving shirt for him to iron. I was lucky to have Baz Hilcock as my cabin mate. He was kind, funny and always in a good mood. He shimmied as he ironed, humming some catchy show tune. He was eighteen and from Australia. When we reached Sydney he was off on shore leave for a month.

'Three more days, I'll be with Teresa,' he said, giving me a wink. Teresa was his sweetheart. Her picture was taped to the wall beside his bunk. She was in a daring one-piece bathing suit, laughing, her skin all tanned, and she looked so womanly that it made me uncomfortable to gaze at it too long – though I wanted to – as though I was peeping at something I shouldn't. Baz liked talking about her, reading out bits of her letters, and I mostly liked listening, glad he confided in me.

Baz looked up from his ironing and grinned at me.

'Know what, mate? I'm going to propose to her.'

'You are?' I said, amazed. Getting married seemed big, and more grown-up than I wanted to contemplate. I felt a fierce twinge of sadness, like Baz had just said goodbye to me for good, and was bound someplace I couldn't follow.

'Sure,' he nodded, buttoning up and checking his hair in the tiny mirror that hung from the back of our door. 'We've been talking about it, and I figure, it's high time. I've got a good job, in all likelihood I'll make second steward in a year or two when Cleaves finally jumps overboard. Sooner probably, he looks so frazzled.'

I laughed as I pulled on my blue trousers. I looked at my shoes and decided they could go another night without a polish. I slipped on my vest.

'So what's up with you?' Baz asked. 'You looked glum when you came in.'

'I'm not junior sailmaker,' I said, and told him about my talk with the captain.

'I think I've seen the fellow,' Baz said. 'Ten to one he'll fall off the ship before we make land. I'm sorry, Matt. Doesn't get more rotten than that.'

'The captain says he went to the Academy.'

'Oooh, yes, the great Academy,' sang Baz in a high fluting voice. 'The Academy where one learns how to say please and thank you while in flight.'

I chuckled, but the fact was, I longed to go to the Academy. A place where I could learn how to be a rudder man or an elevator man, and be certified. But it was expensive. Most of my wages I sent back home to my mother. She and Isabel and Sylvia needed it more than me. I didn't need money up here – all my meals and clothing were taken care of by the *Aurora*.

Baz winked at me. 'Don't fret, Matt. You're a sailor through and through. There's no keeping you back. I bet my molars and a leg you'll be flying the *Aurora* within ten years. And remember, you're still young! The baby of the ship! Why I remember when we first brought you aboard, wrapped in swaddling clothes. Ahhh, those were sweet days, when I got to bottle-feed you—'

'Oh shut up!' I said, laughing.

'We're all so proud of how you've grown up, young Matt,' he said, dancing out of the way as I tried to bullwhip him with my tie. But his good humour and confidence cheered me up.

'Come on,' he said, handing me my white shirt,

warm and freshly ironed. 'Get your tie on and let's grab some dinner!'

The crew's mess was on B–Deck, beside the kitchen and bakery. It was a cozy room with six large booths that sat about a third of the crew at any one time. The officers had their own mess farther along; they got roomier tables and china place settings and napkins – but exactly the same food. Meals were heaven aboard the *Aurora*. Crew and officers ate as well as the first–class passengers – no point in having the cooks prepare more dishes than necessary.

Baz and I sat down after checking out the menu posted on the wall. Tonight it was venison cutlets and Yukon mashed potatoes – so creamy not even the tip of your tongue could feel a lump – and asparagus spears glazed with lemon butter. There were pitchers of fresh milk and water and ale for those going off duty, and jugs of gravy for the mashed potatoes, and dishes of butter balls glistening with dew and baskets of granary bread baked fresh that afternoon.

I went to the kitchen window to collect my dinner and Baz's. I always liked watching the bustle in there. And I was riveted by the chef, Vlad Herzog, who happened to be cooking downstairs that night.

'Watch out for that one,' Baz had told me on my very first day, three years ago. 'Chef Vlad, he's volatile.'

The word had stuck with me. It made me think of nitroglycerine. In my years aboard the *Aurora*, I'd spent plenty of time around the kitchens, and believe me, Vlad was scary. He had some kind of Transylvanian accent, and Mr Lisbon, the chief steward, had a completely different accent, just as thick, and the two claimed they never understood each other. This was a problem, seeing as they needed to communicate pretty much on an hourly basis. It led to some interesting misunderstandings during mealtimes.

It wasn't that Vlad was crazy, not in any obvious way. He didn't shout or clatter pots and pans or yank his hair out by the roots. Not at first anyway. He always started out very calm, and when he was really angry, he got even calmer and quieter and spoke so slowly you thought he was falling asleep between words. A few weeks ago, just as an example, there had been some confusion over the dinner menu.

'You want that I what?' he had whispered politely to Mr Lisbon. 'You want that I cook duck? Duck? Duck?' He muttered the word softly, as though he didn't know what it meant. Mr Lisbon began to explain.

'No, I know what duck is, many thanks to you,' said Vlad, giving a terrifying smile. 'I make good acquaintance with duck. Little water bird, splash splash, yes? No, that is not my problem. Problem, Mr Lisbon, is this. Problem is DUCK IS NOT ON MENU TONIGHT!'

All the kitchen help casually took a few steps back, but pretended that nothing was the matter.

Mr Lisbon had insisted that duck was, in fact, on the menu.

'Oh,' said Vlad, tossing his hands up in the air. 'Well,

just let me DOUBLE-CHECK!' He made a big show of looking at a sheaf of papers on the counter. 'No. Duck is not on menu TONIGHT. That is TOMORROW. You what? You have CHANGED the menu. Without telling me, I think? I see. I understand now that you change menu without telling me. Yes, I see. Thank you very greatly for this. Good.'

Then Vlad had reached over to his block of big cutting knives, and started laying them out ominously on the counter, arranged by size.

'Duck,' he muttered to himself. 'Duck. But today is Tuesday. And duck was for Wednesday.'

Everyone knew to leave him alone when he got all his knives out like that. He would spend several minutes checking them over, testing their sharpness, and this seemed to soothe him. Then he had taken the duck from the icebox and started cooking.

And it had been wonderful.

Chef Vlad might be loony, but it would be a sad day if he ever left the ship. Or was dragged off kicking and screaming in a straitjacket, as Baz said was more likely. Tonight he seemed fairly calm, and he even smiled at me when he placed the two plates on the counter. Just the smell alone was enough to feed you.

I often thought of my father during mealtimes. He had once eaten at this very table, with many of these same people I now rubbed shoulders with. They'd known my father. They'd known he'd served dutifully and well aboard the *Aurora*. Some had been his friends. I liked being near them all. I didn't need to talk about my father with them, I just liked knowing he'd been here.

I was finishing off my second helping of mashed potatoes when the mess door opened and a crew member I'd never seen before entered. I knew right away it must be the Lunardi fellow. The potatoes nearly stuck in my throat, and I had to swallow them down with a gulp of milk. Lunardi looked around a bit uncertainly, and then sat down at the end of my table.

'Hello,' he said. He was seventeen or eighteen and, I noticed dejectedly, as handsome as a matinée idol. There was no denying it. In fact, he looked like the hero in the last swashbuckler I'd seen. I felt my mouth go dry with indignation. Well, I supposed money could buy anything, even good looks. He sat down, and the first thing he did was knock over a pitcher of milk. Unfortunately, it was nearly empty and only wetted his lap a bit. He mopped it up with his napkin, ears burning red.

'Not too swift, was it?' he said, attempting a laugh, looking right at me.

I couldn't meet his eyes, just kept staring at the junior sailmaker insignias on both corners of his jacket collar. A small gold steering wheel stamped into the fabric. Surely he must know who I was, what he'd done to me. But maybe he didn't. Maybe no one had told him and the blinking oaf didn't know.

'I'm Bruce Lunardi,' he said to everyone. 'I'm the trainee sailmaker.'

Everyone nodded and said polite hellos, nothing more.

Some of them looked at me, checking my reaction to this. Wondering what I'd do. Well, if they were expecting a show, I wasn't giving it to them. Next to me, Baz gave me a friendly wink and nudge. I said nothing. Just slowly drank another glass of milk.

'So you're Otto Lunardi's boy then?' one of the machinists asked.

'Yes, I am,' he said.

'D'you think your father would give me a raise?' someone asked, and laughter rose from the table.

'I'll be sure to put in a good word for you,' Lunardi said. 'But he's a stingy old goat, I can tell you.'

This brought more laughter, but it wasn't against Lunardi this time, and even I couldn't help smiling and giving a quick sniff of amusement.

Meals were a delicious, but quick affair aboard ship. No one really had time to linger, except those coming off watch and willing to trade sleep for company and some friendly gab. Anyway, I'd lost my appetite, even though there was crème caramel for desert, served with fresh Brazilian strawberries and vanilla cream. I nodded goodbye to the other crew and made my exit, relieved to get away from Lunardi.

I wished he'd come to the table bold and cocky, crowing about his position, complaining about the ship and his cabin and the discomfort he now had to endure compared to his palatial mansion ashore. But no, it looked like he might be a decent fellow, and that made things worse somehow.

Upstairs, the first-class lounge was filling up as most of the passengers finished off their dinner. All the gentlemen were in their black jackets and wing-tip collars and bow ties, and the ladies in their long evening dresses and jewels. Mostly it was the ladies in the lounge, as the men seemed to prefer the smoking room where they could breathe some smog and take their drinks and talk about important matters like profits and the price of things.

At a table by the windows sat Miss Simpkins and Kate de Vries. I was stunned at the way Kate looked. She was like a different person altogether in her silk gown. She wore her hair up this evening, and around her throat was a simple sparkling necklace. Her shoulders were showing. When I'd met her this morning she'd been a girl, and now she was suddenly too much like a woman. Beside her, drinking tea, sat Miss Simpkins, her hair in some kind of terrifying beehive. Kate saw me and smiled, and her smile I recognized at least. I nodded as I made my way to the bar to replace Jack Mobius.

'Watch out for the woman with the scary hair,' he whispered to me, as we traded places.

'I know all about her,' I whispered back.

'Said her tea tasted like a fish had bathed in it.'

'Should have taken the poor fellow out earlier,' I told him. 'Then she wouldn't have known.'

'Night, Matt,' he said with a laugh.

Baz came up later to play the baby grand. A marvel it was, all alumiron if you can believe it, and weighing only a couple of hundred kilos. And Baz was a wonder himself, the way his hands waltzed and tangoed across the keys.

'This music's too loud,' I heard Miss Simpkins complain. 'It's too raucous. Completely inappropriate for young ears.' A few minutes later, she stood up to leave, and Kate reluctantly stood as well. Kate caught my eye, and held it for a moment, like there was something she wanted to tell me. Miss Simpkins, I noticed, took her time walking out, pausing to look at the paintings and glance at the last red wash of the sunset on the ocean. She walked like someone who expected people to watch her, and funnily enough, a few of the men were. They seemed to find her pleasing, and I suppose she was an attractive woman. I guess they hadn't talked to her yet. Maybe they didn't think her hair was as scary as I did.

Kate had a lot of hair, and it was piled up on the back of her head. A lovely mahogany it was. But it was her eyes I liked best, the way there always seemed to be something going on behind them, sparks and swift gusts. A right little thunderstorm, in her head.

A table of gentlemen had struck up a conversation with Miss Simpkins about one of the paintings, and Kate casually left her chaperone's side and walked across the lounge to the bar.

'Good evening, Mr Cruse,' she said.

'Would you like anything to drink, Miss?' I said. 'Hot chocolate, tea. Brandy?'

She smiled. I decided I'd try to make her smile as much as possible.

'How long are you on duty here?' she asked.

'Till midnight, Miss.'

I was trying to stay polite and professional.

Over her shoulder, I saw Miss Simpkins turn and see Kate. She came striding over.

'Shall we retire then, Kate?' she said, cocking a suspicious eye at me, as though I'd just tried to drug and kidnap her young charge.

'Goodnight, Mr Cruse,' Kate said to me.

'Goodnight, ladies. Sleep well.'

I was sad to see her leave – and frustrated too. How was I supposed to find out more about her grandfather at this rate?

The evening went on. The lounge filled as people arrived from the smoking room and cinema after the late show ended. I served coffee and tea and then more port and sherry and Scotch and brandy and Baz's playing got more and more passionate and there was ragtime and honky-tonk and then Mr Lisbon whispered in his ear, and Baz began playing Bach funeral music, sitting stiff and waxy and doing his best to look like a cadaver. One by one the passengers left the lounge to return to their staterooms for the night.

Midnight was coming on, and I was alone in the lounge, wiping down the counters when I heard a thunk in my message tube. I lifted out the canister and saw from its markings it was from the Topkapi stateroom. I unscrewed the top and unrolled the note.

Two hot chocolates, please.
Kate de Vries

Smiling, I finished cleaning up, and then steamed some milk and melted the chocolate and mixed in the sugar and put a dollop of whipped cream on both and some chocolate shavings. I put them on a tray and set off for the stateroom.

I'd been expecting Miss Simpkins to open the door, and was surprised to see Kate standing there. She was wearing one of the burgundy dressing gowns that came with the stateroom, and I was glad to see her hair was down and braided. She looked young again, after being all grown-up at dinner.

'Hello,' she said.

'Where should I put them, Miss?' I asked, stepping inside.

She looked around before pointing to one of the coffee tables. 'There, please.'

'Where's Miss Simpkins?' I inquired.

'Oh, she's been asleep for ever.' She pointed at the closed door of her bedroom.

'Who's the second one for, then?' I asked, nodding at the hot chocolate.

'You.'

I blinked. 'Thank you, Miss, but I can't.'

She looked genuinely surprised. 'But I thought you were off duty now.'

'I am. But I'm crew, not a first-class passenger. I can't just sit down in your stateroom!'

'I don't see why not if a first-class passenger invites you.'

She seemed quite miffed, and I understood then that hers was a world where she got her own way, and nothing was impossible. For a moment I almost disliked her. Could she even imagine how other people lived? Could she guess how it felt to be poor and miss an opportunity because of a rich man and his son?

'It's not really allowed for crew to fraternize with passengers, Miss,' I said stiffly.

'Well, it seems a silly rule,' she said, but she gave me an apologetic smile. 'I don't want to get you into trouble. I just wanted to talk some more. It was a bit intriguing, where we last ended up, wasn't it? Aren't you a bit curious?'

'I am,' I said, sharing her smile. 'Of course I am. But what about Miss Simpkins?'

'Don't worry about her, she hardly ever wakes up before she's had nine hours.'

I wasn't altogether reassured, and knew I couldn't stay long. I shuddered to think what would happen if I was spotted coming out of her stateroom after midnight.

I noticed that all the curtains were drawn back and that a wooden tripod had been set up before the windows. Atop it was a camera, a great boxy thing with an accordion-like lens. Wooden crates were set out nearby on the floor, containing all manner of flasks and receptacles.

'Is that all yours?' I asked.

She nodded. 'It's a bit of a hobby of mine. I'm quite good.'

'What is it exactly you're hoping to take pictures of?' I half knew the answer.

'You've never seen them, then?' she asked me.

'No.'

From the coffee table she picked up a fat leather-bound notebook, held together with a ribbon.

'It's my grandfather's log,' she said. 'It's all in here, what he saw. He made some sketches too.'

Outside, clouds scudded past, ablaze with moon and starlight. The warm smell of chocolate filled the room. The ocean whispered through the open windows.

'Kate?' came a sleepy voice from behind the door. 'Is that you?'

A jolt went up my spine. Miss Simpkins. It sounded like she was getting out of bed.

Kate pressed the journal into my hands. 'Take it. I know I can trust you. Read it and bring it back to me when you're done.'

Inside Miss Simpkins' bedroom I heard the sound of slippered feet moving over the carpet.

'Kate? Are you there?'

I grabbed the tray and high-stepped it out of there.

'I've put a bookmark where he first sees them,' Kate told me.

'Goodnight,' I said.

Kate smiled at me as she closed the door.

I stood in the deserted hall for a moment, looking at

the notebook. It had been on the balloon when I'd swung over, a year ago. Maybe it had been amongst the things scattered across the gondola floor. Maybe I'd even seen it as I'd crouched over Mr Benjamin Molloy. It seemed strange to be holding it now in my hands, all wind-warped and rain-swollen. I took the tray back to the kitchen, then went to my cabin and started reading.

5

THE LOG OF THE ENDURANCE

The journal's spine was cracked and flabby, and there was a hair ribbon round the book, holding it all together. Moths danced around in my stomach as I climbed up to my bunk and stretched out. Baz was on crow's-nest until four. I turned on my reading lamp. I untied the ribbon and carefully turned back the cover. The pages were all scabby, like the book had been soaked by rain, then baked in the sun.

Small neat lines of ink covered each page: date, position, wind speed, altitude, observations. There was a little preface telling about how he, Benjamin Molloy, planned to do a complete west-to-east circumnavigation of the globe in his hot-air balloon. I read quickly over these first pages, not because they weren't interesting, but because I could see Kate's bookmark up ahead, and it made my stomach feel swirly, wondering what was written there. It was hard to concentrate on the stuff beforehand.

Kate's grandfather had started out in Cape Town to catch the jet stream, and travelled quickly eastwards over the Indian Ocean. But over Australia his luck ran out, and he got shunted off course to the north-east.

There was no sign of panic in his log. His days were busy with keeping the balloon shipshape, managing his supplies and provisions, taking weather readings and bearings. He described the countries and landscapes he was sailing over. Some days there were just co-ordinates and weather conditions, other days he had lots to write about: birds, the changing light, the landscape of the passing nations beneath him, the creatures below the ocean's surface. He seemed interested in everything.

I was keeping an eye on his co-ordinates and realized he was drifting along a flight path not too far off the *Aurora*'s from Sydney to Lionsgate City. With every day his course veered more to the east, as he tried to catch favourable winds at different altitudes. Not for the first time I felt a sense of dread for him. I loved being aloft, but to be completely at the mercy of the winds, with no other means of power or steerage – it was a frightening thought. Obviously Kate's grandfather had a stouter heart than mine.

I lost track of how long I'd been reading, I was so caught up in the day-to-day journey. There weren't a lot of clues, but little bits of the man crept through, even in his log. He liked watching the weather coming; he hated the tinned baked beans but ate them because they were nutritious and portable; he enjoyed Shakespeare; he loved his granddaughter. He'd mentioned her often in his log. 'Must remember to tell Kate,' he'd write. Or: 'Will send Kate a postcard when I set down in Cape Town.'

With a start I realized that Kate's bookmark was just a page's turn away.

I put the journal down, climbed off my bunk, and went down the corridor to have a pee. At the sink I splashed cold water on my face. Not that I was sleepy. It just seemed like the thing to do when you were up in the wee hours of morning, reading the log of a strange, doomed voyage.

Back in the cabin, I slid down into the warm furrow of my bunk and took a glimpse at the stars out of my porthole. With a deep breath, I picked up the journal and turned the page.

September 2nd

15:23
An island in the distance (171'43" west, 2'21" north) veiled in mist. Possibly volcanic given the cone-shaped silhouette it presents. It looks a tropical place, with a crescent-shaped beach behind a green lagoon, and densely forested.

Sighted two albatrosses foraging over the ocean, plucking fish and squid from the water's surface with their long hooked beaks.

17:45

Closer to island now. Huge flock of albatrosses in distance. Most unusual to see so many together. Perhaps island is nesting ground. Their colouring is odd, no dark coloration on their wing-tips or bodies. Their plumage seems a misty white, so that against cloud and sky, they are scarcely visible. Only when they are against the ocean or the island can I make them out with any clarity.

18:02

Not birds.

It sent a tingle through me, those two words, and I had to look up from the book. I imagined Benjamin Molloy peering through his spyglass, his hand tightening around the gondola's rim. What was it he'd seen that told him these creatures weren't birds?

Their wings are not feathered. I was mistaken about their beaks; they have none. Considerably bigger than either magnificent frigate birds or albatrosses. One of the creatures broke from the flock and made a slow circle of the *Endurance*, quite high at first, then spiralling down closer to the gondola. It seemed very curious. Its body is easily two metres in length, and closely furred, its forelegs seem to turn into wings, like a bat's, with a single protruding claw at the wings' leading

edge. The span I would estimate as two or three metres across. Its rear legs are stubby, but with wickedly sharp curved claws. I feared for the balloon, should it collide with it. How can such a creature stay aloft? It looks too heavy. It is fiercely agile in the sky, dipping and spinning and diving with ease, its wings infinitely versatile. It fairly seems to leap through the air. Saw scarcely anything of its face. A gleam of sizeable incisors on upper and lower jaws. A flash of intelligent green-flecked eyes. Then it veered off, hurtling back towards its fellows.

An undiscovered species?

I turned the page and there was a picture, a pencil sketch. Just looking at it made my heart flutter, and I had to sit up and catch my breath. He'd put the rim of the basket in the foreground, and the silhouette of the island in the background to give a sense of scale. The creature's wingspan was huge. He was a deft hand, the grandfather, that was certain. Couldn't have had much time to get it down, but his lines were swift and assured. It was the strangest-looking thing, half bird, half panther.

September 4th

I have dropped into a calmer stratum of air so I can hover over the island and observe them. They float. They face into the wind, and scarcely need

beat their wings. I watched one move not a muscle for hours, sleeping maybe, bedded down on the air itself. They cannot weigh much.

Across the next two pages were drawings of skeletons.

The first one was human, I saw that clearly enough, the ribcage, the hips, the skull atop the neck. Next to it was a skeleton that looked at first glance not so very much different. Excepting the hands. The bones of the fingers were all long and flared. Freakish it was to look at, until I read Benjamin Molloy's caption underneath. Bat, it said. Next to this was a third skeleton, and it seemed some sort of bizarre combination of the two. Shortened legs, like the bat, and instead of arms, the same weirdly flared finger bones of the bat. But the skull on this one was no bat's; nor was it human. The skull was flatter, with sharp teeth. Littler yes, but certainly no one would mistake this for a bat, and never a bird. The drawings were made with scientific care, all shaded and with a length scale to the side. He was a clever man, Kate's grandpa, no questioning that. Seemed to know something about everything. Underneath were all sorts of Latin words.

September 5th

09:15
Still playing the air currents around the island, so I can watch them. They have a great curiosity for

my balloon, circling high, but rarely drawing too close to the gondola. Difficult for me to see their bodies or faces more clearly. They seem wary of me; the sight of my spyglass makes them scatter in an instant. I wonder why?

With a start I wondered if these creatures were responsible for damaging his balloon. Had they tested the material with their sharp claws, torn enough little gashes to make it sink?

17:47
They do not land. In all the time I've been observing, they haven't landed in the trees or on the water. They feed low over the island, preying on all manner of birds. They are voracious hunters. They also eat fish, strafing the water and plunging their rear claws into the sea as they brake. They come up with fish or small squid. They lift it high, then flip it up to their mouths and take it whole. Sometimes they drop their prey, and then dive down and snatch it into their mouths.

September 6th

11:17
I have counted twenty-six of the creatures.
   I wish Kate could see them, the way they

gambol and swirl through the air. I've never seen an animal look so at home in its element. Like dolphins or porpoises or whales, they clearly love to play. Why has no one ever seen these before? Their natural camouflage is excellent, but with so many airships aloft now, surely someone else must have seen these creatures? Or are there very few? Are these the only ones in existence?

On the next page was another sketch, of a great flock – or a herd, I wasn't sure what to call them – of these things circling over the coast of the island.

September 7th

13:40
They birth in the air.

One after another, one of the creatures – a female I now realize – would soar to a great altitude, 2,000 metres or so. I increased my lift so I could rise with them, and keep watch. The female put her head to the wind and angled her wings so she was hovering. Then something dropped from her hindquarters. It happened so quickly all I was aware of was a small dark bundle plunging away from her. At first I thought it was merely her droppings. But I quickly realized it was too large. And the female's behaviour was most curious. Immediately she went into a dive too, keeping pace with the falling object.

The object wobbled in the air and seemed to enlarge, even as it fell past me. It was spreading its wings. It was no bigger than a kitten, but its wings, as they unfurled, were many times the width of its body. Out went the wings, and angled instinctively so that the newborn's plunge began to slow dramatically. After a moment or two I saw the wings lift and push tentatively, then again, and again, each time with more force.

It was flying.

From the moment of birth, it knew how. How could such a thing be possible? Incredible! But then, does not the newborn whale, born into the element of water, know instantly how to swim? Why could it not be so with this creature then? Only air, and not water, was its element.

The mother flew close alongside its child, as if giving advice, monitoring its progress.

I watched more females make the climb to the birthing altitude, and then release their newborns into the air.

The sixth birth was different.

The newborn fell, and only the right wing unfurled to its full length. The left seemed stuck, or crimped somehow, and the newborn went into a spiral, out of control. It could not pull up. The mother flew around it frantically but there was nothing she could do. She made a sound I had not heard them make before, a plaintive shriek. Down the newborn fell, flip-flopping in the air. Finally its wings were both out, and I thought it must be slowing, though it was impossible to tell from so high above.

I lost sight of it above the dense foliage of the island. I waited and watched the skies for a time, but only saw the mother circling overhead. No sign of the newborn. It must have fallen to its death.

Wonder how many must die like this, unable to learn the air instantaneously?

Of the fourteen births, this is the only failure.

The newborns cling, upside down, to their mothers' bellies to nurse, and she flies for both of them.

September 8th

12:51
All are feeding today with a new kind of urgency. Are they on some kind of migration? I wonder where they're going? Where they come from? I suppose the sky is their home; they need no terrestrial haven. Perhaps they simply move from hemisphere to hemisphere looking for the

warmest skies, and the birthing season coincides with their arrival in southern latitudes.

19:35
They're departing. Would like to follow, but they're too fast. With tailwinds, I would estimate eighty knots. Amazing creatures.
  Gone now.
  Weather changing.

Maybe it was me, but I thought he sounded pretty dejected. When I turned the page I felt a bit queasy. Most of the handwriting was smeared, by torrential rain, I supposed, and I could make out only a few words. It seemed a tropical storm had overtaken him, and kept him in its fist for some time. I think I saw the word 'damage' in one entry, and a mention of a problem with the envelope. A hot flush swept my back. Was it leaking? Had the creatures torn his balloon, or was it just the storm?

Benjamin Molloy had stopped dating his entries, and his co-ordinates and weather observations seemed half-hearted now. His handwriting was all tilted over, the letters slewing into one another. I remembered that we'd found him on September 13th, so that left five days after his last dated entry. I wondered if he'd now fallen ill, too weak to repair his ship, or keep his log properly. There were some more sketches of the creatures, and then, suddenly, the sketches became stranger, covering more and more of the pages.

Creatures with the faces of lions or eagles or women. Creatures with human faces, and fur and wings that, even not fully extended, dwarfed their bodies. These were imaginings, surely, for they were so different from his earlier sketches, but drawn with such detail you'd have thought he'd had them right before his eyes.

Surely he was ill, or disturbed by now. Seeing angels, maybe. Seeing his own death fluttering down to gaze upon him with her hypnotist's eyes and carry his soul off.

'They were beautiful,' he'd muttered to me before he died. 'Did you see them?'

There was only one more written entry in the log.

Airship in the distance. Will signal for help.

I looked for the date, but found none. It must have been the *Aurora* he'd sighted, but I'd certainly seen no signal from his gondola. Perhaps he'd passed out before he could signal. Doc Halliday had said he'd had pneumonia, and possibly a heart seizure too.

I stared at that last page for a while, the final words, the nothingness after it, and it got me feeling strange, so I had to close the book. I felt a keen disappointment. It was hard to know what to make of it all. At first the log had been so clear and reasonable, but by the end, especially with those pictures, it seemed he was dreaming it up. When did the real end, and the conjurings of a disturbed mind begin?

It was pushing two in the morning now, and I felt thoroughly ill at ease. I put the book on the shelf and eventually slept.

And dreamed all night. Of me and Kate de Vries and winged creatures that looked like cats, and Benjamin Molloy, and Captain Walken, and there were others swirled into the dream: the Lunardi boy, and Baz and a great sense of peril hung over us all, but also exhilaration. My father was there, too, and we were suddenly in a gondola, this great group of us, with winged creatures careening all around. Some watched the creatures with intense amazement, some with fear, others with only mild curiosity. But they were flying closer to the balloon, ever closer, and I saw their great curved claws and teeth and was worried they would tear the balloon and we'd no longer be airworthy. Keep back, I shouted at them, but closer they came. Keep back, I shouted again, but they would not heed me.

I woke feeling as if I hadn't slept at all, head thrumming like a symphony. I sprang off the bunk, eager to get the journal back to Kate and talk to her. But it wasn't until lunch that I had a chance. At breakfast I was serving, and Miss Simpkins was at the table the whole time, and then she whisked Kate out before I could even hand her the journal. Then there was the clearing up and the preparing for lunch.

Around midday we were passing over the Hawaiis, and the captain slowed down and took us lower so the passengers could get a good look. On other trips we sometimes made stops, but this was a direct passage, so everyone had had to content themselves with peering down at the lush foliage and hearing the shriek of macaws and spider monkeys and toucans and cockatoos, and smelling the heady scent of flowers that reached us even at thirty metres. We were close enough so people on the ground waved and cheered, and bathers on the beach shielded their eyes with tanned hands to look up at the great ship as it painted its massive shadow over the sand and water.

We were cruising over the outer islands when the captain entered the lounge, grinning.

'Ladies and gentlemen, a point of interest. Off the starboard side, we're passing Mt Mataurus and if I'm not mistaken she is about to erupt.'

Nearly everyone put down their forks and knives and rushed to the windows. In the distance was the island with its volcano, a great heap of stone, looking more like the devil's anvil than anything, despite the green hue of its lush vegetation. Great puffs of grey smoke were billowing up from its jaws, and getting darker by the second.

'Thar she blows!' shouted Baz.

Black bits of rock came shooting out from the cone, and then the sound hit us a second later, a deep thunderous vibration that passed through the entire ship and rattled the windows. Best view in the world it was. We were upwind of it, or we would have soon been choking on the ash and smoke the volcano was venting high into the sky.

Soon it was spitting out sparks, and then a glutinous tongue of black and orange lava oozed over the crater's rim and started a leisurely slide down the slope, incinerating everything in its path. Good thing this was an uninhabited island.

'Amazing, isn't it?'

I glanced over and Kate was beside me. She was looking out the window but I knew she wasn't talking about the volcano. There was no sign of Miss Simpkins nearby, and there was no one else around us; everyone was watching the eruption anyway, and talking and pointing excitedly and snapping pictures.

'Incredible,' I said, and faltered, uncertain what to say next. I took the journal from my inside breast pocket and passed it to her. 'Thank you.'

'You don't believe it,' she said coldly.

'I'm not saying that. It's just, I'm not altogether certain your grandpa really knew what he was seeing.'

'How can you say that? He spent days watching them and taking down notes like a scientist. He couldn't have made up all these things. Not in such detail!'

It did seem an awful lot to imagine, even if he was delirious. I remembered his drawings. A weak, shaking hand couldn't have spun those lines.

'He always saw them from a distance,' I pointed out.

'True, but think what he saw! The feeding, the birthing!'

'Those pictures towards the end.' I had traversed the skies over Atlanticus and Pacificus and never had I seen such creatures. How to tell her that her grandpa had been ill and his fevered brain had projected these things on to thin air for his failing eyes to see? I thought of all her camera equipment, her bottles of chemicals, and could not find it in my heart to speak the truth.

'You think like the others,' she said, and there was a new hardness in her voice.

'I think your grandfather was unwell and saw things. Maybe,' I added. All the friendly light in her eyes had frosted away and it made me feel sick.

'No. He saw them. He'd been watching them for days.'

She clenched the journal in both hands, knuckles white. 'He was sick by then, I suppose,' she said. 'But maybe he didn't mean us to think those last drawings were real. He was just imagining.'

'Your grandpa's not the first to see such things. They're called sky kelpies. You see them from time to time, reflections on the water, mostly. All sorts of weird atmospheric things. Airshipmen used to report them all the time. It's like how sailors used to think there were mermaids. They were just porpoises and narwhals and such.'

I could see she didn't like this much. I was insulting

106

her. But what else could I say? I was just telling her the facts.

'Maybe you should talk to the captain about it,' I suggested. 'I'm sure he'd talk with you, Miss.'

Captain Walken surely must have read the journal last year when we took the gondola on board. I wondered that he'd never spoken of the strange things it contained – but of course he wouldn't have. He would never have divulged the contents of another captain's log to any but the relevant officers and authorities. It was confidential. He wouldn't go blabbing to the crew and cabin staff about it.

'I don't need to talk to the captain about it. I expect I'd get much the same as what I've just heard from you.'

'It's not that I haven't looked,' I blurted out as she turned to leave. 'I've looked, for all sorts of things, you can take my word on it. Every flicker in the sky.' I shook my head. 'I've never seen anything. But I'd love to. What your grandpa described is amazing. It sent shivers across my belly and then up into my armpits.'

'Me too!' she said, nodding with a frown. 'That tingly feeling. I get it every time I read it, and I've read it a hundred times now.'

All the passengers in the lounge, including Miss Simpkins luckily, were still crowded around the windows, riveted by the eruption. The volcano was putting on quite a show. Half the island was aflame now, lava crackling and steaming as it poured itself into the water.

'Have you shown the journal to anyone else?' I asked her. 'Your parents, surely.'

I saw her nostrils narrow as she sucked in an angry breath. 'They're embarrassed by the whole business. Mother's always thought he was odd. The travelling, the balloons. Just silly. They always thought he was a bit of a nutter. Hallucinations, that's what they said. Let's just forget the whole thing. That's why I had to send the letter to the Zoological Society myself!'

I blinked.

'I couldn't let my parents stop this from getting out to the world! This is a major discovery — a new animal! I wrote them a letter describing more or less what my grandfather saw, and asked them if they'd care to see a facsimile of his journal.'

'Did they reply?'

'Oh yes.'

From her handbag she produced a letter. It was folded square, the creases so worn you could tell she'd folded and unfolded it many times. I could imagine her face when she read it, getting mad all over again. It wasn't a long letter and I read it quickly:

Dear Miss de Vries,

Thank you for your letter. Firstly, let us say how sorry we are to hear of the death of your grandfather. We wish you and your family the best in this trying time. We appreciate your taking the time to tell us about your grandfather's

observations on his balloon voyage, namely the sighting of 'some kind of winged mammal'.

We feel strongly that should such a creature exist it would surely have been sighted and documented long ago. Every year there are hundreds of unsubstantiated sightings of monstrous creatures in land, air and sea and we feel it is our duty as men of science to remind you gently that your grandfather was not trained, and in his state of health, he may have suffered additional deficiencies of observation . . .

'Additional deficiencies of observation,' Kate scoffed, reading over my shoulders. 'They mean he was seeing things. Why don't they call him a senile old goat!'

I turned away a bit so I could finish the letter.

Our suggestion to you would be to put your grandfather's writings out of your mind, and turn your interests elsewhere, to more comfortable young ladies' pursuits.

'Did you get to the "young ladies' pursuits" part?' she demanded.

'Just now, yes.'

'I suppose they mean darning socks and needlepoint or making iced butter balls for the dinner table.'

'Most likely,' I said. 'Can I just finish—'

'You're taking a long time,' she said.

I whisked the letter down. 'With you interrupting!'

She seemed to realize she was being a pest, and her haughty gaze fell to the carpet.

The rest of the letter was all yours sincerelys and thank you for your interest in the Zoological Society etcetera etcetera. It was signed Sir Hugh Snuffler. I saw him in my mind's eye. Short and balding with a big loud voice.

'Arrogant old farts,' Kate muttered. 'As if they've explored every inch of the planet. As if anyone has! And what about you?' she fairly shouted.

'What about me?'

'You've flown for years, yes?'

'Well, three.'

'And how much of the actual sky have you traversed?'

'Not much, when you put it that way.'

'Exactly. Ships have their routes and, as you say, deviate from them only when necessary. That must leave millions and millions of kilometres of unexplored sky and sea!'

'I imagine you're right,' I said, nodding.

'And how long have airships really been flying?'

'Fifty years or so now.'

'Hardly any time at all, in other words. So how can they possibly say they don't exist?'

'Especially out here over the Pacificus,' I said, surprising myself. 'The skyways and sea lanes are much less well travelled, compared to the Atlanticus.'

'Exactly,' she said, beaming.

'Do your parents know you wrote to the Zoological Society?'

'Heavens, no! They would've locked me in my room without pen or paper! They'd have been mortified! Telling someone outside the family! Spreading his mad rantings! I wish he'd been my father and not Mother's. Wasting all his stories on her. She hasn't an imaginative bone in her body!'

'But you do. Question is, is this all imagination, or real?'

'The co-ordinates he wrote down, for the island. Do we pass over them?'

'I'd have to check, but I think no.'

'Will you check, though?'

'Yes,' I said.

'And if we don't pass over, will you tell me when we'll be nearest the spot?'

'I'll do that.'

'Will you really?' She seemed amazed.

'Yes.'

'Grandpa thought they were migrating, and this is the same time of year. We could see them.'

I thought of her fancy camera.

'And what if you get a picture? What'll you do with it?'

'I'll send it directly to Sir Hugh Snufflynose at the Zoological Society. That'll set him straight!'

I laughed. 'I'm sure it will, Miss.'

'I wish you wouldn't call me Miss.'

'What should I call you?'

'Kate, of course.'

'If I start calling you Kate now when it's just the two of us, I might slip up in public, and that'd be seen as impertinent.'

'Silly rules.'

'People like you invented them. Not me.'

'Good point,' she said appreciatively, a thoughtful crease in her brow. 'Really good point.'

'Here's what I'll do,' I said. 'When I get off duty, I'll check the charts and find out when we'll be closest.'

'Thank you. I just hope it's during daylight.'

'I hope you see them,' I said. 'I really do.'

6

SZPIRGLAS

Back in the crow's-nest, nestled beneath the stars. Trying to imagine winged creatures above me, creatures who never needed to land, who'd never felt earth beneath their feet. Sitting under that glass dome, looking up at the sky's bigger black dome, always put me in a talkative frame of mind. Of course it was all talking to myself.

Before starting my watch I'd gone down to the navigation room and Mr Grantham had patiently let me gawk at his charts. Our projected route was a dotted line, with a few little zigzag markings so far where we'd deviated because of wind and weather. I looked for the co-ordinates Kate's grandfather had written in his journal. There was no island marked on Grantham's charts, not even a little dot. I could imagine Kate's look when I told her that. Her nostrils would narrow a bit, and her chin would lift and she'd say something like, 'Surely, Mr Cruse, you're not suggesting that every drop of the ocean has been charted?'

And she'd be right, of course.

'What is it you're looking for, lad?' Grantham had asked in his friendly way.

'What's over here? Much?'

'Don't think so. We try to stay out of that region actually.'

'Why's that?'

'Winds are capricious all through there, that's why it's called the Sisyphus Triangle. There's been airships that went in and never came out. I've heard rumours about garbled distress calls, compass needles spinning madly, instruments all screwy. Luckily, there's not much need to use those airways. They don't lead anywhere of particular interest.'

I looked at the dotted line of our course, and made a quick calculation. Tomorrow at breakfast we'd be as close to the invisible island as we were likely to get.

At dinner, I'd left a note in Kate's napkin, telling her what I'd learned. Baz caught me folding it up. He didn't say anything, just gave me a look, like a cat that had taken an entire budgie in its mouth and was sitting very still, hoping no one would notice. Then he winked and walked off. I blushed –

And almost blushed again now in the crow's-nest as I remembered it. I liked talking to her, but sometimes I'd feel her eyes on me and I'd be painfully aware of the way my words sounded, or of my body hanging around me like a big floppy suit of clothing, and I wouldn't know how to stand properly, and what was my arm doing there, and was there a bit of spit on my upper lip?

I wondered if she was awake, sitting up already at her stateroom windows, camera ready, waiting for first light. Midnight was long past; the passengers were all asleep, and only the crew and the *Aurora* were awake, working and moving through the sky.

At night, when the sky is scalloped with clouds, and the moon does a vanishing act, you fall back on instinct when looking for moving objects. Almost like looking for shadows on shadow.

I was gazing off our port stern when I felt one of those little shifts in the sky. From the corner of my eye, some of the stars seemed to disappear. I looked back, and of course there was nothing. But it spooked me some. My imagination was all riled up from Kate's story and her grandpa's journal.

Then more stars were suddenly snuffed out, and a long slash of darkness tilted across the sky. I blinked. At first it was impossible to tell how big it was, or how close, and I was squinting, face pressed so close against the glass dome I was starting to fog it up. The moon slid out from behind the clouds and I fell back in surprise as an enormous pair of dark wings soared over me. I swirled around, nearly braining myself against the glass, but the moon was blotted out once again, and all I had to see by were a few listless stars.

Something had landed on the *Aurora*.

In shadow it hunched there, not fifteen metres from my observation post. Its enormous wings were half folded back like some fearsome gargoyle. An eye flashed

115

as its head turned slightly. It took a step towards me. I lost my wits, I'll admit, and my mind flooded with nightmare thoughts. I should call the bridge, I should call Kate, I should get down that ladder faster than a fireman on a pole! It was one thing to think about mysterious creatures, another to have one a few feet away.

It took another step.

The moon came back and the creature's white feathered body gleamed in the light. Right away I noticed its beak, a long hooked thing. It had webbed feet.

It was nothing more than an albatross. It folded its wings against its body and took a few more steps towards my post.

I was mightily relieved I hadn't called the bridge. I could imagine my half-throttled voice reporting a giant seagull. The jokes would become legendary. Young Matt Cruse gave himself a bit of a fright when a seagull flew by. I heard it was a budgie. But you know how much bigger things look at night! Perhaps we should've allowed him to take his teddy bear on watch with him.

I looked at the albatross. An impressive thing it was, the sheer size of its feathered body. Made me realize right then how easy it would be to mistake these birds for something more, for mysterious winged mammals, for flying cats even. It made me sad.

I'm not sure if the albatross even saw me beneath the

dome, watching it. It hunkered down atop the *Aurora*. With its wings folded, it didn't look nearly so huge; in fact it was hard to imagine where all that wing came from when they were folded up. I didn't want to scare it, but I didn't want it on the ship, putting a nick in our skin with those pointy feet.

I rapped sharply on the glass.

The bird's neck straightened a bit, and its head turned a smidgen.

I rapped again.

This time the bird just lowered its head into its body, settling down for a nice snooze. Happy to let someone else do the flying for a while. I was sure it must be tuckered out, this far over the ocean. Look at it, comfy as could be, its feathers didn't even look ruffled, even though there was a stiff wind blowing on it.

'Come on, clear off,' I said, waving my arms and hands.

The bird looked at me, unimpressed.

Being ignored by a bird, even as grand a one as an albatross, is rather hard on the self-esteem. I had to get it off, but carefully. No one liked the idea of maltreating an albatross. Before sailors took to the air, there'd been an abundance of stories about the bad luck that would befall any who harmed an albatross. 'The Very Longe Poeme of the Venerable Mariner' was one of them. The lads in that one, they shot an albatross, cooked it up for dinner, and had no end of bad luck.

I took the speaking tube.

'Crow's-nest.'

'Yes, Cruse.'

It was First Officer Rideau on duty. Lucky me.

'Sir, there's an albatross landed atop the ship. I've tried to scare it off but it's going nowhere. It's near the crow's-nest. Permission to open the hatch and shoo it off.'

'Very well. Take all precautions, please. And report back when you're finished.'

'Very good, sir.'

Carefully I unlatched the hatch, put my goggles on. I clipped a safety line to my belt and tipped the domed hatch up and back. The wind met my face at 130 kilometres an hour. I turned my head slightly so I could breathe. The simple movement of the hatch made the albatross stand up in surprise. And when it saw my head and shoulders rise up out of the crow's-nest, it shuffled back a bit.

'Go on, clear off, mate!' I shouted. The wind hurled my words back over my shoulder. I doubted the bird could hear me. So I waved my arms around over my head.

This was one stubborn bird.

I knew I'd have to let it see who was the boss. Standing up, the bird was no midget. Its head came to my waist, and I didn't fancy getting snapped at with that beak.

I stepped over the rim and on to the *Aurora*'s broad back. The wind met me full on. There was a guide line along the ship's spine, and I took it with one hand, crouching, keeping my head low so the wind shot over my neck and shoulders rather than catching me full in the chest.

I took a few steps towards the bird. It took a few steps back, wings arched threateningly. I had to admire its nerve. Was it was planning to walk me all the way along the ship to the bow and see who could fly better? I wasn't afraid of falling. Heights didn't mean a thing to me, never had. But I did start to wonder if this bird and I were in for a long game of follow-the-leader. This wouldn't do.

In the end, I made my meanest face and lunged at it. Those amazing three-metre wings swelled open and the albatross lifted off the *Aurora*. I watched it for a moment, before it banked sharply to the east, and as it turned it unblocked a view of something else in the night.

An airship, still distant, but headed right for us.

I stared for a moment, to make sure. Then, hunched over, I ran back to the crow's-nest and jumped in, pulling the hatch closed after me. I yanked the speaking tube to my mouth.

'Crow's-nest,' I panted.

'Are we bird free, Mr Cruse?'

'Sir, there's a ship headed towards us!'

The airship was small, and I could now see why I'd not picked her out earlier. Her skin was painted black, and she carried no running beacons anywhere on her.

No light emanated from the control car either. Her side bore no markings, no name or number. It was only her dark sheen from the moon's light that made her visible at all.

'She's at ten o'clock and sailing straight for us, a kilometre away.'

'Bear away,' I heard the first officer tell his rudder man. 'Elevator up six degrees. Summon the captain.'

That meant we were going into a climb. The *Aurora* was responsive as a falcon. Stars streamed to my left as the ship began her turn, angling heavenwards. I swivelled in my chair so I could watch the smaller vessel. As we turned and climbed, she turned and climbed with us, keeping herself on a collision course. This was no mistake. She was chasing us. She was smaller and faster than the *Aurora*, and I could feel the vibration of our engines at full capacity. We would not be able to outrun her.

'Where is she, Mr Cruse?'

'She's changed course, but still coming right at us. Closing, at eight o'clock.'

'Raise her on the radio!' I heard the first officer shouting out to the wireless officer.

'She's not responding.'

A collision seemed sure now, but for what purpose?

'Distance, Cruse!'

'Some 180 metres, sir.'

'Send out a distress call,' I heard Mr Rideau instruct the wireless operator.

'We're too far out, sir,' Mr Bayard's voice replied.

It was clear there was no shaking her, this sleek black raptor shadowing us through the night sky.

'She's angling up, sir,' I said into the speaking tube, 'as though she means to overshoot us.'

'Take us down, Mr Riddihoff, take us down five degrees, with haste!'

I felt the *Aurora* pivot, and her bow dip. My ears popped and heaviness rose through me. I swirled in my seat, peering up and almost over the ship's stern now as the airship pulled closer, altering course as seamlessly as if she'd anticipated our moves.

'Forty metres off our stern!' I shouted into the speaking tube. 'Thirty, twenty . . . she's pulling up over our tail!'

And so she was, this predatory airship, skimming over our tail fins and gradually overtaking us, only a dozen metres overhead.

'She's directly overhead now, sir, matching us.'

We were levelling out now and so was the other airship. Less than half our size, she was like some agile black shark hounding a whale.

'Hard about, please.'

Through the speaking tube it was the captain's voice I heard now, and I felt a surge of confidence to know he was on the bridge. He would see us through this. Again the *Aurora* swivelled, trying to throw off her predator, but once more the smaller ship matched our movements, slinking over the top of us like a shadow. A spotlight flared from its underside and I saw ropes springing from open bay doors and unfurling towards the *Aurora*.

'She's dropping lines on us!' I shouted into the speaking tube.

Pirates. That was all they could be.

'They're trying to board,' the captain said. 'Dive and roll to starboard, please.'

The lines were weighted, for they hit the ship and didn't slide off. I saw six men already dropping down towards me. But then the *Aurora* banked sharply, dipped, and the lines slewed off the *Aurora*'s back, leaving the men dangling in mid-air.

'Ha! You'll not have us!' I shouted, shaking my fist.

But the pirate airship was already adjusting its course, keeping pace, and as it forced us closer to the waves, we would have less space to manoeuvre. There was a great flash from the pirate ship's underbelly and a thunderous volley of cannon fire scorched the night sky across our bow.

A voice carried by bull horn shuddered the air.

'Put your nose to the wind and cut speed.'

There was no need for me to repeat this into the speaking tube for I knew they had heard it in the control car. There was a moment of silence, and I could imagine them all down there, standing very straight and still, the elevator men and rudder men watching the captain, awaiting his command. He had no choice. That cannon could sink us in an instant.

'Level off and put her into the wind, please,' said

Captain Walken. 'Throttle back the engines to one quarter. Thank you.'

The pirate ship glided over us. Once more the boarding lines hit the *Aurora*'s back, and down them slid six men, clothed in black, with more already on the way. The first set touched down and made fast their lines to mooring cleats. Spotlights swept the ship, giving the pirates light. We were connected now, the *Aurora* and this diabolical little ship. She had us like a harpooned whale, and there was nothing we could do to throw her off. At 120 metres over the waves we cruised along in tandem.

'They're on us, sir,' I said into the speaking tube. 'Six of them and six more coming. Maybe more, I can't tell.'

Half were heading towards the aft hatch, the other half towards mine, single file, hunched over, hands barely grasping the guide wire. They were quick. In the spotlights' glare, the man in the lead was a terrible sight to behold, his hair tied back, his face hollowed out by shadow, eyes narrowed against the wind. He must've seen me, for he gave a most unpleasant smile that made my stomach roll over. I caught the dull sheen of metal in his belt: a pry bar, and beside it, a pistol.

'Mr Cruse,' came the captain's voice. 'Did you hear me? Lock the hatch and leave your post, please. Assemble in the keel catwalk outside the passenger quarters.'

'Yes, Captain.'

It felt cowardly to abandon my post, but my heart was clattering and the urge to fly beat in every muscle of my body. The men would be here soon. I locked the hatch, though I knew it would only slow them for a moment. My last glimpse was of yet more men sliding down the boarding lines and landing on the *Aurora*'s back. I started down the ladder as quickly as I could.

From below came the slow whoop of the alarm klaxon. Overhead I heard the hatch being wrenched, then a crack. Heavy footfalls rang through the ladder. I took my feet off the rungs and slid with both hands the rest of the way. I hit the axial catwalk running.

'We're boarded!' I gasped to two of the sailmakers. 'They're coming through the fore and aft hatches.'

'How many?'

'Too many. They've got guns.'

The ship's alarm filled my head. I saw one of the sailmakers look at the long wrench in his fist. He grimaced. We were no match for armed men.

And then the pirates were all around us.

'You! All of you! Don't move. Let the wrench go. Hands where we can see them. That's the way.'

More and more pirates sprang down on to the axial catwalk, their pistols cocked. Dressed in black trousers and shirts, the pirates brought with them a malodorous breeze of gunpowder and oil and sweat as though they'd just burst out through the gates of Hades. Their belts swung with tools and knives and gunny sacks.

They rounded up whatever crew was unfortunate enough to be up here and forced us down the ladders with them, wedged in by pirates above and below so there was no chance of escape. Where would we escape to?

All along the keel catwalk the pirates surged, corralling more of the crew and marching us forward at gunpoint, our hands in the air. At the end of the catwalk, Captain Walken stood with his first officers before the locked door to the passenger quarters. Across his chest he held the ship's rifle. Last time I'd seen it, it was nestled in its glass cabinet in the captain's cabin. There were no other arms aboard.

The pirates came to an abrupt halt, and for a hopeful moment I wondered if they were cowed by the sight of the captain and Mr Torbay and Mr Rideau and Mr Levy and the ship's rifle at the ready. The pirates looked back down the catwalk, to the nearest companion ladder. Tall gleaming black boots stepped nimbly down the rungs. Dark riding pants and coat followed. The man jumped to the catwalk and the pirates parted, shoving me and the other crew to one side as he passed, walking towards the captain. He looked as if he could have just dismounted a horse at a nobleman's manor. He was smiling, as though about to be reacquainted with an old friend.

I recognized him at once, for I had seen his likeness sketched in newspapers the world over. He was a handsome man, with a high, intelligent forehead, tightly curled hair, large eyes and pale skin. His name was Vikram Szpirglas and he was as much legend as man. No one in my acquaintance had actually encountered him, but everyone knew someone who had. The stories were many, and all terrible. He sailed over the globe, he had no fixed home, and had never been caught. He boarded freighters and passenger ships and looted them, killing if he needed to.

'Sir,' said Captain Walken, and I marvelled that his voice betrayed not even a tremor. 'This is the most scandalous breach of aeronautical law I've ever encountered. Explain this behaviour.'

'It needs no explanation, surely,' said Szpirglas to the chuckles of his pirate crew. 'We've boarded your ship. We mean to pillage it. And then we will depart.'

'You'll not enter the passenger quarters.'

'Sadly, we must. We want to get at all the jewels and pretty trinkets your rich passengers carry aboard.'

The captain raised his rifle.

'Sir,' said Szpirglas. 'Please. Let us not play-act. Firing that gun would wound your ship. My men are fine aims, sir, finer than you, but once we all start firing, there would be too many holes in her belly to stay aloft. She's a fine ship, and we have no wish to harm her or any aboard. You have my word.'

A suave gentleman he was, to be sure. To hear him speak, you'd think he was the ambassador of Angleterre.

'We'll also be wanting access to the cargo holds, to have a look about.'

His men were everywhere now, dozens of them ranged along the catwalk, crouched atop ballast tanks and ladders, and in the rigging, all with their pistols drawn, and pointed at the crew and our captain. Cowardly, it was. To come aboard an unarmed passenger vessel with such might, and hold her crew at gunpoint. It was almost more than I could bear to watch the captain. He had no easy decision to make – for truly he had no choice. What he did not give to these pirates they would take, by violent force.

'You will allow my crew to assemble the passengers in the lounges,' Captain Walken said severely. 'We will instruct them to leave their valuables in their rooms. They will not be harassed in any way.'

'Agreed,' said Szpirglas, 'as long as they all behave and don't try to ferret away some of their favourite baubles in their silk pyjamas. We have a deal, my good captain – ah, and one last thing of course. No heroics from your men, if you please. No daring counter-attacks, or attempts to send distress signals.'

'Very well,' said the captain. He lowered his rifle, and one of the pirates stepped forward and snatched it from his hands. Captain Walken turned and unlocked the door to the passenger quarters, and the pirates pressed forward, driving us with them. At the base of the grand staircase, the captain summoned the other stewards. I caught Baz's eye as he stared, bewildered, at the sight of all the pirates fanning out through the entrance lobby.

'You will escort these gentlemen through the ship,' the captain told his cabin crew. 'Please wake the passengers as gently as you can, and reassure them.'

The pirates shadowed us as we dispersed through A- and B-decks. I was coupled with a tall rangy fellow with only one hand, but that looked big enough to strangle a rhino with. Right now it was closed around a pistol, his meaty fingers so big they made it look like a child's toy. A gunny sack was tucked into his belt.

'We will be collecting bracelets, timepieces, necklaces, brooches, rings,' Szpirglas sang as we proceeded up the grand staircase to the A-Deck. 'In particular we are fond of anything with precious stones, and gold and silver. Though rest assured we will not be asking for gold fillings tonight!'

His crew erupted into raucous laughter, as though this were all the best of fun.

'I would also like keys to the ship's safe, if you don't mind, Captain,' said Szpirglas.

It was unpleasant work, rapping on people's doors at four in the morning, and telling them the ship had been boarded by pirates, and they were requested to please throw on a robe and come to the lounge while their rooms were pillaged.

'I'm sorry,' I told a frail lady and her sister. 'No harm will come to you. They only want things.'

'But . . . we're very fond of our things,' said one of the ladies wistfully.

'Don't be daft, Edith, they're welcome to whatever they want.'

In went Rhino Hand, rummaging through their steamer trunks and bureaus and stealing whatever he wanted. I left him to his work and proceeded down the corridor. By this time, with the alarm and noise, many were already awake, opening their doors and sticking out their heads. I reached the Topkapi stateroom at the end of the corridor. I'd barely raised my knuckles to rap when the door opened.

It was Miss Simpkins. Her hair was tied up in rags, and she wore a scarf round her head, so she gave me a bit of a shock. Without her make-up she looked quite different, puffier, and her eyes seemed smaller.

'You must come, Miss,' I said. 'Pirates have boarded the ship.'

'Pirates!' she said in outrage, as though we'd somehow planned this just for her inconvenience.

'You and Miss de Vries must come to the lounge now.'

'We'll do no such thing, young boy. Now shoo, I'm about to lock my door.'

A great boot hit the door, bursting it open, and nearly mashing Miss Simpkins, who gave a squeal as Rhino Hand strode into the room.

'You heard the young lad,' the pirate told her. I hadn't known he was capable of speech, but he had a very fine British accent as it turned out. 'To the lounge, please, ladies. Sorry for the inconvenience. Lashings of apologies.'

By this time, Kate had appeared in her nightdress. 'What does this mean?' she whispered to me, face pale, her eyes huge.

'Don't worry,' I said. 'We've been boarded, but they've promised to do no harm as long as we co-operate.'

She hesitated, looking stricken, as the pirate poked about her camera, deciding whether to take it or not. He didn't in the end, and was more interested in the wardrobe drawers where there were plenty of sparkly things to put in his sack.

'Come along,' I said, and led them to the lounge, where most of the other passengers were now assembled, sitting stiffly in the wicker chairs, looking like wax dummies under the electric lights. All these people who I normally saw in dinner jackets and evening dresses, laughing and eating, were now in their pyjamas and bathrobes, small and bewildered. A few people tried to talk, but silence weighted the room like thunderclouds. Watchful guards stood at the main entrances. Szpirglas perched on the bar and helped himself to a drink.

'I can guarantee you're all insured, ladies and gentlemen, and this will be, at worst, an inconvenience. We mustn't get too attached to our worldly possessions, after all, must we? What are they but things, baubles, trifles, bits of stuff?' He thumped his heart. 'It is here we must find our treasures and store them up. And these things know no price.'

A real comedian he was, this was as much a vaudeville performance as a robbery. But if newspaper reports were to be believed, his sense of humour could shrivel up in a second. From a laugh to a gunshot without any warning.

The pirates were efficient, I'll give them that. It seemed hardly any time at all had passed before they were back with bulging gunny sacks, and big smiles. Then another pirate entered the lounge, a great bearded mountain of a fellow, pushing the chief radio officer, Mr Featherstone, ahead of him at gunpoint.

'What's this, Mr Crumlin?' Szpirglas asked.

'Caught him down in the wireless room, trying to send an SOS,' Crumlin said.

'Ahhh,' Szpirglas said, as though confronted with a particularly stubborn child. 'Sir, I thought we had something of a gentleman's agreement,' he said, turning to Captain Walken. 'You would let us go about our work unmolested, and we would leave you and all aboard unharmed. But trying to radio for help, this is breaking the rules, wouldn't you agree?'

'He knew nothing of it,' Mr Featherstone said. 'I was acting on my own. Sorry, Captain.'

'Very noble of you,' said Szpirglas, 'I commend you for your honesty. But this does distress me, it truly does. I'd been quite enjoying myself until now.' Everyone in the lounge was sitting rigidly, listening, and Szpirglas addressed us all, as if we were an audience and he was on stage. 'You must understand, all I have in the world is my good name. People know me, they know that I might come aboard their ships and take their goodies. They know that I am a pirate. To be an effective pirate, one must be respected and feared. So what would become of me if people started to think they could put one over on old Szpirglas? Try to trick me, try to catch me. No, that wouldn't do at all. I must protect my good name at all costs.'

He drew his pistol, and shot Featherstone point–blank in the head.

A great gasp from all of us sucked the air out of the room as the wireless officer fell to the floor. People were crying and screaming. Doc Halliday was at Featherstone's side in a second.

'He's dead,' he said.

'Listen to me!' Szpirglas shouted. 'I will not be trifled with. I do not relish killing, but I will do it if I must. If you do not show me the proper respect, you force me to earn it! I bid you all farewell.'

He turned and left the lounge, and his men went with him. We all stood frozen for a moment. My insides were ice. I don't think anyone really knew what we ought to be doing. Some part of me thought we should be following them, seeing what they were about, making sure they did no mischief to the ship, but no one was keen to anger Szpirglas further.

Captain Walken nodded at Mr Torbay and Mr Wexler, and they cautiously began to follow the departing pirates. I wasn't supposed to, but I went too, falling into step behind the officers as they headed down the grand staircase and through the access doorway to the keel catwalk. Overhead, I could see the pirates climbing the companion ladders towards the axial catwalk. I wanted to make sure they kept going; I wanted them off the ship without harming her.

'I can follow them,' I said to Mr Torbay. 'They won't see me.'

'You'll do no such thing, Mr Cruse.'

'They won't even know I'm there, sir,' I persisted. Mr Torbay had seen me swing over the ocean on a piece of rope; he knew I could climb and hide myself amidst the ship's rigging.

'You do not have my permission, Mr Cruse,' he said kindly. 'Do not follow us, is that clear?'

'Yes, sir.'

They started up the companion ladder to the axial catwalk. I would not follow them. I would go aft and climb up through the rigging, unseen by officers or pirates. It was unlike me to disobey an order, but there was something going through me, a terrible fear that the ship might be in danger, my home, and I could not just sit in the passenger lounge, blind, hoping everything would be all right.

I raced aft, and scampered up the wiring and braces. I could swing my way around the ship like a spider. Up I went, hidden, towards the axial catwalk, my feet springing from wire to wire. Almost level with the catwalk I could see the pirates now waiting their turn at the next ladder, climbing up to the forward observation hatch. It seemed they really were leaving – without any other evil design on the ship or her passengers – and I felt my heart begin to calm. Maybe it was truly over.

As the last pirate began his climb, I ran down the catwalk and hurried up the ladder to the aft crow's-nest, past the shimmering gossamer skin of the gas cells. I peered out through the domed hatch. The remaining pirates were crouched along the *Aurora*'s back, grabbing at boarding lines, uncleating them and then holding tight as they were hauled back to their airship. We were free.

But when I looked beyond Szpirglas' ship, I saw a great dense mass of darkness against the night sky and knew, just by the *Aurora*'s vibrations, that we were heading into a storm front. Rain started clattering against the ship's skin, and the *Aurora* bobbed sharply as the wind hit it.

Above me, Szpirglas' ship gave a mighty downward lurch before steadying herself. We were free of the pirate ship, but not of the elements. Ploughing through a front, you sometimes got a microburst, an intense downward column of wind that could drive you suddenly lower. I snatched up the speaking tube.

'Crow's-nest reporting!'

'Mr Cruse?' came the captain's voice. 'What the devil are you doing up there?'

'Sir, the pirate ship has cast off, but we're heading into a storm front.'

'I'm aware of that, Mr Cruse. Now get down from there.'

'Sir, the other ship, she's awfully close—'

At that moment the wind took the *Aurora* in her grip and gave us a mighty downward shove. I heard our engines roar to full throttle, felt the elevators struggling to keep us level. But from above, I saw Szpirglas' ship, a fraction of our size, come hurtling down towards us, driven by the same wind.

'She's coming down on us!'

I felt the *Aurora* start to dive and roll, but we were too late. The pirate ship veered into us, tried to pull away, but another gust of wind pushed us together again, I saw and heard Szpirglas' propellers come towards us, two great whirling blades on her starboard side, slashing the night and then –

The *Aurora*. The propellers caught in our skin and kept cutting, through the taut fabric, through the gas cells inside. The propellers slashed through our port side, from stern to amidships. I felt the horrible chainsaw vibration rattle the entire ship.

'We're breached!' I hollered into the speaking tube.

The pirate ship slewed away from us, and came back once more, its propellers racing right towards me. I dropped down the ladder, and was nearly thrown off the rungs when the blades cut through the hull. Then they were gone, wrenched back into the sky. I clung to the ladder, panting, listening to the roar of the propellers fade.

And then there was a new sound.

The mango-scented gush of escaping hydrium.

7

SINKING

We all knew what had happened, and what needed doing. The sailmakers were charging along the catwalks, pulling toolbelts and patching kits from the storage lockers, springing up into the ship's rigging to start repairs on the torn gas cells. The reek of mangoes made my eyes water. The whole ship was exhaling, like the last long sigh of a dying man. From underfoot there was a metallic creak as the ballast tanks along the keel opened, and tons of water tumbled out to the sea below. The captain was trying to lighten the ship.

I saw another team of sailmakers heading for the upper hatches and ran over.

'Cruse, you'll help?' asked Mr Levy, the chief sailmaker.

'Yes.'

'Good lad. We could use you up top.'

He tossed me a safety harness and pointed me towards the locker. I kicked off my shoes and slipped my feet into snug rubber-soled slippers. I grabbed a helmet, tested the lamp mounted on top. Tightening a tool belt around my hips, I crammed it full of patching materials. Bruce Lunardi was already in his gear, looking pale as he mounted the ladder. I climbed up after him, my feet dancing up the rungs.

We'll see who's the better sailmaker, I thought, even at that moment.

We came out the aft hatch on to the ship's back. Her massive dorsal fin towered above us like a mountain peak. I could see the *Aurora*'s elevators angled high, trying to keep the ship's nose up. Over the wind in my ears, I heard the fierce drone of the four engine cars at full power, straining to fly us level as the *Aurora* gushed her precious hydrium. Below, all around us, the sea was dark as mercury, and closer than I liked.

'Cruse, you're over here! Starboard side!' shouted Mr Levy. I hurried along the ship's spine to where I was needed. I hooked my safety line to the cleat, fitted the goggles over my face, and turned on my lamp. The sailmaker passed me a bucket of patching glue and a small satchel of patches, and I clipped them both to my harness. Then I walked backwards, down over the ship's side, paying out line. My rubber-soled shoes gave me a fine grip, even though the wind pushed at me. All across the *Aurora*'s bulging flank were other sailmakers, hanging from their lines, examining the ship's fabric skin. I swept my lamp back and forth, searching for gashes.

They were all too easy to find, huge jagged swaths, hissing angrily as hydrium escaped from the torn gas cells within the hull. It gave me a pain in my chest to see them.

I tied my line to one of the many safety cleats across the ship's flank. Then I got to work. With my brush I swiped glue over the skin, pressed hard with the patch and counted to five. It was fast-setting stuff, this glue, and you had to work quickly, and make sure every edge was sealed tight. Hydrium was restless, the lightest thing in the world, and if it saw a way out, it would take it. Brush, press, hold, listen, move on. I liked it when the hissing sound stopped, or at least grew fainter. Little by little, I was helping heal the ship. Every breath of hydrium saved was more to lift the *Aurora*.

Inside, the sailmakers would be frantically sewing and stitching the actual gas cells. They'd be wearing masks by now, breathing tanked oxygen so they wouldn't pass out. Hydrium wasn't poisonous, but it would push away all the air, fill up a space fast, and you'd suffocate.

I moved along to another gash ripped by the pirate ship's propellers. It was like a terrible wound created by a monster's claws, ribbons of torn skin flapping in the wind. Warm mango scent washed over me. It was really too big to patch, but I'd just have to do my best. Even with five patches across it, I could still hear a quiet hiss leaking from it. No time to do better, I had to move on. Everywhere my lamp's beam touched there were more holes. I wondered how much hydrium we'd lost.

I heard a distant clatter of water and looked down to see more ballast hit the sea. The sea. How had it gotten so close? Surely there could be no more ballast. The captain wouldn't have dumped so much unless he was quite certain . . . that we were sinking.

A gust hit, and the *Aurora* rolled to starboard. I drifted away from the ship's side, dangling over the water for a moment before the ship righted herself. I bounced back gently against her flank. I heard a yell and looked off to my left to see Bruce Lunardi, upside down in his harness, arms flailing. He must have done a somersault. He was hollering and kicking and not having much success righting himself.

I sighed, then pushed off and swung towards him. I got halfway, fastened my line to a new safety cleat, then took another run at it, paying out line as I swung the rest of the way to Lunardi. My rubber-soled shoes gripped the hull. I cleated myself off on his right side.

'Take hold of my hand and pull.'

His grip was painful as he dragged himself upright in his saddle.

'Thanks,' he muttered, wiping his face with his sleeve. I think he'd thrown up.

Without another word he went back to work. I glanced at his patching. It was excellent, tidier than mine. But I doubted he'd done as much as I had; he was spending too long.

I nodded goodbye and swung myself back to my place. Like a spider I scuttled across the ship's flank. Brush, press, hold, listen, brush, press, hold, listen. I hollered up for a second bucket of glue. The gashes seemed endless.

'That's my girl,' I said to the ship, as I pressed another patch on to her skin. 'You'll be good as new soon. See if you aren't.'

'Come aboard!' someone was shouting down at me.

'I'm not done!' I cried back.

'Doesn't matter! Come aboard!'

I looked down and saw the sea, thick and colourless in the coming dawn. We were lower than ever. This was an altitude I usually only saw when we were coming in for landing. Hand over hand I hauled myself up to the ship's back. After hanging, weightless for so long, my body felt heavy as a stone gargoyle. I crouched, catching my breath, looking at all the other crew, pale from exhaustion. Lunardi nodded at me, too tired to speak.

Inside, Mr Riddihoff waited for us on the axial catwalk.

'We need to get the passengers to their muster stations and into life jackets,' he said. 'You all know the drill.'

But this wasn't a drill.

'Are we ditching?' I heard Lunardi ask.

'We've lost too much hydrium,' Mr Riddihoff said, his skin waxy. 'We can't stay aloft.'

'Is there no land nearby?' someone else wanted to know.

'We're in the middle of the Pacificus. The pirates rode us way off course. Nearest charted island is at least 1600 kilometres. It's a water landing, gentlemen.'

There was nothing left to say, and we all headed in

our different directions, keeping our fears bottled up inside us. Airborne, nothing frightened me. But the idea of crash landing on the sea, water filling us, made my stomach churn. The *Aurora* was my home and I couldn't bear the thought of abandoning her to the waves.

I shrugged off my harness and patching gear, and quickly made my way back to the passenger quarters. With every step, my senses kept track of the angle of the ship. Each movement passed through my feet and into my brain. Right now she felt level enough, but I could tell by the weight in my stomach and the tautness of my eardrums, we were slowly but surely losing height. I had to keep moving.

I vaulted up the grand staircase, knocking on doors, making sure everyone was out of their cabins. Most of the passengers were still assembled in the upper lounge, many with a drink in their hands.

'Ladies and gentlemen,' the chief steward said, 'the captain has informed us that we will be making a landing over water . . .'

I started handing out life jackets, trying to block out the rest of the steward's message, and the cries of dismay and fear that rose up from the passengers. I saw Kate and Miss Simpkins across the room, and worked my way towards them. Kate was sitting with a book in her lap – her grandfather's log, I noticed. She looked pale but composed.

'All right?' I asked Kate quietly.

'Of course we're not all right,' said Miss Simpkins, fussing with the straps of her life jacket. 'We're about to sink to the bottom of the ocean!'

'We won't sink, Miss,' I said, helping her fasten her straps. 'The engines and helm are unharmed, and the winds are very light. The captain will set us down gently, and all you need do is step into the life-raft. We'll take care of everything.'

I hoped I was right. The *Aurora* was not watertight. Captain Walken would need to keep her nose into the wind, and hover just above the ocean's surface for as long as he could. For once the ship touched down, and started taking on water, she would not heed our commands any more. She would sway and spin and flood and begin to sink.

I checked Kate's life jacket to make sure it was snug, and started over to the next group of passengers.

'You're coming back, aren't you?' Kate said.

'Yes. You're part of my muster group. We'll be on the same boat.'

Nearby, a young boy was crying. 'Don't you worry,' I told him. 'Our captain will see us through. I've sailed with him three years. There's no better than Captain Walken. He's been through worse than this.'

As I was helping a woman on with her life jacket, she turned her scared eyes to me and said, 'I don't know how to swim.'

'You don't need to, ma'am,' I told her with a smile. 'There are more than enough life-rafts for everyone.

They're quite roomy, you know. And with enough provisions to have bang-up meals for weeks, if need be. We've made sure there's a chef on every boat. You'll be fine.'

She touched my cheek. Her fingers were cold. 'You're a good boy,' she said.

Just then I caught the scent of her perfume, and it was my mother's perfume. I had to turn quickly away, a sudden tremor in my throat. I looked out the window at the approaching sea. I didn't know how to swim either. We were close enough to hear the ocean's impatient sigh, see the thuggish slouch of her surface, calm enough, but no hiding the immense strength of her mile-deep muscle. It was a clear day and the rising sun was painting jittering diamonds on the surface.

I didn't want to touch it.

Jump now. You won't fall. You'll stay aloft. You'll fly clear.

Your father did.

Stupid thoughts.

Everyone was in their life jackets now, just waiting for the captain's order to proceed to the emergency hatches. The life-rafts were ingenious things, packed into small bundles in the ship's hull. A pull of the handle and they would inflate instantly with a burst of compressed air, all the paddles and emergency provisions already stowed away in their lockers.

I walked amongst the passengers, checking their life jackets, trying to comfort them. It was like trying to soothe some great wild beast, to keep it from breaking free of its chains and going on a rampage. Some were holding hands, others crying quietly or praying. A few were being sick. I wished I were in the control car with the captain. I wished I were there serving fresh coffee and pastries, and hearing the captain's calm voice giving orders, and knowing exactly what was going on. It would keep the fear at bay.

The emergency phone was ringing.

I looked at the chief steward. Our eyes met. He picked it up.

'Mr Lisbon here, sir.'

I could not bear to watch his face as he heard the order to evacuate, so I turned to the window again. I squinted. Dead ahead a dome of bright mist hovered on the horizon. Mist at sea meant . . .

'Land ahoy!'

It was me that shouted it, for I'd just caught sight of a bony peak jutting above the mist, and then through the mist itself, a darker outline spreading across the water's surface.

'An island!' I exclaimed, turning to the chief steward.

'Very good, sir,' he said into the phone, and hung up. He was smiling. 'Ladies and gentlemen, I'm very pleased to inform you that we've sighted land and will be setting down shortly. The captain's asked that you all remain seated.'

I looked at Kate. She was smiling. I was smiling. Miss Simpkins had her hands over her face and was weeping.

It was like a thundercloud had just passed out of the lounge.

I opened up a window and stuck my head out as far as it would go. The mist was burning off quickly and I could see that the island was sizeable. A gaunt peak poked into the sky. The coastline sloped gradually upwards into hills. Before us, the sea broke in a ragged white line against a coral reef, protecting a turquoise lagoon and a long crescent of sand. Back from it sprouted palm trees, sparsely at first, and then more densely as the verdant forest took over and shrouded the island in a canopy of green which continued up the hills and into the mountains.

The beach, I thought. That's the natural landing site. It was flat, and wide enough and deep enough to accommodate the *Aurora*. And likely it was the only flat place on the whole island. That's where Captain Walken would bring us down.

Luck was with us. We were coming at the island with the wind at our nose, perfect for an approach. But we would have only one chance. We were losing too much hydrium to come round again. No question, it would be a tricky landing: an unknown airfield, no ground crew to grab the lines and tether the ship, no mooring mast to keep her secure.

Already the captain was bringing us down, quite sharply, the engines' pitch deepening as we slowed. The phone rang again. I knew what the call was about and was already heading for the exit.

'All hands to their docking stations,' the chief steward called after me. 'Prepare for landing.'

Down at the bay doors, the crew were waiting, scrambling for every inch of spare line we could muster. Baz was there and it was good to see him. He grabbed my shoulder and squeezed hard.

'Quite a time we've had lately.'

'You'll have a story to tell back home.'

'Too true,' he said.

The bay doors opened and we could see the water, sparkling below, and getting closer. Head pressed against the hull, I watched the coastline approaching. We were over the reef now, surf crashing, then the jewelled lagoon and we were coming down lower and lower. Enormous fish, in colours I've never known, flitted beneath the clear water. Then the sand of the beach. The engines gave a great roar as they went into reverse, and you could feel the whole airship straining as she pulled back.

'Ready now, men,' said Mr Chen.

I looked down and the sand was no more than two metres below me.

'Spring to it!' shouted Mr Chen, and we were out the doors in a second. All across the *Aurora*, stem to stern, starboard and port sides, sixty of us hit the ground at once, each with a line uncoiling behind us, holding the great ship steady. I hit the ground and almost stumbled, the earth strange under my feet. I felt heavy, clumsy, my nose filled with unfamiliar scents. The sand sent me staggering, and I reeled towards a stand of palms. The air was thick. I'd already forgotten how much I hated being landlocked. Twice I wrapped my line around a palm trunk, awaiting orders from the second officer. A sudden morning breeze pummelled the ship, and the line burned through my fingers, sending smoke from the tree's bark.

'Hold tight!' came the cry, and for a moment I was afraid we'd lose her as she lifted and leaned back out towards sea, as if lonesome for the sky. She was still lighter than air, just, but she was as big as an ocean liner, and when she moved, she moved hard. I dug in with my heels and prayed for her to stop. She did.

'Starboard side, pull her tight!' came the officer's call, and with all my might I tugged my line, winching it round the trunk.

An incredible sight it was, this massive airship nested down on the shores of a tropical island, palm fronds brushing her flanks. A steamship in the middle of a desert could not have looked more out of place. Amidships, where she was fattest, her belly was almost scraping the beach. Her lower fin was badly crumpled, its tip buried in the sand. The *Aurora* swayed in the humid air. She seemed a mirage.

The great ship's nose pointed inland. On her starboard side the palms grew quite close, and we'd been tying up her lines to the trunks. Off the *Aurora*'s port side, there was nothing but beach, so the crew was tethering her lines to mooring spikes, driven deep into the sand. I hoped she would hold.

'I want more lines on her!' the captain called from the window of the control car. 'Every extra inch I want holding her. Stem and stern and breast lines. See to it, please! We may not have a mooring mast, gentlemen, but I want this vessel tied down as tightly as Gulliver! Houdini could not shift her, nor a typhoon! See to it, men! Heave on those lines and make her snug as if she were in dry dock!'

Still shouting his poetry, the captain dropped down from the control car and rolled up his sleeves and hammered ties and pulled lines along with the rest of us. My knees were all shaky. I blinked up at the sun, which had just cleared the hills to the east. I felt unpleasantly hot, the light bouncing off the sand and into my face. I sucked in a big breath, wishing for more breeze.

'She's snug!' the captain pronounced after a good twenty minutes. 'Thank you, gentlemen.'

I headed back to the ship, wanting sleep. At the windows in the passenger quarters I could see faces pressed against the glass. My eyes strayed to the Topkapi stateroom, and there were Kate and Miss Simpkins at their big picture windows. The tropical light flashed off the lens of Kate's camera. She lifted her hand and waved.

8

THE ISLAND

The ladies stood beneath their parasols, the gentlemen angled their hats against the sun's full glare. In their black patent shoes and high-heeled boots, they were having trouble standing upright in the fine white sand. They tilted and swayed. In their dark clothing they looked strangely thin and insubstantial, wavering there on the beach like heat mirages. Strange birds shrieked from the forest, a coconut thudded to the ground, surf crashed against the reef. Captain Walken stood before his assembled passengers, eyes crinkled benevolently.

'Ladies and gentlemen, first let me apologize for this unscheduled stop in our journey to Australia.'

This brought a few grateful chuckles from the crowd; but most people, I noticed, still looked shaken and anxious, some even angry.

'Luckily, thanks to my able crew, we made an exceptionally smooth landing and are snugly berthed. Our ship is largely undamaged, with the critical exception, of course, that we have lost much of our lifting gas. We have the pirates to thank for that.'

'We're shipwrecked, then!' said one passenger.

'Not at all, sir. Our vessel is in one piece. And she will fly again.'

'When?' a woman with a powerful voice asked. 'We are not children, Captain. Tell us the truth.'

'Indeed I am, madam. Repairs are underway as I speak. Which is why I have asked for all of you to disembark. A temporary measure, I assure you. Right now, I need the *Aurora* as light as possible until we've sealed every leak.'

I looked over at the ship. She hovered, only inches above the sand. Several crewmen were already busy digging her tail fin free. If the *Aurora* lost any more hydrium, she would be forced to start bearing her own weight – something no airship was designed to do. Without enough hydrium, she would collapse upon herself. Inside, the sailmakers would be in a frenzy, seeking out every tear in her gossamer gas cells. And outside, the hull crawled with more crew, patching all those holes we'd missed last night. I wished I was up there with them. Lunardi was up there. But here I was, shimmied halfway up a coconut palm, trying to string a tarpaulin to make some shade for our precious passengers.

'But will we be able to lift off again?' someone else demanded.

'With our current load I am most doubtful. We may need to remove cargo and furniture and other non-essential items. We won't know how much hydrium we have until repairs are finished. At the moment, we have plenty of food and drinking water. The weather is fine and we are all unharmed – with the tragic exception of our chief wireless officer, Mr Featherstone.'

The captain paused for a moment, and I saw him sigh. I don't think anyone who'd been in the A-Deck lounge was able to clear the images from their mind's eye. The way Szpirglas had lifted the gun, so casually and unflinchingly, and squeezed the trigger. An explosion of blood and bone and a life gone for ever.

'We still have cause to be grateful,' said our captain. 'An encounter with the likes of Mr Szpirglas could have been much, much worse. I intend to be underway as soon as possible. I will keep you abreast of all developments. The cabin crew is at your disposal, as it is when we are aloft. The ship's schedule will remain unchanged, with meals served at the usual times. However, your safety is my first concern, so I would urge you to stay within sight of the *Aurora*. The beach looks very pleasant, and the lagoon sheltered. If you wish, please sunbathe and swim, but do keep an eye open for sharks. I must also ask you to refrain from straying inland unless accompanied by a crew member. I hope that you will be able to return to the ship before much longer. I know that our cabin crew will be serving a full breakfast on the beach shortly. Now you must excuse me while I tend to the ship.'

It was a reassuring oration I thought, but the passengers were not all soothed. I heard a fair bit of grumbling and caught plenty of worried looks. I turned back to Baz, who was cinching the other end of the tarp to a palm. It made a good screen, enough to keep the ladies' faces from being blemished by the sun.

The captain had quietly told me, Baz and the other cabin crew to keep an eye out for any island inhabitants. I can't say the idea made me very happy. What if they weren't friendly? So when I wasn't stealing glances into the darkness of the trees, I was watching the *Aurora*, afraid something disastrous would befall her. Afraid she would get blown away, or taken over by cannibals, or more likely, crushed into the sand by her own unaccustomed weight. I didn't want to be here. I looked up at the sky, a deep cobalt blue. A frigate bird circled high.

Baz and I strung up a few more tarps and then set about serving breakfast with the rest of the cabin crew. It was quite an undertaking, laying out blankets for the passengers, setting up the trestle tables for the buffet, then lugging out the plates and cutlery and napkins and food. It all seemed nonsense to me right now, when the *Aurora* was ailing. I kept watching her belly, gauging how much more she'd slumped into the sand.

I didn't even want to be outside. Didn't want to be reminded that I was on an island, and the *Aurora* aground.

I wanted to be inside, helping the ship right now, instead of pampering our passengers.

'How do you expect them to eat?' Baz asked in mock horror when I grumbled all this to him. We were headed back to the ship, teetering with dirty dishes.

'Let them hack open a few coconuts,' I muttered.

'And what next?' he asked. 'Wrangling their own sharks? Buttering their own bread? These people did without fresh croissants this morning, Matt. That's right. These poor people, washed ashore like Robinson Crusoe, making do without croissants. Have some pity, boy.'

'Oh, shut up,' I said, grinning.

He looked at me, then back at the *Aurora*.

'She'll be fine, you know.'

'I know.' I blinked away tears.

'Been a bit much for everyone, hasn't it.' Baz sighed. 'Especially without fresh croissants.'

I laughed. Baz could always cheer me up.

After a hurried breakfast in the crew's mess, the chief steward, Mr Lisbon, told me to get some sleep.

'They could probably use an extra hand up top,' I replied, thinking of the sailmakers repairing the ship's skin.

He shook his head. 'Sleep first. Captain's orders, not mine.'

I was glad there was no one else around to hear this; I knew the captain meant it kindly but it had the ring of being sent to bed by your parents. I got a sudden lump in my throat. My father, who would never send me off to bed again. My mother and sisters back home. The truth was, I didn't want to sleep. On land I never slept well. My lungs didn't get enough air; my heart clattered. I panicked when I could not feel the sky beneath me, when I could not feel my father near. I just wanted to work.

'Were we able to send off a distress message, sir?' I asked Mr Lisbon.

'The pirates smashed all the radio gear. Mr Chaudhuri's trying to repair it.'

'Perhaps he could use—'

'You're off duty, Mr Cruse. I suggest you sleep now when you've got the chance. We've all plenty of work ahead of us.'

'Thank you, sir,' I said. I walked mournfully to my cabin and stood beside my bunk. I felt like a six-year-old, not wanting bedtime to come, afraid of the dark. I could feel how tired my body was; maybe I could sleep just a little. Very slowly I took off my trousers and jacket and shirt and climbed up to my bunk. I slid down under the covers, pushed my cheek against the pillow.

I closed my eyes and tried to pretend we were still aloft, still moving. But the smell of mango permeated the ship, and I could not forget we were leaking. All through the ship I heard the soft thuds of crew working on her skin, crew working above me in the bracing wires, crew coming up and down the corridor. I could feel my heart start beating faster. I swallowed, tried to breathe slow and deep. I was aloft. I could fly. I was soaring alongside the ship. I was falling.

My eyes opened. I felt myself start to shake. Out of my porthole I could not see the clouds or open sky, only palms and a sweep of beach, and some of the passengers promenading on the sand. I heard the waves crashing against the reef. Landlocked.

Shipwrecked.

No, not shipwrecked. We would fly again, the captain had promised. I would fly again. I just had to keep moving.

I threw back the covers, jumped down to the floor, and yanked on my off duty clothes: a pair of trousers, shirt, suspenders and flat-soled shoes. I could not stay here in the cabin; right now it was just like my room at home, motionless, small, collapsing in on me.

I opened the cabin door and practically ran out into the corridor. I nearly collided with Baz and Bruce Lunardi. They looked like they were going somewhere.

'You two need a hand?' I asked.

'If you like,' said Baz. 'The captain's asked us to find some fresh water.'

'We're not out,' I said, with some alarm. 'Are we?'

'Not yet,' Baz said, 'but he had to dump most of it last night. We've got enough to last maybe one more day.'

'We'll be gone by then,' I said confidently.

'Even so we'll need to take on more to make it to Sydney,' Lunardi pointed out. 'Plus we need ballast.'

'I know that,' I said, annoyed he was telling me about my ship; and annoyed at myself for forgetting all the ballast we'd dumped. We walked down the gangway on to the beach, squinting in the sudden sun. Bruce and Baz were walking ahead of me, side by side, and I noticed they were about the same height. I supposed they were about the same age too. I wondered when they'd got so chummy; I'd never seen them together before. Suddenly I felt like a little brother, tagging along, unwanted.

'You all right after last night?' I asked Bruce. 'Seemed like you were having a rough time up there.'

'I was,' he said, turning around and giving me a smile. It wasn't a matinée idol smile, it wasn't cocky enough. This smile was humble and it took me aback. 'Thanks for helping me out,' he said. 'I really appreciate it.'

'It was nothing.'

'I don't have much of a head for heights.'

'You're in the wrong line of work, then,' I said.

'Probably. Do you think there's any hope for me?'

I felt bad. 'It looked good, your patching,' I told him. 'Very tidy.'

'Really?'

I grunted.

'Well, that's encouraging. Maybe there's hope for me yet.'

I didn't want him to feel too encouraged, but I said nothing more.

'Shouldn't be too hard to find water,' Baz said. 'The island looks fairly big. There's got to be a stream somewhere.'

'Let's start over there,' said Lunardi, pointing to the far end of the beach.

We walked along the sand, away from the ship, past the makeshift marquees we'd thrown up to shade the passengers. I caught a glimpse of Miss Simpkins stretched out on a wicker lounge chair. She appeared to be dozing, like many of the others. I didn't see Kate until we were farther along the beach. She was standing close to the water, her back to the lagoon, staring up into the forest and hills. She wore a long white summer dress and a simple white hat with a single magnificent rose on it. Her hair hung around her shoulders in two loose plaits, each tied with a red bow. In one hand she held a parasol, in the other was a book – her grandfather's journal, I now realized. Her chin was tilted up and she was peering off into the distance and occasionally she put down her parasol on the sand so she could write something in her book. She looked very intent.

'Who's that there?' Lunardi asked, squinting. 'She's rather attractive, wouldn't you say, gentlemen?'

'That's Miss Kate de Vries,' Baz told him. 'And you'll have stiff competition from Matt. He's already set his sights on her.' Baz gave me a playful poke with his elbow.

'Don't talk rubbish,' I muttered.

'Kate de Vries,' Bruce said, surprised. 'I do believe I know her.'

'Really?' I said coldly.

'Hmmm,' he said vaguely.

As we approached, Kate looked up and waved.

'Hello!' she called out.

'Are you all right, Miss?' Baz asked. 'Can we help?'

'Oh no,' she said, 'I'm just taking notes.' She smiled at me. 'Hello, Mr Cruse. How are you today?'

'Very well, thank you.'

'Hello, Miss de Vries,' said Lunardi, 'I believe we've met before.' He suddenly seemed much older and sure of himself, almost suave.

Kate looked up at him. 'Yes, I think you're right,' she replied. She thinks he's handsome, I thought forlornly. Plus he was in his uniform, and looked very crisp and sharp. I felt shabby in my off duty clothes. His gold steering wheel insignia gleamed in the sun. Cover those up, I wanted to growl. You haven't earned them. Better yet, tear them off and give them to me.

'Was it at the Wolfram Gala last year?' Kate asked.

'Indeed it was,' said Lunardi. 'Your mother and mine were on the same fundraising committee.'

'Yes,' Kate said, 'of course. How nice to see you again.'

'What are you taking notes on?' Lunardi asked her.

'Oh, just the local flora and fauna,' Kate said, closing her notebook.

'Are you sure you wouldn't be more comfortable with the others, Miss?' said Baz. 'We're off to find a stream.'

'Oh, it's over there a way,' said Kate. 'I spotted it earlier. Not far.'

'Really?' I asked, impressed. 'You've been doing a little exploring?'

'Hardly,' she said. 'You can't miss it.'

Bruce laughed. 'Well, she's saved us a lot of work, gentlemen. Thank you, Miss de Vries. Perhaps we can consult you again when we're foraging for food.'

'Food won't be any problem either,' Kate said.

'Found a nice restaurant nearby, have you?' Baz joked.

'Look at those trees,' she said, pointing. 'Do you know what they are?'

'Can't say I do,' said Lunardi.

'Breadfruit trees,' she told him.

'Breadfruit trees,' Lunardi said with a laugh. 'Very creative.'

'That's what they're called,' she said. I saw her nostrils narrow, and Lunardi's smile dissolved and all his matinée idol suaveness with it. 'See the fruit up there in its branches,' Kate went on. 'They're a tremendously filling food, if you split them open. Starchy, but filling. We're lucky to have them. We won't starve here, gentlemen. And look, coconut, and mango, and I think that's pineapple over there. In terms of other food sources, we've got an abundance of marine life. Just take a peek in the lagoon. We've got many varieties of fish and shellfish.'

We all just stared at her, the three of us, in amazement.

'We're lucky to have you, Miss de Vries,' said Bruce graciously.

'Miss de Vries,' I said, 'please don't tell the captain what useless clods we are, or we'll all be out of work.'

'Your secret's safe with me,' she said, smiling.

'We'd better go take a look at this stream and report back to the captain,' said Baz. 'Everyone's agreed I found it, right, and I had to fight crocodiles and piranhas on the way? Good. Thank you very much, Miss de Vries, you're a fount of wisdom.'

'All from books,' she said.

'I must read them more often,' said Baz.

The three of us said goodbye, and ventured up the beach to find Kate's stream. Before long we caught sight of a little network of rivulets cutting through the sand and emptying into the lagoon. We followed them into the forest where they all joined up and formed a single stream. I bent down and had a taste. Silky fresh. I splashed some on my face. It was cold enough to make my cheekbones ache. I closed my eyes.

'All right?' Baz said to me. 'You look a little woozy.'

'I don't like the way the ground feels under my feet,' I told him.

'You should get some sleep, mate.'

'I'll sleep later. I'll sleep when we get off this blinking island.'

'Don't fancy lugging buckets of water back to the

ship much,' said Baz, turning to see how far it was to the *Aurora*.

'Well, the captain's not giving us that order yet,' Lunardi said. 'He just asked us to find a stream. Here it is. Not going anywhere.'

'Right you are,' said Baz. 'This is good news. We won't die of thirst at any rate.' He sighed and his shoulders sagged a little. 'Bloody hell. I had plans in Sydney.'

'I should get back,' said Lunardi. 'Still plenty of patching to do.'

'Will there be enough hydrium left?' I asked. I didn't like having to ask him, Were I a sailmaker, I would've known. Then I wouldn't have to be making picnic lunches for the passengers.

'I don't know if there's enough,' Lunardi admitted. 'Shall we head back?'

'You two go on ahead,' I said. 'I need some more fresh air.'

'See you back at the ship then,' Baz said, looking at me, asking me with his eyes if I was OK. I gave a nod.

I walked a little farther out along the beach. If I'd seen this view in a book I would've said it was beautiful, an image of tropical paradise. But right now, I felt like a convict who'd just been dumped on a prison island. All my thoughts were of escape.

I turned and slowly made my way back towards the *Aurora*. Kate was still standing alone with her journal, scribbling. It irritated me suddenly, all her intense talk about mysterious winged creatures – it seemed childish right now. What was important was the ship, getting airborne. I felt too sour to speak with her, and would have turned away, but she'd already seen me.

'Hello,' she said with a smile. 'I was hoping you'd come back alone.'

Amazing how a few words can change everything. I felt a bit of air enter my lungs.

'I wanted to thank you,' she said.

'For what?' I asked, confused.

'When you were helping us on with our life jackets—'

'I was just doing my duty—'

'But it was the way you talked to all of us. You made things seem like they were going to be perfectly all right.'

'I was lying,' I said.

'I thought you were, but it was still immensely comforting.'

'I shouldn't have said I was lying,' I added hurriedly. 'I don't want you to think we lie all the time or anything. And everything did turn out all right, didn't it? Maybe not perfectly all right, but—'

'I understand.' She smiled. Despite her parasol, her cheeks were flushed from the sun. Her hair looked redder in the full light. Maybe it was just the red bows – girls knew how to do these things.

'A desert island,' she said, as if it was the most fabulous thing in the world. 'Do you have any idea where we are?'

'They said it was uncharted.'

'Uncharted,' she repeated with real zest. 'Do you think we're the first people ever to set foot here?'

'Can't say I've given it much thought.'

I gazed over at the *Aurora*, bellied up on the sand like a beached whale. Palm trees shifted in the warm breeze. My feet felt alternately heavy as cement blocks or so light they barely touched ground. The whole world looked swimmy to me, unreal.

'Well,' Kate was saying, 'I read this terrific book a few months ago, about a girl shipwrecked on a desert island. Completely alone.'

'No chaperone?' I asked.

'Actually I think she did have a maid, but that was it. They had to build their own shelter and hunt for food. It's really fabulous.'

'I'm glad being shipwrecked appeals to you.'

'Captain Walken made a point of avoiding that word.'

'Well, he was trying to keep everyone jolly, wasn't he? It's no good having everyone running around screaming and eating each other.'

'I wouldn't run around screaming,' she said. 'I can see eating someone in a pinch, though. If it really came down to it, I mean.'

'I don't doubt it.'

'Come on, Matt Cruse, don't you find it just a bit exciting, being here?'

'No.'

She looked at me as if I'd suggested we stop breathing for a few hours.

'Well, I'd expected more from you,' she said.

My heart raced with anger. 'In case you hadn't noticed, we've been boarded by pirates, had one of our crew murdered, and crash-landed on a desert island no one knows exists. The ship might not fly again. Me, I find this upsetting. But go ahead, think of it like a voyage, tropical beach holiday and fairy tale, all three for the price of one.'

Kate looked at the sand, contrite, and I almost regretted my sharpness. 'I'm sorry. How obtuse of me. You must think me a complete fool.'

I couldn't help smiling.

'Although,' she said, looking off into the distance again, 'I guess technically it's not really a desert island. That would imply very little flora or fauna, which is obviously not the case here. Are you off duty?'

'For a time, yes.'

'Well, here's what I'm thinking, Matt Cruse. I don't think we're the first people to lay eyes on this island.'

'No?' She had that look. There was no turning away when she shone her eyes on you like that. I should have known we weren't just in for a simple little chat on the beach.

'No.' Sand and palm trees and blue sky blazed in her eyes. She patted the journal. 'Did you read Grandfather's description of the island?'

'Skimmed over it mostly. I wanted to get to the creatures.'

'Completely understandable. Just listen to this.' She opened the log – she must have had a bookmark, for she didn't even need to flip pages. She just started reading: 'It looks a tropical place, with a crescent-shaped beach behind a green lagoon, and densely forested.'

She closed the book and looked up at me triumphantly. No wonder she was so chipper. We'd crash-landed in the middle of nowhere, but she was in high spirits because she actually thought we'd ended up on the same island where her grandfather had sighted his winged creatures.

'Miss, that would—'

'You're supposed to call me Kate.'

'Kate. That would describe pretty much every volcanic island in this part of the Pacificus.'

'Yesterday you said our course would take us close to his co-ordinates. Sometime in the night you said?'

I sighed. 'Anything's possible, but let's say I think it improbable.'

She frowned and opened the book again, turning pages, looking for more evidence.

'I could ask Grantham if he has co-ordinates for the island,' I offered. 'He might not have exact ones; I don't know how much time he had to chart our course with all the business last night.'

'Would you?' she said, looking up.

'Yes,' I said, but then something in the log caught my

eye. It was one of the drawings of the creatures. In the background Kate's grandfather had sketched a bit of the island. I hadn't really paid attention to it before.

It was the mountain, the bony peak poking into the sky. I remembered the outline of that peak as we'd made our dawn approach. Startled, I looked back at Kate.

'We're here,' I said.

9

BONES

I'd scarcely uttered the words before Kate was walking across the beach, away from the ship, away from the other passengers, towards the forest. I fell into step beside her as she strode through the palm trees.

'Where do you think you're going?' I asked.

'We need to explore.'

'The captain doesn't want us wandering off.'

'That's not what he said.'

'That's what it sounded like to me.'

'No. He said to make sure a crew member accompanied us if we ventured inland. Are you a member of the crew?'

'You know I am.'

'You're accompanying me.'

'No, I'm not. I'm not coming.'

'Goodbye then.'

We'd left the palms behind and were now in a bamboo grove, the yellow knobbly trunks as thick as my body, towering thirty metres in the air. The white sand had given way to soil and ferns. Before us hung the dense green veil of the forest. Just looking at it made my breathing feel all hemmed in.

'What about Miss Simpkins!' I cried.

'Her? She'll sleep for hours. She excels at sleeping.'

Not much of a chaperone, our Miss Simpkins.

'Look, you can't just wander off alone!'

'Are you going to stop me?'

'Yes.'

'How?' She stopped and looked at me, genuinely interested. 'Would you grab me and drag me back?'

I blushed at the thought of it.

'Do you have handcuffs?' she wanted to know.

'Of course not!'

'You'd have quite a job if I struggled.'

'I suppose I would, yes.'

'Do you think you could flip me over your shoulder and carry me?' She puzzled over this for a moment. 'I'm not sure you could manage it, if you don't mind me saying so. Otherwise, you'd just have to drag me. Really, it seems hard to imagine you bringing me back unless I co-operated.'

I laughed despite myself. 'I was hoping you'd listen to a bit of reason.'

'Reason,' she said. 'How's this for reason: this is the same island my grandfather saw. The creatures flew around this island. Remember, he saw that newborn fall into the trees. If it died, its bones should still be here somewhere. And surely there are others who died here. Bones, Matt, that's what I'm after.'

'Fine, but we can't just go wandering into the forest. It's not safe.'

'It's perfectly safe.' She kept walking.

'Miss de Vries, I must insist you come back.'

'I'll be fine,' she called over her shoulder with a cheery wave. 'Don't you worry about me.'

I folded my arms across my chest, and smiled. She would stop. When she realized I wasn't about to rush after her, she would have second thoughts about pushing on into that forest alone. By this point she was getting quite far away, and showed no signs of faltering. She pushed through some thick fronds, and I lost sight of her altogether.

I started counting. By ten she'd be peeping out from behind the foliage to see if I was coming.

By twenty she hadn't reappeared.

'Bloody hell,' I muttered, running to catch up.

The foliage was so high and thick now I couldn't see the sky. The humid air pressed against my chest. Great pine-like trees, with slender drooping branches, bristled with spiky flowers. Ferns and fronds and vines and brilliant petals were everywhere. A shrieking parrot flashed by, scarlet and green. Insects chattered in the perfumed heat. I kept looking for the light between trees, the brightness overhead, just wanting to punch through it all. Just wanting a horizon.

'Brilliant, you've decided to come,' said Kate, with barely a backward glance as she kept walking.

'Miss de Vries—'

'You said you wouldn't call me that any more.'

'You haven't travelled much, you said so yourself. But I've been all over.' I gave her a smile which I hoped she'd see as sophisticated and world-weary. 'I've been all over the tropics and there's things you've never even heard of. All kinds of wild animals—'

'I've read up on it actually,' she said briskly, whacking away foliage with her furled parasol. 'We shouldn't run into anything too fearsome. Plenty of birds. Bats. Skinks. Lizards. Big toads. You won't be seeing any big mammals, no tigers or lions or bears. Possibly a wild pig.'

'How can you know all this?' I demanded, keeping pace with her.

'How do you think? My grandfather flew over the Pacificus and I wanted to know all about the world he saw. I read up on Oceanica. Especially after I read his log. I've stared at pictures and memorized the names of the animals and trees and plants. What else was I supposed to do with myself?'

She looked at me defiantly, challenging me to contradict her.

'What about snakes!' I said, jabbing a finger at her. 'Pythons!'

'Not indigenous.'

'Boa constrictor?'

'No.'

'Anaconda!'

'That's South American. You won't find any snakes here at all.'

She did have a way of stealing the wind right out of your sails. But I wasn't quite finished with her yet.

'Just stop a second, will you? There may be people living on this island,' I said ominously. 'And who says they'll be happy to see us?'

She didn't slow down. 'Good point. But we mustn't be governed by our fears, Matt Cruse. We have a duty, you and I.'

'A duty?'

'To science, absolutely. If there are bones on this island, we must find them.'

I sighed. I was still far from convinced these winged creatures even existed. But I could see she was hell-bent on looking for them, and I couldn't very well leave her to go off by herself. Yes, Miss Simpkins, I saw her go skipping off into the woods. No, I didn't go after her. Why would I? She seemed perfectly fine on her own. Wasn't at all worried about her, no.

'It's a big island, Kate.' I was starting to feel quite defeated. 'You can't explore it all. Where do you intend to start?'

'We just start,' she said. 'Bones could be anywhere, if the creatures just fell from the sky. Of course, they might have been picked up by other animals. Unlikely though, there are probably no substantial mammals on the island.' A little furrow of concentration appeared over each eyebrow. 'But all animals feed on carrion.

So: around trees with bird nests, or the lairs of skinks and lizards.' She paused. 'That's fun to say. Skinks and lizards.'

The ground was rising now, and she was getting a bit puffed with all the walking and talking. Heat sifted through the trees and fronds. My back was wet. My heart felt loose in my chest. I'd never heard such a ruckus of birds. They were chirping and warbling and hooting and tooting and screaming non-stop. You only had to look up to see a swoop of bright feathers and flashing tail plumage, and you couldn't take many steps without getting pooped on by one of them. Cheeky things they were, and obviously had no fear of people, for they would sit and stare until we came quite close, crashing and slapping our way through the foliage. A truculent little budgie waited until I nearly trod on it before flitting away.

'You'll get tired of holding that book,' I told her. She'd got it in a little purse with a braided strap that she had slung over her shoulder.

'It's not heavy,' she said, with a shrug.

I kept waiting for Kate to get worn out. Her dress looked like cotton, airy enough, but it went all the way down to her ankles, and she kept hiking it up with one hand so she could move more easily. She was bound to get hot and want to go back to the breezy shade of the beach. But she didn't. I marvelled at her stamina. When needed she scrambled over rocks and up little hills. She kept going.

I was not at all sure of the sense of this, but part of me was glad to be moving, relieved to be busy rather than lying still in my bunk, welded to the earth. Every few minutes I would turn round to take a sighting, so we'd be able to find our way back. It was hardly necessary, though. I was good with directions, like I had a lodestone in my skull. You could spin me round and I could tell you the bearing without opening my eyes. I felt the compass, cool in my pocket.

Kate never looked back once. She was only interested in what was in front of her. Her eyes swept the ground, and she'd often stop and kneel to push back some ferns and peer about closer to the earth. Sometimes she'd look up into the tall, strange trees, or just listen. She seemed to know what she was doing, but so far we hadn't seen any bones, big or small.

It was midday now, and hotter than ever. The air was thick and perfumy. My temples streamed. I wished we'd brought water. But we hadn't brought anything. We hadn't planned. We were walking aimlessly through the tropical forest, in search of the bones of a creature that might not exist. I'd have to be back in a couple of hours. Not that Kate seemed at all aware of my duties and obligations.

'If I can collect a set of bones from this creature, imagine that!' she said. 'Pictures, photographs would be excellent too, of course. But the Zoological Society might pooh-pooh them. Fakes, like the fairies, they'd say, like the Schlock Ness monster. Imagine the furore when I show them real bones. "How do you explain that?" I'll say to them.' She already saw it playing out in her mind like a cinema reel.

'I'm expected back soon,' I told her.

'Turn back any time you need to,' she said absently.

That was rich, I thought, feeling grumpier with every step. She'd taken no note of her path; she had absolutely no hope of getting back on her own. But maybe she knew that, just like she knew I would stay on with her and be her navigator. And she was right. I felt disgusted at my own powerlessness.

'You're different here,' Kate told me. 'On the ground, I mean.'

I said nothing.

'I think you're more frightened down here than you were when the ship was about to crash.'

'You're right,' I said. 'I don't like being on the ground. I don't feel at home.'

'Do you think it's because you were born in the air?' she asked. She looked at me as if I were a picture in a textbook.

I didn't reply. I didn't much like her calling me frightened.

'I can't go back without you,' I told her impatiently. 'You'll get lost.'

'I'll be fine.'

'Which way is it then?'

She paused, frowning, as if this were all a terrible and needless annoyance.

'I'm not ready to go back yet.'

'But when you are.'

She sighed. 'I know my way.'

'Just point.'

Her chin lifted and her nostrils narrowed. I tried to narrow mine too. I'm not sure it worked.

'That way,' she said.

I nearly hooted with delight. 'Quite wrong. You're off by forty degrees or more.'

'Forty degrees,' she muttered disdainfully. 'I'll just walk downhill. That'll take me back to the coast.'

'There's a lot of coast on an island.'

'I'll just walk round.'

'Simpler if you just knew where you were going.'

We looked at each other. I was waiting for her to ask me the right direction, but she didn't.

'Listen,' she said. 'Water.'

A little way off was a sizeable stream, half hidden beneath ferns. I reckoned it was the one that emptied out near the lagoon. We knelt down to drink. The water was clear and cold.

'Well, this makes things simple, doesn't it?' Kate said jauntily. 'We'll just follow this upstream, and when we're ready, let it lead us back down to the beach. See, now we know exactly how to get back.'

'I already knew.'

'Maybe you'd better go back to calling me Miss de Vries. I'm not accustomed to being spoken to so boldly.' For a moment I thought she was serious, but I caught the light dancing in her eyes. 'You're quite right. I'm hopeless with directions. I'm lucky you're with me.'

I scratched my cheek, looking into the forest.

'I'm not frightened here,' I said. 'Not exactly.'

'I didn't mean you were scared. I just thought it was interesting you felt more at home in the sky than on the ground. With most people it's the complete opposite. That's all. It's really quite fascinating.'

'I'm fascinating now, am I?' I said.

'Absolutely.'

'I just like to keep moving,' I said. 'On land I feel like I'm going nowhere. I'm not good at standing still. I'm like a shark: if I don't keep moving forward, I can't breathe.'

'A shark,' she said, raising her eyebrow at me. 'That's quite a comparison. I wouldn't say you're really very shark-like, deep down. The dangerous, carnivorous man-eating Mr Cruse!'

'I suppose not, no.' I blushed. 'I just meant the moving part.'

We walked on, and after half an hour seemed to have reached a bit of a plateau. More light was getting through the forest canopy. The birds really were tremendous here, and by now I was used to having them so close overhead, their quick shadows soaring over me, blinking out the sun.

Kate sighed and for the first time looked discouraged.

'Nothing,' she said.

'It's a big island. It would take years to search it properly.'

'And we don't have years.'

'There might be time for another look around.'

I couldn't believe I'd gone and said that. It's just that she looked so crestfallen and I wanted to cheer her up. But she was smiling at me now, and I had the uncomfortable feeling I'd just been juggled.

'Really?' she said. 'You'd have another look around with me?'

'If there's time,' I muttered. 'Maybe. I can't promise.'

'Thank you so much. I know you'll try your best. Well, I suppose we should head back soon. I don't want to get you into trouble.'

'I'm sure that's uppermost in your mind,' I said.

Something slithered past my foot, and I stepped smartly out of the way. 'I thought you said there were no snakes here.'

It was curled innocently under a big fern frond. It seemed a harmless little thing, not more than a few inches, and a pretty bright red – a daft colour for a snake amongst all that greenery, you couldn't miss it. Any bird of prey would see it a mile off. A dainty little tongue lapped the air. This was no anaconda, no king cobra, no boa – I'd seen those snakes, and they were enough to make you run.

'Don't move,' Kate said, her face pale.

'What?'

'I think that one's poisonous.'

'This little thing?'

Then, in the unfriendliest way possible, it jumped. It launched itself sideways, and arced through the air, straight at my face. Kate squealed, and I gave a shout, not a very polite one, and staggered backwards. The snake landed not a metre from my shoes. Kate and I danced back some more, and that little red demon jumped again like it was half pogo-stick and scarcely needed to touch earth. I wouldn't turn around to run, for fear it would land on my back without my knowing. So I ran backwards, shooing Kate on ahead of me. The snake sprang again and this time lighted on the toe of my shoe. I gave a great footballer's kick and sent it spinning through the air and into the distant undergrowth.

'It's gone. It's OK,' I panted, standing with my arms out, knees bent, watching. There was nothing to see, not so much as a ripple of leaves.

'Wasn't he just the sweetest little thing?' I said, and started giggling.

'I'm sure he only wanted to say hello,' Kate added, giggling too. 'I must remember to bring one back for Miss Simpkins.'

'There's no snakes here, by the way,' I told her. 'I'm completely sure of it.'

'Well, there shouldn't be,' she said stubbornly.

'Then how'd you know that one was poisonous!'

'I'm pretty sure I saw it in a book,' Kate said, and then screamed.

I whirled to see the snake springing up from the ferns and bouncing towards us, fast. This time we turned and ran. Kate hiked her skirt up high and held it bunched in one hand so she could take proper strides. Every time I looked around, the snake was still there. I wanted to laugh and scream at the same time. The little creature was ridiculous. It was terrifying, and it was also gaining on us.

'The tree!' Kate gasped, heading for an enormously thick tree with huge jutting branches.

'That safe?' I shouted.

'Think so!'

'*Think* so?'

'Snakes can't climb.'

Which I didn't think was at all true, but Kate was already at the tree and trying to get up on the lowest branch. It was about two metres off the ground, and her boots skittered off the bark, and her skirts kept getting in the way. I looked over my shoulder and there was our little red friend sailing towards us and only needing two or three more leaps before we had a happy reunion. I grabbed Kate's waist and heaved her up, giving her backside a push for good measure. One of her heels caught me in the cheek, but she was up, and then it was my turn.

'Make room!' I shouted. It was an easy jump for me, up in a trice, and sliding my belly over the branch.

Below I could see the little red snake bounce straight up at my face, and I thought it was going to bite me on the nose. I recoiled, scrambling into a sitting position. The snake was a few inches short of the branch, and down it fell, but then it just bounced up again, and again, intent on reaching us. This snake was no quitter.

'Maybe one more,' I said to Kate, nodding at the next branch up. It was a great broad flat thing, sticking out horizontally from the trunk, and mostly shrouded in a cascade of hanging vines from high above. There was an easy way up to it, for many stunted branches stuck out from the trunk, making a kind of spiral staircase.

'This way!' I stepped up the little branches towards the bigger one. I glanced down and couldn't see the snake any more. It had given up jumping.

'Never climb a tree in a long dress,' Kate panted, coming up behind me.

'I'll remember that,' I said.

She had hiked her skirt up again, so high that I could see her gartered stockings. I tried not to look. She had knotted the skirt around her hip so she would not need to hold it.

We climbed. Crouched over, I pushed my head through the curtain of vines. Something hard knocked against my cheek and I jerked back with a grunt.

'What?' I heard Kate shout behind me.

But I could not answer. I had stopped breathing. It was just inches away from my face. I could only gaze at the head that was staring at me from its eyeless sockets.

Its fangs seemed enormous in its fleshless jaws. I forced breath into my lungs.

'It's dead,' I said.

I made room for Kate on the broad branch, and cautiously she crawled through the vines.

'Oh my goodness,' she breathed.

It was not just a skull, but an entire skeleton, hunched down against the branch like something about to pounce. I wondered how long it had been here. Insects hummed and trilled and danced in the heat. Light slanted through the vines. The bones gleamed. Its claws were locked deep into the bark in its final death grip. Its flesh had been picked clean, but its bones were still miraculously attached, bound together by sun-cured sinew and leathery bits of muscle. It was easily two metres from head to tail. It had died on this very branch. It had been here for ever, just waiting to be discovered.

I looked at the long, flat skull, the fangs curving from the upper and lower jaws.

'It's a panther,' I said to Kate.

'No . . .'

'Or some other kind of big cat, it's got to be.'

'It's not.'

'We should get out of here. There might be others around.'

'Look at it, Matt.'

I didn't understand what I was seeing. The skeleton was all crumpled up along the branch, collapsed in on itself. I could make out the long, knobbly chain of vertebrae clear enough, and the ribcage, though some of the bones there were cracked or flattened. The legs I wasn't too sure about, for they were folded at odd angles alongside the body, getting mixed up with the other bones.

'Its front legs,' I said, frowning.

They weren't right. They were too long, especially the lower bones. They went on for ever and ended not with a proper foot, but with a spray of whip-thin bones fanning out across the branch, trailing over the sides. I'd never seen anything like it.

'Those aren't legs,' Kate said. 'They're wings.'

She was looking at me, her face flushed and shiny with sweat. Her breath came in little shaky pulses.

'How do you know?' I said. 'How can you tell they're wings? It's just bones now.'

She scrambled closer to the skeleton. 'Those are its fingers,' she said, pointing at the long thin bones. 'They help support the wing. Have you ever seen a bat's skeleton? It's a bit like that. These are wings.'

I nodded, remembering the sketches in Benjamin Molloy's journal. I'd seen giant flying foxes in the Dutch East Indies. They sometimes had wingspans of two metres, but their bodies were no bigger than a rat's. This creature was much, much larger.

'This is no bat,' I said, swallowing.

'No.'

The exact same thought must have been bounding

through both our heads, but I wasn't ready to say it yet.

'But how could a creature this big fly?' I asked.

Kate leaned in close, and gingerly picked up a large piece of fractured rib bone that had fallen on the branch. She smiled, and handed it to me. My hand actually floated up as my fingers closed around it, for I'd been expecting something heavier. This bone was light as air. I held it balanced in my palm and could barely feel its weight.

Kate took it back.

'Look,' she said, holding the fractured end up for me to see. In the slanting light, I could see the bone wasn't solid inside. It was a honeycomb of air and slivery struts.

'Like a bird's,' she said. 'To make them light. Imagine, if all its bones were hollow, it wouldn't weigh much. And those wings. I'm trying to imagine them all stretched out. Over a metre each, what do you think? A two-metre span?'

'More. Three metres, I'd say.'

'Enough for flight?'

I nodded. 'Enough sail to take it airborne.'

Her eyes widened. 'And look here.' She was pointing around the creature's ribcage. 'Look at its breastbone, see, it's got a kind of keel on it.'

'To hold the ribs together, to make them stronger,' I said. I knew what a ship's keel was for.

'And to give the wings strength,' Kate added. 'That's

where all the muscles would attach. Birds are the only creatures that have them.'

'How do you know all this?'

'Books,' she said.

I looked again at the skeleton. 'So you're saying this is some kind of big bird now?'

'Absolutely not. In a bird's wing the metacarpals are all sort of fused together so it looks like just one digit. This creature clearly has five.'

I shook my head, not understanding.

'It doesn't matter,' she said. 'Just look at the skull. If it's a bird, where's its beak? Do you know any bird that has jaws or teeth like that?'

'Or a long tail,' I said, looking at the skinny line of vertebrae trailing on the branch. I needed to touch it again. I lifted the broken rib bone in my hand, felt its weightlessness. I felt weightless too, and hungry. I would drift right off the branch soon, up into the sky.

Since I'd last slept, pirates had boarded the *Aurora* and sunk her, we'd crash-landed on a desert island, and Kate and I had discovered the skeleton of some strange creature halfway up a tree. It had a bat's wings, the hollow bones of a bird, the head of a panther. It was like nothing anyone had ever seen. I touched the dry hard bone of its skull. I didn't know what it was, or what to call it.

'It's one of them,' said Kate. 'It's just the way he described in his log. You can see that, can't you?'

I remembered her grandfather's careful sketches of skeletons. The human. The bat. And then the weird hybrid creature. It was just as he'd imagined. 'Yes,' I said.

'It's real, isn't it?' Kate said.

I nodded.

'They exist. They really exist.' She was staring at the skeleton. She was crying.

'What's wrong?' I asked.

'He was right,' she said. 'Grandpa.'

I nodded, surprised. Had she ever doubted him? She'd seemed so sure always. Or maybe it was just relief and excitement and exhaustion all swirled up together. It made me feel like crying. Kate wiped her eyes, sniffed. I wanted to touch her, but didn't dare.

'It seems almost wrong to disturb it,' she said. 'It's so perfect. But I want the bones. I'll need to take some photographs first. Just as it was when we found it. That way we'll know how to put the bones back together. We could number them, too.' She nodded, pleased with this idea. 'Yes, we'll number them. I've got a special wax pen that should work.'

'You do?'

'I do.'

It seemed she had no end of scientific gear with her. I marvelled that it all fitted on the ornithopter that brought her to the *Aurora*.

'You'll be able to find this place again, won't you?' she asked me.

I couldn't help smiling. 'Well, I haven't really been paying attention to where—'

'Oh, don't joke!' she said, grabbing my arm.

'Yes,' I said, 'yes, I'll be able to bring you back.'

She let go of my arm. I liked the way it felt when she'd squeezed it.

'Bit of a slog carrying your camera and gear up though. I suppose we could get someone to help.'

'No.'

She said it most emphatically, and I didn't understand.

'We'll tell no one.'

'What about the captain?'

She shook her head gravely.

I laughed. 'We've got to tell the captain at least!'

'Why? Is it ship's business?'

'Well . . .'

'It has nothing at all to do with the ship or her well-being.'

'I suppose not, but why keep it secret?'

Her face had a hardness I'd not seen before. 'If we go back and tell the captain, you know what will happen. He'll forbid us from coming back to take pictures.'

'I don't know about that.'

'Or at best he might send some of the crew to come and collect the bones, and then it'll be taken from me. Put into the right hands, they'll say. Let experts take care of these things.'

'The captain's a fair man.'

'I'm sure he is. But you remember the letter they sent me, those important gentlemen from the Zoological Society. Turn your attention to more ladylike pursuits. They'd just take it away from me, and I won't put up with it. This is our discovery, Matt. We tell them, they'll take it away from us. They'll treat us like children.'

She had a point.

'Promise me you won't tell.'

I said nothing for a moment, uncomfortable. I felt like she was making me choose between her and the captain, her and my ship. But maybe she was right: strictly speaking this had nothing to do with the *Aurora*. It was something else entirely.

'So we'll just come back to the ship with a big bag of bones. Look at all the mangoes we collected, everyone.'

'No one has to know what's inside.'

'They might not be too keen to take on more cargo.'

'It'll be light,' she said with a grin. 'I'll make room in one of my steamer trunks.'

'All right,' I said. 'It's a secret.'

'Our secret,' she said. 'And when I get back home I'll contact the Zoological Society. I'll have photographs, the bones, the journal. They'll have to believe me and my grandfather then.'

The *Aurora* was beached like a whale, but getting home was a certainty for Kate. She'd already leapfrogged time in her head, not just to her homecoming, but to some glorious future. I wondered where I'd be then.

'I almost hate to leave it,' she said. 'Afraid it won't be here when we get back.'

'It's not going anywhere.'

As I stared at the skeleton, I imagined muscles and sinews and tendons fusing with the bones, skin and fur growing over it all. I looked at the skull and pictured the jaws opening wide, a flash of life in the eye sockets. A bird shrieked, and I jerked.

'Come on,' I said, 'we should be getting back now.'

10

SHIPSHAPE

I'd been hoping that when we returned, Kate would just melt back in with the other passengers on the beach, and I would slip unnoticed aboard the *Aurora* and report late for duty. And that would be that. But as we neared the beach we could hear Miss Simpkins' voice. We peeped out from behind a palm. She was yelling at Mr Lisbon. Worse luck, the captain was nearby, talking to some of the other passengers, and he had turned to see what all the fuss was about.

'What do you mean, you don't know where she is!' Miss Simpkins was shrieking at the chief steward. 'She might have been eaten by savages, or a snapping turtle, or some other monstrosity on this island you've crashed us on!'

I hung back behind the tree.

'Come on,' said Kate, 'let's get this over with.'

'I'm not sure it's a good idea.'

She strode ahead, and there was no point me lurking alone behind a palm all afternoon, so I fell into step beside her.

'Hello,' Kate called out with a cheery wave. 'I'm terribly sorry. Have you been looking for me? I didn't want to wake you, Marjorie, you looked so fabulously peaceful, and I know how you hate to have your naps interrupted.'

'Kate, where on earth have you been! I've been worried sick!'

'Yes, I'm sure. I went for a stroll, just along the beach and then in amongst the trees for a bit. The scenery really is extraordinary here.'

By this time, Miss Simpkins' gaze had settled on me with the weight of an anvil.

'He was with you, was he?'

The captain was nearing us, hands clasped behind his back, looking on.

'Of course,' said Kate. 'He accompanied me.'

'Captain Walken!' said Miss Simpkins. 'This is quite improper. Don't think I haven't been keeping an eye on all this. Your cabin boy there has been forcing his attentions on Miss de Vries.'

I blushed just to hear the words spoken.

'He's done nothing of the sort,' said Kate severely. 'I asked him to escort me on a walk into the forest and he kindly did so, on his off watch. He was a credit to his ship and captain.'

Miss Simpkins looked no less displeased. 'Surely, Captain Walken, fraternizing with the passengers is forbidden the crew.'

'It seems to me, Miss Simpkins,' the captain replied,

'that Mr Cruse was only trying to accommodate a passenger's request. Although it might have been more sensible to stay within sight of the ship.'

'Exactly what Mr Cruse said,' Kate agreed. 'He was most sensible. It was my idea to go farther afield. I'm sorry, Marjorie, for the worry I caused.'

'You were gone several hours!' protested the chaperone, gripping her hair as if it was about to blast off her head.

'Miss de Vries,' said Captain Walken, 'perhaps it would be best for all involved if you stuck a little closer to home from now on, what do you say? Spare your poor chaperone the worry – and your parents too, no doubt.'

Kate looked at me. 'Mr Cruse, thank you so much for escorting me, and I'm sorry for the trouble I've caused you.'

'Not at all, Miss de Vries. Good day, Miss Simpkins.' I gave her a nod and turned back to the ship, Captain Walken at my side.

'Am I right in saying this is the first time you've ever been late for duty, Mr Cruse?'

My ears felt hot. 'Yes, sir, I believe so.'

'After the rigours of last night a bit of sleep might have been in order.'

'I know, sir. But I couldn't sleep.'

'Fair enough. But we need you safe and sound, Mr Cruse. You're too valuable to us to be off sight seeing. I see no need to make a note of this in your record. You may go about your duty.'

'Thank you, sir.'

He could have been much harder on me. Being late for duty was taken very seriously aboard an airship, and it was usually put in your record. The captain strode on ahead, then turned round.

'Ah, Mr Cruse, I've got a bit of good news for you.'

'Sir?'

'We've enough hydrium to lift off. Ah, see, I thought that would please you. But we'll need to lighten first. And there's more repairs yet to do. But she'll fly again, Mr Cruse. She'll fly. Now to work!'

And back-breaking work it was, lightening the ship. The officers and captain had already made up a list. We had to shed thousands of kilos, and the cargo holds were the obvious place to start. The bay doors were wide open, and the davits were swung out over the sides, lowering crates on to the sand. After that, we had to shift it by hand. We had no fork lifts or trolleys. Try lifting a heavy crate with a team of other men, your feet sinking and slewing about in the sand and the tropical afternoon sun beating down on your neck, and sweat making your palms so slippery you worry you'll lose your grip, and all of you staggering off towards the shelter of the trees to stack the crates as neatly as you can.

Still, every kilo I lifted was a kilo lighter for the *Aurora*. With every crate we took off, she would rise a little higher off the sand. The sailmakers had been working like galley slaves to seal off the leaking gas cells and were still patching the ship's outer skin. It was my turn now to help heal the ship.

Knees aching, I helped lower yet another crate to the sand. I leaned against it, catching my breath. On the side was stencilled *McGahern's Rubber Hosing*. This was the fifth one we'd shifted now, and who'd have thought it would be so heavy. It almost made me angry. We were breaking our backs carrying out crates of useless rubber hosing. How much rubber hosing did the world need?

'All right?' Baz asked, looking at me.

'Rubber hosing,' I grunted.

'I know, it's absurd,' he sniffed and we headed back to the ship for more. Across the beach passengers were sipping cocktails and chilled fruit juices now. It wasn't often I wished I was serving rather than working on the ship, but now the thought was tempting. Off a way from the main group I could see Kate. She'd brought out her camera and had it set up on a tripod. It was tilted towards the sky and had some big long lens which was probably telescopic, attached to it. Her hand shielding her eyes, Kate swept the blue-bleached sky. I knew what she was looking for. I looked up too, but saw nothing except wispy cloud.

A beefy gentleman with one of those irritating bristly moustaches was standing beneath the cargo bay doors, watching us unload. He'd been there for a while, smoking a foul-smelling cigar. Now he was jabbing a sausage-shaped finger at the crate being swung out on the davit.

'Be careful with that one, all of you,' he commanded, spewing out noxious smoke. 'That's personal effects in there. Antiques. I don't want any of them damaged. They're in mint condition.'

'We'll be as careful as we can, sir,' said Baz.

'And look here, I don't like where you're putting them. You can't just leave it all out in the open like that. My antiques will warp in the heat, they'll bleach in the sun!'

'We'll cover them all in tarpaulins when we're through, sir,' Baz grunted as we lifted. There were six of us on this crate, it was so heavy.

'See that you do,' said the man, circling around us as we carried his crate across the sand. 'It's disgraceful, this whole business.'

We could leave you behind instead, I wanted to say. But we can't promise you won't get warped in the heat.

'And how do you propose we're to get our belongings back?' he demanded. 'Have you thought of that?'

'A ship will be dispatched once we reach port.'

The man sniffed. 'First pirates steal our valuables, now we're expected to abandon the rest! And what if they're ruined in the meantime?'

'Your insurance will cover the loss, sir,' I gasped as we staggered towards the trees.

The gentleman blew cigar smoke at me, his face screwed tight. 'Fine for you to say. I don't see you lot putting your things out on the beach.'

'Well, sir,' came the captain's voice behind me, 'the lad, like most of his crewmates, has the clothes on his back, plus a second set, toiletries and a few books and letters from home. That wouldn't make much of a difference now, would it? But if I asked them to, they would part with every last thing willingly. They know it would be in the best interest of the ship and all who sail on her.'

The gentleman said nothing, puffing on his cigar before turning on his heel and walking back to the other passengers.

'Please carry on, gentlemen,' said the captain, 'you're doing fine work.'

The sun was low in the sky, and pretty much the entire crew was out on the beach, manning the *Aurora*'s lines. In a few moments we'd see if she would fly again. Baz and I were off the ship's starboard side. I'd untied my knot and left a few turns around the palm trunk, and we were both leaning back on the line, awaiting orders.

'Slowly now!' the captain called out, holding tight to his own line near the ship's bow. 'Let's see how she's doing.'

I knew she was stronger right away. I could feel the pull of her through the taut line. Hand over hand we let it out. My eyes were fixed on the *Aurora*.

She shivered.

And then she lifted, and my heart lifted with her.

A huge cheer burst from all of us, crew and passengers alike.

She was lifting, and we were all cheering, and her belly, which had been nearly grounded, was now a metre or so off the sand.

'That's my girl,' I said under my breath.

'Let her come!' cried the captain. 'Let her rise now! She's our phoenix. She's our homesick angel! Steady now!'

Her tail fin, badly crumpled, lifted free of the sand. We let the *Aurora* rise. She was properly aloft now, landlocked no more. My eyes were ablur but I dared not take my hands off the line to wipe them. I watched as, centimetre by centimetre, she lifted higher.

'And hold her there!' cried the captain. 'Tie her off, gentlemen, with your best knots, make tightropes of each and every line!'

We tied off. The *Aurora*'s belly had about two metres of clearance now. She hovered there over the beach and there was no finer sight to me in the wide world and all her skies and seas.

'Good heavens, look at you,' Baz said, clapping a hand on my shoulder. 'She's all right, you know.'

'That's why I'm blubbering,' I said, coughing away my tears, swiping at my cheeks. I glanced up at him and saw his eyes were shining too.

'You've got me all emotional now,' said Baz, laughing. 'Get a grip on yourself, young Matt Cruse. We're all of us going home.'

'You'll be a married man after all,' I said to him.

'She may not have me, now I've gone and kept her waiting.'

'You had the very best of excuses.'

'Pirates!' he said.

'Murderous pirates and a sinking ship and a crash landing on a tropical island!'

'And let's not forget my valiant acts!' Baz added. 'I served cool beverages in blazing heat; I helped shade the rich and privileged.'

'You're a proper hero,' I assured him.

We were making our way back towards the ship, where the captain and officers were already inspecting her underbelly. It was not a pretty sight.

'We can mend scrapes and broken bones well enough,' Captain Walken said. 'Mr Chen, what do you make of the tail fin and rudder?'

'A day's work, sir.'

'Make it tomorrow's work, then, Mr Chen. I've worked you all like pack horses, today. Aside from essential watch duty, and cabin crew, you've all shore leave for the evening!'

'Permission to give you three cheers, Captain?'

'If absolutely necessary.'

We all gave the captain three great cheers.

'Now then,' he said, 'I believe that our esteemed chef, Mr Vlad, has been preparing something wonderful for dinner. I urge you all to enjoy it. My heartfelt thanks to you all for your labours. Now I must go relay the good news to our passengers.'

The captain had allowed all the passengers back on board, and everyone in the dining room was in a merry mood that night. In the kitchen, I'd never seen Vlad happier. Earlier in the afternoon, he'd sent his four assistant chefs into the lagoon to catch fish, and had been slow-cooking them in great pits on the beach.

'Look at this,' he'd said to me, pointing a cleaning knife at an enormous colourful fish laid out on the kitchen counter. 'Have you ever seen anything so lovely? Look at the texture of her flesh, here. You see? She is beautiful. The fish here are finer than any I've seen anywhere.' He sucked in his breath and looked across the kitchen at some distant mirage. 'I could stay here, yes? Stay here and open a restaurant. People would come from all over the world to eat fish such as this.' He pointed his knife at me. 'You, Mr Cruse, would you travel across the world for such a meal?'

'Yes,' I said.

'Good boy. You're a good boy. Now go and tell my idiot cooks to hurry up with those mangoes.'

After they'd spent hours fishing, Vlad had sent them climbing trees to gather coconuts and mangoes and pineapples. Judging from the smells coming from the kitchen, and wafting across the beach, we were all in for an exotic feast.

All the windows in the dining room were thrown wide, and the warm, perfumed night air filled the lounges and dining rooms. It still amazed me, the view from the windows: palms and sand and a turquoise lagoon, still aglow even as the sun sank below the horizon.

And there was Kate, sitting in her usual seat, but where was her chaperone?

'How is Miss Simpkins this evening?' I asked as I put the napkin on her lap.

'She's feeling poorly. She's retired to bed with a violent tropical headache.'

'Tropical headache?' I placed a hot roll on her side plate.

'Thank you. That's what the ship's doctor said, but I think he was just simply kind. I think she just wanted to get back into her comfy bed. The beach was a little too stressful for her. Your ship's doctor's rather dashing, isn't he?'

'Is he?' I said, taken somewhat aback.

'He is,' Kate said firmly. 'Now look what I found.' She had a fat little book in her hand – how many books had she brought? – and flipped its pages.

'I always thought Doc Halliday was kind of odd looking,' I muttered.

'There, look at this,' Kate said, pointing.

It was a tinted picture of the little red snake that had sent us running through the forest.

'Perfectly harmless,' she said, smiling, as she read the description. 'Apparently it jumps like that to frighten off predators. It's not at all poisonous.'

'Cheeky devil,' I said, pouring some water from the decanter into Kate's glass.

'I'm very grateful to the little fellow. If it weren't for him, we might not have found the skeleton.'

'Maybe you'd like one as a pet?'

'Well, at least we know it's not poisonous. So when we go back, no worries.'

Going back, I looked over to the captain, seated at the head table with his officers, and a number of passengers.

'Would you like the fish or the suckling pig tonight, Miss de Vries?' I asked with professional courtesy as Baz swirled close by with three plates balanced in his hands.

'The fish, of course. I've been smelling it baking for the last hour.'

'Very good, Miss.'

'We'll talk later,' she said, eyes twinkling as I moved away.

We didn't get the chance to talk again until much later. Dinner had been served and eagerly devoured. The desserts trolleys had made their rounds; the men had retreated to the smoking room, the women left behind in the starboard lounge to await their partners' smoggy return. People headed off to bed earlier than usual, no doubt exhausted by watching the crew work all day. I tended bar. Kate stayed behind, reading. One by one, the passengers left, until it was just Kate sitting there. I started wiping down tables. I wasn't sure I was ready for Kate just now.

'Aren't you going to do this one?' she asked, when I'd cleaned every table but hers. 'You're not avoiding me, are you?'

'Of course not.'

'When do you get off duty?'

'I'm not sure it's a good idea, going back.'

'Of course it's a good idea. We need to take pictures and gather up the bones.'

'The captain asked you to stay near the ship.'

'Yes, but I'm under no obligation to obey him. I gave no promise.'

'Well, he had a word with me afterwards.'

'Did he forbid you from leaving the ship?'

'Not exactly.' I recited our brief conversation to her.

'Well, I don't see what the problem is,' she said. 'You wouldn't be disobeying a direct order. He just wants you to be safe, he doesn't want you to be late again. You won't be.'

She was just shaping things the way she wanted, I knew that.

I said nothing. Her voice was low and urgent when she next spoke.

'Matt, you promised.'

'I know.'

'This is something the world has never seen. We can't just leave it here. We've discovered something amazing, you and I!'

I liked the 'you and I' part. I felt all tugged in different directions.

'I want to help you,' I said miserably. 'I want to get the bones, I do. But the captain wants me with the ship.' It wasn't just disobeying orders; I couldn't help feeling that if I left the ship, some disaster would befall her. It would be tempting fate. 'Don't ask me to choose, please. It's not fair. You or the captain. You or the ship.'

'It doesn't seem a very difficult choice to me,' she said, her nostrils narrowing. 'Anyway, I don't see what the ship's got to do with this.'

'It's my home.'

'It's not your home,' she said impatiently, 'it's where you work, that's all.'

I looked at her, not trusting myself to speak. She didn't understand anything.

'Fine,' she said. 'I don't want to force you. I can ask Mr Lunardi.'

'Mr Lunardi.'

'Yes, I'm sure he'd be delighted to accompany me.'

'You don't mind sharing your little secret then?' Our secret. My heart was beating slow and hard and angry.

'I'm sure he can keep a secret. He seems a perfect gentleman.'

'A much better bet than a cabin boy, you're quite right. I'm sure you'll be much more comfortable with Mr Lunardi. Good night, Miss.'

I turned and walked away, trembling inside with rage. I'd been useful to her, that was all. That was the only reason she was friendly to me.

'Matt,' she said, when I was near the door. I stopped. 'I'm not going to ask Mr Lunardi. You know I wouldn't do that. You're the only one I trust.'

I gave a hollow laugh, unconvinced. 'And what if I say no?'

'I suppose I'll just have to go by myself.'

She would too. I almost smiled, half in vexation, half in admiration of her pig-headed wilfulness. She'd go and get lost, and then I'd feel it was somehow my fault. There'd be a big search party, and that would waste even more of the ship's time. And she might get hurt. I sighed. If I went with her, it would only take a few hours.

'I'm not on duty again till noon,' I said, without turning to face her. 'We can leave at first light. We'll have to be quick, though.'

'Thank you,' she said, walking over. 'Thank you so much, Matt. I'm sorry. I didn't mean to insult you. I didn't mean to imply that Mr Lunardi was—'

'—any better than me? Well he is, isn't he? Let's not pretend. He's wealthy, he's older, he's handsome, he's a junior officer . . .'

'Is he?'

'Of course he is,' I fairly shouted. 'Assistant sailmaker. Didn't you notice the insignia on his collar?'

'I didn't, no.'

'The golden wheels? Blazing like little suns?'

She shook her head. 'All those insignia look the same to me. Everyone seems to have them.'

'Not me,' I said hotly.

'And I don't find him handsome, by the way.'

'You don't?'

'I don't,' she said firmly. 'His type of looks are not at all to my liking. You know, the only problem with first thing in the morning is the light might not be at its best in the forest.'

'Take it or leave it,' I said. 'There might not be another chance before we take off.'

'It's fine,' she said. 'I've got a flash anyway.'

'What about Miss Simpkins?' I asked.

'Oh, she'll be bedridden.' Kate said it without a trace of sympathy. 'I know all about her headaches. Half the time they're just to get off work.'

'Well, her work is particularly horrible,' I said.

She looked put out for a moment before she realized I was joking.

'Marjorie won't even know I've left the ship,' she said. 'I'll leave her a note telling her I'm at breakfast, and then reading in the lounge so I won't disturb her rest. So that's all taken care of.'

It was a bad decision I was making, I knew that. But I couldn't have her cavorting alone in the forest. Besides, I did want to see the bones again, and I wanted her to have them. It made me feel good to help her.

'About six thirty then,' I said. 'Meet me at the base of the grand staircase.'

I was exhausted, and I should have fallen asleep the moment my cheek touched the pillow. But I could not. I tried to lull myself to sleep with images of flight. I imagined the *Aurora* lifting off into a cloudless sky, imagined myself at her controls, flying her. But every time I almost dozed off, some part of my mind would start to panic and jerk me away from sleep, and my heart would race. It was just like being back in the cramped, low-ceilinged apartment in Lionsgate City.

I hated it, feeling this way about my beloved cabin. It was small, but that didn't matter: when the *Aurora* was aloft the cabin was big as the sky, and in a single night it gave me a sleep as wide as continents and deep as oceans.

Now it was a cell.

It was four in the morning before my body could finally endure no more, and I slept despite the turbulence in my brain. I slept –

– and dreamed I was running along the beach. The skeleton was bounding after me, its bony wings flared, its legs stretching long as it soared weightlessly over the sand. Its jaws gaped.

I was so slow, so weak. I could barely lift my feet from the sand to take a stride. Why couldn't I go faster? It would be upon me in a moment. What was wrong with me? I should have been able to fly free, but I could not leave the earth.

11

THE ONE THAT FELL

I tore at the vines hanging down around the branch, trying to let more light in. I felt strange doing it, and kept glancing over at the skeleton, half expecting it to shift, angry at having its long, sheltered slumber disturbed. It seemed smaller somehow, once the view around it opened up and the morning sun bathed its dry bones. It looked dejected, no longer so ready to pounce, all slumped and crumpled along the broad branch.

'That's brilliant, much better,' said Kate from the ground. I moved back against the trunk, and she took a photograph from down there. She said it was important to give a sense of exactly where the specimen was found. She was using a smaller camera than the one I'd seen in her stateroom. This one was a compact box, with a large mirrored bowl lamp mounted on the front. When she took the picture it gave a mighty flash, stunning the bugs of the forest into a momentary silence.

The camera and flash all fitted snugly inside a leather

case with a moulded interior. Kate had carried it slung over her shoulder as we'd worked our way up through the forest in the early morning light. I'd offered to carry it for a while, for it did look cumbersome, but she kept saying she was fine, that it was her gear and she would manage it, which quite impressed me. She did let me take the carpet-bag though. She'd insisted on bringing it, to carry back the bones. I felt absurd hiking through the ferns and foliage hefting a carpet-bag with a pattern of roses on the outside. 'I've left quite a lot of clothing in there,' she'd told me, 'for padding.' Bones were fragile things, especially these ones, she'd told me. She didn't want them getting scraped or cracked.

It had taken us over an hour to reach the tree.

'Can you stand close to it,' she called up to me now, 'without touching it, of course.'

'Why?' I asked.

'Scale.'

I still felt uncomfortable being near the skeleton, but reluctantly crouched beside it and stared at the camera's big dark eye. Flash!

'Terrific,' she said, 'I'm coming up.'

She passed the camera up to me first, and then I helped pull her to the first branch. She wore a white cotton tennis dress, and the skirt was daringly short, just below the knees, but it meant it wasn't always getting underfoot, and she could get around the tree much more easily. On her feet she wore flat-soled sandals with good grips. Her legs were bare, and earlier when I'd first noticed, my cheeks flushed. It was most unconventional, even in the tropical heat, for a young lady to go bare-legged. I was trying to keep my eyes off them. They were very pale, and bruised purple in places from all our running and tree climbing the day before.

Before she started taking pictures, she first measured the skeleton with a cloth measuring tape. She took the length and width and height and a bunch of other measurements that seemed quite unnecessary to me, and wrote them all down. I noticed she was using her grandfather's journal, continuing the work he'd started last year. I liked watching her hands as she wrote, the way her fingers held the pencil. She had lovely long fingers, but they looked strong too. Probably got lots of exercise turning the pages of books.

Then it was on to the photographs. Kate wanted close-ups from every possible angle, so she'd have no trouble reassembling the bones once she got them home. It was quite a job, manoeuvring around the skeleton, and she clambered about on all the nearby branches to get the views that pleased her best, and I followed after her anxiously, holding the camera until she was ready and, once or twice, grabbing hold of her whenever she was about to teeter off the tree altogether.

'How do we know they don't live on land?' It had been bothering me all morning. If there was one here, there could be others, alive this time, teeth and all.

'My grandfather said they never landed. Anyway, he saw them head south, remember? They just feed around here. They're not land animals, Matt. Take a look at the legs and arms. They can't walk. They don't want to be on land.'

'Right.' I wanted to be reassured. 'So this one must've just died in flight.'

I looked up through the tree. I supposed it was possible. Directly overhead I could see a patch of clear sky. It died in the air, spiralled earthwards like a dry leaf, just happened to thunk down all neat and tidy on this branch. A bit far-fetched maybe but . . . No. Impossible. Its claws were locked into the bark. It'd been alive when it landed. I tried to imagine it. It was too weak or ill to keep flying, and had started to drop, leaving behind its home, its sky, every metre lower a metre it would never regain. By chance the island was below it and into the trees it went, clutching at things with weak claws until it crumpled against this big old branch. It dug in, hunching down as death took it. No bird dared come near the body: they'd never seen such a thing. Only the bugs, after a time, went to work on the carcass.

Kate fired off another blinding photo.

'Surely you have enough now,' I said, conscious of the time, and wondering how long it would take to label and wrench apart all the bones.

'Yes,' she said. 'I think I have enough.'

She hung her camera carefully by its strap from an overhanging branch. Then we brought up her carpet-bag. The branch was broad enough for us to crouch side by side, and put the suitcase behind us. Kate produced a special wax pencil, which she said she never travelled without.

'I suppose you never know when you might stumble on some ancient relic or skull and need to label it right away,' I said.

'Quite,' she replied. 'Really, it would have been more useful to label the bones first, then take the pictures, then take the skeleton apart,' she said. 'Never mind. Gosh, there really are a lot of bones, aren't there?'

'Lots of bones,' I said.

'I've never done anything like this before, you know,' she told me gravely.

'Really?' I said. 'You amaze me.'

'Oh be quiet,' she said, smiling a little. 'Here's what we'll do. I'll label the bones, and then you start taking them apart and packing them into the bag.'

'It's what I've trained to do all my life,' I said. 'It's my heart's desire.'

'No need to be sarcastic, Mr Cruse.'

She started with the skull, which was closest after all, and worked her way down the vertebrae. I took a deep breath and grasped the skull on either side. I joggled it gently.

'You're being careful, aren't you?' she asked.

'I think so.'

'These are delicate things.'

'Would you rather do it?'

'No, no, I trust you. Just be gentle.'

With a snap the skull came free from the spine, and I was suddenly holding it in my hands. It was incredibly light. The lower jaw dropped off its hinges, and I nearly lost it altogether.

'That was close,' said Kate.

'Stop watching me,' I told her, 'I'm absolutely fine.'

A few teeth fell out, and I caught them in my hand at the last moment. I gingerly lifted it all over to the bag and put it inside.

On we worked, Kate labelling, me dismantling. I was wrapping bones up in handkerchiefs and knickers and stockings and bits of ladies' clothing I'd never seen before and certainly never handled. And then I realized, of course, they were also Kate's things, and my cheeks started to burn and I felt most improper. I got back to work on the vertebrae, fiddly little things, but they popped out fairly easily.

Kate looked over and gave a snort, and at first I thought I was doing something wrong.

'I wish we had some proper packing materials,' she said.

'I'm surprised you didn't think to bring some.'

She smiled. 'We'll just have to do the best we can.

Given the circumstances, I think we're managing rather well.'

'Those wing bones aren't going to make it,' I said, nodding at the whippy bones at the end of the creature's arms.

She grimaced. 'I know. They're bound to break. Just do the best you can wrapping them up.'

We worked on in silence. I still didn't like being in the forest much, still felt it pressing in on me. The air was thickening as the sun climbed. Every one of the creature's bones passed through my hands, and I marvelled at the lightness of them, as if they were filled with hydrium and only wanted to be released from my grip to fly. Lighter than air. I smiled to myself.

'Amazing creature,' Kate kept muttering as she worked her way down the skeleton with her wax crayon. 'Amazing. I was reading about pterosaurs, do you know what they are?'

'No.'

'Winged lizards. Or at least that's what they thought. Lizards that died out eighty million years ago. But not everyone agrees. Maybe they weren't reptiles at all. Perhaps they were mammals, or that they at least developed into mammals . . .'

I knew nothing of the matter, so said nothing. It made me feel rather downcast, all this knowledge locked away in books that I didn't know, and likely never would. I loved books, but they were expensive and heavy and reading them took time I rarely had. It seemed Kate had read practically everything.

'Imagine how many animals used to exist,' she was saying. 'All the ones that are extinct now. Not just the dinosaurs, but all the other animals that must have once flown and crawled and walked and hopped across the earth. Maybe this is one of them that's managed to live on in secret. Don't you love the idea of it?'

'I love how it never has to land,' I said.

'You would,' she said with a laugh, then looked at me quite seriously. 'Born in the air, just like you. I'd never thought of that.'

I hadn't either.

'You two have a lot in common.'

'I'm not quite as bony,' I said.

Kate contentedly went back to her labelling. I went back to packing bones in her undergarments.

'When I write my scholarly articles,' Kate was saying now, 'I'll mention that you and I discovered the bones together, and that you were instrumental in their preservation.'

'Thank you, that's very kind of you.'

'Fair's fair,' she said, 'and if you ever decide to go to university, it'll stand you in good stead.'

'I've never had any desire to go to university.'

'No? Well, what do you wish for then?'

'I want to fly airships.'

'I suppose you're already well on your way.'

'Not really,' I said, and I told her. I probably shouldn't

have, but I told her how I'd been expecting to be made assistant sailmaker at the end of the voyage, and how Bruce Lunardi had taken my position because of his rotten father. So I was still stuck as cabin boy.

'That's really terribly unfair!' she said indignantly. 'I like that Lunardi fellow even less now.'

I couldn't help smiling. I couldn't have asked for a more satisfying reaction.

'I shall write a letter!' Kate said, still fuming.

'No, please don't,' I said.

'I hate it when things are unfair,' she muttered. 'You must go to the Airship Academy too, when you're older.'

'It's not quite as easy as that,' I said.

'Why isn't it?'

'It costs money, and I haven't much of that. None, in fact.'

'Surely there are scholarships for promising students.'

I nodded, saying nothing.

'You must get a scholarship,' said Kate, solving all my problems for me. 'And after your training you can proceed to sailmaker, and then on to officer and then captain. It would be such a terrible shame if someone of your obvious ability didn't succeed.'

I didn't feel like talking about it any more. Even if I won a scholarship, the Academy training was at least two years – two years during which I would be making no money to send back to my mother and sisters. They relied on me. Even if the Academy offered me a place,

I'd not be able to take it. But somehow I couldn't tell Kate this. I felt ashamed. Around her and all her wealth, the very idea of being poor seemed ridiculous. Impossible. She meant well, but I doubted she had any notion of what the world was like outside her moneyed bubble.

I looked up at the sky, noted the sun's angle, and sighed.

'We would've been approaching Sydney Harbour by now,' I said.

She turned to me. 'What happens when we don't arrive?'

It seemed to be the first time she'd given it any thought. I'd been dreading it, forcing it from my mind. Up till now, my mother and Isabel and Sylvia hadn't known anything was wrong. They hadn't worried. That would all change, if not today, then soon. I wondered if my mother could bear it, after what happened to my father.

'We'll be reported missing. Everyone will assume we've crashed into the ocean and drowned.'

'Gosh,' she said.

'Your parents will be worried sick.'

She went back to the skeleton. 'Well, they'll put on a good show anyway.'

I stared at the back of her head, not quite sure I understood.

'They'll call all the important people they know,' Kate went on, 'and demand updates and answers, and an extensive search.'

'Well, that's something,' I said.

'Mmmmm.'

'Do you have any brothers or sisters you're fonder of?' I asked. 'Or did you eat them all?'

'I think one child was all my parents could endure.'

'Well, you are quite wilful,' I said.

Her head whirled round, and she fixed me with those eyes of hers. Then her face softened. 'Yes, I suppose I am. I rather like the sound of it, though. Doesn't it sound intriguing and exciting? The wilful Kate de Vries!'

'I'm starting to feel rather sorry for your parents,' I said.

'You needn't,' she said. 'They don't have to deal with my wilfulness much. There's Miss Simpkins, and before her there were all sorts of nannies. None of them stayed on very long, now that I think of it. My mother is wildly busy fluttering about in high society, and my father manages things.'

'What exactly does he manage?'

'Other people's money, mostly. It seems to take a great deal of his time and energy.'

'Ah.'

'Oh, there's nothing wrong with them,' she said. 'They're perfectly normal, I suppose. Crushingly normal. They wouldn't let me go with Grandpa on his balloon trip.'

'Was your grandfather actually willing to take you?' I asked, startled.

'Well, no, he wasn't. But even if he was, my parents

wouldn't have allowed it. They certainly don't want me to study at university. All they want me to do is dress and behave appropriately and not embarrass them. My interests seem to embarrass them. And my talking. I'm always being told I'm saying the wrong thing, or at the wrong time, or too boldly. "Kate, you are too bold," my mother always says. She hates being embarrassed. She'd rather have the Black Death than be embarrassed. Though I suppose having the Black Death would be rather embarrassing in high society. The coughing and drooling and so on.'

'I'm wondering if maybe your parents paid the pirates to sink our ship.'

To her credit, she laughed.

'I'm sorry. I talk too much, everyone says so. What about your parents? They must miss you, being away so much.'

'Well, I suppose my mother's used to it. My father worked aboard airships too. He died three years ago.'

'I'm very sorry to hear that,' she said, looking stricken. 'Your poor mother. She's going to be frantic when she hears about the *Aurora*.'

'I know,' I said, feeling sick. 'She's a worrier. She never wanted me to take the position.'

'Weren't you awfully young?'

'Twelve's not so young to start as cabin boy. It was a good job. We needed the money, too.'

'So you started right after your father died?'

I nodded. 'The *Aurora* was my father's ship too. I think Captain Walken must have felt sorry for us – but I'm not sure Mom ever forgave him for offering to take me on.'

'It's what you wanted though, wasn't it?'

'Yes.' I'd never been able to tell my mother how comforting it had been to work aboard Dad's old ship. Everyone knew about my father, and they were all very kind to me, especially Captain Walken. Baz took me under his wing right away – the older brother I'd never had. I felt like I'd discovered another family aloft. And my father always felt nearby too, visiting me often in my dreams. I kept this all to myself, though, for I couldn't bear being disloyal to Mom and Isabel and Sylvia.

'Do you get home much?'

'We get shore leave regularly. I've got two sisters, almost as terrifying as you. I should go home more,' I said guiltily. 'It's hard now, with Dad gone.'

'He was the storyteller.'

I nodded, surprised she remembered.

'Took you everywhere in your head. Like my grandpa,' she said. 'Oh, look, I meant to show you this.'

She shifted past me, and climbed down to the ground. From a side pocket on her camera case she slid out an old photograph. Back in the tree, she showed it to me. It was a class photograph of schoolboys on the front steps. They all wore uniforms, shirts and blazers and shorts.

'Can you tell which one he is?' Kate asked.

'Your grandfather?'

'You met him.'

'He was a bit older by then!'

'Go on, look. It's so obvious!'

I conjured up the image of the old man in the hospital bed, tried to take him back to his childhood.

'I don't know,' I admitted.

'Honestly.' She pointed to a boy. 'He looks just like me.'

'He does?'

'You can't see that?'

'Ah, yes, long auburn hair, pleated skirt . . .'

'Boys are so hopeless at this. Isn't he adorable, though? Look at his ears, how they stick out. And did you notice he's the most rumpled-looking? All the other boys look fairly trim, but his uniform's all crumpled like he just rolled down a hill.'

'Already off having adventures,' I said.

She looked down at the picture. 'Yes,' she said sadly.

'He has your eyes, you're right,' I told her.

She looked up at me, beaming.

'This is going to prove him right,' she said, nodding at the skeleton. 'No one will think he was crazy after this, not even my mother.' She looked at her wristwatch. 'We're making good time. It's just past ten o'clock.'

'We should start back in half an hour. I need to be on duty at noon.'

We carried on with our work, dismantling the

skeleton bone by bone. I have to say, I felt odd doing it, like we were stealing. A carpet-bag seemed no fit place for the bones of this creature. The last vertebrae from its tail went in. I clasped the bag, lifted it. The bag scarcely felt heavier than it had when I'd carried it empty. I looked at the naked branch. We were done.

'I do hope we can manage to reassemble it,' Kate said.

It made me smile the way she said 'we' for I would not be around for that, and was about to remind her of this when a terrible throttled shriek pierced the forest, alarmingly close.

The birds stopped singing, the bugs thrumming. Even the wind bottled its breath. Everyone and everything in the forest was listening. Kate and I looked at one another.

I heard the soft rustle of something pattering through leaves. It was in the tree next to us. I caught sight of it almost right away because it was so brightly coloured: a parrot's wing, not attached to a parrot, fluttering down through the branches. It disappeared into the ferns on the forest floor, and I could just see a flash of its colour through the greenery.

I stared at it for a moment, my mind's pistons firing at half speed.

Something had just eaten that parrot.

Something had swallowed it whole and spat out the wings.

There was the wing in the grass.

Sound returned to my ears. My gaze slowly lifted, climbing the tree beside us. High up, something moved fast. Like a slender wisp of fog it seeped through the branches and disappeared behind the veil of vines and leaves. My heart clattered.

'I see it,' Kate whispered.

It jumped.

It was so quick it was hard to focus on it. It was long and lean and had sleek cloud-coloured fur and as it soared through the air between trees, its wings flared open for just a second and suddenly it was huge, a completely different creature. And just as quickly the wings pulled in and it was mist again and vanished amongst the branches.

I could hear the rasp of my own breathing. When I spoke it sounded like someone had a good grip round my windpipe.

'It's in our tree.'

We had our heads tilted back, and hands shielding our eyes, trying to spot it, but the sun was too bright. I had to keep blinking and looking off to one side. All I caught were vanishing wispy bits of the creature through all the greenery. My whole body was filled with liquid lead.

High up, I saw a fringe of cloudy white fur against the thick dark trunk and realized it was clinging to the far side, almost completely hidden. Then it showed itself. Sinewy as a snake, it came slyly creeping around, its whole body flattened upside down against the trunk.

I felt Kate's hot hand close around my arm.

It was a pale panther. It was a bat. It was a bird of prey. It was sleek, almost scrawny. It had jutting shoulders and a humped back, but then I realized these were its massive wings, bundled tight. From head to tail it was no more than a metre and a half. Its face was a cat face, only longer, with a lower forehead, the nostrils more pronounced and dark against the pale fur. It was a panther's face but altogether more streamlined, designed to cut through wind. Its large eyes danced with intelligence and sunlight. It was exquisite. It was terrifying.

'I need my camera,' Kate whispered. Her face was pale and she was trembling.

'Stay still,' I hissed.

But Kate started slowly to stand. I grabbed her arm to hold her back, but she pulled away. I saw the creature tense above us, and did not know whether it was merely startled, or about to leap at us. The camera still hung by its strap from an overhead branch. Kate took it in her hands, and tilted it upwards. She pressed the plunger and the camera gave a blinding flash.

The creature screeched and pounced on to a higher branch, sprang once more to its tip, then soared out of the tree.

'Come on!' Kate said, scrambling down. I jumped after her. I didn't know how wise it was to follow this creature, but Kate was already off. For a moment it seemed we'd lost it, and I couldn't help feeling a bit of relief, but then Kate jabbed up her finger and I caught the quick cloudy flash of it as it pounced into another tree.

It definitely had its own course set, for it was travelling in a straight line now, pouncing, and barely touching down before springing again. The branches did not shudder as they took its weight. Sometimes the creature, when crossing between trees, opened its magnificent wings a little, white fur bright in the sun.

And I understood now how we could've missed them, all of us sky sailors over the years. Against the green of the trees they were easy enough to spot, but against a cloudy sky they blended in almost completely. Even in a blue sky your mind would've told you it was just a little wisp of cloud; the same with water: just a bit of foam on a wave's crest. Maybe I'd even seen them before, and simply never realized it.

We ran after it, heads tilted, trying to track it as it soared through the forest. But it was faster than us, and I knew that it would soon leave us far behind.

The trees thinned and then disappeared abruptly and we saw the creature launch itself into the air, wings spread, and drop out of sight. I gasped. We moved as close as we dared to the edge of the high bluff. Below us we could see it as it pounced down the cliff, wings flaring from scraggly treetop to treetop as it jumped. As the ground levelled out, it continued to leap across the forest canopy.

'It doesn't know,' Kate said. 'It doesn't know how to fly.'

'Its left wing,' I said. 'Look.'

Every time it flared its wings, the right shot out

to its full length; but the left never quite made it. Perhaps it had been injured, or maybe its left wing was unnaturally stunted, making it incapable of flight. Maybe it had just never learned. Any creature capable of flight would not be leaping from tree to tree; it would be soaring high above them. We watched as the silvery creature got farther and farther away, and then dropped out of sight altogether into the distant foliage.

'I bet that's where it lives,' Kate said. 'I bet that's its nest! Can we get down there?'

'We've got to get back.'

'You know what it is,' she said.

'Yes. I know.'

'It's the one Grandpa saw,' she said. 'It's the one that fell.'

We couldn't stop talking, our words piling up one atop another. Talking about the creature, about what we should do next. Kate wanted to keep going, to see if we could find its nest, but the terrain was too steep here, and we were out of time. We had to start back. I was going to be late as it was. As we walked, our words spilled out to fill the humid air.

'He fell and survived somehow,' she said.

'It's incredible. That the fall didn't kill him. That he could slow himself down enough to land.'

'But he never learned to fly.'

'I think one of his wings might be deformed,' I said.

'But would that stop him from flying?'

'Or maybe after the fall he just never had the confidence,' I said.

'They never came looking for him.'

'They just left him. The mother abandoned her own baby.'

'Nothing she could have done,' Kate said. 'She couldn't carry him.'

'They can lift big fish out of the water, your grandfather said as much.'

'Maybe they just assumed he'd be dead, or that he was so unfit what was the point of rescuing him, he couldn't survive if he couldn't fly.'

'Seems a bit harsh,' I said. 'Maybe it just needed some extra time. To heal or to learn. Then it would've been a fine flier.'

'They're animals,' she said. 'They don't think like us. It's all survival of the fittest with them.'

'Even animals feel love for their offspring,' I objected.

'True,' she said. 'I've seen chimps much friendlier than my parents.'

We laughed and then walked on in silence for a bit, our minds churning.

Kate spoke slowly, her brow furrowed, thinking things through. 'He fell down and landed in a tree or somewhere soft. He had no mother to nurse him. Somehow he stayed alive eating birds and bugs and all sorts of little things here. Berries, fruit. It's an incredible tale of survival.'

'There was nothing here to hunt him,' I pointed out, wanting to be clever and methodical too. 'There was luck thrown into it as well.'

'Yes,' Kate agreed. 'But he's adapted to his environment so well – the way he leaps from tree to tree. Did you see his legs, the way they pushed off from the branches? Very strong. They'd have no need to be that strong in the air. He's gotten stronger in different ways here, so he can survive.'

'He doesn't fit in though. His fur, it's the wrong colour for here. He stands out. He'd be easy to catch if there were predators.' I sighed. 'He should be flying, not leapfrogging around the forest. He was built to fly.'

'But he wasn't, not this one. Maybe he has a deformity, like you said, maybe his wings don't really work. This is all he's got.'

I felt sorry for him, landlocked. At least he had never known flight. He had nothing to miss, nothing to yearn for. I wondered if he remembered the terrifying plunge that started his life.

We reached the tree and Kate repacked her camera in its case. I picked up the carpet-bag filled with bones.

Kate stopped and looked back. 'What if I never see him again?' she said miserably. 'We'll probably be leaving today or tomorrow. The photograph I took won't come out. I wasn't even aiming properly. And it moved so quickly. At best it will just be a blur. I need to be closer.'

'You've got the bones,' I reminded her. 'And the pictures of the skeleton.'

She snorted.

'But you said they'd be enough!' I said. 'You said the bones would be conclusive!'

'Oh, the bones are fine,' she said dismissively, 'but there's a living one, right here! If I could get some shots of him up close . . .' She trailed off, distracted. 'Isn't it funny how we both started calling it him?'

'I didn't even think about it.'

'We have no way of knowing whether it's a he or a she. But of course we just call it him. Just another big important male of the species.'

She looked at me angrily, as if this were all my fault, somehow.

'Let's call it she then,' I suggested.

Her frown disappeared. 'All right. Good. She.'

'Did she look the way you imagined?' I asked.

'No. Yes. I'm not sure. She was beautiful, wasn't she?'

'She was.'

'Beautiful creatures, just like Grandpa said. Oh, Matt, I want to see her again.'

'I do too.'

She looked at me and smiled.

'But we've got to leave,' I said. 'And maybe it's just as well. It might be dangerous, trying to get close to her.'

'You think she'd attack?' The thought seemed completely new to her. 'They didn't attack Grandpa.'

'That's true. Still, she's a wild animal.'

'She seemed gentle enough to me.'

'Just a nice big pussy cat, was she? You need to take a look at the teeth in here,' I said, holding up the carpet-bag.

'Well, I don't think she'd attack humans.'

'You've come face to face with lots of wild animals, then, have you?'

She laughed. 'Not really, not . . .'

'Taking close-ups of pumas, or maybe a Komodo dragon from Indonesia, just for fun?'

'What should we call her?' she said.

'The creature?' I laughed. She was already imagining her name in science books. 'I don't know.'

'She should have a name. And since we've discovered her, we need to give it to her.'

'You think of something,' I told her, 'something with lots of Latin in it.' But in my head I was thinking: Cloud cat. I was afraid to say it aloud though, in case she thought it was too simple, too unscientific.

I paused and blinked. I felt the weather change in my skin and looked up with a start. Up through the forest canopy I could see a big swath of sky, and it was no longer blue. When had this happened? It was like nothing I'd ever seen, the weather changing so fast. Twenty minutes ago pure blue and now it was stacked high with dark-bellied clouds that looked like the vaults of hell. I hadn't even noticed until now. A fine lookout I was. Weather watcher. Ship's eyes.

'We've got to hurry,' I said. 'Come on!'

We started running. I could already hear the wind coming, and all I could think was:

My ship.

And then the weather was upon us.

12

SHIPWRECKED

The wind and the rain hit at the same moment, bending trees, blasting us along, trying to knock our feet from under us.

I summoned the *Aurora* before my mind's eye, tried to count her mooring lines. I felt them strain against their anchor spikes deep in the sand, felt them chafe hotly around the palm trunks. All those taut lines were moaning and wailing like an infernal stringed orchestra. I could hear the first crack, and then the next, as the lines started to break and the ship slewed. I could think of nothing else as we lurched through the forest.

Kate stumbled and I took her hand, slippery as an eel. Bent double we staggered on, weighed down by the camera case and carpet-bag, stumbling whichever way the wind let us. A snapped tree suddenly fell not three metres before us, and its impact bounced us off our feet. I hadn't even heard it falling above the smashing rain and banshee wail of the wind. I could barely see through the slits of my eyes.

It got worse. Branches spewed water like gargoyles' jaws. Waterfalls crashed down tree trunks. The wind shook heaven and earth. I hardly knew what we were doing or where we were going. We moved as best we could, heavy with rain, our clothing clinging to us, making us clumsy and slow. Branches sailed through the air. We would come to harm soon.

Through the grey veil of solid rain I saw a shadow and moved towards it. There was a dense tangle of undergrowth and a dark opening below a hump of earth and rock. I dragged Kate towards it and pushed her through the flowering vines which covered the entrance. It was a small cave, just big enough for us to sit side by side. How far back it went I didn't know, for it was very dark, and I had no yearning to poke about. It was more or less dry inside, and gave us quite a lot of shelter from the wind and lashing rain. Kate fussed over her camera case and the carpet-bag full of bones, checking to make sure the contents weren't drenched, pushing them behind us so they wouldn't get any wetter. I stared back over my shoulder, letting my eyes adjust to the darkness of the cave. I could see a little further in now, enough to realize it went back quite a way.

We sat together, saying nothing for a while, just wiping water from our faces, and plucking at our sodden clothes, and staring in awe at the fury of the storm.

'The ship'll be hurt.' I could barely hear my own voice above the wind and rain.

'It'll be all right.'

I shook my head. There was no doubt in my mind. If they had managed to get the *Aurora*'s head into the wind in time, the damage might be small; if the wind broadsided her, she'd act like a giant sail, and pull herself off her moorings. And if she got torn, we would lose the little hydrium we had left. Without hydrium, the *Aurora* was just a crumpled hull.

The wind had a voice and it was howling and cursing and whenever it died down for a moment I would pray that this was finished, that it had spent itself, but then the rain would crash down with renewed hatred, and the wind would shriek again as if all the heavens were its bellows, aimed at our island.

I felt in my pocket for my compass. It was a point of pride to me that I rarely needed to consult it. After so long aloft, I always knew which way we were headed. Sometimes, when I felt the ship shift in the night, I would test myself by plotting our new heading, then checking the compass. Mostly I was right on the nose. But I needed it now. Before we'd taken shelter we'd been so swirled about by the wind I'd lost all sense of direction.

I looked at it now, the needle shimmering with the rumble of earth and air. My mind's compass set itself, and I knew the way back to the lagoon and the ship. Kate was looking at the compass. I held it out to her and she took it in her palm.

'It always points north, doesn't it?'

She had to talk right into my ear to make herself heard.

'Yes.'

'Which way is the tree?' Her breath was warm against my face.

'South-south-west.'

'And the bluff,' she asked, 'where we last saw the creature?'

'Almost due south-west from here, I reckon.'

I wondered if she was trying to cheer me up, finally taking an interest in her whereabouts. We were side by side, our shoulders touching. Even in the midst of the storm the air was perfumed heat. I think some of it came from Kate's hair and clothes. The smell of mangoes was strong here too, and it made me crave the sweet fruit. I'd seen plenty of mango trees around, and I was both thirsty and hungry after the labours of the long morning.

I looked out, desperate to get going. I felt claustrophobic in the cave, beside Kate, in this suffocating forest. I wanted some space around me. I wanted to be on the beach again, to be near the ship, and know how she was. I covered my face with my hands, feeling ill.

'It'll be all right,' I heard Kate say.

I didn't answer. She knew nothing.

'You'll see, it'll all turn out fine.'

'No,' I moaned. 'No.' It was worse than being back at my mother's in Lionsgate City, the sleepless bedroom wrapping itself around me and crushing me.

'Tell me why you're so frightened,' Kate said, a long way away.

'I need the ship,' I said. 'If it's wrecked, nothing's good any more. I can't stand still. I've got to keep flying.' I was babbling like a child, fighting tears, but I couldn't help myself. Knees drawn up, arms wrapped around, holding on tight, for I knew that if I let go I'd go running out into the typhoon like a madman, frantic to get away from myself.

'Why do you need to fly so much?' she asked.

'If I don't, it'll catch up with me.' The words just came out.

'What will?'

I took my hands from my face, panting. I stared out at the storm.

'Unhappiness.'

Kate looked at me, waiting.

'When my dad died, I was afraid I'd never ever be happy again. But I was. Once I started working on the *Aurora*, I loved it. It's the world I was born into. It's all my father's stories. I dream about him up there, and I never do on land. It feels like home aloft. But on the ground, it all catches up with me. So I've got to keep flying, do you see?'

'Everyone has to land sometimes,' Kate said.

'Not them.'

'The creatures?'

I nodded.

'We're different,' she said, a bit sadly. 'You can't fly for ever. Anyway, do you really think you can outrun unhappiness?'

'Maybe until it runs out.'

'Well, perhaps you're right,' she said. 'I miss my grandpa too. At home I was happiest when I was thinking about him and his trips, and what he saw. Planning my own adventures.'

'See, you like to keep moving, too. On the ground, at night, I can't sleep,' I told her, 'I get all—'

I stopped myself. I'd told her too much already. All this babbling and panic wasn't dignified. It wasn't at all manly. At least I hadn't bawled.

'We'll be all right,' she said. 'I just can't believe things could ever be too bad, not with you around.'

'But I'm not around,' I said miserably. 'Not where it counts anyway. The ship, that's where I should be. Not gallivanting around the forest, playing scientist and wrapping up bones in your knickers! I've never seen so much underwear!'

'Some of it belongs to Miss Simpkins, I'll have you know!' she retorted angrily.

We both looked at each other in surprise and started laughing.

'You took her underwear too?' I asked.

'I needed padding,' Kate giggled. 'What else was I to do?'

'Listen,' I said. 'It's a bit quieter.'

I peered out into the forest and could see farther than

before. The wind had settled to a constant moan, and the trees seemed to be shuddering less. We'd get drenched and blasted about still – and there might yet be more and worse to come at any moment – but I wondered if we should make a run for it anyway. We were already soaked to the skin.

There was a hissing sound behind us.

Was this new? Or was I just hearing it for the first time, now that the storm was a bit quieter? I jerked round and peered into the darkness of the cave.

Sssssssssssss.

There was something back there.

'Get out!' I shouted to her. I snatched the carpet-bag and camera case and we lurched out of the cave. The raindrops were as big as hailstones, but at least we weren't blown off our feet. When we were some distance from the cave I turned and looked back. I saw nothing emerge.

'It sounded like a snake,' Kate said.

'Just another friendly little snake on your snakeless island.' I felt all out of sorts, tired and embarrassed. It was hard to look her in the eyes, now that she'd seen me all laid low and whingey in the cave.

'The other one didn't hiss like that,' she pointed out.

I shrugged. 'Maybe it was some new kind of *flying* snake. Nothing would surprise me on this island any more.'

The smell of mangoes was still strong in the air, and I looked up into the trees, trying to spot some of the bright red and green fruit. I thought maybe I could shimmy up quickly and snatch a few. But I couldn't see any anywhere. It was just as well. We needed to get going. I needed to get back to the *Aurora*.

It made me gulp when I saw her, so deflated she looked like some emaciated animal, ribs sticking out piteously. She was slumped on the beach, scraping sand again, only worse than before. There was a great gash in her flank. Flaps of flayed skin hung off her. Her lower fin was terribly bashed up again. She looked sunk.

'Oh,' I whispered. 'Oh.' I stood there gaping stupidly.

The ship was listing slightly to starboard and the crew were all around her on the beach, pulling lines and trying to bring her upright. Mr Grantham and Mr Torbay glanced over at me, but they were too busy to stare long at a stupid cabin boy. Then I saw the captain, and his head turned and I knew he was looking at me. Me, standing there beside Kate, a camera case slung over one shoulder, a pink floral carpet-bag in my hand, like I'd just returned from a picnic. Before he turned away I caught the look on his face: not anger, but a weary disappointment.

Burning with shame, I swallowed and turned to Kate. 'Could you take these please,' I murmured, putting down the camera case and carpet-bag.

'Yes, of course.'

I wanted to run back into the forest, but I forced my steps towards the ship. At least she was here. She had not blown away; she had not been rent in two. I picked up my feet and tried to run, but my clothes were still soaking, tight against my legs, and I fell and was instantly coated with sand. I scrambled up and hurried on.

It was raining and still blowing a bit, and the passengers were all huddled beneath the palms for shelter, watching the crew. I looked away, not wanting to see Miss Simpkins. Things could not have gone worse. Our return was meant to be invisible. Early this morning, with the ship healed, and everyone on board again, I'd thought it would be simple for Kate and me to slip back inside and go our separate ways. A more conspicuous entrance than this I could not imagine.

Off the ship's port side I spotted Baz and took hold of his line with him.

'How bad is it?' I asked.

'Pretty damn bad.' There was no lift in his voice, no light in his eyes. 'We tried to hold her, but the wind was too strong. She broke her lines and her stern went sailing into the trees before we could tie her down again.'

I should have been here. I could have helped hold her.

'Have they patched her?'

Baz shook his head. 'No way anyone could climb up, she was whipping around too much. Passengers got tossed around pretty bad. We only cleared them out when the worst was over. Captain's worried about the frame now.'

Without enough gas to help support the ship, the alumiron frame, strong as it was, would start to crumple under the immense weight. The *Aurora* would crush herself.

I stared at the ship, and felt like a big storm system was flooding me, filling my guts and head to bursting. Shipwrecked. There was no more terrifying word to me. We were truly shipwrecked now, here on the island with its crushing heat and suffocating forest, and how would I ever get back up into the sky? I closed my eyes; I wasn't getting enough air.

'She's right again! Tie her off, gentlemen!'

The captain's shout brought me back to myself, and Baz and I set about making our line fast to a mooring spike.

'At least she's level,' I muttered. Somehow she didn't look quite as desperate now she wasn't leaning over.

'Hate to break it to you,' Baz said, 'but you're in a keg of trouble.'

'You don't say.' I had a feeling what was coming next.

'Before the typhoon hit, that scary chaperone was raising Cain with the captain.'

'I thought she was bedridden.'

'She mustered the strength to go screaming through the ship, asking where Miss de Vries was. Then it turned out you were missing as well. I suggested it was merely a coincidence, but no one was too impressed by that.'

'Thanks for trying.'

Baz was shaking his head. 'This is no time to be undone by a girl, Matt.'

Even in the tropical heat I could feel the flush that swept my face.

'I'm not undone by her,' I said.

'She's a fine-looking girl, no question, but you two have about as much future as a fish and a kangaroo.'

'Am I the fish or the kangaroo?'

'It doesn't matter. You know, you're a bit young to be getting this talk at all. You can't go carrying on like this.' He was trying to sound firm like a big brother, but he was also looking at me strangely, as though I'd done something amazing and he couldn't quite believe my daring. 'Plus, she's a passenger, first-class, and you're crew.'

'You've got it wrong,' I said. 'She's curious about the island; I've just been helping her.'

He laughed and looked away. 'Must be something pretty grand to take you away from your ship.'

They stung me, his words. I wanted to tell him, but I'd promised Kate I'd keep it secret. Why was I doing this? It was the cloud cat. It was Kate de Vries. It was both, all tangled up.

'It's not like you think,' I said. 'I wish you'd just believe me.'

He nodded, but still looked unconvinced. 'All right.'

I looked at the *Aurora* and everything else seemed suddenly, colossally, unimportant. All that had happened in the hours before – the bones, the cloud cat – faded like a bleached photograph.

'Oh Lord,' I said, feeling hopeless, 'look at her. Look at our ship.'

* * *

'The condition of our ship is doubtless no mystery to you,' Captain Walken said.

It was standing room only in the officers' mess, all the crew assembled for an emergency meeting. We were a dispirited-looking bunch, with our sodden uniforms and sand-crusted faces and hair. I slouched at the very back, feeling I had little right to be here.

'The ship's frame is still intact,' the captain said, 'and the chief sailmaker and I believe we have enough lifting gas left to support the structure and allow the passengers back on. We're solid. But that, sadly, is an end to the good news. We've lost too much hydrium, gentlemen. We can't fly.'

'Is there no possibility of lightening her some more, sir?' asked Mr Chen.

'We could remove every crate of cargo and stick of furniture, and every passenger for that matter, and we'd still not have enough lifting power to hop across the lagoon. In our current state it would take the hand of Zeus to lift us. So now we must investigate our options.' He turned to the second wireless officer. 'Mr Chaudhuri, what is the state of our radio equipment?'

'Well, sir, the pirates were quite thorough. The transmitter was pretty much destroyed.'

'What chances of repairing?'

'I've been working on it, sir. But even with a fully functioning transmitter, I don't think we'd be able to send a signal very far from down here.'

'Continue work on it. A radio can only be an asset to us. We did send out a distress signal when we were about to be boarded by the pirates, but we heard no reply. So I fear we were out of range of any other vessel.'

'We'll be reported missing by now, sir,' said the first officer.

'They'll not have much luck finding us along our route,' said the captain. 'The pirates were careful to drive us far off course. Grantham?'

'It was hard to keep track, sir,' the navigation officer replied. 'They led us on such a firefly run, but I calculate over 320 kilometres off our flight path. We're in an obscure little corner of the Pacificus here. Chances of seeing any other air traffic are close to nil. And we'll have no joy waiting for a rescue, I'm afraid. There's too much ocean. They'll think we crashed and sank without a trace.'

This was not a cheering bit of news, and I could see the shoulders of some of the crew visibly sag.

'Well then,' said the captain, 'I believe this may be a good time to organize a party to explore the island.'

'There may be inhabitants, Captain,' said Mr Rideau.

'Precisely what I am hoping,' said the captain.

'They may be a savage lot, sir, with no love of visitors.'

'We shall have to be exceptionally charming, then,' said the captain. 'It may be that they have a means of transport that we can use, perhaps not to carry all of us, but at least to carry a message for help. Who knows, perhaps they even have a wireless. We must make it our business to find out.'

I could see the captain's eyes trawling the crowd. I looked away.

'Mr Cruse, you've seen something of this island, I believe.'

'I have, sir.'

I could hear a few quiet snickers.

'Have you seen any signs of habitation?'

'No trace of other human beings, sir, not on the eastern slopes of the island, and up to the central plateau. But the island is large, and stretches many kilometres to the west.'

'There may be a settlement on the windward side of the island, then,' said the captain. 'Mr Cruse, you'll be with the exploratory team we assemble.'

'Yes, sir.'

I felt my heart lift a bit. I could still be useful, and the captain did not mean to confine me to the ship from now on – a fate I had fully resigned myself to. But perhaps I was fooling myself, in thinking the captain wasn't displeased with me. We were truly shipwrecked now, and our situation was dire, and if he had need of me, he would use me. It did not mean he trusted me.

'There are the life rafts,' Mr Levy suggested. 'Some of us could go for help.'

Mr Grantham was shaking his head. 'No. It's over

1000 kilometres to the nearest port, and you'd be working against the trade winds.'

'Too risky, I think,' said the captain.

'Sir?'

I recognized Bruce Lunardi's voice amongst the crowd.

'Mr Lunardi?'

'We studied a similar case at the Academy, sir,' he said.

A few of the crew made little impressed titters at this, and the captain's eyes flashed angrily.

'Gentlemen, there is no one in this room who is too wise to learn. Mr Lunardi, please continue.'

I heard the tremor in Lunardi's voice, and felt sorry for him. 'Well, sir, in this case the ship was grounded from loss of hydrium. But the crew managed to stitch together a crude balloon from her gas cells, and vent the remaining hydrium into her. It was enough to carry a gondola and three or four crew.'

'I remember this incident,' said Captain Walken. 'Only one made it back to shore.'

'Yes, sir. But I was wondering if there might be some way we could balloon back into the shipping lanes, wait there for a passing vessel, and signal for help.'

'Very good, Mr Lunardi, it is an intriguing idea. Again, riskier than I would like. I have little confidence in air balloons.' I saw the captain sigh, and for the first time, there were obvious traces of sadness on his face. 'And your plan means cutting open our hull to extract the gas cells. I am loath to cannibalize the *Aurora*. But if she truly is of no use to us, perhaps your idea is the best we have so far. I thank you for it. Let me consider it.'

The idea of the ship being sawed up like a cadaver made me feel faint. My home, left in ruins, never to fly again. But even I could see it might be our only chance. I wished I had some brilliant idea to win the captain's praise – and save the *Aurora* from such an undignified end. But I had nothing to offer.

'If I might interject, sir, there may be another use for such a balloon,' said Mr Bayard, the junior wireless officer.

'Let's hear it,' said the captain.

'If Mr Chaudhuri and I are able to salvage a transmitter, we might be able to send a distress signal. If we could rig an antenna to the balloon, and float it high above the island, our range could be considerable.'

'Good,' said the captain. 'It looks as if we all entered the wrong profession, gentlemen. We were all destined to become balloonists. Very well, we will turn our hands to it. Now then, immediate concerns. I know that we've located an ample stream, not far from the ship, but as for food, how are our supplies, Mr Vlad?'

'We will not starve!' cried Vlad happily, and some of us laughed gratefully at his good cheer. 'The lagoon alone holds enough food for all.'

'Not all the passengers like fish,' Mr Lisbon pointed out.

'I am very sorry, but this I did not understand,' Vlad said to the chief steward.

'I merely said that not all of our passengers enjoy fish.'

'Fish, yes, fish is what I am conversing about.'

'Not everyone likes it!' shouted Mr Lisbon.

'I will teach them to love it!' Vlad said fiercely. 'I will make many dishes and soups and delectable things – that is a word, yes? Delectable? – and make us all fit and harmonious. Some of our passengers, yes, could lose a little weight, if you know what I mean, Captain.'

'Thank you, Mr Vlad, I'm sure they'll be very grateful.'

'Our supply of fresh meat is almost out,' Mr Lisbon remarked.

Vlad glared at him. 'Meat! Yes, yes, yes, meat is fine, it is delicious, I agree, but what is meat when we have fresh coconut and breadfruit and mango and bananas! Better fruits they did not have on Mount Olympus!'

'They'll be without bread within two days,' the chief steward told the captain. 'We'll have no more flour or yeast by then. That will have them howling.'

No fresh croissants, I thought with a smile.

'This is a blessing,' Vlad shouted, 'can you not see this? This is opportunity for a culinary rebirth!'

'We look forward to it, Mr Vlad,' said the captain, eager to stem an all-out battle between his chef and steward. 'I am encouraged to know that we will not go hungry with you in charge.'

Vlad stalked off, shooting a serrated look at Mr Lisbon,

and muttering about breadfruit and jackfish and crabs and how unappreciated he was. He'd go off and lay out all his sharp knives and feel better.

I wished I could feel better.

We were shipwrecked and discussing how best to get rescued, how best to survive. And it seemed our only course of action was to skin and gut our beloved ship and fashion a balloon.

I was on water duty, hefting buckets back to the ship from the stream. The winds had calmed since the typhoon, but were still stiff enough to make you curse as you trudged against them, a heavy sloshing bucket of water wobbling in each fist. I wondered if this was some sort of punishment, or at least some way of keeping me solitary and busy and out of trouble. The captain had said nothing to me after the meeting; it was the chief steward who had glanced at me and said simply, 'Mr Cruse, we're getting low on water. See to it, please.'

I wondered how Kate was getting on in the Topkapi stateroom. Would Miss Simpkins have her locked in the bedroom? Would she dare? Kate would tell her nothing. But if the chaperone discovered what was in Kate's carpet-bag, what could Kate possibly say? 'My goodness, how did those get there? Marjorie, do you have any idea what these are?' Even if Miss Simpkins didn't see the bones, sooner or later she would notice some of her undergarments missing. 'Kate, have you seen my beige petticoat? I can't find it anywhere.' 'How odd,' Kate would say, trying not to smile. 'How very unusual.'

It made me smile, thinking of it, though mostly all I felt was angry with her. But I'd gone willingly enough. Now was no time to be undone by a girl. Maybe Baz was right. I'd let myself become foolish. Had I just been another one of her servants, temporarily useful to her?

A bucket slammed against my shin and I swore. Surely there was a better way to get the water to the ship than this. Then I remembered the crates we'd unloaded, the heavy ones marked rubber hosing. I wondered if the captain would agree to cracking them open and running a pipeline between stream and ship. I'd mention it to him when I had a chance; maybe it would help redeem me in his eyes.

It was clearing overhead, sunlight slanting through from the west, and making the trees and silver airship glow against the dark clouds. Suddenly there was a rainbow, the biggest and most complete I'd ever seen, looking like it had been constructed by the bridge-builders of Eden. It had all the colours a rainbow is supposed to have, but never does. I stopped to stare at it, so stupendous a thing it was, arching over the island. It made things seem not so bad.

Then my smile faded. Two sailmakers were repelling down the port side of the *Aurora*. I knew what they meant to do. I did not want to see this. The very thought of it sent a razor's shiver across my belly, as though it was me about to be slit with a knife.

Captain Walken had emerged from the control car with Mr Rideau, and was standing back to supervise the work.

I was quite close to the ship now, and I realized I'd stopped walking, was just standing there, staring. I tried to look away but couldn't. They'd chosen a section where the skin was already limp against a punctured gas cell. I saw the sailmakers take out their knives, their blades flashing. In went the tips. I felt myself flinch. No. No. I couldn't bear it. I was close enough to hear the tearing fabric, and the hiss of the last escaping hydrium. The wind carried the distinctive scent to my nostrils.

And I suddenly remembered the cave: the hiss of the snake, the smell of mangoes.

'Stop!' I shouted up at them. 'Don't!'

The sailmakers paused and looked down at me. The captain and first officer turned.

'What's the matter, Cruse!' Mr Rideau said irritably.

'You don't need to!' I cried out.

'What?'

'There's hydrium!'

'What're you on about, boy, we're busy!'

'Don't cut the ship! There's hydrium here on the island!'

'Sir, the boy's fast becoming a nuisance,' said Rideau.

'Let him speak,' the captain said. 'Why didn't you mention this earlier, Mr Cruse?'

'I thought it was just mangoes at first, sir, but when I

looked there were no trees anywhere around. And it wasn't mangoes – hydrium smells a bit sweeter. Getting a whiff of it just now made me realize.'

'Where was this?'

'We took shelter in a cave, sir, during the typhoon. I could smell it then, and later when the storm was shushing down I heard a hiss. I thought it was a snake and we hightailed it out, but it wasn't a snake at all. It was hydrium, venting from the cave!'

The captain said nothing. The two sailmakers were poised overhead against the ship's hull, looking down and listening. Mr Rideau glared at me.

'Be sure of this, boy, for it would be a terrible thing to raise all our hopes.'

'Truly, I'm almost positive,' I said, though felt less sure now under Rideau's steely gaze. 'The cave went way back, and deep. It must've been coming from a vent.'

'This is remarkable news you bring, Mr Cruse,' said the captain.

'I can take you there, sir.'

'I think that would be a good idea.'

'Even if it's there, what use is it to us?' said Rideau to the captain. 'It might be a crude variety, unrefined. And in any event we've no way of transporting it through the forest to the ship.'

'But we do!' I said. 'We've got miles of rubber hosing! I helped shift it from the cargo hold yesterday. We could run a line from the cave to the ship. With one of the

251

ship's pumps to draw the gas along, we could easily refill the cells once they're patched!'

'Should we proceed with our work, Captain?' the sailmakers called down.

'Absolutely not,' said the captain. 'Hold off until we've visited this cave and seen if Mr Cruse's hunch is correct.' The captain laughed, and clapped me on the shoulder. 'I have a lucky feeling it is, knowing you, Mr Cruse. Was there ever a more remarkable cabin boy?'

13

HYDRIUM

The chief sailmaker, Mr Levy, had only to take a sniff at the cave's mouth and a huge smile soared across his face. 'Mr Cruse,' he said, 'this is more welcome to me than striking gold.'

I smiled too, as much in relief as anything else. A terrible thing it would have been if I'd been wrong, and all I'd led them to was a particularly smelly mango tree and a nest of vipers.

We crawled into the cave on our hands and knees, the sailmaker and I, our electric torches splashing light over the walls, looking for the source. The hiss was loud and insistent, and I was amazed I had not heard it sooner, in spite of the wind's wailing. As we went deeper I started to feel a little queasy with the smell. The hydrium was forcing out all the air. There wasn't enough oxygen to breathe. The roof of the cave slanted down into a dead end.

'There she is,' said Mr Levy, fixing his circle of torchlight on the back wall. I could see a narrow gash in the stone. I was closer, and I scrambled towards it. I put my hand over the crack, and felt the gush of escaping hydrium, rushing up from beneath the ocean floor.

'We can fit a collar to the stone,' Mr Levy said, 'and lock the rubber hosing to it.'

From his belt he took a small sack made of goldbeater's skin, the same material the gas cells were made of. He held the opening of the sack against the crack in the stone. The sack filled quickly, and Mr Levy gathered the bottom in his fist. We awkwardly backed out of the cave. Captain Walken waited with Mr Rideau. I took deep breaths, glad to be out in the open.

'It's the finest hydrium I've ever smelled, sir,' Mr Levy announced. The sack of goldbeater's skin ballooned from his hand, straining skywards. He let it go, and it shot up into the trees like a rocket. The sack flared open at the bottom, releasing its hydrium to the sky, and then fell back down into the sailmaker's hand.

'This stuff's purer than what comes from the refineries in Lionsgate City.'

'Well done, Mr Cruse,' the captain said. 'Well done once again.'

'Three kilometres back to the ship is my guess,' said Mr Rideau, managing to look put out despite the good news. 'We'll need all that hosing.'

'We're losing the day now,' said Captain Walken. 'We'll work through the night, patching, and by first light, we should be ready to lay the pipeline.' I was nodding and smiling.

They wouldn't have to butcher the ship.

She would fly again.

The news spread through the ship faster than hydrium through air. I walked into the crew's mess to grab a quick dinner before I went on duty, and suddenly everyone there was on his feet.

'Here's to Mr Cruse!' one of the mechanics said.

Dozens of glasses lifted high into the air.

'To Mr Cruse, the finest ship's boy you could have!'

'Lighter than air, that's our Mr Cruse.'

I didn't know what to say, so I just smiled and looked down at the table and wished they would put down their glasses and go back to their meals.

Chef Vlad came in from his kitchen with a steaming plate of smoked Muscovy duck, scalloped potatoes and asparagus, and put it before me.

'Your favourite, Mr Cruse.'

'How did you know?'

He looked insulted. 'You do not think I watch people as they eat my food? I am a chef! I could tell you the favourite foods of everyone in this room!'

'Thank you, Mr Vlad,' I said. 'Thank you very much.'

'It is my understanding that you've saved the ship,' said the chef. 'Really, I should be angry. I could have dwelt here, I could have cooked fish for these people. It would have been a marvellous thing!'

'We can always leave you behind, Mr Vlad!' one of the crew called out.

'And who would cook for you, imbecile!' Mr Vlad looked at me and smiled. 'You're a good boy, Mr Cruse. You understand food, not like some of the lunkheads in here!'

I set to my dinner, and I can't remember a time when I'd enjoyed my meal more. It was like I'd never tasted these things before. The rich savoury flavours filled my mouth, and a tremendous sense of well-being spread through me as my stomach filled. I'd been missing meals, with all my time in the forest. I paused and took a deep breath. My head was aswirl. The crippled cloud cat leaping through the trees, the storm hurtling branches through the air, the ruined ship.

I'd been holding myself so tightly the past few days, and now I could feel a little tremor going through me, and I suddenly felt like I was going to bawl if I wasn't careful. I was unfit, really. This island had completely undone me.

But we had hydrium now, and with hydrium we could fly away.

Everything was going to be all right again.

I fell.

I was a slick wet bundle of bone and hair and I was in the sky, falling. I knew I should fly; knew I was meant to. But my wings would scarcely open. I tried to flap, but I was so weak, I could barely push against the tower of air thrusting past me. Why couldn't I do this? Every bit of my body was born to do this, so why couldn't I?

My wings would not move.

But the ground flew up towards me.

I woke myself from my mango-scented nightmare, and it was still dark. With dismay I saw that it was not far past two o'clock. I tried to lure sleep to me, but she just slowly shook her raven tresses and would not come back. Despite all the good news, my weather eye could still glimpse a big black cloud of panic on my brain's horizon. If I stayed in bed, eyes closed, fretting, I would be engulfed.

Quietly, so as not to wake Baz, I swung myself off the bunk and dressed. Closing the door behind me, I slipped out on to the keel catwalk. One of the things I loved about night aboard the *Aurora* was how the ship never really slept. There were always crew about, sailmakers working their shifts along the axial catwalk and shafts, machinists manning the engine cars. In the bridge, the captain and officers were bathed in the deep orange glow of their controls. Beyond the windows it was dark, but we were always flying towards dawn. The bakery and kitchen staff would be up before long, preparing for the first meal of the day. Listen, and you could hear footfalls; take a breath and you would soon smell the ambrosia of baking bread. It made me feel better, just being out amongst it all.

Even airborne, there were times when sleep evaded me, though I never panicked then. I liked reading in my bunk, or just dreaming, content to be carried through the night. And sometimes, I did what I was about to do now.

I let myself back into the passenger quarters, climbed the grand staircase to A-Deck, slipped through the dim, deserted lounges and reception rooms to the cinema. With my ring of keys, I let myself into the projectionist's booth. I fitted the first reel of the movie on to the projector and warmed up the powerful tungsten lamp. I pressed a button and the curtain in the cinema lifted. When the lamp was ready, I started the film going, and hurried back into the cinema to take my seat in a red velvet-upholstered chair.

Baz and I would do this sometimes when we couldn't sleep, discombobulated from too many night shifts, or just too excited after leaving some exotic port. We'd start the movie and sit side by side smack in the middle of the deserted cinema and let the movie just wash over us. And sometimes I'd do it by myself. Once the movie starts, and if it's a good one, you sort of forget if you're alone or not. The cinema smelled of perfume and cigar smoke and roasted almonds.

Gilgamesh. I hadn't seen this one yet, though judging by the tall stack of reels in the booth, it would be a good juicy long one. The Lumière triplets always made good ones. Light played on the screen and, as always, the movie pulled me right in. There was a creature called Enkidu, half man, half animal who falls from the sky, and the cruel king Gilgamesh is jealous of his power over people and animals, and wants to kill him.

I sat riveted, except when I had to change reels on the projector. I'd race back, pull off the old one, and slap on the new one and hurry back to my seat. Near the end of the movie, Enkidu travels to the city to confront Gilgamesh, and they start to fight high atop the city's towers.

My heart was pounding, my hands clenched the armrests and I was leaning forward towards the screen. The tower was impossibly high, there was a terrible storm blowing and clouds scudded past, and it was almost as if they were airborne. They were fighting closer and closer to the edge of the tower, lightning flashed, thunder rolled, and Gilgamesh slipped. And fell.

I shouted in surprise.

Gilgamesh fell so slowly, arms spread, right off the tower's edge and towards the clouds, but somehow Enkidu grabbed hold of him. He seized him around the wrist and was so strong he could lift him back over the edge and on to the tower.

I didn't really see the end of the movie. I was having a good cry in the dark.

My father fell.

But no one could save him. There was no one close enough. He was coming back from Kathmandu on the *Aurora*. Over the East China Sea there was a storm, and part of the ship's skin ripped away near her tail flaps. He was a sailmaker, my father, just a junior one. After years working cargo ships for the Lunardi line,

259

he'd been offered a position aboard the *Aurora*. It was Captain Walken who'd hired him.

A team of sailmakers went out on to the ship's back in the storm. My father was among them. The wind was fierce, but my father did not falter. The ship's back was slick with rain, but he did not slip. He was doing some patching, when a big panel of ship's skin tore free and struck him in the head. He was knocked unconscious, and the weight of his fall ripped his safety line from the cleat. The others tried to reach him in time, but couldn't. They saw him fall off the ship's back and soar down through the stormy sky. They saw him disappear into the low cloud churning above the sea.

They were never able to recover the body, the seas and skies were so rough. They told us that, from such a height, the impact on the water would have killed him instantly. But I liked to think of him sailing clear. I liked to think of him soaring around the world, crossing paths with me.

Morning came and I was on the pipeline crew, guiding them to the cave. It seemed strange to be trudging through the forest without Kate, but, I had to admit, I was relieved to be free of her. I had not seen her last night in the dining room; Baz later told me Miss Simpkins and Kate had taken their dinner in their stateroom. It seemed the chaperone had Kate under lock and key, and I couldn't help thinking it was good sense. I knew she would want to go back and see the cloud cat again, and I was worried I would not have the strength to say no to her. A proper weakling I'd become down here.

It was slow, hot work, unrolling the heavy rubber hosing through the forest, like wrestling with some mythological boa constrictor. It was noon before we reached the cave, and the sailmakers had attached the end of the hose as best they could to the collar on the hydrium vent.

'Back to the ship!' the chief sailmaker told me, 'and tell them to turn on the pump!'

I raced back. The end of the pipeline fed directly into the forward gas shaft in the *Aurora*'s bow. A pump had been rigged to suck the hydrium along the pipeline, and into the shaft. From there the captain could fill each and every gas cell simply by opening the valves that connected all the cells.

'Prime the pump!' I yelled to the mechanics. 'She's ready!'

I heard the pump start, and then went back out on to the beach to watch.

It was silly, because I knew that it would be a slow process, not like watching a party balloon get blown up. The rubber hosing was thin, and I'd heard the sailmakers say it would take at least a full day to completely replenish the *Aurora*. All through the night, the sailmakers had been working, once again patching the *Aurora*'s skin. By this time she looked like a bit of a Frankenstein's monster, stitched together so that both flanks and back were covered with raised scar tissue. That could be fixed. Back in harbour, all that could be taken care of.

I watched. I wanted to see something happen.

Mr Nguyen, one of the machinists, came out to tell me the hydrium was feeding in just fine.

'What are you looking for?' he asked.

'Just watching her, that's all.'

'You're crazy, Mr Cruse. It'll be hours before you see any difference.'

I went aboard, and no sooner had I set foot on A-Deck when Miss Simpkins came dashing around the corner as fast as her long skirt would allow, waving a bone in the air. I flattened myself against the wall: she looked to be in a running-down frame of mind.

'How dare you poke about in my room!' Kate hollered, barrelling around the corner after her chaperone.

'This is too much!' Miss Simpkins said, rounding on me. She waved the bone in my face. 'What is the meaning of this!'

'Give it back!' shouted Kate. 'You'll damage it!'

Miss Simpkins, it seemed, had just discovered our bones.

As luck would have it, the captain was strolling out from the upper lounge, and Miss Simpkins went straight for him.

'Captain Walken!'

'Miss Simpkins, I trust your tropical headaches have eased, under the care of our fine doctor.'

'My head is simply throbbing!' Miss Simpkins declared, 'and likely to get worse given recent events!'

'Perhaps we could talk somewhere more private,' the captain said gallantly. 'Please, will you all join me in my cabin? You, too, Mr Cruse.'

'Yes, very well,' said Miss Simpkins, turning to Kate. 'Come along!'

Kate glared at her chaperone and then turned to me.

'Hello, Mr Cruse. How are you today?'

'I'm well, Miss de Vries. And yourself?'

'Quite angry.'

We followed the captain down the catwalk and into his cosy cabin, where he offered Miss de Vries and Miss Simpkins the two chairs. I stood.

'Captain,' the chaperone began, holding the bone out before her as if it were the most gruesome and gore-soaked thing imaginable, 'to have my charge and your cabin boy cavorting about the forest is quite bad enough, but now I find that they've been grave digging!'

'You had no right to open that carpet-bag, Marjorie,' said Kate. 'I am terribly, terribly vexed.'

'She refuses to tell me how she came by these bones, so I am hoping her sly accomplice, this cabin boy of yours, might be more forthcoming!' said Miss Simpkins, patting at her hair.

'We haven't been grave digging, Marjorie,' Kate said, with a disdainful toss of her head. 'The idea is quite absurd.'

'Then explain this, please!' she said, shaking the bone.

'That is a femur.'

'I don't care what it's called. I want to know where it came from and why you have it.'

'We just found it,' she said. 'In a tree.'

'A tree! You see, Captain, she's quite unbalanced.'

'Mr Cruse,' said the captain, 'I know I can rely on you to shed some light on this matter.'

I looked at Kate. Her face was giving nothing away. I knew I'd promised to keep it secret, but my captain had asked me a direct question, and I would not go against him any longer.

'She's right, sir, we found the bone in a tree. Actually we found an entire skeleton.'

'I take a great interest in bones,' Kate cut in at this point.

'Bones!' said Miss Simpkins with a shudder, finally setting the femur down on the captain's desk as though it might come alive, snakelike, in her hand. 'This is not a healthy pursuit, Kate. It is morbid.'

'It isn't,' Kate protested. 'It's a perfectly fine pursuit. I plan to become an archaeological zoologist.'

'This does not have the approval of her parents, I can assure you,' Miss Simpkins told the captain.

It seemed that we might get away without telling them what kind of animal the bones came from. It did feel a bit dishonest. I would not lie, but I didn't think I needed to volunteer information. I'd leave that up to Kate.

The captain picked up the bone and examined it thoughtfully.

'Sizeable,' he remarked, looking at Kate, 'I hadn't thought there were any large animals on these Oceanic islands.'

'How my head throbs!' wailed the chaperone.

I was awfully grateful to Miss Simpkins: she was doing a wonderful job distracting the captain from the matter of our bones.

'Would you like me to arrange a visit from our doctor?' the captain asked, sounding amazingly sympathetic.

'I feel as though I'm likely to be laid low again,' Miss Simpkins said piteously.

'I'll have him come to your stateroom immediately,' the captain told her.

'Since you're going to be out of commission, Marjorie,' Kate said, 'I was rather hoping we could have your permission to make another excursion.'

Miss Simpkins' jaw fell. 'You must be mad, child. Not only will you stay away from the forest, you will be locked within the stateroom until we leave this wretched island.'

'That's imprisonment!' Kate protested. 'Captain, surely you can't allow that.'

'I have no authority over this matter,' said the captain. 'But if truth be told, Miss de Vries, you have not exercised sound judgement. Harm could easily have come to you in that typhoon; you might have been lost, or attacked by some animal. I'd prefer to have everyone aboard the ship now. It won't be long till we depart and I would hate to miss favourable winds because one of the passengers was unaccounted for.'

'But locking me in my room, I think it's most unfair,' said Kate. 'My parents will be most displeased—'

'To learn of your shenanigans, yes, they will,' her chaperone cut in. 'Digging up bones!'

'We didn't dig them up, Marjorie.'

'I expect you to be rid of them before we leave! They're not coming with us.'

'They most certainly are,' Kate said.

'Perhaps you can continue this discussion in the privacy of your stateroom,' said the captain, standing. 'I must see to the ship. Thank you, Mr Cruse, for joining us.'

'And Captain,' said Miss Simpkins, 'I would appreciate it if Mr Cruse here would keep his distance from my charge. I fear he is a poor and perverse influence on her.'

'Marjorie, that is quite uncalled-for!'

'Did you know that it was Mr Cruse who discovered hydrium here on the island?' the captain asked her. 'He's saved us all, Miss Simpkins.'

'That was awfully clever of you,' Kate said to me, beaming. 'Where?'

'The cave.'

'The cave! You mean that hiss was hydrium? Oh, well done, Mr Cruse!'

'You two were in a cave together?' said Miss Simpkins in horror.

'Yes,' said Kate, 'and it was very, very dark.'

'Ladies, a pleasure as always,' said Captain Walken, opening the door.

'Captain, I want these two kept apart,' insisted Miss Simpkins. 'I will do my part, and I will hope you can do yours. Come along, Kate.'

Kate sighed and paused only to pick up the femur from the captain's desk. She cradled it carefully in her hands as she left. I was about to follow them but the captain called me back.

'I'll ask no further questions, Mr Cruse, but please, stay with the ship. Let's fix her up, you and I, shall we, without any further distractions.'

'Very good, sir. I'm sorry.'

'No apologies, Mr Cruse. If I had my way you'd be first officer by now.'

She was filling. I'd nipped outside to check on her, and I swear I could see the difference. Her worst sections, once saggy and torn, looked decidedly firmer now. It was like watching an old woman stand up unexpectedly from a wheelchair. More than that, it was like watching her shed her years before your eyes until her skin was smooth and beautiful again. I just stood there for a few more minutes, staring. Her belly no longer rested so heavily on the ground. Work crews were repairing her lower rudder. Everyone was busy, making the ship whole again.

There was a great burst of light from the Topkapi stateroom, and I looked up and saw Kate standing at her bedroom window, waving. She'd used her camera flash to get my attention. Reluctantly I walked closer. The windows on A-Deck were some ten metres overhead. Kate opened her window a crack and sent a little paper airplane gliding out. It tailspun to the sand. I looked around, making sure no one saw this, for I felt a proper fool running after a paper airplane.

I unfolded it. Written on the paper was:

Am locked in. Help.

I glanced up at her and she stared down at me, silently reproachful.

I shrugged. What could I do?

Another paper airplane came down and hit me in the forehead.

You're the cabin boy. You have keys.

I shook my head.

I swear I could see her nostrils narrow, even from this distance.

She scribbled furiously on her notepad, tore a piece off and dropped it out the window. It fluttered down and I snatched it from the air.

We need pictures of her!

I sighed, shrugging once more. I couldn't bear Kate's baleful gaze on me any more, so I turned away, and hurried back inside the ship, back to my duties. The two females in my life seemed strict taskmasters, the *Aurora* and Kate de Vries, and there was no pleasing both of them. I felt angry with Kate. I wanted to be happy now. Why did she have to go and make me feel guilty, when all I wanted was for my spirits to soar like hydrium?

14

NEST

I slept. The ship filled all through the night, and even in my dreams I could sense it. I could feel her shifting on the sand as she became lighter, and at some point she came free of the ground, and was floating again. Air moved beneath her belly once more, and in my sleep I soared all around her. I waited for my father, but he did not come.

I was only half dressed when Baz burst into the cabin.

'Oh, thank heavens,' he puffed when he saw me.

'What's wrong?'

'Kate de Vries has gone missing.'

I nearly fell over, one leg in my trousers, staggering around the room.

'I thought she was locked in!'

Baz couldn't keep a smile from pulling at his lips. 'Apparently your Miss de Vries is quite determined. She made a run for freedom – after drugging her dear chaperone.'

'No!'

'A few too many drops of the sleeping elixir Doc Halliday prescribed for Miss Simpkin's tropical headaches. When she finally woke up, Miss de Vries was long gone.'

'She's completely capable of it,' I muttered.

'Quite a future she has ahead of her, your sweetheart.'

'She's not my sweetheart.'

'A criminal mastermind in the making if you ask me. And what's all this about grave digging?'

'How long's she been gone?'

'No one knows. Miss Simpkins only woke up about half an hour ago. She got Mr Lisbon up, and he had all the passenger areas checked.' Baz shook his head. 'So then the captain got called in, and they wanted to find out if you'd gone off with her again.'

'Oh no.'

'They wanted you to go to the Topkapi stateroom if you were here.'

I tied my shoes, skipped brushing my teeth, and hurried forward to A-Deck, combing my hair with my fingers. I could just imagine Miss Simpkins, sitting in an armchair and puffing and fanning herself. And when Mr Lisbon opened the door to the Topkapi stateroom, and let me in, Miss Simpkins was in fact collapsed in an armchair, gulping air and fanning herself.

The captain was obviously relieved to see me. 'Mr Cruse,' he said, 'I'm very glad to find you aboard. Mr Hilcock no doubt told you of our missing passenger.'

'Yes, sir.'

'Did you have any prior knowledge of this?'

'None, sir.'

'But perhaps you have an idea where she might have gone?'

I took a deep breath. 'Perhaps, sir.'

'Then you shall go find her.'

'I certainly don't approve of that idea,' said Miss Simpkins primly. 'I think he's spent quite enough time alone with Miss de Vries.'

My face was burning, but I dared not say a word. Any objection I made would only seem to confirm her suspicions, and perhaps spread them to the captain. I stood looking at the floor, furious with Kate for sneaking off like this.

'Mr Cruse will not go alone,' the captain replied. 'Mr Lunardi is off duty; he will accompany him.'

'Just the two of them?' protested Miss Simpkins. 'Surely you can—'

'I can spare no more,' the captain said. 'The ship's repairs are my chief concern. I need all hands here. Mr Cruse knows the island better than anyone, and I suspect he also has a good idea where to look. He will find her more easily than a team of thirty men. Bring this reckless girl back, Mr Cruse. Once the ship is airworthy I plan to depart immediately.'

'Yes, sir.'

'Change into your shore clothes and report to the main gangway at once. I'll have Mr Lunardi meet you there.'

The captain was annoyed, and I did not blame him. This business with Kate de Vries, and me too, I suppose, had gone from being an annoyance to a danger to the ship. We had already been blind-sided by a tropical storm; the captain knew it would be foolhardy to stay any longer than necessary. He did not want to be delayed by a wilful young lady with a talent for disappearing into the wilderness.

Back in my cabin I hurriedly changed out of my uniform and rushed to the main gangway. As I stepped down to the beach, I was pleased to see the ship had a good two metres' clearance now.

It was just coming up to nine o'clock. First light would have been no earlier than six. Kate would not have ventured into the forest before then. At most she had three hours on me. I knew where she would go. Down into that valley where we'd seen the cloud cat disappear. She thought its nest was there. She'd go there to take pictures.

If she could get there. For the first time I felt afraid for her. She had a terrible sense of direction. She'd get lost. And if she did, what hope had we of finding her? I was about to go back and ask the captain for more men to help us look, when I remembered the cave. How she'd asked for the bearings of things. Still, that would be no use without –

A compass.

My hand darted to my pocket. It was not there. My thoughts flew back to the cave when she had handled it.

273

I could not remember taking it back from her, could not remember its smooth cool shape returning to my pocket. I had been without it since then, and too preoccupied to notice.

Kate knew how to follow the stream to the skeleton tree, and from there she might well remember the direction we'd taken as we'd pursued the cloud cat. That would get her to the bluff overlooking the valley. But how she would descend the slope was another matter, and then, when she was down amongst the trees, would she have the sense to chart a course for herself, and keep to it?

Bruce Lunardi vaulted down the gangway, and smiled uncertainly at me.

'I understand we're on a rescue mission,' he said. 'I brought some gear. Do you have a compass?'

'I did.'

'Never mind, I've got quite a good one,' he said producing it from his pocket. 'Lead the way.'

I still wasn't happy about having Lunardi tag along. I wondered if the captain had done it to placate Miss Simpkins; or whether he truly didn't trust me now. The thought made me gloomy. He'd sent me off with a chaperone of my very own, just to make sure Kate and I didn't get up to any more mischief. My ears burned at the unfairness of it. Your girlfriend, Baz had called her. They all thought we were off in the forest whispering sweet nothings to each other. I tried to imagine Kate whispering a sweet nothing to anyone, and couldn't.

I led Lunardi to the stream and then into the forest.

'So where do you think she's gone?' he asked me.

'Likely she just went off to scribble in her notebook,' I muttered, not feeling much like talking. Of all people, why had the captain chosen Lunardi to accompany me? It did seem a bit cruel; then again, he was off duty, and he could be spared. The captain wasn't concerned with supplying me with a charming picnic companion.

'What is it she's so interested in?' Lunardi asked.

'Oh, just the local flora and fauna.'

'She takes photographs, too, judging by that camera of hers.'

'She's a keen one for the pictures.'

'She should be careful wandering around alone,' he said. 'There might be poisonous snakes about.'

'There's a little red one that jumps,' I said.

'Really?' he asked.

'Deadly, apparently. One nip's enough to take down a hippo. I'd stay sharp. You see anything move down there, sing out.'

'Thanks,' said Lunardi, his eyes dropping to the undergrowth.

We walked on a bit in silence.

'It's not really poisonous,' I said, feeling bad. 'But it does have a spring to it. Gave me a fright, I can tell you.'

He laughed. We walked on in silence. He took a compass reading. In his crisp khaki trousers and shirt he looked like some dashing jungle explorer stepped out of a cinema screen.

'This is something, eh?' he said happily. 'Bit of an adventure.'

'Bit too much,' I said. 'We don't usually get pirates and a shipwreck on every trip. Don't go getting used to it.'

'No, I suppose not,' he said with a chuckle. He was quiet a moment, and then he said to me, 'You're lucky, you know.'

I looked at him, irritated and surprised all at once. 'Why do you say that?'

'Because you love what you do. I can just tell. Your whole life, you've wanted to work aboard airships, haven't you?'

'Yes.'

'I see you around the ship, doesn't matter what you're doing – you just look content, like you're doing the right thing. My problem is, I can't figure out what the right thing for me is.'

'You don't need to.' I said it before I could stop myself.

'Why do you say that?'

'Because you're rich,' I said. 'You can do exactly as you wish.'

He looked astonished. 'No, I can't. My father expects me to help run the family business. That's not what I want. I don't have any interest in that. And I don't have any talent for it either. I'm not at all sure I have a talent for anything. My father's quite disgusted with me. Says I can't stick at anything. So he decided to stick me somewhere himself.'

'You didn't want to go to the Airship Academy then?'

I would have given my molars and as many fingers as I could spare for such a chance.

Bruce shook his head. 'My father and I made a bargain. I'd train at the Academy, and spend two years on board a ship, and afterwards, if I still wanted, he'd let me try something I chose. Providing he approved, of course.'

'And what would you do?'

'That's just it. I don't know yet. There's plenty of things I'm interested in, for a little while anyway. But nothing I've got a passion for. That's why I think you're so lucky. You just know.'

I sniffed. I wasn't as lucky as he thought.

'Look, they told me what happened,' he said. 'Me getting your place, I mean. Stealing must be how you think of it. And you're right. You earned that position. I'm sorry.'

'It's not your fault,' I said uncomfortably.

'I'd transfer ships if I could,' he said, 'and get out of your way, but my father made me sign a two-year service contract with the *Aurora*. If I even change ships, he'd see that as quitting, and he wouldn't give me a chance at anything else. I'd end up working for him at the company for the rest of my life.'

'Why can't you just quit and do what you want?'

'I'd be in disgrace. He'd cut me off without a penny, I'm quite sure of that.'

'You'd just make your own way.'

'A bit scary, when I don't know my own way. I'm not

like you, Mr Cruse, I don't have much of a talent for anything.'

'Everyone has a talent for something,' I said.

'I hope you're right. I'm sorry for the trouble I've caused you. I hope you'll not think too ill of me.'

I couldn't quite understand why he just didn't do what he wanted – but it's easy to give advice to others, until you try to imagine yourself in their skins. Going against your father, feeling alone and helpless in the world: these were not easy things to bear.

'Seems we're stuck with each other for a couple of years then,' I said. I tried to say it kindly, but could not keep the bitterness from my voice.

'Perhaps you could transfer ship?' he said. 'I could speak to my—'

'Please don't.'

'But then I wouldn't be holding you back!'

'Why should I change ship?'

'So you could be sailmaker, like you wanted!'

'The *Aurora*'s my ship.'

'Yes, but you can't limit yourself to—'

'She's my home. You should be the one to move.'

'But I just told you I—'

'I know, I know,' I said. 'Let's not talk about it any more. Let's just find Miss de Vries.'

We fell into an uneasy silence. I was sorry for my outburst; Bruce was only trying to be kind, but I didn't feel like apologizing. After several minutes we reached the skeleton tree. Bruce took a compass reading, and we set course for the bluff where Kate and I had last seen the creature. It was farther than I thought, but of course, last time I'd made the trip, I was running.

'It drops off up there,' Bruce said.

We walked to the edge and looked down the slope. I gazed at the treetops, trying to remember exactly where it was we'd seen the cloud cat disappear. I pointed.

'She'll be down there.'

'How do you know?'

'She wanted to go down there a few days ago, but we ran out of time.'

'She'd have a job getting down there,' Bruce said.

'Oh, she can take care of herself just fine,' I said, hoping I was right.

It was possible she'd never even made it this far. What if she was lost and bumbling around in the forest? Somehow I doubted it. This was a young lady who could drug her chaperone and steal my compass. While we were together, she might have been secretly taking her bearings the whole time, thinking ahead to when she'd be rid of me. For her sake, I hoped this was the case, for if she were lost, we might never find her. I looked both ways along the bluff, trying to guess which was the easiest way down.

'What do you think?' I asked Bruce.

'This way,' he said.

I saw no reason to disagree, so we headed north-east along the bluff.

'Drink?' he asked, offering me the canteen. I'd seen it

earlier, slung over his shoulder. He'd filled it at the stream back at the skeleton tree.

'Thanks. You're all kitted out,' I said.

'I know,' he laughed. 'My mother gave me the compass too, before I shipped out. Looks like I should be exploring the Amazonia instead of flying on a luxury liner. Ridiculous, isn't it?'

'Still, awfully useful,' I said, grateful for the long drink of cool water.

'Look at this,' said Bruce. There was a fresh slash in the bark of a tree. 'She's cut a blaze.'

'Good for her,' I said.

Before long we came across another blaze, marking a path that ran steeply down the side of the bluff. Of course it wasn't a real path, only a kind of notch that zigzagged crazily down into the valley.

'She went down that way,' said Bruce with some admiration.

It was no simple feat even for us, and we weren't carrying camera gear. When we were still up high, I took a good look across the valley, for I knew that once we were down amongst the trees it would be easy to get lost. I sighted the spot we were heading for, and set my mind's compass. Bruce, I saw, sensibly took his own bearing. We didn't speak, just concentrated on our footing. The first bit was the hardest, and then it got a lot easier, with plenty of strong branches and vines to grab hold of as we staggered down. The climb back up would be hardest.

At the bottom we paused to wipe sweat from our brows, and have a drink from Bruce's canteen. We spotted another of Kate's blazes, showing us the right direction.

'Should we start hollering for her?' Bruce wondered aloud.

'Probably a good idea.'

'Miss de Vries!' he shouted.

I added my voice to his. I was glad he was with me. I would have felt odd belting her name out into the wilderness by myself. There was no echo. The sound just disappeared, swallowed up by the trees and the hot, heavy air. I was amazed Kate had had the nerve to come so far alone. I turned back and could no longer see the bluff, the foliage was so dense. Trees and snaking vines and flowers everywhere. Our voices sent rainbow-plumed birds crashing through the leaves and branches. The sun was well overhead now, the air almost too thick to breathe.

'Miss de Vries!' I hollered.

'Here!' came a pleasant sing-song voice.

Bruce and I both looked about, and then up into the trees.

'Up here!' Kate said.

We walked towards an enormous tree with thick branches, hairy with moss. Resting at the base was a familiar carpet-bag with a pink floral pattern. It smelled quite awful. I peered up into the verdant foliage. There, in the highest branches, was Kate, reclining against the trunk, legs swinging. A spyglass hung around her neck, along with a compact camera. In one hand she held her notebook. If she hadn't been swinging her legs and waving, it would have been most difficult to see her. She was wearing a pair of outlandish, emerald green harem pants with sequined cuffs, and a reddish brown tunic. I could see that it was good tree-climbing gear, snug at the ankles, with no long skirt to tangle her up. And the colours couldn't have blended in better. A real thinker, my Kate.

'Are you quite all right up there, Miss de Vries?' Bruce asked.

'Perfectly comfortable. The view's fine. You should come up and see.'

'Actually,' I said, 'we were hoping you would come down and return to the ship now.'

'She probably needs help down,' Bruce said to me, starting to climb.

'She doesn't need help,' I told him. And I certainly didn't want Bruce to be the one to help her.

'I'll just nip up,' he said.

'What about your head for heights?' I said, loudly enough for Kate to hear.

'I should be all right in a tree,' he muttered.

I went after him. It was quite an easy one to climb, the branches just the right distance apart. I made sure to outstrip Bruce and reach Kate first. She was perched right near the top. I saw her close the notebook as we neared. She gave me a withering look as if to say, 'How

282

clever of you to have brought someone else along: what on earth were you thinking?'

'Hello, Miss de Vries,' said Bruce.

'Wonderful to see you again, Mr Lunardi,' Kate said, suddenly the perfect hostess.

'We were sent to bring you back,' I said, by way of explanation. Bruce and I stood on the branch beneath hers, so all our heads were at roughly the same height. I had to give it to her, she'd picked an excellent vantage point. Near the tree's summit the branches and leaves thinned, as had all those of the surrounding trees. She had a view deep into the forest around us for about forty metres.

'See anything interesting?' Bruce asked.

'Plenty,' she said. 'All manner of birds. The vantage point is really quite splendid.'

'I can see that,' said Bruce.

'We should head down,' I said. 'Mr Lunardi here might get a little woozy with the height.'

'I'm fine, thanks,' he said.

Kate was all smiles up there in the tree, quite the little actress. You'd never know she was worried about our secret getting out, someone else horning in on her scientific breakthrough.

'Good job finding your way here,' I said. 'My compass help you out, did it?'

'It was awfully useful. I did mean to give it back.'

'I'm sure.'

'But I was under lock and key at the time, as you know.'

'Unfortunate. Well, we should really be heading back now.'

'I'm not quite ready just yet, thanks,' she replied.

'You've created quite a scandal back at the ship,' I said, losing my patience.

'I don't see why,' she murmured, and peered through her spyglass.

'You drugged Miss Simpkins!' I exclaimed.

'Drugged! Honestly! You make it sound so extreme! All I did was give her a dose of her own sleeping elixir. Four drops in her water glass before bedtime. Maybe it was eight, I can't remember. No more than eight. What choice did I have? You weren't about to help me. How else was I supposed to get out? She kept the keys clutched in her fist in a death grip. I knew I'd have no chance of wiggling them out unless she was in a good deep sleep.'

'She's in a terrible state. And the captain is displeased as well.'

'I was being held prisoner! It's probably illegal, not that you seemed at all concerned about my welfare.'

I rolled my eyes. 'You're to come back with us immediately.'

'How are you enjoying this island, Mr Lunardi?' she asked, turning her smile on Lunardi. 'Quite a paradise, isn't it?'

'It's very beautiful,' he replied.

He was smiling up at her, with a completely contented look on his face. I didn't much care for that look. Not that Kate wasn't striking. In her emerald green harem pants and mahogany blouse, she looked like some exotic bird of paradise. But I didn't see why Bruce had to pick this moment to be all suave and matinée-idolish.

'Really, I'm surprised no one's ever settled here,' he said.

I half expected him to ask me to fetch them drinks.

'It's not near anywhere,' I said impatiently. 'It's off all the main trade routes. According to the charts, the nearest sizeable island is over a thousand kilometres away.'

'Still,' Bruce said, 'it seems to me someone could live here quite comfortably.'

'Perhaps your father might buy it for you as a vacation home. Shall we head down now?'

Kate turned to me. 'I'm not leaving until I get pictures.'

'Pictures of what?' Bruce asked.

'We are out of time,' I told Kate. 'The captain wants to leave as soon as possible.'

'Then this is my last chance, isn't it? I want to get a good clear shot of her.'

'Her?' Bruce said.

'Ah! So you're happy to share your little secret with Mr Lunardi, are you?' I said to Kate. 'We're allowed to tell now?'

'What secret?' Bruce demanded.

Kate looked at me, immensely pleased with herself.

'I've found her nest,' she said.

'Some kind of rare bird?' Bruce asked impatiently.

'Where?' I said.

She pointed. 'Do you see it?'

I followed the line of her finger, deeper into the trees, not exactly sure what it was I was looking for. Branches, flowering vines, leaves, fronds, getting thicker and darker the further back my gaze ventured.

'It's just trees,' I said.

Kate pulled the spyglass from around her neck and passed it to me.

'Keep looking, Mr Crow's-nest,' she said.

Eyepiece pressed tight, I adjusted the focus. It still looked like nothing extraordinary, and I felt my impatience with Kate rekindle. Then I noticed a strange weave of branches. They'd not grown together naturally, not those. It looked as if many small pieces of branch had been carefully arranged into a kind of screen. And there were feathers woven into it too, of all different colours, and bits of sod, and clumps of leaves. I was just seeing the screen from one angle, but it seemed that it continued around in a full circle, a high-walled nest, unlike anything a bird would build, more like the nests squirrels build for winter. It looked as if it might even have an overhang or something to keep out the rain. I noticed, too, that the windbreak was angled against the prevailing winds.

I lowered the spyglass.

'She built that,' Kate said.

'Why would she make a nest?' I said. 'Birds make nests to lay eggs in; squirrels do them for winter.'

'She needs a place to live,' Kate said. 'It's incredible really. She's not a land mammal, she started with no experience, but instinctively she thought to make herself a kind of shelter. She's smart.'

'Do you mind if I take a peek?' Bruce said, reaching for the spyglass.

Before he could put it to his eye, something happened. Something long and cloud-coloured appeared in a distant tree. I saw the flare of a wing.

Kate fumbled her camera to her face, but the cloud cat was already moving again. She leapt away into another tree, her amazing wings flashing open and I could hear Bruce gasp in surprise. I probably gasped too because it was still a surprise to me, the way the creature suddenly became huge and glorious and powerful in that one second her wings spread. And then they folded up again and she touched down on another branch and swiftly glided amongst the foliage and then disappeared behind the wall of her nest.

Kate exhaled loudly through her nose.

'Missed it. I wasn't ready,' she said crossly. 'You two got me all distracted!'

I looked at Bruce. He was staring, his whole body hunched in the direction of the cloud cat. His mouth was open.

'I've been waiting all day for her to come back,' Kate said. 'You hollering through the forest probably didn't help.'

'What on earth is it?' Bruce said, his voice dry.

'We don't have a name for her yet,' Kate told him.

'Cloud cat,' I said absently.

Kate looked at me. 'That was the name I thought of too!' She smiled. 'We thought the same thing.'

'I thought it would be too unscientific for you.'

'No, it's the first thing that leapt into my head.'

'It's some kind of giant bird, is it?' Bruce asked.

'No, she's a winged mammal,' Kate told him.

'You've seen it before?'

'Once, yeah,' I said. Obviously we weren't bothering to try to hide this, which was a relief. I couldn't really see the point of pretending any more.

Kate had her spyglass to her eye again, and was peering at the nest. 'She's in there, I can see her moving. But I can't get a clear shot from here.'

'How did you find the nest?' I asked.

'Luck mostly. I figured she would live somewhere around here, so it was just a matter of finding a good waiting place. But around her tree, the one her nest is in, there was a lot of debris on the ground. Bird bones, wings, beaks, fish heads. She must pick fish out of the water from the bank of the stream or lake, or maybe she glides over!'

'Incredible.'

'She's an omnivore. She eats fruit, too, I saw some mango pits and coconut shells. She must carry them up and smash them to pieces on a rock. Quite a varied diet. Seems to like fish the best though.'

She opened her notebook to write something down,

and I saw it was filled with jottings, and little sketches she'd made.

'This is amazing,' Bruce said.

'That's why I need a good clear photograph,' said Kate.

'It'll have to wait,' I told her.

'Look, I'd probably have one by now if you and Mr Lunardi hadn't come yodelling along and scared her off. You owe me a photo at least.'

I was about to tell her I didn't owe her anything, but Bruce said, 'Have you seen it fly?'

'Her,' said Kate firmly. 'And no, she can't fly. She's crippled, we think.'

'Who knows about this?'

'The three of us,' Kate said. 'And we'd like to keep it that way, if you don't mind.'

'This is going to send the scientific world into a furore,' Bruce said.

'Do you think so?' Kate said, pleased.

'Absolutely. No one's ever seen anything like this; you've made a huge discovery here. You'll want to come back, to make a proper study.'

'Ideally,' said Kate.

'My father funds a lot of scientific research, you know,' Bruce said.

'Does he?'

'This is exactly the kind of thing that would spark his interest. He's a keen collector, especially of freakish oddities.'

I felt a stab of indignation. Oddity. I didn't like that

word. The cloud cat wasn't an oddity. She was a real animal, one that was meant to fly, only couldn't because of a mistake at birth.

'My father keeps a whole wing of one of our houses like a kind of museum. All sorts of taxidermy and so forth.'

I looked at Kate, hoping she'd object, but she was just nodding, listening, swept up in the promise of glory.

'If your father's after a hunting expedition, this isn't it,' I said angrily.

'No, no, I just meant he's interested in all sorts of things. He could set you up with a proper expedition, you know.'

'Do you think?' Kate asked, enthralled.

'Absolutely. With lots of equipment and experts.'

'I wouldn't want to be shuffled out of the way, though,' Kate insisted, her nostrils narrowing just a touch.

'Of course not,' Bruce said. 'We'd make it a condition.'

Bruce couldn't stop talking. His enthusiasm was like a big balloon that was stealing all the air from mine. I didn't mind so much that he'd seen the cloud cat – but I did mind that he'd stolen something that, hours before, belonged just to Kate and me. He'd stolen our discovery, just like he'd stolen my position aboard ship.

'Well, that's all grand,' I said. 'Everything's taken care of. You'll all be famous. But right now, we need to get back to the ship.'

'I still need a picture,' Kate insisted.

It would have been nice if Bruce had echoed my wishes, but he wasn't doing anything; he was peering through Kate's spyglass at the cloud cat's nest. He seemed quite happy to let me continue in the role of party pooper, and suddenly I felt extremely angry.

'No,' I said to Kate. 'You're coming back now and I'll carry you kicking and screaming if need be.'

'You wouldn't.'

'I would.'

'You couldn't.'

'I could, and I will. There's two of us here, and we're acting on Captain Walken's express orders.'

Kate fluttered her fingers dismissively. 'I don't believe for a second someone of Mr Lunardi's breeding would pick up a struggling lady and lug her around like a sack of rice. Would you, Mr Lunardi?' she said, smiling as if they shared some wonderful cosy secret.

'I certainly wouldn't, no,' he said, still peering through the spyglass.

My heart was pounding. My voice shook. 'Lunardi, we take orders from our captain, not from some spoiled girl!'

'I resent that!' said Kate.

'You know,' Bruce said, looking over at me, 'this really is an amazing thing she's discovered here.'

'Yes, and with your father's help, she'll come back again. You'll come again. I'll come again so I can serve you all lemonade. But right now, we need to go.'

'I need a photograph now,' said Kate. 'I need the proof.'

'When all this started, you were happy with the bones and the photographs of the skeleton!'

'Yes, but if I get pictures of her, I can get into any university I want; I can head an expedition.'

'I thought you just wanted to see what your grandfather saw. Beautiful creatures. Now you want to be all famous.'

'That's not fair,' she said hotly. 'You think I'm being selfish, don't you? That I'm rich and have nothing but choices. But I'm a girl, and girls don't get choices. No one's going to give me a chance unless I force them to. It's not enough to just be smart and curious. It's just like you, being poor. You and I have to try harder and be better to get ahead. I have to have something amazing like this before they'll pay attention to me.'

No one said anything for a moment.

'She's right, you know,' said Bruce.

'Terrific,' I said. 'So touching when the rich stick together.'

'It is a huge scientific breakthrough,' Bruce said again.

'I suppose disobeying orders means nothing to you,' I said. 'Why would it? Lose this job and you can always just get your father to find you another. Don't mind that you're getting me in trouble too.'

'You go back then,' he said. 'I'll stay with Miss de Vries.'

That made me even angrier, the thought of her alone with Bruce while they took their pictures of the cloud cat. My cloud cat. Not just Kate's.

'Stay, Matt, please,' said Kate. She looked anxious, but I wasn't sure if it was genuine, or just a face she put on to keep me here. 'I promise it won't take long. I've got a bit of a plan.'

'What's that?'

'To lure her out into the open. Up here I'll never get a clear shot, especially with her moving around the way she does. But if I could get her on the ground, it might be easier. She'd be slower, and the camera would be steady. I've brought a tripod.'

'How would you lure her out?'

'I brought some food.'

'You brought some food?'

'A fish actually. The cooks set their catch out on the beach, and I nabbed one as I was heading off. There was no way I could get anything out of the kitchen. There were too many people around. But I didn't think they'd miss just one fish. It's a nice big one,' she said enthusiastically. 'I left some money for it.'

'They'll appreciate that. Where's this fish?'

'All wrapped up in the carpet-bag.' That explained the smell. 'I wrapped it up in leaves as well as I could. It's probably good and stinky by now. She'll smell it instantly.'

'You're going to lure her out into the open with the fish?'

She nodded.

'And you'll be hiding nearby with your camera, ready to take her photograph?'

'I won't use the flash this time. That just scares her off. We take a picture or two and then it's back to the ship, lickety-split!'

She was a planner, you couldn't fault her there.

'Seems sound to me,' Bruce agreed.

'I don't like it,' I said. 'What if she sees us? She might be dangerous.'

Kate looked amazed. 'Her? She ran from us, remember?'

'She's a wild animal.'

'She's gentle as anything, isn't it obvious? She's shy.'

'Why not just set a little saucer of milk out for her?'

Kate looked at me. 'I'd like to get on with this if you don't mind, Mr Cruse. We *are* expected back at the ship.'

'Sorry to hold you back,' I said, and saw that her eyes were smiling at me.

'Half an hour, that's all,' she promised.

I nodded. 'Let's get down from here, and find a good place to take this photograph.'

15

THE CLOUD CAT

The fish stank. And in the middle of the small clearing, under the noonday sun, it was certain to stink even more soon. Any living creature with or without nostrils would sniff it out before long.

'Won't she be suspicious?' I asked. 'Oh look, a dead fish in the middle of the forest.'

'I don't think she'll ask too many questions,' Kate said.

Bruce stank too. He was the one who'd taken the fish from the carpet-bag, unwrapped it, and placed it on the ground. He kept rubbing his hands on the grass, but the smell was stubborn and clung to him.

Trees and stacks of fern grew thickly all around the clearing. We crouched down, hidden. Kate found a narrow gap in the fronds and set up her camera in front of it. She peered through the viewfinder.

'This will be perfect,' she said. 'I've got a good wide shot through here. If she comes to the fish, I've got her.'

We waited. We were not far from the tree which held the cloud cat's nest. Surely it couldn't be long before she smelled the fish. I could smell it – or maybe that was Bruce. I wished he'd move a little farther away. On Kate's instruction, we stopped speaking altogether. Part of me wanted the cloud cat to hurry up and come; the other part was afraid she would. I was not so sure of Kate's assumption she had a gentle soul. Why should she, any more than an eagle or panther?

The day gathered heat. Even sitting in the shade of the trees and ferns, my body was filmed with sweat. The air was so filled with moisture it was hard to imagine there was any room for oxygen. My heart ran hard. I leaned back against the tree trunk, closed my eyes, listened to the heat. I listened to the symphony of birds and bugs. I listened to the breeze high up in the treetops. For a moment I thought I could hear the ocean, but that was probably my imagination. And then, most strange, I thought I heard the sound of propellers. I opened my eyes. Already it was gone. It had been very faint.

'Did you hear that?' I whispered to Bruce. 'Sounded like propellers.'

His eyes lifted to the sky and he listened and shook his head. 'No.'

'Shhh,' said Kate.

A branch creaked. Something brushed leaves.

The cloud cat was coming.

Kate held her hand up.

Very slowly I moved my head so I could see through the ferns. At the far side of the clearing, trees rose up in a solid wall. Suddenly, there she was on a low branch in

296

full view. I blinked. She must have dropped down from on high. It was the first time I'd seen her, tip to tail, the whole glorious length of her, and she was truly beautiful, sleek and regal and exquisite, her fur silvery grey and soft-looking. You could imagine exactly how it would feel if you stroked it. She was not much more than a metre in length. She was like a princess robed in a fur mantle, bunched around her shoulders. With her wings furled, she didn't seem so large. She was like a strange cat. Her eyes were flecked green. I wanted to look at her for ever.

She gingerly paced along the branch to its skinny end, and still it didn't bow, she was that light. Nimbly she pounced into the clearing, landing several metres back from the fish. She crouched frozen on the earth, and then took a single step closer.

She wasn't meant for walking, I could tell right away. Her wings were her front legs and she had a funny hunched way of moving on the ground, shoulders swinging, face closer to the earth than her rump. She was a bit like a cat when it's stalking a bird, ready to pounce. But on the ground she had nothing of her feline grace when soaring from tree to tree. Her legs were all wrong for walking, even though she'd strengthened them with a life in the forest. I hated seeing her walk. She slouched, she slunk, as if revolted by the feel of the earth beneath her feet. I wished I could help her. I knew what it was like to have your wings clipped.

Closer she came to the centre of the clearing, where the stinking fish shimmered in the sun's gaze. Before now, we'd only seen her from a distance, veiled by leaves and branches and moving quickly. The cloud cat took one more step and then stopped. I could see her ears twitching. She was listening. Could she hear our breathing, the creak of our bones as we tried not to move? The cat, I noticed, had never once put her back to us. She approached on the far side of the fish, her head pointed towards us. Surely she couldn't see us. Not for the first time I wondered at the wisdom of coming so close to her home. I'd seen crows attack people when they innocently walked beneath a tree holding the birds' nests. But that was because there were hatchlings, and the parents were protective. This cloud cat of ours had nothing to protect – but herself.

Then, in three abrupt, slinking steps, she was upon the fish. With her curved front claws she impaled the fish at both ends, tail and gills. Her jaws opened and we saw her teeth and everything changed.

We saw her teeth and suddenly she was no longer a sleek, shy cat.

We heard her wet panting sounds as she ravenously tore into the meat with her fangs and she was suddenly full of threat and power. I'd seen the teeth on the skeleton, but it was impossible to imagine them in motion, powered by her massive jaws, ripping into the fish. Now that she was so close, I could smell her, a rank chicken-coop heat of fur and sweat and fish and old meat and excrement. I swallowed, but my mouth was so dry I almost gagged. I glanced over at Bruce. He was shaking. Kate's face had gone very pale. Her hands trembled atop the camera.

We'd made a terrible mistake.

It was no more than four metres in front of us, and I felt a tremendous fear in me. I could see the fish's broken spine on the ground, its severed head and dead eye jerking with every pull from the creature's jaws.

It ate the fish. It could eat us.

The picture was not important. All that mattered now was getting away safely.

The cat finished with the fish and looked up. Its nostrils flared. I looked at Bruce's hands, could practically see the smell of the spoiling fish, rising like steam.

Kate had put her eye to the camera's viewfinder. Her finger was on the plunger. I reached out to try and stop her, but too late.

The camera clicked as its shutter contracted and opened.

It was a small, precise little metallic click, but it was a sound completely foreign to the forest, and it might as well have been thunder. The cloud cat's head snapped up as if yanked by a chain. Its gaze was levelled at the ferns. That was all there was between us, a few centimetres of soft, drooping leaves.

Be very, very still.

I heard a low, dangerous, liquid purr. I crouched frozen, floating outside my body, just staring at the cloud cat's face. It was not a cat's face really. It had altogether more intelligence and intent.

It will not see us it will not smell us it will not hear us.

Bruce ran.

He did it so suddenly there was no hope of holding him back.

'C'mon!' he snapped.

He pivoted and ran straight back from the ferns, bent low, hoping he would not be seen. I could see the cloud cat's ears flare and swivel, its chin tilt up. Its rump dropped, and then it sprang. Kate and I fell flat, my hand raised across my face to ward off a blow, but the cat was not interested in us, perhaps didn't even see us. Bruce was its prey. The cat sailed towards us, wings flaring immensely. It landed on a thick branch above me and Kate. In the brief second it touched down I saw the way its claws gripped the bark, and smelled the pungent odour of its belly and breath and wings as they folded and flexed. Its nostrils flared again as it sniffed and then it launched itself after Bruce, leaping from tree to tree. Bruce ran headlong, but he would not be able to outrun it. I saw the cloud cat pounce on to a branch directly over Bruce, and then spring down at him. It made a terrible shriek and caught him in the legs. Bruce fell.

I looked frantically round for a stick or a rock, some kind of weapon, but saw nothing. My eyes flicked over Kate's spyglass, and suddenly her grandfather's scribbled words burst from my memory – 'the sight of my spyglass makes them scatter in an instant'. I snatched it up and ran.

'Stay here!' I shouted at Kate.

Bruce had rolled over on to his back, kicking with his feet to keep the cloud cat at bay. The cat squealed, its jaws wide, feinting with its head. Bruce shouted; I shouted, too. I scooped up a stone and hurled it. It struck the cat's flank, and the creature turned clumsily. Bruce scrambled back, and I caught a glimpse of his torn trousers, ragged with blood. I stood, a few metres from the cat, my arms spread wide, brandishing the spyglass like a sword and cursing to clear a Tasmanian pub. The cloud cat froze, its eyes following the frenzied motion of the spyglass.

'Go on! Get out of here!' I bellowed, churning my arms, trying to look big, and make enough noise to scare it off.

But it did not flee. It stood its ground, watching me, fur bristling.

Bruce was slowly crawling backwards. Shakily, he stood.

'Run, Bruce!' I shouted. 'Go!'

He ran. He was injured but he could still run. The cat kept its eyes fixed on me. The spyglass wasn't as terrifying as I'd hoped. The creature was spitting and hissing, and its rump kept dropping and I flinched every time, waiting for it to pounce. I stepped backward, never taking my eyes from the cat, slashing the spyglass through the air. The cloud cat stayed put. Back I went another step.

'Kate!' I shouted, without turning.

'Here,' she said.

'Stand up slowly.'

'I'm standing.'

I hoped Bruce was good and far away now. I hoped he had the sense to keep running and not stop until he reached the ship. He had his compass. Kate had mine. We wouldn't get lost.

'Don't move suddenly,' I said, still walking backwards. I felt Kate's icy hand take mine. The cloud cat was still in sight, hunched on the ground, making an unearthly growling sound.

'Leave your camera behind.'

'But—'

'Leave it.' My eyes did not stray from the cat. 'You'll need to run.'

'Yes.'

'Walk slowly backwards with me. We're just going to disappear nice and easy into the forest.'

We took two steps and I tripped. I landed heavily on my rump and the spyglass leapt from my hand and disappeared in the dense undergrowth. When I looked back up, the cloud cat was gone. Then I saw a cloudy flash overhead in the trees, and it was leaping towards us, clawed wings flared, jaws parted, shrieking.

I grabbed Kate's hand and we ran, hurtling through the trees. We didn't have long. It would outrun us in less than a minute and we'd have to face it, try to scare it off somehow. We were bigger and heavier than it, but it was stronger and faster. Its teeth.

I risked a look back and saw it crackling from tree to tree like flame through a parched forest.

I wanted to scream. Kate did. Up ahead I saw the trees thinning and what looked like an open field on the far side. I tugged at Kate's hand, leading her towards it. That was our chance. The cat liked trees. It felt safe in them. If only we could get free of the forest, we would be out of danger.

16

RESCUE

We burst from the trees and were in a field of tall grass. Before I could even check to see if the cloud cat was following, the sun was blotted out and I heard a great droning sound behind us. I spun and saw the belly of an airship passing overhead, so low I could feel the powerful wash from its propellers, and smell its engine fumes. The ship cast a great shadow over the field. In the trees at the forest's edge, I caught a glimpse of the cloud cat cringing against a branch, watching the ship, watching us.

I whirled back to the airship. It took my mind a few seconds to catch up, for at first I thought it was the *Aurora*. But how could it be? This ship was much smaller, only a third its size. It came in for landing in the field, nose to the wind. Rescue: someone had been searching for us and now they'd found us! She slowed herself swiftly, and crew were hopping out from the hatches and taking the lines and holding her down. In the centre of the field was a tall mooring mast, and there atop its peak were two men catching hold of the nose lines as the ship nudged up against the locking cone. Then I knew.

I pulled hard on Kate's hand, trying to turn her back to the trees. I recognized the ship's night-coloured skin, the complete absence of any markings on her rudder or belly, and I knew what she was and who she carried.

'What're you doing?' Kate demanded, trying to pull free. 'We've been rescued! Hello! Hello!' she shouted out, waving.

'Shut up!' I hissed. 'It's the pirates!'

But it was too late. One of the landing crew had turned in our direction. We'd been sighted. Now it was Kate's turn to tug at me, but I stood stock still, grasping her hand tight.

'Matt? Come on! Run!'

'Keep waving,' I told her, and I lifted my hand and waved at the pirates. 'Hello there!' I hollered. 'Hello!'

'What are you doing?' Kate sobbed.

I kept waving. 'If we run, it tells them we know they're pirates. It means we might have friends to warn. They'll chase us; they will search and find the ship and we will all be lost. Do you understand?'

'Yes,' she said quietly.

'There's nowhere to run anyway,' I said. 'The cat is still in the trees.'

I saw her take a glance; I'm not sure if the cloud cat was still there at the forest's edge. It didn't matter.

We jogged towards the pirate ship, still waving.

'Here's the story,' I told Kate, inventing as we ran. 'We were bound for the Hawaiis in a small airship out of Van Diemen's Land. We got caught in that terrible typhoon and were sunk. I'm the cabin boy. You're a passenger. We are the only two who survived. All others were lost, including your mother. We washed up here on the island. Smile. We think we've just been rescued by nice friendly people.'

'But won't they recognize us from the *Aurora*?'

'No.' I was gambling they wouldn't have had the time or interest to notice what we looked like; they'd been intent on other things.

If we could lie, if we could make them believe we were castaways, perhaps we would have a chance. After our run through the forest, we looked bedraggled enough, our faces sweaty and streaked, our clothes rumpled and torn in places. It was good luck that I was not in my ship's uniform to give us away, and that Kate had decided on a streamlined outfit rather than a sundress. A proper dress would have sunk her to the ocean floor in heavy seas, and made our story a farce. In harem pants, though, it was possible she could have swum. Thank heavens we were not carrying the camera equipment and spyglass. Now I only prayed that Bruce would not come running out after us and give us all away.

My belt.

'Run ahead of me for a second,' I urged Kate. 'Block their view.'

I pretended to stumble in the tall grass, and as I hit the ground, I ripped my belt out through the loops and left it. On its buckle was the Lunardi Line insignia.

I scrambled back up and continued running. We reached the landing field proper, where the grass had been scythed low. The pirates, I saw, had laid down a rail track in a great circle around the mooring mast, so that the airship, fixed at her nose, could pivot with the wind, her stern rolling along on its set of landing wheels. It had taken a great deal of work, and it had been done well. The field's placement was ideal for keeping the ship hidden, ringed around by hills and forest on either side. It would make a difficult approach and landing, but the ship was small, and manoeuvrable as a tiger shark. I remembered her agility as she'd stalked us through the night skies.

'Thank goodness!' I called out when we were near the crew. 'We worried we'd never be found! Are you from the Sky Guard?'

Their eyes were on us, and I prayed again we would not be recognized.

'Who the feck are they?' I heard one of the pirates mutter to his comrade.

It was quite something to be running towards a group of pirates, trying to look as overjoyed as a child unwrapping Christmas presents. Many of them wore little more than cut-off trousers and undershirts, their muscled bodies greasy with sweat. Their faces were whiskery.

'Where'd you two come from then?' one of them asked, striding forward.

This was the one Szpirglas had called Mr Crumlin, and I assumed he was first mate, if air pirates went by such titles. He was a great grizzly bear of a fellow, his bare shoulders and arms sprouting more hair than seemed decent or practical in such heat.

We stopped before him. I was puffed as I began my story, and I was glad, for it made it harder to feel nervous about the lies I was spewing. And as I talked another conversation started its chatter in my head. What good could come of this? These were the wretches who had murdered our officer, who'd been happy to leave us to a watery grave after their ship slit us stem to stern. What chance have we of getting away alive from them? Maybe we should have taken our chances in the forest with the cloud cat; we should have run until our lungs burst. But I kept all these worries imprisoned in my skull and finished my tale of storms and shipwrecks and castaways.

'We'd better let the captain hear this,' said Crumlin.

But he had no need to summon him, for down the gangway came Vikram Szpirglas himself, looking dashing, I had to admit, striding towards us as though he had a mastery of all four elements. He was a handsome man; he should have been someone admirable and good, but all I could see in him now was the murderer who'd held a pistol to Mr Featherstone's head and pulled the trigger.

'They say they were wrecked in the typhoon,' Crumlin told his captain.

'Good heavens!' said Szpirglas, all concern.

And so I repeated my story for him. 'You're from the Sky Guard, aren't you?' I asked, trying to appear dim-witted.

Szpirglas smiled benevolently. It made my skin crawl. 'Of course we are, dear boy. I'm Captain Anglesea. It was a bit of good luck that you happened to be swept to this island where we have a large station. It's quite an establishment really. You two are very fortunate indeed.'

Almost every second I thought: He is playing. He knows.

'Mr Crumlin,' he said to his mate. 'Take them to the village and make them comfortable. I'll be along shortly after I oversee the docking.'

Village? I thought.

'Are you hungry?' Szpirglas asked us. 'You poor creatures must be ravenous.'

'We found some banana trees,' Kate said quietly.

'Very good. Clever children. But you'll still be wanting a proper meal after so long. I'm ready for a good meal myself. We'll have a feast together and I want to hear about your mishap.'

Szpirglas strode off to oversee the berthing of his ship. His crew were already smartly getting on with the business of unloading and loading and refuelling, inspecting her skin for wear and tear. It might have been a scene from any harbour around the world, but it did not comfort me now. From the cargo bay doors and gangplanks came metal barrels of Aruba fuel, crates of food, a squealing pig, and other unmarked crates which surely must contain the pirates' despicable loot.

Crumlin smiled at us, but it came out like more of a grimace. He did not share Szpirglas' talent for malignant fakery.

'This way then,' he said.

As Kate and I followed him, my plan came to me. The *Aurora* wasn't ready to fly yet. But by tomorrow, midday, she'd be fully refuelled and airworthy. We would have to bide our time today with the pirates, making sure they believed we were the two sole survivors of some shipwreck. They would not be suspicious of two grateful and gullible children. And tomorrow, in the early hours of the morning, while they all slept, we would make our break, cross the island, and warn the *Aurora*. By the time the pirates noticed us missing, they would have little time to launch a search of the entire island, and by then we'd be airborne.

Crumlin led us to the edge of the landing field and on to a well-maintained path into the forest. Of all the islands in the Pacificus, we'd had the misfortune to crash on the one Vikram Szpirglas had made his secret base. But this was no makeshift hideaway. At my first glimpse through the trees, I saw that village was indeed the right word for it. There was a large bamboo lodge, a wide generous veranda on all sides, with lots of proper windows and a high-pitched roof of palm fronds, and arranged all around it were well over a dozen smaller bamboo huts and houses. There were fenced pens with chickens and pigs snuffling about, and more people milling around than could have come from the airship just now. With a start I realized there were women here too. They were dressed in saris and sarongs and all manner of loose-fitting clothing, their arms and necks and ears bejewelled, and they ran to embrace their pirate mates and were hugged and kissed and swirled around through the air. And children! Some of the women carried babies in their arms, and toddlers ran about underfoot.

This place was a proper home. It must have taken years for the pirates to establish it. They had cleared as few trees as possible, and I realized that even if you were to fly low overhead, you would not see their habitation. Beyond their buildings, the forest thinned and I saw that we were high on a promontory overlooking the island's windward shore.

It looked as if the village had taken a bit of a beating in the typhoon, sheltered as it was behind the trees. Men were up on the roofs, repairing the thatch. One shed was tilting over crazily, and there were palm fronds strewn all around the village. Despite all that, the place had an undeniably trim and tidy look to it. Clearly there was a ground crew who stayed on the island when the others were out pillaging. A little kingdom Szpirglas had created for himself here. The thought made me go all queasy, for I knew how the pirates would guard the secrecy of this place. What were the chances of them letting us escape, even if they did think us harmless children?

My plan seemed a paltry thing now. We ought to have run when we had the chance. I thought of Bruce limping wounded through the jungle. I thought of the ship, filling, but not yet ready to launch. I felt as close to despair as I ever had in my life. But when I looked at Kate, I pulled myself together. It had been my plan, and she was playing along with it, and I must do my best.

Crumlin led us to the main lodge and up the steps to the veranda, which was veiled all round, most civilized, with mosquito cloth. We sat at a large table and Crumlin told us we could wait here for the captain to return. There followed a great deal of grunting and satisfied moaning as he unlaced his great black boots and set them thunking on the bamboo deck. He had the biggest, hairiest toes I'd ever beheld, and it made me quite ill just looking at them. His big toe alone could squash a coconut. I wondered that any airship would support a man of his bulk.

The late afternoon breeze off the water blew amongst the trees and cooled us. I longed to talk properly with Kate, but we had no chance with that great hulk Crumlin there, massaging his feet. I was glad we were upwind. Looking through the doorway into the lodge itself, I saw a large hall that was obviously meant for a dining room, arranged with tables and chairs. Then I caught sight of something on the wall, and stared in amazement.

'What're you looking at, then?' said Crumlin suspiciously, turning to follow my gaze. He chuckled. 'Oh, that. Never seen one of them before, I'd wager.'

Kate had seen it too now, and I shot her a look so she wouldn't say anything.

It was the head of a cloud cat, mounted on the wall like a trophy. Its wings had been nailed up on either side.

'What is it?' I made myself ask.

'Freaks of nature, is what they are. You only see them in these parts. They fly over the island a couple of times a year. Shot that one meself, right out of the sky. They're fast. Damn hard to hit, I can tell you. We all have a go at them whenever we can. Good sport. Four or five we've brought down over the years.'

I pictured Crumlin, a rifle to his face, and suddenly understood why the cloud cats had been afraid of Benjamin Molloy's spyglass. When he'd raised it to his eye, they must have mistaken it for a gun.

'I don't think it's very sporting at all,' said Kate. 'They've done nothing to harm you.'

Crumlin gave a low growl of laughter. 'Not so, young Miss. There's one that lives here on the island. He used to come slinking around our village sometimes. He'd throttle our chickens, and gut our pigs alive. Had a go at me once too. Look here.' Crumlin rolled up a trouser leg to reveal a long red crescent of scar tissue on his hairy calf. 'He's saucy as a cat, with as many lives too. Don't know how many shots we've taken at him. The winged devil's learned his lesson, though; he stays away from the village now.'

'Well, it's lucky we didn't come upon him,' I said, looking at Kate. I was worried she might go saying

313

more, but she just grunted, looking faintly ill. I wondered if the cloud cat was naturally vicious, or whether it was the pirates who had taught it to attack people. I couldn't help thinking of Bruce and his own injured leg. I hoped he was all right, and that he was well on his way back to the *Aurora*.

More and more men and women were filing into the lodge and there were a good many celebratory whoops and clinking of mugs, and it seemed a merry time was going to be had tonight, which suited me just fine. It would be all the easier to sneak away from pirates sunk in a drunken sleep.

Just then Szpirglas returned, jogging into the village amidst a general cheer from his men.

'Another successful mission for the Sky Guard, ladies and gentlemen!' he shouted grandly, to more applause. 'And look, we've just discovered these two castaways who had the courage to make it ashore after their ship was wrecked.'

He leapt up the steps to join us, as if he'd long been anticipating this meeting with the utmost glee.

'There you are,' he said, sitting down. 'Mr Crumlin, have you offered them some refreshments?'

Crumlin forced that grimace on to his face. 'Where are my manners,' he muttered. 'What shall I get for you?'

'Fresh mango juice I think,' said Szpirglas. 'To wet their parched tongues,' he added, and I thought I saw Crumlin suppress a smirk.

'Very good, sir,' he said and went off inside the lodge.

'Now, tell me everything,' said Szpirglas.

'We'd given up hope, hadn't we?' I said to Kate. 'And right here on the island, a Sky Guard station!'

Szpirglas smiled, but it was just a mouth smile, his eyes were cold and concentrated, and I knew my storytelling powers were about to be sorely tested.

'What was your vessel?' he asked.

'*Pegasus*, sir. She was twenty-five metres long, twin engine, G class. She was mostly for cargo and private charter. Eight crew under Captain Blackrock, and only two passengers. We were two nights out of Van Diemen's Land, heading north-easterly for Honolulu.'

I did not know how carefully these pirates monitored air traffic over Oceanica – for all I knew they could have flight plans of every ship within a thousand kilometres, or else how could they pinpoint their prey so accurately? But a small vessel could more easily slip through the cracks. It would not raise any suspicion, or so I hoped. My answer seemed to satisfy him.

'And you say the typhoon brought you down.'

I watched him as I spoke, alive to every movement of his face, every blink, every lift of his eyebrows and twitch of his mouth. The typhoon was unquestionable; it had been real, and would have posed a grievous threat to any small vessel caught in its bellows.

'The winds must have damaged one of our props. We were having engine trouble, sir, and losing altitude. We were levelled off at only thirty metres, but we might have been all right if it hadn't been for the wave. It was one of them rogues, sir, a big cliff of water from nowhere, working against the wind, and it came and clipped us as it crested. Knocked off our engines, our fins, and sent us spinning down.'

'God in heaven,' said Szpirglas, all amazement and sympathy. 'It is surely an airshipman's worst nightmare. I'm amazed anyone survived. Did you have time to make a distress call?'

'I was not in the bridge, sir, I don't know. But I would doubt it. It all happened so quickly.'

I knew what he wanted to discover. If we'd sent a distress call, and it had been heard, there might be a search under way. And a search might come close to his island kingdom. I didn't want him to think we were bringing danger to him.

Crumlin returned and put two mugs of mango juice before us. For Szpirglas there was a crystal glass of ruby wine. I drank, for I was truly thirsty. It was a sweet concoction, but cool and refreshing, and I drained the mug nearly to the bottom in one breath, and broke away, panting more than I needed to.

'You must be parched,' said Szpirglas. 'Poor lad.'

He did not recognize us, of that I was quite certain now. I'd been watching him as he watched me, and could see no flicker in his face. A huge relief it was, for if he remembered us, all was instantly lost.

'Are you sure you were the only two to survive?' Szpirglas asked.

'I don't know,' I said. 'We were all tumbled around terribly, it seemed to happen all in a trice.'

Like any game of pretend, you had to half believe it to play properly. All I had to do was remember my fears as the *Aurora* had come close to crashing in the sea. 'We hit the water, and I must have lost consciousness for a few moments. The ship was already starting to fill. It was only by chance I came across Miss Simpkins here.'

It was not a good choice of name, but it just fluttered into my head, and I seized it. Kate did not even flicker. Through all my talking she'd dutifully hung her head and her face had a crumpled look – which was not hard to fake right now. Just looking at her made me feel like bawling. Kate was born to this kind of play-acting, probably came from all her reading and fanciful stories. I could have handed the whole thing over to her and had a nap.

'We got out only just in time,' I said.

'If it weren't for Mr Cruse here, I'd surely have perished,' said Kate, and she said it with such gratitude and conviction that I wasn't angry she'd spoken out. I'd wanted to do all the talking, so we didn't start contradicting each other, but I'd doubted she'd be able to stay quiet so long, and let me hog all the story spinning. I supposed it didn't matter she'd used my real name. It meant nothing to the pirates.

'You had a lifeboat of some kind, surely,' Szpirglas asked.

'No, sir, there wasn't any time to deploy them. We just

cracked into the drink, and scrambled up on to a bit of busted hull that was like a kind of raft, and we clung to that. We didn't see anyone else.'

At this Kate covered her face with her hands; she didn't sob, she just shivered, and made a kind of whimpering sound.

'Her mother was aboard too,' I explained to Szpirglas. 'She was our other passenger.'

'You poor thing,' said Szpirglas. 'Well, it's too early to give up hope, Miss Simpkins.'

'Do you think?' Kate asked, staring at the table and lifting her big eyes slowly. 'Might she still be alive?'

'We will do all we can to find out,' said Szpirglas in soothing tones. 'This region isn't very well charted, but there are countless little coral atolls dotting the ocean. It's possible, yes, she might be safe and sound somewhere else, and just awaiting rescue. As soon as our ship is refuelled and my men fed and rested, and we have a day's light ahead of us, we will set a search in motion.'

Kate beamed at him, with such sincerity that I felt momentarily confused.

'Thank you,' she said.

It took me a moment to puzzle it out, why Szpirglas was being so kind to us. Why did he bother wasting his time on this game? Then I understood. He wanted us to relax; he wanted us to feel safe and content; he wanted to know everything we knew, in the hopes of gaining something from us. It wasn't simply a matter of him finding out if there would be others searching for us.

Maybe he also wanted to know what our ship was carrying. Was there any precious wreckage that might have washed ashore?

'You have no idea where you are, then?'

I knew I must be very careful here. I did not want Szpirglas to think the secrecy of his base was at risk. He would surely never release anyone who could give its co-ordinates away.

'No, sir, we were tumbled around so much I haven't a clue.'

'But your bearing before the typhoon?'

'I don't much take an interest in that,' I said, trying to look sheepish. 'Captain says I'd get lost on the ship, if I weren't told where to go, I've got no sense of direction.'

'No matter, no matter,' said Szpirglas. 'You're safe with us.'

Another pirate came and put some new mugs of mango juice before Kate and me.

'There's food coming, don't fear,' said Szpirglas merrily. 'I can smell a feast cooking and it won't be long before it's served, eh, Mr Crumlin?'

'That's for certain, Captain,' said the bearish mate. 'Pork.'

'Excellent,' Szpirglas winked at me. 'I can't abide anything that swims, I'm afraid. Rather awkward on an island, don't you think?'

Kate and I both made ourselves chuckle. There was a brief silence, and it seemed Szpirglas had lost interest in us, but I knew our interrogation was far from over.

'A long flight for a small vessel, Van Diemen's Land to the Hawaiis,' Szpirglas mused. 'Your captain must be an experienced one.'

'Yes, he is.'

'Strange then he didn't see the warnings of the typhoon.'

'It seemed to come out of nowhere,' I said, and almost felt defensive, for I had missed it too, weather eye that I was.

'It did come on sudden, I'll grant you that. We caught just the tail end of it, and it gave us a shake, did it not, Mr Crumlin?'

The mate gave a curt nod. 'I'll see what's what with dinner,' he said, and went inside the lodge.

'Weather does come on quickly in these parts, you are right,' Szpirglas said. 'Well, you two are lucky you survived and we must be hopeful there will be others. Whereabouts did you two wash up then?'

He was watching me carefully, and for the first time I felt myself falter. He would want to see if there was wreckage there to confirm our story.

I sighed and tried to look abashed. 'I'm not quite sure. We've walked about quite a lot, looking for inhabitants, and I've got turned around. It was a rocky stretch, not shallow, and we had to swim for it. We're lucky the seas were calmer then, for we could easily have been dashed against the rocks. As it was, our bit of raft floated off and we were left to scramble up on to the rocks. I think it was somewhere off that way.' I pointed, and made sure to point in the opposite direction to the *Aurora*.

Szpirglas nodded without so much of a flicker in his eye. 'And that's where you've made your camp?'

'Well, we didn't really bother with a proper camp or anything.' I didn't want him checking for signs. 'Couldn't even make a fire.'

'We tried with some sticks,' Kate offered, 'but neither of us had any luck.'

Szpirglas gave a hearty laugh. 'It is a deucedly hard business, making fire without matches, I agree.'

'We just slept there the first night, and waited the next day, hoping we'd see some others. But,' I looked over at Kate, in consideration of her missing mother, 'then we moved on, hoping we'd find someone, or get to higher ground where we'd have a view of something or other.'

They would check the coast, and would find nothing. But that was why I'd been careful to mention the raft had floated off. I wanted to make sure I left no loose ends to my story.

'Ah, there he is!' cried Szpirglas suddenly, and I looked over my shoulder to see a striking, tall, raven-haired woman walking towards us. But it was not the woman Szpirglas beheld with such pleasure; it was the small boy she led by the hand. Not more than four, this boy, I'd say, and pulling free from the woman's grasp now so he could charge headlong up the veranda steps and into Szpirglas' waiting arms.

'I've missed you, lad!' Szpirglas said, lifting the boy on to his lap. 'Thank you, Delilah,' he said to the woman, and she nodded obediently and departed. 'This,' he said proudly to me and Kate, 'is my son, Theodore.'

I could feel my surprise, like an earthquake's tremor, about to ripple across my face, but hoped I managed to stop it in time. It seemed impossible that a cold-hearted thief and murderer like Szpirglas should have a son. And a handsomer little fellow I'd never seen, with huge brown eyes and a perfect bowed mouth, and wavy hair that would become curly like his father's one day, eyebrows that made his whole face seem intent.

'Hello, Theodore,' Kate and I said, in almost perfect unison, with the same forced jollity.

'Did you have good adventures?' Theodore asked his father.

'The things I saw!' Szpirglas exclaimed.

'Well, go on and tell me,' the boy said with studied patience, as though this were a game they were both used to playing.

'Well, there's a great deal to tell. Do you know what I saw though?'

'What?'

'A night rainbow. I did, I swear.'

'What did it look like?'

'Like a normal rainbow, only cast by the moon's glow it was, all across the midnight sky. All the colours you can imagine, it spanned one horizon to another.'

'I want to see one!' the boy said indignantly.

'You will. When you're older, and we're flying together, we'll stay up late on the perfect night of a full moon and wait for one.'

'What else?'

'I saw the seahorse again.'

'The giant one?'

'And he wasn't by himself any more. We were sailing low over the ocean and that water was clear as crystal and I could see them all below the surface. There was a whole herd of them this time. Brilliant orange they were, each as big as a dolphin, flying through the water.'

I listened, momentarily swept up in the beauty of his tales. Szpirglas' face and voice were completely altered as he talked to his son, with none of the sharp, mocking humour I'd seen in him aboard the *Aurora*, none of the danger. His eyes were as wide and guileless as those of his boy. Theodore listened, rapt. My father had once told me such stories.

It made me angry that such a man should have a son. This boy did not know who his father was, the things he'd done – and if he did, would it even have mattered? What did any of that have to do with him? Here was his father, the man who had adventures, who told glorious stories and held him on his lap and kissed his head. There was nothing else of importance.

'I brought you something,' Szpirglas said, 'and then it's off to bed with you.'

'What is it?' the boy asked, sitting bolt upright.

'I hope I didn't forget it . . .'

'Papa!'

'No, no, here it is.' Szpirglas rifled through his breast pocket and brought out a small gold astrolabe. I recognized it at once, for it used to rest in the display case of the *Aurora*'s A-Deck reception lounge. An artifact from airship days of old.

The boy took it in his small starfish hands.

'An astrolabe,' he breathed.

'Very good. With this, you can cross all the skies of the world, with nothing but the stars. Handsome thing, isn't it?' he said, looking at me.

'Very, sir,' I said.

'Now then, where's Delilah?' Szpirglas asked. She appeared as if conjured, and took Theodore's hand. The boy didn't want to leave his father.

'I'll see you first thing tomorrow,' promised his father. 'Shall we have breakfast together? You come and wake me the moment you're up, and we'll dine just you and me. But now, it's late for you. Goodnight, my son.'

I couldn't look away as he gathered his son once more in his arms and kissed his cheek. The boy kissed him back.

'His mother died in childbirth,' said Szpirglas as he watched his son led away by his nurse. 'He's a fine lad, don't you think?'

'Yes,' Kate said. 'He'll look like you when he's grown.'

'Do you think?' Szpirglas asked, pleased.

'Oh, yes.'

Dinner was served. The pirates were eager enough for it, judging by the surge of cheering from the dining hall. It looked like pork, but at a glance, I could tell it was overdone, and the rice looked a tad singed too. Chef Vlad would have had a fit if he'd seen it. He wouldn't have served it to the ship's cat, if we'd had one.

The pirates didn't mind. Through the doorway I could see all the men and women assembled inside, and they gave a thumping chorus of approval and set to it happily, cheered no doubt by the frothing mugs upon their tables.

Kate and I ate. We were castaways: we'd eaten next to nothing in two days. We were half starved. I sluiced the meal down with the mango juice that kept filling up our mugs, and felt better than I should have after eating such fare. Indeed, I felt almost relaxed and couldn't account for it. My thinking was clear and fast, and our situation didn't seem as dire as it had earlier. We were fooling Szpirglas; we would continue our play-acting and tell our shaggy dog stories, and then slip away under cover of night, back to our ship, and be gone.

The evening was cooling, and it was amazing how much fresher the air was here on the windward side of the island. For the first time in days I felt my sense of claustrophobia lift. From the veranda I saw the sun near the horizon, searing the ocean. The wonderful low light slanted through the trees, bathing everything red.

Szpirglas' wineglass sparkled as he raised it to his lips.

Inside the lodge, the women sang. The mango juice was delicious. The food did not taste so dry.

Suddenly my stomach clenched.

I was getting drunk. Some flavourless alcohol had been added to our mango juice, and I'd been guzzling it down like an idiot. So that was Szpirglas' game – he wanted the truth from us, and wasn't above gliding it out of us with drink. I looked at Kate, and she smiled back at me, her cheeks flushed. How pretty she looked. But we would say something foolish soon if we were not careful. I took a deep breath, tried to sharpen up my mind.

'How many other passengers were you carrying?' Szpirglas asked me.

'Just the two, sir. Miss Simpkins and her mother.'

'It was a private charter, then, was it?'

I nodded, and perhaps it was the lift of Szpirglas' eyebrow, but suddenly I realized my mistake. All along I thought it would be easier to explain away a smaller ship and fewer passengers. There would be less wreckage, fewer survivors who might wash up on the island. But Szpirglas saw what I hadn't. A private charter meant wealthy passengers. And if Kate was wealthy, how wealthy? Who would be glad to get her back? How much would they be willing to pay?

'Your wristwatch,' Szpirglas said to Kate, 'does it still work?'

I turned in dismay; I'd forgotten Kate had a wristwatch, concealed beneath the sleeve of her tunic up until now. It was a fancy-looking thing, too, the strap inlaid with some kind of jewels: I did not know their names, but they looked sparkly enough, and no doubt Szpirglas had instantly totted up their value in his head. Only someone wealthy would have a wristwatch as fine as this one. I felt sick.

'It does work, you know,' said Kate. 'Isn't that amazing, after being waterlogged and thrashed about?'

This was a clever bit of covering up on Kate's part, for the chances of a wristwatch surviving a shipwreck and sea journey aboard a raft were next to nil.

'A miraculous piece of machinery,' said Szpirglas. 'Swiss perhaps?'

'Icelandic, actually.'

'Now then, you must have loved ones you're both eager to contact,' said Szpirglas, putting down his fork and pushing back in his chair.

'Is it possible?' Kate asked, eyes widening with hope. 'My father will be desperate. He was waiting for us in the Hawaiis. Mother and I were visiting my aunt.'

'You all live in the Hawaiis, do you?' Szpirglas asked.

'Yes. Not originally. We moved there for my father's work.'

'And what work does your father do there?'

'He's the chief superintendent of police,' said Kate.

'Is he?' said Szpirglas, smiling.

'His work is very demanding, or he would have come with us on our trip.'

I did not know what to think of this invention. Was

she trying to deter Szpirglas from harming us, thinking he'd fear incurring the full wrath of the police? I did not like it – it might easily have the opposite effect on a man like Szpirglas. Worse, he might actually know the name of the police chief, in which case we had just been discovered as liars. But it was out now, and I would have to abide by its new rules. I wished Kate were not so enthusiastic at this game of deceit.

'Mr Crumlin, bring pen and paper for these two so they can write messages.' He turned to us. 'Make sure to include the address so we can telegram them for you.'

'Would you?' said Kate.

'And your family, too, my lad. Let them know you're all right.'

I nodded eagerly too, but a worry sprang into my head. No doubt they did have a wireless on board, but this was just a ruse. What they really wanted was to check on Kate's identity.

'We'll radio in the morning from our ship. We'll take off first thing and you can show us to the crash site – as close as you can recall anyway, and we can begin a search for your dear mother. After that, we can arrange for your passage on to the Hawaiis.'

'You're very kind, sir. Thank you,' said Kate.

'Not at all, Miss. It's a pleasure to assist such fine young people.' He looked at Kate as he said this, and I did not care for the look.

'Now, tonight, all you need do is rest yourselves. Our accommodation is a bit humbler than you're used to, no doubt, Miss Simpkins, but please take my private cabin for yourself. It will give you some comfort.'

'Oh, no, that's quite unnecessary.'

'I insist. Mr Cruse, you won't mind bunking with Mr Crumlin and me?'

'Not at all, no. Thank you.'

I'd feared as much. I'd assumed Kate and I were to be separated; but I hadn't counted on sharing a room with Szpirglas and his mate.

Mr Crumlin appeared with some dog-eared bits of paper and a bottle of ink.

'There you are,' said Szpirglas. 'Just a brief note to let them know you're well. No point in adding more worry to your traumas.'

What was I to do? I scribbled some note, and invented an address in Lionsgate City.

'And now you, Miss,' said Szpirglas, moving the nib and bottle over to her.

I could not imagine what she would write, but prayed she would invent some address. The message itself did not matter, but I wondered if Kate was thinking clearly.

'My father will be so relieved,' she said, 'and most grateful. Is there some way we can make a donation to the Sky Guard in thanks? I can think of no more worthier institution than yours.'

'You're very kind, Miss.'

'My father is most influential, and I'm sure he'd be only too happy to sing your praises.'

I wished she'd shut up about her father and all his money. She was not helping.

'Now then, let me speak to my steward and see about your cabin, Miss Simpkins.'

He and Mr Crumlin left us alone at the table. The other crew were still swilling and eating inside, the windows tipped open. There was much loud singing and cheering from them. We could speak together.

'Shush about your father,' I told her.

'Why?'

'He might think you're worth holding on to for a ransom.'

'We're escaping,' she said jauntily.

I frowned. Typical of her to have the fairy-tale plan. Easy as that. Let's just escape. Never mind that I'd be cooped up in a room with Szpirglas and his mate.

'Got it all figured out then, do you?'

'I do, actually. Can I finish off your mango juice?'

'No.' I pushed the mug away from her reaching hand. 'It's spiked with something. He's trying to get us drunk so we'd slip up if we were lying.'

'Good luck to him,' she said. 'I'm not in the slightest bit slipsy.'

'You just said slipsy.'

'I know. I was just teasing. Now listen,' she whispered, 'when everyone's asleep, we'll slip out of our rooms and get back to the ship. It'll be ready to take off by morning, won't it?'

She wasn't as dopey as I'd thought. 'That's what I'm

hoping,' I told her. 'Can you find your way across the landing field to the place we came out of the forest? Do you remember the way?'

'Of course,' she said, her nostrils narrowing a bit. 'I'm not as hopeless as you like to think.'

'Good. We'll meet there.' I thought briefly of the cloud cat, but it would be long gone by then, and surely it was not nocturnal: we'd always seen it during the day.

'Shall we set a time?' Kate asked.

'No point. These lads may be up to all hours whooping it up. Wait until it gets quiet, and make your run when you can. It'll be a big moon tonight, and clear, so keep to the shadows, there may be lookouts. Then just wait for me in the trees, if I'm not already there.'

I wished the plan could have been better. If I'd known where we were each to be lodged, we might have made a rendezvous sooner; as it was, we'd just have to do our best alone.

I saw Szpirglas coming back towards us and all I had time to say to Kate safely was, 'Don't fall asleep', and then we shut up. There could be no more planning. I only hoped that we'd played our parts well enough, and that Szpirglas thought us ignorant, and would not be expecting us to flee the village in the dead of night.

17

THE PIT

'You take the hammock, my lad,' Szpirglas said. 'It's sure to give you a good night's sleep, and you need it.'

'Oh, no, Captain Anglesea, sir, you should have it,' I said, trying to hide my dismay.

'Won't hear of it,' said Szpirglas, all courtesy. 'I've had my fill of hammocks aboard ship anyway. I'll be happy as a king to sleep on solid ground tonight.' He nodded at a reed mat on the floor. It was practically beneath my hammock.

'Thank you very much,' I said, feeling greasy with all the pork and potatoes and mango juice. 'You're very kind.' I protested no more, for I did not want to make him suspicious.

A hammock is a tricky thing to get into. Perch on the edge and it will flip you off. You've got to get right into the middle, fast. I hopped in backwards, and the ropes creaked like the devil's own accordion. You'd think the thing was spun from rusted gossamer. I swallowed. Getting off quietly would be next to impossible, especially with Szpirglas directly underfoot.

Crumlin was settling down into a second hammock. The room was actually his, and was off the dining hall in the big lodge. It was well past midnight and the last of the pirates had now left for their own huts and bunkhouses. I could only hope they would sleep deeply after all the grog they'd gulped.

Szpirglas looked at me and laughed.

'Do you mean to sleep in your boots, then?'

'Oh.' There they were, still on my feet. I tried to look surprised and laughed, for I had left them on in the hopes that no one would notice. I would need them in the forest, and I didn't want to waste time fumbling for them in the middle of the night.

With a heavy heart I unlaced them and carefully dropped them on the floor near the top of the hammock. I hoped I would not have to leave them behind.

'You'll sleep better for it, lad,' said Szpirglas, taking off his own boots.

I couldn't believe I was bunking down with pirates. Not an everyday sort of thing. It was a wonder to me they even slept; I couldn't imagine such men at rest, their faces smooth and innocent despite the wickedness of their hearts.

'You're an impressive lad, to survive what you did,' Szpirglas said, as he doused the oil lantern. 'You might give some thought to working for us, you know. Now that your own ship has been lost. We've need of a good cabin boy. Our last decided to leave us.'

At this Crumlin chuckled mirthlessly.

'That's very kind of you, sir. It'd be an honour to work with the Sky Guard.'

It must have been nerves, but I almost giggled in the dark. Maybe my chances of promotion were greater if I did ship out with pirates! I was assuming there might be more frequent opportunities aboard ship, what with crew members getting shot or thrown in jail. Surely Szpirglas could use an extra sailmaker.

I lay on my back, cradled by the creaking hammock. In the darkness I could feel Szpirglas' eyes boring into my shoulder blades. I didn't like being parted from Kate. I wasn't even sure where her cabin was; I'd visited the latrines earlier, and tried to get a sense of the village's layout, and imagined that Szpirglas' hut would be one of the nicer-looking ones, but one bamboo hut looked much like another to me. How typical of Kate de Vries to get the private cabin. I hoped she was nice and comfy, and feeling grateful she didn't have to smell Crumlin's boozy breath and whiffy socks. Probably she wasn't at all frightened. What could be more exhilarating than a pirate capture? It was something right out of her books.

Crumlin was already snoring, the great yak. Below me, Szpirglas was silent, but to me it sounded like the silence someone makes when they are pretending to be asleep. There's just something too still and rigid about it. My heart clattered so loudly I was worried it was making my hammock swing. I tried to smooth my breathing. I thought of the *Aurora*. I pictured the rubber hosing shuttling the hydrium from the cave and shushing it through the forest towards the ship. I imagined its whispered hiss as it filled the gas cells. I saw the gas cell slowly swelling, and the *Aurora* growing firmer and stronger. And the hissing sound got louder and louder and my thoughts streamed off up into the air and stars and –

I had to seize hold of myself and yank myself back awake. No more calming thoughts for me now. I prayed Kate would not let herself fall asleep, for the urge was so strong. I cursed my own stupidity at guzzling so much of the pirates' drink. It might well have been poison. And why hadn't it been?

I was fairly certain now that Szpirglas meant to keep Kate for ransom, but he would have no use for me. Unless he meant to press me into service. But no, I doubted his intentions for me were so sunny. If I did not escape, he would dispense with me.

Was he hoping I'd sleep, or hoping I'd make an escape so he could follow me? It was a sickening thought. He'd put me in this infernal hammock for a reason. Maybe he wasn't sure I'd bolt, but if I did, he wanted to know about it.

I wondered how Bruce was making out. His leg would slow him down, and night might have fallen before he'd reached the *Aurora*. Would he keep walking through the darkness, or wait for the dawn to continue?

I rolled on to my stomach. What a noise that made, but I figured they'd be even more suspicious if I made no sounds at all. Everyone shuffles and shimmies about when sleeping. I cracked open an eye and looked down at Szpirglas. His eyes were closed and his breathing calm. He seemed genuinely asleep.

In the smudgy darkness of the room, I looked about at my possible exits. There was the door which opened out into the hall of the lodge. And there was a window, big enough to get through. It was hinged at the top and held open with a bamboo stick. The door was out of the question. Earlier someone had slumped drunkenly against it and fallen asleep in the hallway. His shadow blotted out the crack under the door, and I heard his great racking snores.

It had to be the window.

My hammock was bolted to the wall, quite close to the window. I didn't dare try to swing myself out of the hammock, for I feared the noise it would make. The hammock would have to be my tightrope.

Now was the time.

I looked down at my boots. If I stretched, I might just grab them. But I would have to lean way over, and that would make the hammock rock, and I might end up getting spilled out with a rusty pirate-rousing shriek. Even if I could snatch them up, I'd just have to hold them, and I needed both hands free now. I never thought I'd look at a pair of boots with such longing. I removed my socks and placed them quietly on the hammock. I must be barefoot for the acrobatics I was about to perform. My stockinged feet would get awfully bloodied and bruised in the forest, but that would be a small price to pay for freedom.

Flat on my belly I dragged myself up along the hammock, towards the wooden dowel from which all the netting was strung. The hammock creaked quietly. It wanted to roll. It wanted to pitch me off across the room and on to Szpirglas' chest.

I would not let it.

With my hands on the dowel, I slowly knelt, bringing one knee up at a time, keeping perfect balance. I stood, feet planted wide.

The hammock sighed.

I fixed my eyes to the window.

Below me Szpirglas gave a snort. I dared not look down for fear of losing my balance. I stood, hovering above him, an acrobat. If he'd seen me, he would speak. If he said nothing, he was still asleep.

He said nothing.

I stepped nimbly on to the ends of the dowel, my feet curling around the rope and wood. There was a metre between me and the window.

I leapt. I spread my arms like wings and when I landed on the windowsill I made myself believe my bones were hollow and I was so light the wood would scarcely know my weight. My feet gripped the narrow sill and my hands reached up and touched the window's upper frame.

Lighter than air I was.

But not light enough, for with a rattle, the stick

holding the window jiggled and slipped and fell outside on to the veranda. The window started swinging down; in less than a tick it would slam shut.

I took one of my hands off the frame and caught the window with my spread fingers against the glass. The hinges gave a little whine. I closed my eyes, breathed, waited. Behind me, Crumlin and Szpirglas made not a sound.

I have walked the back of the *Aurora* in a gale.

I have swung across the ocean from airship to balloon.

I can do this.

Someone was sleeping outside on the veranda, just to the right of the window.

I held the window up as far as it would go and jumped through. I kept my arm up high so it would catch the window as it fell back shut, and as my feet cushioned my silent fall on the veranda, the window swung back and pincered my hand against the sill. But there was no sound: the shriek of pain was only in my head. Gingerly I took my fingers out, found the stick lying against the belly of a sleeping pirate, and propped the window back open. I padded across the veranda, climbed the railing and sprang off, picking for my landing site a place without crackly leaves or branches. I landed in a crouch and froze, looking all around, drinking in the darkness and watching for movement.

I wanted to find Kate's cabin, but I did not know which one it was, and I was afraid of wasting time. I would just have to hope she'd get out on her own.

I started moving, seeking out the shadows for cover. And then I was into the trees.

I ran. My eyes had adjusted to the dark, sharp as an owl's. I saw by starlight and moonlight filtered through the branches and leaves. The air was velvet. I could run all night, I felt that strong. I was a wolf. My feet barely touched the ground. They did not hurt. I was free of the pirate's room. I flew through the forest. In the landing field the moon shone darkly on the moored airship and the tall grass. I would stick to the trees, and run all the way around to the far side where Kate and I had first emerged. Without my belt, my trousers were a bit loose around my hips. Every once in a while I had to give them a good tug. But my lungs did not burn. I had no cramps. I kept running.

I was on the far side of the field now, and I slowed. I listened for Kate. I whispered her name. I looked around. I went a little deeper into the forest and whispered her name some more. I stared at the stars, and knew it was well past two. I pictured Kate in her cabin, peering through her window, about to begin her run.

I sat down against a tree near the field's edge and hugged my knees and waited. Cloud blotted out the moon for a moment, and it was truly dark. She would come before I counted to a hundred. But she did not. I gave her another hundred and then stood and walked along the field's border, whispering her name, fearing she was lost.

But she was not so helpless. She had found her way

from the ship across the island, down the bluff into the valley quite happily. She was capable. If she'd left her cabin, she would be here. Unless she'd been caught. Unless something was wrong.

My throat felt thick. I did not want to go back to the pirates' camp. I was free here in the woods. I felt I belonged to the night air, and I did not want to venture back and risk being caught. I wanted to run to the ship, my ship, and warn her and cast off.

I took a breath, stood, and started towards the pirate village.

I decided to risk it and run across the landing field, for it would be faster. I entered the village quietly as a deer, for I feared a trap. I lingered at the edges, looked towards the bungalows. There was no one in sight. I went to the first that seemed likely and found a window and saw half dozen men sleeping on mats and hammocks. I went to the next, and through the window saw the nurse Delilah sleeping on a mat near Szpirglas' son, Theodore. The next hut over was the right one. It was a proper little house this, with furniture and a desk and a sofa and a bed, and on the bed was Kate fast asleep.

I skirted round the bungalow to the door and pulled at the handle, but it was made fast from the inside. I dared not knock. Back to the window I went. Luckily it was not locked. I pushed it all the way open, and hoisted my belly over the sill. Headfirst I slid into the room, landing in a handstand.

I went to her side and put a hand on her shoulder. The fragrance of deep sleep was all around her. I whispered her name in her ear. She made a small sound, and her eyelids crinkled like she wanted me to go away and leave her be. I gave her a rough shake and said her name again, this time not so gently.

Her eyes opened and she looked at me most reproachfully for a few seconds. Then her eyes flicked around the room in horror.

'I fell asleep,' she breathed.

'Come on now.'

'I fell asleep,' she said again in disbelief. 'I'm so sorry.' She was fully dressed at least. I headed for the door.

'Do I have time to visit the toilets?' she asked.

I stared back at her, incredulous. 'You can go in the forest later.'

'I certainly won't,' she said.

'Suit yourself.'

'All very well for boys,' she muttered.

I turned the latch and opened the door.

Szpirglas stood before me.

'This is most improper,' he said.

I had no words.

'I thought I recognized you,' Szpirglas said, 'but I wasn't sure, and you play-acted so well. I thought to myself: if they try to get away, they know who we are – and they've got another way off this island.'

'I don't know what you mean, Captain Anglesea!' I said desperately.

341

He struck me hard across the face. 'You know my real name, boy! Why didn't you run when you first saw us at the landing field, eh? You're protecting someone, and something.' He shoved me back and strode into the bungalow, followed by his mate. 'Mr Crumlin, rouse a search party immediately. We may have a ship to salvage. Where is the *Aurora*?'

'Your props tore us to shreds!' I told him. 'The ship crashed. Only some of us got off.'

'No. You're lying. Where is she?'

I stopped talking.

'Perhaps your fancy friend here will be more co-operative. What do you say? You seem attached to the girl. It might upset you to see us torture her. Tell me what I need to know, and save her from torment. How does that strike you?'

He was smiling as he said this, as though it was another of his gentlemen's jests, all in the best of fun.

'To the north-west,' I lied.

Szpirglas looked at me with disgust.

'There's no place there where a ship could land. I see you don't take me at all seriously, lad.'

'The ship did not land,' I said doggedly. 'She ditched and some two dozen of us made it ashore.'

I saw in his face that same cold anger as when he'd shot Mr Featherstone. His gun was holstered through his belt, and I knew he could use it on me at any moment.

'Let's take them both to the pit, Mr Crumlin.'

Szpirglas seized Kate by the arm, and Crumlin grabbed me in his butcher's block fists and marched me out of the bungalow. Even if I could struggle free they'd shoot me in the back. We crossed the village and took the path towards the airfield, then turned off on to another path I hadn't noticed before. The smell of mangoes bloomed heavily in the air. In the speckled starlight I saw huge spools of hosing near a great stony mound. Set into the stone's face at an angle was a narrow metal hatch. In its middle was a round collared opening, capped right now. Crumlin grabbed the hatch's handle and pulled it open. Hydrium hissed out loudly from the dark shaft.

The entire island seemed porous with hydrium. No wonder this place was so precious to the pirates. Hidden, and with an eternal supply of lifting gas.

'Your ship was gutted,' Szpirglas said as if I'd personally insulted him. 'She should have sunk.'

'She did sink.'

'I think you managed to save her somehow. Or slow her enough to land here. I applaud your captain and crew. You must have been mending her at a furious pace.'

I said nothing. Szpirglas was smiling, as though marvelling at our ingenuity.

'Now then,' he said nodding at the shaft, 'the fall isn't much, just enough to bruise you up some. It's the hydrium that will kill you. There's no room for air down there. You start telling me the truth, or you both go down.'

343

My entire body burned with cold. Not even in my worst nightmares had I imagined such powerlessness. My legs were weak. I could not run. I could not fly.

'You first then,' said Szpirglas to Kate. 'If I'm to ransom you I'll need your parents' particulars, not that pretty address in Honolulu you concocted.'

'I'll not tell you,' said Kate, giving him one of her nostril-narrowing gazes. I was amazed she had the courage at such a time.

'Excellent,' said Szpirglas. 'I'm most impressed. Of course, the alternative for you is a particularly nasty death.'

She said nothing, only looked at me. I nodded. She told Szpirglas her real name and address.

'A fancy address for a fancy girl. Very good. Now, Mr Cruse, the whereabouts of your ship.'

'There's no ship,' I said once more. 'Only some survivors, on the island's leeward side.'

He looked at me thoughtfully, almost sympathetically, I thought. 'Take heart, Mr Cruse, there are only three or four places on the island where one could land a vessel the size of the *Aurora*. It will not be hard for us to scout out.'

'You'll not find any ship,' I said, lying in vain even now. The sickly gush of hydrium was giving me a headache.

'It's a shame,' Szpirglas said. 'I had no intention of damaging the *Aurora*. You must blame Mother Nature and her storm winds. I take no pleasure in killing. As it is, you must know I can never let you leave the island. I've got a whole village to take care of, men and women and children. My own son. This is my home. I can't have anyone giving me away. Last year, some benighted fool in a hot-air balloon came bumbling over the island and had a good long look. We had to go after him and slit his envelope and make sure he'd never see land again. He was a sick old man; I don't think he would have lasted long anyway. I didn't enjoy doing it, but it was not a choice I had.'

I looked at Kate, pale in the starlight, staring with silent hatred at the man who'd helped kill her grandfather. I now understood the last entry in Benjamin Molloy's journal: 'Airship in the distance. Will signal for help.' It hadn't been the *Aurora* he'd signalled, but the pirates' airship.

Szpirglas looked at Kate. 'Your parents only need to *think* you're alive for me to ransom you,' he said, and he gave her a shove that sent her sprawling down the shaft into darkness.

'No!' I shouted, but already Crumlin had me by the shoulders and was half lifting, half pushing me towards the shaft opening. I kicked and struggled and jammed my feet against the sides, but they battered me until finally I was dangling over the pit, and then with one great push I was sliding down on my backside. Darkness gobbled me up. The steep slope fell away altogether and there was a big drop and I hit the ground. All the breath was knocked out of me.

Only the faintest pulse of light slanted down from the open hatch, at least ten metres overhead. Kate lurched towards me, wheezing. The cave floor was scored with countless little hydrium vents, and the gas boiled invisibly all around us, leaving no room for air. When the metal hatch clanged shut we were plunged into a blackness more total than I had ever known. I had Kate by the hand. An hour ago I was free in the forest, running through the night.

I forced myself up, staggered forwards until my outstretched hand hit a wall. Too steep to climb. I kept moving, smacking at the rock. Too steep, no footholds, no way out here. A geyser of hydrium blasted me in the face, making my head spin. I tripped and fell, my nose in the dirt and –

Breathed.

Air, a little pool of it, lay silent and heavy against the earth, undisturbed. I grabbed Kate and pushed her head to the ground. She struggled at first, thinking I'd gone mad.

'Breathe,' I croaked.

It wasn't much, just enough to keep our hearts kicking, for a little while.

'What now?' was all she could say.

I shook my head, grunted. Didn't want to waste air on words. This was a cruel way to kill someone. Much better to be shot, or thrown off a cliff into the waves.

I felt a little eddy of hydrium slip into my shirtsleeve, the fabric ballooning. Its lift was so powerful, my arm started to rise. My sluggish brain began to work.

'Take your harem pants off!' I told Kate.

'What?'

'They're perfect,' I gasped. I grabbed at the waist of her harem pants and yanked them down. I heard her give a yelp. I was too breathless and too muddy-brained to explain more. The material of my own trousers and shirt was too porous, but Kate's pantaloons were silky, just like the ship's impermeable gas cells. They were baggy and a bit stretchy and they'd carry a lot of hydrium.

'Balloon,' I wheezed, and luckily she seemed to understand, because she stopped struggling and helped me peel the pants off. In the dark I worked as carefully and quickly as I could. I knotted both legs tightly at the ankles.

'This way,' I said, dragging her over to a hydrium vent. I felt its gush and held the harem pants, waist down, over it. Within seconds they were ballooning with gas. The pull started dragging me off my feet.

'Hold tight!' I gasped at Kate, guiding her hands to the waistband.

We rose very slowly, but up we flew, dangling beneath the ballooning harem pants. It was lucky we were slender, but even so the weight of us both was almost too much for it. I kept pushing off against the walls with my bare feet, trying to give us a little more lift.

Lighter than air, I thought groggily, that's our Mr Cruse.

After a moment I felt our balloon nudge up against something, and we were no longer moving. We'd hit the top of the shaft. Now where was the hatch? I kicked about with my feet until I hit something metal.

I prayed the hatch was not locked, but I could not recall seeing any bolt or bar on it. My lungs were ready to burst. I kicked harder, and the hatch jumped a bit, moonlight gilding the edges. I hoped the pirates had left us to our death, and we would not find them waiting for us. I'd need to kick harder to fling the hatch wide.

'Hold on,' I grunted to Kate.

I started swinging to get a bit of momentum, then gave a big kick and the hatch lurched open. Night. Sky. Air. The pent-up hydrium in the pit burst out in an eager rush, carrying Kate and me with it. Our harem-pant balloon bobbed us up out of the pit.

We collapsed on the ground, sucking air greedily. No pirates. I thought my lungs would never feel full. My heart clattered sickeningly. I looked at Kate and her lips were blue, her face white as cream. Slowly our bodies came back to themselves. I crawled over to where Kate's pants had fallen and brought them back to her. Like a sleepwalker she unknotted the legs, and pulled them back on over her knee-length cotton knickers. My body felt so heavy. Before my eyes, the night forest pulsed and shimmered. I closed the metal hatch; no sense giving notice we'd escaped.

Run, I thought but did not say, I was still so short of

breath. Back to the ship. Warn them. The pirates would be looking for them. We staggered into the trees. We were weak as newborn kittens – had the pirates been close at hand they could have lifted us by the scruffs of our neck and drowned us. I lurched along, Kate keeping pace at my side. Some part of my brain must have remembered the way. I was trying to calculate how long we had been gone. Since yesterday before noon. It was coming on dawn now. Almost eighteen hours. The ship might soon be refuelled and repaired, ready to go aloft.

We moved, and kept moving. Trees and leaves and birds blurred around us. It grew lighter. At the bank of a creek we crumpled together and drank. Neither of us could take another step.

'Just a few minutes,' I said. I put my forehead against the mossy ground and told myself I must not sleep, not yet. There would be sleep later, waiting for me in my cabin on the *Aurora* when we were aloft.

Kate was crying. I looked up and she was shaking her head and dragging her hands over her face and saying it was all her fault Bruce Lunardi had been hurt, and the pirates knew about the ship now, and that she'd put us all in danger. I grabbed her hands and tried to calm her. But she shut her eyes so tightly her eyelids were just crinkled slits. She pulled her hands free, and her lips trembled and were wet with her tears.

I kissed her mouth.

I wanted to do it, so I did it.

She stopped crying and opened her eyes and looked at me.

'That kiss could get us both in a lot of trouble.'

'Worse than what we're in?' I said.

'Do it again.'

I kissed her again, and for longer this time, and when she pulled back her head she was smiling. She looked off past me into the trees.

'That was very nice,' she said. 'That was the second time I've been kissed.'

'You were kissed before?' I said jealously.

'Yes, just now, by you, but I thought I'd count each time.'

I wanted to kiss her some more. I don't know why, for there could be no less suitable time. Maybe it was pure relief that we were alive and away from the pirates. Maybe it was jealousy, because she and Bruce had seemed to get along so well. Mostly it was just because I wanted to, and had for days.

'You ready?' I asked.

I was anxious to keep moving. I didn't fancy another run-in with the cloud cat. We both trudged on across the island, back towards the ship. My bare feet were raw and bleeding now, but it did not matter. All I wanted was to get back to the *Aurora*. I kept track of the time through the treetops, watching the rising sun.

'Hurry,' I said.

I was trying to feel the wind in the clearings, studying the edges of the clouds. The wind was right. The *Aurora* could take off without risk of being blown towards the island. She would have a good launch.

In another hour we reached the hydrium cave. The rubber hosing still ran out from the mouth into the forest, but there was no crew about. I wondered if this meant the ship had already been refilled. It made me nervous, seeing that hosing disappearing into the trees, like a trail leading straight to the *Aurora*.

I squeezed Kate's arm at the sound of footfalls. We huddled down amongst some thick ferns and held our breaths. A thin pirate flashed through the forest, coming from the direction of the *Aurora*. He was a natural runner, his strides smooth and long, and he ducked and veered through the undergrowth like he was well used to the terrain. His breathing came in quick smooth bursts. I watched him disappear and waited until I could no longer hear the crunch of his feet on earth.

'Hurry,' I said to Kate. 'He's seen the ship.'

'How do you know?'

'He's a scout. He's going back to the village to tell them. They'll send everyone.'

She looked a little ill.

'What time is it?' I asked her.

She checked her watch. 'Half past nine.'

I didn't want to waste time taking the easy path by the stream. We went downhill the fastest way I could think of, and it was steep and uncomfortable, bumping down on our bottoms, clutching hold of roots and creepers. I kept casting a wary eye into the higher branches, to see if the cloud cat was prowling above us.

Light filtered in from the open beach. The trees thinned. We came out into the palms and sand. The lagoon sparkled. There was the *Aurora*, and my heart swelled to see her looking so well, hovering in the miraculous way of airships, two metres off the sand. Her frame had been repaired, and her rudder, and she looked as taut and full and well-fed as a blue whale.

She was snugly tethered, but there was no one about, which made me nervous. Was she about to depart? But she couldn't, not without ground crew ready to cast off the lines.

We had to warn them they'd been spotted. We had to leave at once.

Keeping to the palms, I led us closer towards the *Aurora*.

Her gangways were shut tight.

The control car was empty.

I looked across to the windows of the starboard passenger lounge.

A figure moved past the glass and I could see his face.

It was Szpirglas.

18

SHIP TAKEN

'Cruse.'

The voice reached us as a hiss from the trees, and I whirled round expecting the worst, but instead saw Bruce Lunardi, hunched over, beckoning to us.

'I saw the whole thing,' he said.

We moved towards him, in amongst a thick screen of ferns and trees which completely shielded us from the *Aurora*. Bruce's lips were unnaturally red in his pale face, his skin greasy with sweat. I looked at his leg and saw that it was still bleeding through the rough bandage he'd torn from his shirt. He looked terrible.

'Are you all right?' I asked him.

'I was worried about you two,' he said. He seemed anxious to explain. 'When you distracted the cat, I ran until I was sure it wasn't following. Then I stopped and went back a way, to try and find you.'

'How's your leg?' Kate asked. She glanced at me, looking worried.

'It started hurting pretty badly in the night,' Bruce said. 'I'll live. But listen. I should have stayed and helped you fight it. I did try to find you, but I didn't want to call out. Then I thought I heard it moving around in the trees again, and it seemed pointless to wander. I started back for the ship.'

'That was sensible,' I said, to reassure him. I wondered if he was a bit feverish.

Bruce shook his head. 'I got lost on my way back, even with the compass, and then my leg was slowing me down so I had to rest all the time. By then it was night-time, so I waited until first light. Didn't get any sleep, all I heard were things moving around; it was deafening. Eventually dawn came and I found my way back to the beach.' He nodded towards the ship. 'They got here just ahead of me.'

'You were lucky, then,' I said. 'Those are Szpirglas' men. They have a base on the other side of the island.'

'We spent a very pleasant night there,' said Kate. 'I had the captain's private cabin.'

Bruce looked at her as if he wasn't sure if she was telling stories or not. His face was so bewildered I felt sorry for him.

'We got away, but not fast enough,' I said. 'What happened?'

'I was just about to walk out from the trees on this side. I could see some of our crew working on the ship, and then suddenly this other group appears, and they're running and shouting and waving pistols.'

'How many?' I asked.

'Half a dozen, maybe more. More I think. Szpirglas

led them. They worked pretty fast. I backed up into the trees. The pirates held the crew at gunpoint, tied their hands behind their backs. They marched them inside, the crew in front as hostages and shields. They pulled the gangways up after them. There were a couple of gunshots,' Bruce said, looking sick. 'And then the starboard gangway opened for a second, and one of the pirates, a tall rangy fellow, went rushing out, back into the forest.'

'We saw him,' I said. 'He'll bring the rest.' If he was headed back to the pirate village, it would take at least six hours before they returned in full force. Unless they brought their airship.

I peered through the bamboo at the windows of the starboard lounge and could see nothing against the sun's glare. I wondered if the pirates had gathered all their hostages in there.

'We've got to free them.' Kate said.

'Yes, but how is the question,' I said. 'If the pirates spot us, they'll kill us without blinking.'

'We must kill them first,' she said fiercely.

I looked at her in shock.

'They tried to kill us, Matt. They killed my grandfather. They'll kill everyone on board, you know they will.'

She was right. I opened my mouth to speak, but nothing came out.

'If we can get to the captain's cabin, we can get the ship's gun,' Bruce said.

I shook my head. 'It's gone. They took it away the first time they boarded.'

'Then we'll take some of theirs,' said Kate. 'We'll get inside and make some noise. They'll send one man out to investigate. We wait for him. We whack him—'

'Whack him?' I said.

'Yes, bash him with something very hard, like a frying pan or a lug wrench, right in the skull.'

She said it with such ferocity, her hands balled into fists, that I winced.

'He's knocked out, we tie him up, take his pistol and then go in and surprise the other pirates and shoot them through the hearts.'

Bruce scratched at his chin and smiled. I looked at Kate and shook my head in disgust.

'Perhaps we could work in a little swordplay first,' I suggested. 'You wouldn't want to cut short your swashbuckling.'

'What's the matter?' she said. 'Are you saying it won't work?'

'Do you have much experience, shooting a pistol?' I asked.

'How hard can it be?' She made a gun of her thumb and forefinger.

'Well, I've never fired a gun in my life,' I told her.

'I have,' said Bruce, and both Kate and I turned to him in surprise.

'In a shooting range,' he added with a sheepish grin. 'I was a pretty lousy shot actually. It's trickier than it looks.

I don't know that I'd trust myself to shoot straight in a pinch.'

'Exactly. These men were shooting before they could walk. We'd be dead in a second.' My body felt hollow and weak. 'I'm being honest. I don't think I could shoot a man, even one as bad as Szpirglas.'

'I'm not so squeamish,' Kate said, and the expression on her face frightened me.

'There must be other ways,' I said.

'The fact remains,' Kate said, 'we've got to separate these men from their guns, and I don't see any other way to do that.'

'She's right,' said Bruce, 'about the whacking part at least. If we can lure them out one at a time, maybe we have a chance. Knock them out, tie them up, take away their guns.'

'You're not in much shape to whack anybody,' I said.

'I've got some fight in me.'

'I'm sure you do, but I just don't fancy our chances trading blows with pirates. Your leg's chewed up.'

'Don't you worry about that. And remember, I've got a few years on you,' he added pointedly.

'And fifteen kilos, I know that. But I'm not about to go playing fisticuffs and pistols with pirates.'

'I'm also the senior member of crew here.'

I stared at him in amazement. 'What are you saying, Bruce, that you should take charge?'

'By the books, yes.'

'Well, I don't think we have any books on hand, and besides, you don't know this ship like me. You've been on her three days, not three years.'

'I outrank you, it's a fact.'

'Your rank's bought and paid for,' I said, my teeth barely parting.

'This isn't helping,' said Kate.

I rubbed my forehead hard.

'They think we're dead in the hydrium pit,' I said. 'We have surprise. I know every inch of this ship. I've got a spare set of keys in my cabin. I get those, and we can go anywhere. I can open doors, lock them. If we can lure the pirates into certain cabins and bays we can lock them up. Then we can free the officers and the captain and fly out of here before the other pirates arrive.'

'Ambitious,' said Bruce.

'We'll probably still have to whack a few pirates,' Kate said.

'One or two if it makes you happy,' I told her. 'But I don't want to squander our surprise. Before we do anything, we need to get aboard and have a look around. We're no use out here. I reckon in about six hours we'll have the whole godforsaken crew of them aboard, and there'll be no hope of escape then. Are we agreed?'

'Yes,' said Bruce.

'How do we get on board?' Kate asked.

'Tail fin.'

The *Aurora*'s stern was close to the water. We stayed buried in the trees off her starboard side, and worked

358

our way back until we were directly across from her fins. From here, we were almost out of sight from the passenger windows. We ran. Set into the bottom of the vertical tail fin was a rectangular hatch, about two metres off the ground. The landing gear gave me a foothold, and I heaved myself up on to the step and tried to open the hatch. To my huge relief, the handle turned and I opened the hatch as smoothly and quietly as I could. I took a quick peek inside, then climbed in.

I was inside the narrow tail fin, crouched on a metal catwalk, waiting for my breathing to calm. I listened. All was still. I turned back to the hatch and nodded, then reached down and helped Kate scramble up.

'All right?' I asked Bruce.

'Yep,' he said, through tight lips. He used his good leg to get his footing, and then pulled himself up. I helped him in. He was wincing. I didn't like the look of his leg at all. The bandage was sodden with blood.

We were all inside. I slid the hatch silently shut. Light came from three portholes, and from an electric lamp overhead. Oh, it was good to be aboard her again, even under these terrible circumstances. Just the feel of her around me cheered my heart.

The ship's auxiliary control room was built right inside the bot.om of the tail fin. If there was ever a breakdown in the main control car, the *Aurora* could be flown from back here. My eyes moved across all the rudimentary instruments and silent control panels arranged on either side of the cramped walkway. There was the elevator wheel, and the rudder wheel. A gyro compass was positioned above the rudder, and an altimeter beside the elevator wheel. Ignition buttons, throttles. There was the ballast board with gauges telling you how much water you had, and in which tanks. Over to one side was the gas board, telling you how full each of the twenty-six gas cells was. I peered up at them. The ship was ninety-nine per cent full in all her cells. She was airtight and sound.

Bruce's breathing was coming quick and fast.

'Let's take a look at that wound,' Kate said.

Bruce just shook his head.

'Come on,' said Kate. 'I won't swoon.'

He unwound the bandage. Silently I sucked back air. It looked terrible. The cloud cat had raked his left calf with its claws and clamped its teeth around his ankle, sure enough. It was all red and inflamed and, more worrying, yellow from pus.

'We need some disinfectant for that,' I said, 'and fresh bandages. I'll try to get into the infirmary.'

'Shouldn't I come as well?' Kate asked, and the look on her face was that of a small child, afraid to be left alone at night.

'I'll be faster alone. Safer too. I want to find out where the pirates are, where they've got everyone. You two stay here.'

'What if someone comes?'

'Get out through the hatch and back into the trees, all right?'

'What about you, if something happens to you?'

'Nothing's going to happen to me. I know every centimetre of this ship. She'll hide me. I'll be fast.'

'Lighter than air,' Kate said, 'is that right?'

'Lighter than air.'

She grabbed my hand and held it so tight for a moment, I winced.

'It'll be fine,' I said. 'We'll all be fine. Check the lockers down here. See what you can find. Maybe some rope and things for gagging them and tying them up . . .' It made me feel queasy even to think of what we must do.

'Good luck, Matt,' said Bruce.

Even now, I felt a pang of jealousy leaving them alone together. But I could still feel the imprint of Kate's hand upon mine.

There was only one way out of the tail fin, and that was a tall ladder which angled up steeply to the keel catwalk. I took it silently, and before my head came level with the corridor, I stopped and listened. I pressed my ear to the metal and waited for vibrations. There were none. I tipped my eyes over the rim and looked.

The keel catwalk stretched forward, lit overhead by electric lamps. It was clear. I climbed up and started running. My bare feet made no noise. I kept my head cocked, listening, breathing silently. I liked being alone. No one's eyes on me, expecting me to make things right. Just me and the ship. The *Aurora*'s intricate anatomy

361

scrolled before my mind's eye. I knew every passageway, every hatchway, every crawl space and vent.

Quickly I made my way to the crew quarters. I put my ear to the door of my cabin and listened before opening it and slipping inside. My pass keys hung from a hook by the mirror. I pocketed them. For a moment I didn't want to leave. It was my room. I looked at my bunk. Part of me wanted to crawl into it, and pull the covers over me and sleep and pretend that everything was all right. On the wall by my pillow were the pictures of my mother and sisters and father. I'll be fine, I told myself.

Running again, forward along the catwalk. If I kept going, I'd end up at the door to the passenger quarters. There might be a pirate stationed there, since it was near the exit gangways. How was I to get to A-Deck? I had a hunch that Szpirglas would assemble everyone in the starboard lounge. It was the biggest reception room on board, and it made sense to keep all his hostages in one place where he could guard them most easily.

I paused and thought. I couldn't risk creeping around A-Deck, but I could spy down on it from the roof. I'd need to get on top of the passenger quarters, and the only way to get to it was from overhead.

I hurried along to one of the ladders leading up to the axial catwalk. Up I went, wary. Even with the sun high in the sky, it was shadowy along the catwalk, though the outer skin of the ship gave off a luminous moonlight glow, its silver surface reflecting the sun.

Axial catwalk, clear. I stopped at a supply locker, and took a harness and coil of rope and slung it over my shoulder. Forward I went, the walls of the gas cells puckering and sighing all around me. I stopped. I was now directly over A-Deck. Far below me I could see the ceiling. I tied one end of my line to the side of the catwalk and gingerly climbed over the railing in my harness.

Like a spider I dropped, straight down, spinning out my line as I went. Down through this shimmering mango-scented canyon. Gently I touched down on the roof of A-Deck. The bottoms of the gas cells hung only a few feet above, and I had to get down on my knees to move about. Any loud noise might be heard below. Right now I figured I was over the gymnasium – not likely anyone was exercising right now. I shrugged myself clear of the harness. It did make me feel claustrophobic, the hydrium bags hovering above me, rustling against my back as I crawled beneath them.

Silver ventilation ducts formed a network on the roof, carrying fresh air through the passenger quarters. High in the wall of every lounge and cabin were narrow slit-like grilles. I could see through them if I could get inside the ducts. They were large, but it would still be a tight squeeze and slither.

I found an access panel and unscrewed the wing nuts. A gust of air wafted out as I set the metal panel aside. The opening was no bigger than the hole of a kayak. I would have to go in head first for there was no turning around once I was inside. I gazed out over the maze of ducts and plotted my course ahead of time, for I knew it would be easy to lose my bearings. I slid my body in.

I did not like it inside there. It was dark, though at least not airless, for the whole purpose of the ducts was to circulate fresh air. I slouched along, pulling myself forward on my elbows and forearms. My poor bruised and battered toes were sticky with sweat and dried blood, but they gave me good purchase and pushed me on through the ducts. One tight turn to the left nearly dislocated my spine. I took care not to dig in with my knees or elbows, for fear of making the metal dimple and pop.

I could hear voices and knew I was close to the starboard lounge. I took a turn to the right and the duct stretched ahead, light shafting in through all the slit-like vents on its left wall. I slithered to the first one and peered out. The opening was narrow, but when I moved my head, the view it gave me was quite broad.

The lounge was crammed with passengers and crew. The women and elderly were sitting in chairs, and the rest were on the floor. Hardly a square metre of carpet was unoccupied. Every single one of our passengers must have been there. I caught sight of Miss Simpkins in a wicker chair, one hand pressed tragically to her temple, the other fanning herself. Near her feet was the moustached cigar man who'd complained about his antique furniture being shifted. Like the other passengers he was silent, though he looked like he wasn't too far off having a go at complaining. I hoped he had the sense to keep his mouth shut. Pirates strolled amongst them, their pistols tight in their fists.

The *Aurora's* officers and crew had their hands tethered and were lined up together against the outer wall, beneath the windows. I saw Mr Rideau and Mr Torbay, and there was Mr Lisbon, our chief steward, Mr Vlad, our chef, and not far from him, Captain Walken. They didn't look like themselves. It was like gazing at portrait paintings that were all slightly the wrong colour and shape.

I searched for Baz and found him slumped against the wall with Doctor Halliday at his side. Baz's arm was in a makeshift sling, and a bloody bandage around his shoulder. I remembered Bruce saying he'd heard gunshots. These wretches had shot Baz. I felt a great fist of grief in my throat.

'He's in some pain,' Halliday told one of the pirates. 'At least let me get some medicine from the infirmary.'

'No,' said the pirate.

'This is inhumane.'

'Just hope there's no worse to come.'

'I apologize, doctor,' said Szpirglas, coming into view. 'But I can't spare a man to escort you to the infirmary right now. When the rest of my crew arrives, of course, we'll let you. But for now, I need all my men to tend to you here.' He said it with a smile, as though this was perfectly reasonable and he was simply asking for our help in doing his work.

I started counting pirates. A gaunt fellow with a pock-marked face and a glock blunderbuss in his fist, a second fellow who must have fancied himself something of a gangster dandy with greased hair and a carbine. There was Rhino Hand, the one-handed fellow, his thick finger barely fitting through the trigger loop of his pistol. The sight of all these guns took something out of me, I had to admit, all that deadly greased metal. Six pirates I counted, and Szpirglas and the great brute Crumlin made eight. Eight pirates. I hoped there were no more lurking on board.

I looked back at Captain Walken. He must know that these men were not planning on sparing them. But what could he do? Any attempt to overpower the pirates would mean people getting shot. It was not as if he had any chance to devise a plan anyway. The pirates kept circulating amongst them, giving a kick to anyone talking.

I saw Szpirglas give a nod to Crumlin and they disappeared, headed for the kitchen. I wiggled along the vents, wanting to know what they were up to. I heard their voices, tinny through the ducts. Silently I slouched closer and pressed my face to the grille. The kitchen was small, and I could only see the back of Szpirglas.

'Hazlett's fast, he'll have reached them in ninety minutes or so. Three hours, and we'll have the rest of the crew here.'

It was just as I'd feared – only worse. The rest of Szpirglas' crew were coming, but faster than I'd reckoned. They weren't all the way back at the village. They must have been searching another nearby part of the island.

Szpirglas said something, too low for me to hear.

'Why not keep her?' Crumlin asked.

'She's of no use to us,' came Szpirglas' voice. 'She's big and fat and slow, and we'd be inviting capture if we dared to sail her.'

'Seems a shame to scuttle her.'

'Ah, but she's a treasure trove of parts. Her engines, Aruba fuel, wiring. We'll strip anything of use from her beforehand.'

'And the passengers?'

'They stay with the ship, of course. But this time, we'll make sure there's no clever escapes. We'll send her up bled of hydrium, and aflame. Lock them in the passenger quarters for good measure. They'll not be able to reach the controls. In any event, we'll shoot the crew.'

My mouth was so dry I couldn't swallow. How could he talk of such terrible things in so calm a voice? A panicky hot flush seared my back and arms.

'Now let's go tend our flock,' Szpirglas told Crumlin. 'It might be an idea to shoot someone else before long. Keep them meek and obedient. Walken's no fool, he'll know there's no merciful ending to this. I don't want any crazed escape attempts.'

'Very good, sir.'

'And get that chef of theirs in here. Our lads may as well enjoy some fine dining while we wait.'

Their voices faded, and I was left lying in the duct, sick and weak with fear. Then I moved, fast, trying to remember the way back to the access panel. I was afraid my fearful heartbeat would hammer an anthem through the vents of the entire ship. We had not much time.

Out of the ducts and on to the roof of A–Deck again. For a moment I forced myself to be still and think above my mind's noise. Bruce needed medicine. The infirmary was on B–Deck. I crawled along the roof until I came to the edge and looked down. Ten metres below me was the keel catwalk. I could see no one patrolling it, so I scuttled down through the bracing wires and alumiron struts. I padded along the catwalk to the door of the passenger quarters. I put my ear to it and listened, unlocked it with my keys, and slipped inside.

I was in the *Aurora*'s entrance lobby, at the base of the grand staircase which led up to A–Deck. I hurried past it and through the deserted corridors of B–Deck, past the staterooms and lounges towards the infirmary. I unlocked the door and was inside.

Daylight flooded into the room from the row of windows set into the floor. I swiped two rolls of bandages from the shelf, a bottle of peroxide to clean the wound, and pocketed a tube of antiseptic ointment. I knew Bruce was in a great deal of pain, and he needed something to dull it at least. He needed to be strong as possible for what was to come. I went to the medicine cabinet, but the glass door was locked, and that was one key I did not have. From the linen rack, I grabbed a towel and wrapped it thickly around my fist. I hoped it wouldn't be too loud. I took a breath and smacked hard at the glass. It took two tries for me to get it right, and then the glass splintered and big shards fell rattling inside the cabinet. I paused, listening, praying no one had heard.

My eyes quickly drifted across the rows of bottles. I spotted the aspirin powder and as I was taking it, saw a slender flask filled with dark liquid. I read the label, and decided to take that too. I knotted all my things up in a clean towel and listened at the infirmary door before I opened it. Back down the corridor, through the door on to the keel catwalk, and, once I saw the coast was clear, I ran, taking great weightless strides towards the ship's stern.

I soared past one of the ladder shafts leading to the axial catwalk, and my stride faltered. I stopped. My skin crawled. Fearfully I turned and peered back up at the caged ladder. Some vigilant part of my brain had sounded an alarm as I'd hurried past, but there was nothing there, nothing at all. I was sure of it. If there'd been someone on the ladder, I'd have seen him. But I hurried on, faster than before, to the ship's stern.

Before I went down the ladder to the fin, I paused and took a good long look around to make sure I wasn't being watched. Then down I went, whispering, 'It's me, Matt,' so they wouldn't panic when they heard feet on the rungs. Kate and Bruce both smiled when they saw me.

'Let's get that leg of yours sorted out,' I said.

There was no glass of water to mix the aspirin powder in, so I had Bruce stick out his tongue and shook a good dose on to it. He grimaced as he swallowed it down, for it was bitter stuff.

Gingerly I started unwinding the makeshift bandage, talking as I worked, telling them all that I'd learned.

'Eight of them,' I said, 'including Crumlin and Szpirglas. This'll likely hurt,' I said to Bruce, 'so hold your tongue if you can.' I poured half the bottle of peroxide over the livid gash, and it fizzed mightily as it cleaned out the wound. I could feel Bruce's entire body clench, but he made no sound save for a low grunt. It was an ugly wound, no question, and just looking at it you knew it was gouged by the jaws of an animal, for it was ragged and deep.

'That needs sewing up,' said Kate. 'It won't close like that.'

I noticed she looked at the wound without any sign of squeamishness. She regarded it much the same way she beheld the bones of the cloud cat, with keen interest.

'No,' I said, 'it's best left open so it can drain. Don't want to trap the infection inside.'

Kate looked at me, impressed. 'Is there anything you can't do, Mr Cruse?' she asked.

'Can't sing,' I said.

'Really?'

'Not worth spit. It's a terrible sound I make. Now listen,' I said, dabbing Bruce's wound dry with a clean towel. 'The rest of the pirates will be here soon. I heard Szpirglas and Crumlin talking. They're going to gut the ship, then kill all the crew and send her out to crash. We've got three hours before they arrive.'

I squeezed great globs of the antiseptic ointment into the wound, and then, with Kate's help, started wrapping it up in the fresh bandages, not too tightly. 'Thank you,' said Bruce as we tied it off. 'That feels much better.'

'The aspirin should kick in soon,' I told him.

We sat in silence for a moment.

'Three hours,' I said again.

'Well, are we all ready to whack some pirates?' Kate said.

'We'd better get cracking,' said Bruce, trying to sound decisive, but his mouth was dry.

I took a look around the narrow room: the rudder and elevator wheels, the levers and navigation instruments and control boards, all quiet and dark now, but ready to come alive.

I said, 'We could fly her.'

'What're you talking about?' Bruce said.

'The ship. We could fly the ship. Nothing fancy. Take it up so the other pirates can't come aboard, and then we can set about freeing everyone.'

'Too risky,' said Bruce. 'We can't take off without the captain and crew!'

'We can't afford to wait for them.'

'We're just three people. It can't be done, Cruse.'

'It can be done.'

'I've had two years at the Academy,' said Bruce. 'And there is no way I can launch this ship.'

'I can do it,' I said.

'No.'

'I've spent more hours in the control car than some of the officers. I've watched everything. I know how they do it. I can do it.'

'He can do it,' Kate said to Bruce.

We both turned to her, and I didn't know when someone's words had made me feel so buoyed up.

'You don't know what you're talking about,' said Bruce.

'I have absolutely no doubt he can do it,' she said again. 'Matt can fly the ship.'

'With your help,' I said to them. 'It has to be done, Bruce. We get her up and clear, and we only have eight pirates to deal with. We wait until we have twenty, and that's the end of it. That's the end of everything.'

'He's right,' said Kate.

'How do you propose we do this?' Bruce demanded.

'We need to start casting off lines.'

'Do you know how many lines she's got on her right now?' he said, incredulous.

'Of course I do. She carries twenty landing lines on each side, and each one of those splits into five spider lines. That's 200 lines, plus whatever extra we've put on her.'

'Exactly. We'd need a ground crew of hundreds to launch her properly.'

'We landed her without a ground crew. I know it's dangerous,' I hurried on before he could cut me off, 'I'm not saying it isn't. But we're in luck. There's not a breath of wind right now. We cast off the port and starboard lines first. The bow and stern lines will be enough to hold her snug until we're ready to launch. We'll slip the stern line last, dump ballast and go.'

'The moment the engines come on, they'll know we're here.'

'They'll go to the control car first.'

'Fine, but then they'll come running straight here.'

'We won't be here by then.'

'No?'

'No, we'll be hiding. And they'll be dopey.'

'Dopey?' said Bruce.

I lifted the flask I'd taken from the infirmary and showed it to Kate. 'Is this the same as Miss Simpkins was taking?'

She smiled slowly and gave a nod.

'Your devious little mind has given me an idea,' I said. 'The pirates are hungry. They've got Vlad in the kitchen cooking for them. He'll make them a proper meal – better than the slop they serve themselves. If I can get this to him, he can dump it in the food.'

'He's on A-Deck,' Bruce said. 'How're you going to get past all the pirates?'

'There's no one on B-Deck. I can get into the kitchen down there and take the dumb-waiter.'

'It's tiny.'

'I can be tiny.'

He looked at me, then chuckled, shaking his head. 'You're a madman.'

'How fast does this stuff work?' I asked Kate.

'I don't really know. Quite quickly, I think. But Marjorie never needed much help falling asleep. All she needed was a few drops.'

'They're getting all of it,' I said.

'Well, that should do nicely.'

Bruce nodded. 'If it works fast enough, all we have to do is wait for them to drop, tie them up and free the crew.'

It seemed too much to hope for. 'I'll need someone to go with me and work the dumb-waiter.' There were no controls inside.

'I'll come,' said Kate.

'Good. Bruce, do you think you can start casting off?'

Slowly he stood, testing his leg. 'It's not really 200 lines,' he said. 'If we just slip the main landing lines from the hull, that makes only forty. Safer this way than messing about with the moorings on the beach. They might spot us from the windows.'

'You're right,' I said. 'We'll do the lines forward of the passenger quarters, you take care of the ones aft. Is that all right?' I felt bad for him, with his leg torn up and blazing with pain.

Bruce nodded. 'What about the bow line?'

'I'll take care of that too. Leave the stern line on until we're all back here.'

'Let's do it,' he said.

For just a moment the whole enterprise seemed insane. But it was our only hope, and there was no going back now.

'Take off your shoes and boots,' I told them, 'you'll be quieter.'

'My feet might be a bit whiffy,' Kate said apologetically.

'I promise not to sniff them.'

She unlaced her boots quickly, while I helped Bruce off with his shoes. Then I led the way up the ladder to the keel catwalk. I could smell fish wafting down the corridor. Vlad was already cooking. We had to hurry. It took Bruce quite a while to make it up the ladder. I wondered if he was up to this.

On the keel catwalk we parted company. Kate and I wished Bruce luck, and he limped off down a lateral walkway to the ship's starboard hull. There were access hatches all along it which would let him get at the main landing lines and slip them from their cleats.

Kate and I padded our way forward. We were amidships when I heard voices, and I froze, my senses swivelling to find the source. They were coming from just behind us, from the gangway that led to the aft engine car. Their footfalls were getting louder. They'd come out on to the keel catwalk soon, right behind us. There was no time for running back. Run forward and they might see us before we could get out of sight.

'Slide under,' I hissed at Kate, pointing down. There was a bit of clearance between the metal grille of the catwalk floor and the actual hull of the ship's belly. I pulled her down and helped her swing her legs under the catwalk. I shoved her body beneath, then slid in beside her. It was dark, but there was a tungsten lamp not too far along the corridor, and if anyone was to look directly down, they would see us, stiff and frozen like fossils in a glacier.

The voices grew louder.

'They're beauties,' said one of the pirates. 'Better than ours.'

'Three thousand horsepower each, I'd wager.'

'Szpirglas says we can take three and leave one aboard to power her up and wreck her.'

There were two of them, Crumlin and some other fellow. I could see them as they emerged from the gangway and came towards us along the keel catwalk. They talked about the engines and the best way to strip them. I felt their footfalls through the metal of the catwalk, through the wall of my chest into my heart. I tried not to breathe. Their boots clanged over us.

And stopped, just over our heads.

I was staring up at the pock-marked undersides of their boots. I could tickle the undersides of their boots if I but lifted my finger. I could see up their trouser legs and behold their great hairy calves. The smell was not pleasant.

'That cook's got something on the go,' said the pirate.

'Hungry, are you?' Crumlin asked.

'I'll wager their grub's better than ours.'

'Maybe we should keep the cook.'

They both laughed at this.

Crumlin lit a cigarette and dropped the match. It fell through the metal grille and landed on my cheek, its tip still blazing hot. I screwed up my face and tried to think of my foot, my fingers, anything but the red–hot ember on my flesh. Water flooded my eyes, my nostrils ran. The heat faded. I needed air. I wanted to breathe deeply, but the wretches were still standing over us, gabbing about what else they wanted to strip from the ship. Some cigarette ash drifted down on to Kate's nose. She breathed some of it in and I saw her nostrils wrinkle and knew she was about to sneeze. Her eyes narrowed, her chest quivered. I lifted my hand and pinched her nose with my fingers. She gave a little gasp – but at that moment the pirates started walking again and their boots clanged on the catwalk, blotting out the sound.

Crumlin and his friend kept going. I listened to their fading footsteps, following them forward through the ship. Keys jangled, a door opened and closed, and I knew they'd passed into the passenger quarters.

We crawled out. I was shaken, not just by our close call, but by the fact the pirates were moving about the ship now. I'd become careless, assuming the pirates were still all on A–Deck, standing guard over their hostages. It would make it harder for us to get around, to stay secret. I hoped Bruce was being careful.

'Are you all right?' she said, touching my cheek. There must have been a red mark there, I could still feel it smarting. The pads of her fingers were cool and soothing.

'Fine,' I told her.

The smell of Vlad's cooking suffused the corridor, and my stomach tightened with hunger. It smelled awfully good. We made our way more carefully now, and reached the door to the passenger quarters. The pirates had locked it behind them. I listened, then let us through on to B-Deck.

I led Kate past the crew's mess to the kitchen. Overhead I could hear footsteps, and the faint sounds of Vlad singing and cursing as he cooked in the A-Deck kitchen. I walked over to the dumb-waiter and slid open the door. We looked at it.

'You can't fit in there,' Kate said.

'I can,' I said doubtfully.

It was even tinier than I'd remembered.

'Maybe I should do it,' Kate said. 'I'm smaller.'

'No.'

'In you go, then,' she said.

I handed her the flask of sleeping elixir. I had to go in backwards, for once I was in, there would be no shifting, and certainly no turning around. I backed in bum first, spine and neck bent until I could barely breathe, my knees splayed up on either side of my ears. I felt like a circus freak squeezing into a milk crate.

'All right?' Kate asked, looking at me with concern.

I grunted.

'There's bits still sticking out,' she said and gave me a good shove.

'Gently does it!' I hissed.

'Sorry. Here.' She placed the sleeping elixir in my fingers, and jammed in my right foot, which kept sliding out. 'Don't want it getting caught in the door. Ready?'

'Ready.'

I was boxed. I would rather have swung over the open ocean than this. Sweat prickled across my entire body. Kate slid the door shut and I wondered if my heart would stop. Thank goodness for the little round window at least. I could see Kate peer in at me, smile, then her hand lifted to the control buttons. With a jerk I was moving up. Blackness slid down over the window.

It was only a matter of three metres, I knew, but those were the slowest three metres I could recall. The noise of the dumb-waiter's motor sounded laboured, and I wondered if it had ever carried such weight before. I was light, but not lighter than a rack of lamb.

Good Lord, what if there were pirates in the kitchen with Vlad? What if they were standing guard over him? I'd be delivered to them trussed up like a Christmas goose.

Light bobbed down behind the window, and I was in the upper kitchen. Steaming pots and spitting skillets and vegetables and fish and potatoes were spread out on cutting boards. And there was Vlad, his back to me, whisking something in an enormous soup pot. I tilted my head as much as I could, but saw no one else in the kitchen.

I waited a moment, for Vlad to turn. I'd been hoping

he would hear the dumb-waiter and turn in curiosity, if nothing else. But the sounds of his kitchen must have drowned it out.

I could not open the door from the inside.

I rapped at the glass with my knuckles.

I felt a bat-wing flutter of panic inside my chest.

I was trapped.

I knocked harder and could see Vlad stand taller for a moment. Once more I knocked, and this time he turned, frowning. He bent and peeped into the window and jerked in surprise. He looked hurriedly to the kitchen doorway, then opened the dumb-waiter.

'Yes, Mr Cruse?' he said, as if I regularly made an appearance in the dumb-waiter.

'I've got some—'

He whirled away from me, and went back to the oven.

A pirate staggered in, a near empty bottle of wine in one fist, a pistol in the other. I shrank back into the dumb-waiter. My toes, I was sure, were sticking out.

'Where's that soup!' the pirate roared at Vlad.

'Coming!' Vlad bellowed back. 'A soup you will like. You will adore it!'

'We'd better or we'll bung you in for more flavour!'

'Ha ha!' Vlad laughed dementedly. 'Yes, yes, of course!'

The pirate was beside Vlad now, peering into the great cauldron of soup, his back to me.

'We're hungry, Count Dracula, now get a move on! Cook!'

'Cook, I live to cook!' bellowed Vlad. 'Let me cook!'

The pirate turned. His head was now in profile. With one twitch of his eyes he would see me. He took another long snort from the bottle of wine. He started turning towards me.

'What is that you're drinking?' Vlad said suddenly, placing himself between us.

'Booze, is what it is,' the pirate retorted.

Vlad took the bottle to read the label.

'No! No, no, no!' shouted Vlad, as if impaled on a sword. 'This is the wrong wine for the meal I am about to serve. Open a white, please, a Chablis or a Riesling, the soup will be better, you will see!'

The pirate pushed him away and stomped out of the kitchen.

Vlad turned back to me.

'Peasants, these people. He thinks a burgundy is appropriate!'

He shook his head venomously, as if he'd forgotten the fact we were prisoners, our lives were in danger, and I was crammed in a dumb-waiter.

Vlad sighed heavily. 'Now then, what can I do for you, Mr Cruse? My soup soon is at a critical stage.'

I wondered if Vlad was completely cuckoo after all. My hopes felt all soggy.

I held up the flask of sleeping elixir. He squinted at it, read the label, and nodded. He took it from me.

'Yes, yes, I see. For extra flavour.' He winked at me, and I knew that he understood perfectly. He crammed my foot back inside the dumb-waiter and then, as an afterthought, he filled a bowl of fish soup, popped in a spoon and pushed it into my hands. Then he closed the dumb-waiter's door and pressed the down button.

My last view through the round window was of Vlad uncorking the medicine bottle and dumping the entire contents into the soup, while belting out an opera aria.

Down I went.

It was no easy feat, eating and swallowing in such a position, but I devoured half the fish soup before I reached the bottom of the shaft. I saved the rest for Kate.

With a jolt I stopped.

Light filled the round window.

Kate was gone.

19

AIRBORNE

My eyes darted frantically around the kitchen, but Kate was nowhere to be seen. It could only mean she'd been caught. Beneath the sink, a cupboard door swung open and Kate emerged, a frying pan clutched in her hands. She nimbly leapt out, rushed to the dumb-waiter, and slid open the door.

'Quick,' she said, snatching the bowl of soup out of my hands, then tugging at me roughly. My back and neck sang with pain as my body unfolded itself. I tumbled out stiffly. 'I heard someone. I think he went into the toilets across the corridor.'

I took her hand and led her out of the kitchen. From the men's lavatory we heard a toilet flush. We ran. I fumbled with my keys and opened the door and we were out on to the keel catwalk, near the ship's bow, this time. From here, the catwalk stretched forward to the officer and captain's quarters, and the control car. I started down a lateral passage towards the ship's starboard side.

For the next half hour or so, Kate and I worked along the inside of the hull, opening access hatches and casting off landing lines. I wanted to be quick. With fewer lines on her, the *Aurora* would shift if the wind picked up, and the pirates would surely notice and come to investigate. From the beach they'd see all the slipped lines and know they had stowaways.

Through the walls of the passenger quarters I caught a wave of raucous laughter.

'They've been drinking,' Kate whispered.

'Eating too, I hope.'

'They still seem awfully lively,' Kate said as more guffaws and shouting passed through the walls.

Right now I just hoped most of the pirates were eating in A-Deck lounge, and not skulking about the ship, scavenging. I hoped Bruce was getting on all right. Kate and I worked, silent and intent, along both sides of the *Aurora* until we'd cast off all her landing lines, letting them drop to the sand below.

'Just the bow lines now,' I whispered.

We went back to the keel catwalk and up a companion ladder toward the axial catwalk. Cautiously I lifted my head above the last rung of the ladder and peered about. It was clear. I hurried forward.

Right in the ship's nose were two access panels. I opened one and light flooded in. I stuck my head out and was heartened there was still no breeze against my cheeks. Once I cast off the bow lines, and assuming Bruce had done his work, the *Aurora* would only be tethered by the stern, and anything more than a breath of wind would shift her.

Cleated outside on the hull were the two thick bow lines. They swung down towards the sand and were tied up to palms across the beach. I slipped them off at the cleats and let them fall. It was simpler and faster than risking a trip outside to cast off, and this way at least, there'd be no line left dangling to snag as we took off.

'Let's go,' I said to Kate.

I decided to take the axial corridor all the way back to the stern. I hoped it would be safer, for there was little up here to interest the pirates. We were halfway back when I saw something at the far end of the catwalk.

'What is that?' I asked Kate.

At first I thought it might be a tarp or a bundle of extra goldbeater's skin lying in a heap, but then it shifted, wispy white. The hair on my arms lifted.

'It's her,' Kate said.

She was right. It was our cloud cat, aboard the *Aurora*. I'd never seen any creature look more out of place. Amidst all the metal and cable and wire, it looked like something caged in the zoo. Except it was not caged. It had free run of the ship. How on earth had it got aboard?

'I saw it earlier,' I whispered, suddenly realizing that it must have been the ghostly flash of light I'd spied while running along the keel catwalk.

Curious as a cat, Crumlin had said to us, and Kate's grandfather had noted the same in his journal. They were intelligent, inquisitive creatures. Maybe this one had followed us across the island, invisible in the foliage.

Maybe it had watched the *Aurora* from the treetops for a while, and then the smell of the fish stew had lured it on to the ship's back, and down the open hatch of one of the crow's-nests.

Surely the cloud cat had seen Kate and me now, but it was not moving. The amidships ladder down to the keel catwalk was just before us and I touched Kate's arm and nodded at it. We took it quickly. The cat did not move. Perhaps it was stunned and scared to find itself in such an alien environment.

'This is not a good development,' I muttered, dropping hand over hand down the ladder. Now we had a ravenous carnivore to worry about on top of everything else.

'The pirates will shoot her if they see her,' Kate said.

I was more worried about the cat tearing at the gas cells – or us. With luck, it would find its way back out the way it came, and fast.

I wondered if Vlad had served his fish soup to the pirates yet. How long would it be before they fell asleep? Would their vision swim first? Would they get suspicious? I hoped it took effect quickly and totally, before they could vent their sluggish rage on the passengers and crew. Oh, perhaps it was a wretched plan after all, and would just create more suffering.

When we got back to the auxiliary control room, Bruce was there, slumped against the wall, not looking at all well.

'Just having a bit of a rest,' he said, trying to stand. He

seemed ashamed of himself and I felt sorry for him. 'I got them all off.'

'Good for you,' I said. 'That couldn't have been easy.'

'We should start looking over the controls,' Bruce said.

'Yeah. By the way, the cloud cat's on board.'

'You're joking,' he said, looking at Kate.

She shook her head. 'We saw her up on the axial catwalk.'

'Must've come in through one of the crow's-nests,' I said.

'But I think she's pretty scared,' Kate added, as if trying to reassure Bruce.

'Well,' he said, 'I hope she bloody well gets off before we launch.'

The clock in my head told me we didn't have much time. The other pirates would be here soon.

'Let's get to work,' I said.

Bruce cleared his throat and nodded. 'It's good luck for us they topped up the ballast tanks. She's perfectly weighed off right now. We're just hovering.'

I looked at the ballast board and its row of twenty levers, one for each of the ballast tanks placed evenly along the ship's keel. I was ashamed I hadn't thought ahead to that. Without ballast to dump, we'd go nowhere.

'You know how much to dump?' I asked Bruce.

'Standard procedure is 450 kilos,' he said.

I nodded, though I'd seen the captain dump considerably more when the winds were unco-operative and he wanted to rise more quickly. Today, though, it was perfectly calm.

'We'll need to switch the controls over from the main car,' I said. 'There should be a lever or something.'

'There,' said Bruce, pointing. He looked at me. 'Before you pull that, we'd better be sure what we're all doing.'

He was right, for once we started, I knew there would only be a few minutes before the pirates came running. Unless they were already asleep, which seemed unlikely. All the time I'd been slipping lines I'd been going through the steps we'd need to take, over and over again to make sure it was right, and that I wasn't forgetting anything. There'd be plenty for everyone to do, Kate included.

Bruce and I talked it through, and decided what everyone's job would be. We went through it a second time just to be sure.

'All ready then?' I said.

'Yes,' said Bruce.

'Yes,' said Kate.

I went to the emergency switch–over lever and pulled it. There was a deep low hum of electricity and all the instruments and gauges and control panels lit up a fluorescent orange. She was ready.

'I'll cast off,' I said.

I ducked out through the hatch and jumped on to the sand. The final stern line was cleated just behind the fin's landing gear. It was a devil's knot, untouched for so long that it had hardened and fused together, and my fingers plucked at it uselessly. I'd either have to cut it or untie the other end. It was a great sea serpent of a line and it would be an ordeal to saw through, even with the sharpest of knives. I hesitated only a second then started running across the sand, following the line to the palm where it was tied.

Halfway there I heard a shout and turned.

They were coming.

At the far end of the beach I saw the first of the pirates break from the thick of the forest and stride through the palms. The leader gave a shout, and then there were more of them, rushing for the *Aurora*'s bow. They'd be here in less than a minute.

'Bruce!' I shouted. 'Up ship!'

I was at the tree now, and pulling at the line to untie it. I saw Bruce poke his head out of the hatch, and look about in confusion.

'Up ship!' I bellowed. 'They're coming! Just do it. Don't wait for me!'

There was a great splash, and then another and another, as the ballast tanks opened all along the ship's belly, and water hit the sand. My knot was not quite loose, and already the line was pulling hard as the ship began to rise. In another moment I would not be able to untie it. I put my whole body into it, and pulled one last time, and the line came free, whipping around the trunk.

I sprinted back towards the *Aurora*. Across the beach the pirates were going full tilt towards her bow, yelling and waving and cursing. I was faster, but I knew I would not make it in time. The ship was rising slowly, her fin already several metres off the ground. Kate was leaning out of the hatchway, calling to me. I lunged for the landing gear, missed and sprawled to the sand.

The ship sailed off without me.

I heard Kate scream my name. The stern line slithered past my face, drawn up after the ship. I grabbed it tight and was lifted off the ground, swinging. Twining my legs around the rope, I climbed hand over hand towards the fin. I reached the landing gear, and Bruce's hand was stretching down from inside the hatch and I grabbed hold and he hauled and I pushed and eventually we got me inside.

I stuck my head back out and saw the pirates below us, almost at the ship's bow, and rushing for the spider lines that still dangled to the sand. We weren't rising fast enough.

'Dump more!' I shouted and reached for the ballast levers.

'It's not procedure!' shouted Bruce.

'They'll climb aboard!'

I threw one lever after another and the ship's bow angled up sharply, making us all stagger off balance. But how we rose! I'd never felt the *Aurora* lift so swiftly, and a wave of pure pleasure swept my body.

I looked out through the hatch and saw the beach plunging away beneath us, the pirates becoming smaller and smaller. They were shouting and churning their arms. None of them had reached the spider lines in time.

'Ha!' I shouted, shaking a fist at them. 'We did it!'

We were airborne now and everything seemed possible again – even fighting pirates. I rushed back to the controls and rested my forehead gratefully against the ship's bulkhead.

'That's my girl,' I said quietly. 'We need those engines now,' I told Kate. I'd shown her how to do it before we launched. That was her job, and she was already at work, priming the *Aurora*'s four motor cars from the engine control panel. Usually the motors were started up manually by the machinists, but I'd seen the crew do it remotely during training exercises. It was no easy task.

'We're climbing too fast,' said Bruce. 'We dumped too much ballast. I'm going to vent some gas.'

My ears popped. I glanced at the altimeter. We were at 200 metres now and meeting some wind. I felt the ship starting to slew. But we still had no engines and without engines we had no steerage.

'Kate?' I said.

'Venting in cells one, four, seven and ten,' Bruce muttered aloud at the gas controls, talking himself through the procedure.

'I've got the forward starboard engine going!' Kate said triumphantly, and I heard the distant whine of a propeller through the hatch.

'Rev it up!' I grabbed the wheel and angled the elevators. The nose started coming down. We were levelling off. Quickly I moved to the rudder wheel. 'I'm going to start turning her.'

The ship was heavy with just one engine, and the wind was blowing against my turn. I was making no headway.

'Forward port engine now!' Kate announced.

'That's more like it!' I said. 'Good work! Those pirates are peeing themselves now!'

'We should get out of here,' Bruce said worriedly. 'They'll be coming soon.'

'Not until I finish the turn,' I said.

With two engines now, I could feel the ship starting to respond to the rudder. The important thing was to put as much distance as possible between us and the island, in case the pirates did try to take her back. As I turned the wheel I could hear the great steering chains moving above my head as the flaps angled ever so slightly. I saw the compass needle moving in its liquid globe and felt the ship swinging around in a slow, graceful arc. I turned the wheel a little more, went too far, and then took her back before straightening her out. It was a sloppy bit of steering, but I'd done it. I'd turned the *Aurora* 180 degrees and when I looked out the porthole, the island was behind us, and we were sailing away from her.

'Both aft engines are running now!' Kate said, looking at me, her face flushed.

'Terrific,' I said. Beneath my feet I felt the familiar vibration of the *Aurora* under full steam. I checked the altimeter. We were level now at 250 metres.

'Now, let's get out of here,' Bruce said. Our plan was to hide in the cargo hold until the sleeping elixir put the pirates out. We would wait half an hour, and then carefully make our way forward, tie up the pirates, and free the crew.

We went up the ladder and peered down the keel catwalk. No cloud cat. No pirates.

'Maybe they're already asleep,' Kate said.

'They had wine too,' I said. 'That's bound to make them sleepier.'

'They're coming,' said Bruce. With a horrible jolt I saw them – two pirates, still just dark shapes a hundred metres in the distance, charging aft. They gave a shout. They seemed none too sleepy.

That was our plan scuppered. I'd taken too long at the controls, and now we'd been spotted.

'This way,' I said.

We ran, for a few terrifying moments, straight towards them. I was fumbling with the keys in my pocket, knowing them by feel, for each had a unique shape to my fingertips. At the landing bay doors I slipped the key into the lock and swung the door wide.

'In, in,' I said to Kate and Bruce. Bruce was slow, he could not run quickly. He would not be able to play this game for long. I locked the door after us. This was where Kate and Miss Simpkins had come aboard in their ornithopter – it seemed impossible it was just days ago. In the middle of the floor I saw the seam of the twin landing bay doors. All around were stacked enough crates and cargo and gear to provide shadows and hiding places aplenty.

'Hide,' I told them. 'Over there.'

'What about you?' Kate asked.

'I've got a bit of an idea,' I said.

'Tell me.'

'It's a bad idea,' I told her. 'You two just hide. And stay quiet.'

'What are you going to do?'

There was a banging at the door, and then the even more ominous jingling of keys. It would take them a few seconds to find the right one, but only a few.

'Go,' I hissed to Kate and Bruce. They disappeared behind some high crates on the far side of the bay, and I backed up towards the hull, looking hurriedly at the controls clustered there. It was a mad half-baked scheme I had, and I was afraid that just hearing myself say it to Kate would make me give up. I crouched down behind a row of crates. I fixed my eyes on the hatchway. I heard the right key slip into the lock and turn.

Slowly the hatch swung open and the doorway was filled with the dark bulk of the two pirates. They came through cautiously, their pistols and eyes sweeping the room. They paused, then took a few steps in, and started towards where Kate and Bruce were hiding.

With my fist, I knocked against the deck and made a dull but clearly audible clang. I saw the two pirates turn.

'Out where we can see you! Or we'll have to flush you out!'

They were both coming towards me. A few more footsteps.

Come on, now. Come on, you great lumps. Walk!

I kept my eyes on them, and reached back with my hand for the lever.

'I see him now!' said one of the pirates and let fly with his pistol. The bullet hit the metal floor and ricocheted about before whispering through the ship's skin. There was a sharp precise hiss of air.

Keep coming, I told them silently.

They would kill me. They would kill us all. I did not like doing it, but I had no choice.

They came, and I pulled the lever.

The landing bay doors split apart with startling speed. The two pirates lurched in horror as the floor beneath them parted and the air sucked at their bodies. The first stumbled and plunged into open air, his screams quickly swallowed up by the sky. The second pirate grabbed hold of the edge of the moving bay door, but as it rolled flush with the ship's underbelly, he was forced to let go, or have his hands severed. He let go, and fell. I moved forward cautiously, and looked down into the water, and saw two dots, bobbing on the blue surface. I ran back to the controls and pulled the lever up. The bay doors rolled back together.

'It's all right!' I called out to Kate and Bruce. 'They're gone.'

'Just stepped out for a moment, did they?' said Kate with a shaky laugh. Her face was very pale. 'That was a clever plan.'

'Well, I wasn't sure it would work.'

'Well done, Cruse,' said Bruce.

'That's two down,' said Kate. 'Six left.'

Six was better than eight, but still too many.

'What now?' Kate said.

'We wait. Until the sleeping elixir kicks in.'

'They didn't seem too sleepy,' said Bruce.

'No, they didn't.'

Anything could have gone wrong. 'Maybe they didn't eat the soup. Maybe it got too diluted, or maybe there wasn't enough, or they found out when they tasted it.' I didn't like to think of that; I could imagine what they'd do to Vlad if they thought he was trying to drug them.

'No, they ate it,' said Kate. 'I could smell it on them as they came into the room. Couldn't you?'

'I hadn't noticed.'

'It's extremely fishy.'

'We just need to give it more time then,' I said. 'I say we wait.'

'They'll send more,' said Kate, 'when your two skydivers don't come back.'

I hadn't thought of that.

'They can't send too many,' Bruce pointed out. 'They'll need to keep some with the hostages.'

They'd be nervous now, I realized. The ship was moving. There were people on board flying her. And their numbers were dwindling. I just hoped they didn't start killing the crew in panic. Why wasn't the sleeping elixir working faster? I tried to calm myself. We'd just dumped two pirates into the drink, that was good. The ship was aloft and steaming away from the island at a steady clip. That was good. Now all we had to do was wait another fifteen minutes or so, and then I'd get back into the vents and see if our pirates were asleep. At which point I would hardly be needed, for, without guards, the captain and crew could quickly free themselves and truss up the pirates.

I looked up suddenly.

'What's wrong?' said Kate.

'Ship's turning,' I said. I'd been afraid this would happen. 'Szpirglas must be in the control car.'

'I feel it now too,' said Bruce.

The ship's arc tightened. We were heading up into the wind. I needed no compass to know our course. 'He's taking us back to the island.'

'He'll be out cold soon,' said Kate.

'If he ate the soup,' I said, then remembered. 'He doesn't like fish! He said that when we ate with him. He wouldn't have touched it!'

'Can't you switch back to the auxiliary control room?' Kate asked.

'No, his controls override ours. We've got to stop him.'

'Or stop the engines,' said Bruce.

I looked at him, nodding.

'Close off the fuel lines,' said Bruce. 'We just need to get to the engine cars and shut the valves.'

'And the wind will keep carrying us away from the island, good.'

It wasn't ideal, to be blown along, powerless, but if the wind continued light, we wouldn't have too rough a ride. It was far better than letting Szpirglas take us back to the island and his waiting crew of pirates.

'Can you do the two aft cars?' I said to Bruce. I figured we had some time before Szpirglas sent anyone else to check on his first two pirates. 'Kate and I will go forward for the others.'

'Watch out for kitty,' said Bruce, and hobbled aft along the keel catwalk. Kate and I went forward until we reached the lateral gangways down to the two engine cars.

We started with the starboard. At the hull, I opened the hatch. Air swirled about us. A twelve-rung ladder led down through open air to the pod-shaped engine car. The ladder had only a railing on either side. It wasn't caged. If you fell, you fell.

'You want to wait up here?' I asked her.

She shook her head, pushed past me, and started climbing down, sensibly hooking one arm round the railing. There was little actual wind, but the ship's wind was considerable as we were moving along at quite a clip. Kate's tunic and harem pants were plastered against her. At the rear of the engine car, the four-bladed propeller whirled a pale brown circle in the air.

I started down after her. She was waiting for me inside the din of the engine car, looking a little breathless, but pleased with herself. The car was big enough to stand upright in, and was mostly taken up with machinery. A huge motor spun the propeller shaft, which jutted out the open end of the car. I looked all about. There were a lot of cables and rubber hosing. Of all the parts of the ship, this was the one I was least familiar with. I hadn't spent much time here. It was hideously noisy, for one thing, and the machinists didn't really like sharing the cramped quarters with anyone else. It wasn't what you'd call a social job. They wore leather helmets so they didn't go deaf and crazy.

Kate was watching me, which made me more flustered when I couldn't figure out which was the fuel line. The noise made my brain feel about as useful as scrambled egg.

'It would be this one, I think,' she shouted, pointing. I looked at the hosing coming in through the roof of the car. It fed through the inside of one of the struts that connected the car to the main hull. Kate traced the line with her finger through the air until she came to a circular tap. The shut-off valve.

'I think you're right,' I shouted gratefully. 'Thank you.'

I reached up and started turning. It took about ten full turns before it stopped. But the engine didn't. Kate looked crestfallen.

'There'll still be enough fuel in the engine to keep it

going a while,' I said hopefully. 'I just want to wait to make sure.'

'I'll go do the other one,' said Kate and before I could stop her she was climbing out of the engine car, up towards the ship. I had to give it to her, she wasn't one to sit idly by; she wanted to be a part of everything. I liked that about her.

I watched to make sure she was safely inside, and then turned back to the propeller. It was still whirling as fast as before, but then it gave a cough, and its ghostly circle became darker as the prop faltered and slowed. The pitch of the engine deepened; it was shutting down now for certain. Done!

I hurried over to the ladder, grabbed the rungs and when I looked up, a pirate was standing above me in the hatchway. His pistol rose. The bullet shrieked off the metal railing. I pulled back inside. It was a trap; and I was a fool not to have seen it. Szpirglas must have known we'd come to the cars to shut the engines down.

I peeped through a porthole and saw the pirate coming down the ladder. He came face forwards, one arm crooked round the railing, the other arm free so he could keep the gun trained on the engine car's hatch. My heart was beating so quickly I thought I might pass out. That hatch was the only way out –

But maybe not. I looked out the open end of the engine car. The propeller was slowing, though still spinning vigorously as the motor was starved for fuel. There was not much of a gap between the roof of the engine car and the spinning blade, half a metre maybe. I could see the shadow of the pirate growing in the hatchway; he was almost down the ladder now. I climbed up on the casing of the propeller shaft and started to haul myself up out on to the roof of the engine car. The propeller spun, centimetres from my head, sucking at my body. It wanted to pull me in and spit me out. On the roof there was not much to grab on to so I dug my fingernails into the metal seams and pulled and kicked with my legs, but not too much, for I didn't want them to get chopped off by the propeller. Below me I heard the pirate in the engine car, looking for me. It would not take him more than a few seconds to figure out where I'd gone. I dragged myself further on to the roof and hurriedly brought my legs up, the propeller blades whistling past the soles of my feet. I was flat on my belly, no handholds, no railing. I started to slither, arms and legs spread for grip. The air pulled at me. The ladder was two metres away. I stood in a low crouch and jumped for it. I caught the rungs with my hands and started to climb like a crazed orangutan, my eyes fixed on the hatchway of the *Aurora*.

I was reaching for the next rung when I was yanked down. My hands lost their grip and I slid, the rungs slamming against my ribs. I caught hold and turned and saw the pirate. He was at the base of the ladder, and he had me by the ankle with one hand, and with the other was taking aim at my head. I let go and slid right down at him, kicking like a twister. I was lucky and my foot caught his hand and knocked the pistol from his grip. I saw it go spinning towards the sea.

'Bastard!' the pirate roared, and I kicked again and got him in the teeth this time. He let go and I climbed furiously. At the top of the ladder I got one arm hooked around the handhold inside the hatch. But the pirate had me again by the leg and started pulling. I held tight, the metal handhold digging into my bone, and I knew he'd break my arm clean off. My eyes skittered around inside the ship. I saw an oil can within reach, grabbed it with my free hand, then reached down and squirted the pirate in the face. Cursing, he let go to wipe his eyes, and lost his grip. He fell heavily, crashing in a heap in the engine car. I hauled myself into the ship, lungs burning.

I slammed the hatch shut and locked it with my keys. With luck maybe the pirate would fall asleep and not mess with the engine. I leaned against the hatch to catch my breath.

That was another pirate down. Five left. Just five.

A finger of cold metal knocked against the side of my head.

'Hold up there, lad.'

I turned slowly.

Crumlin's pistol was against my skull.

20

AIRBORN

Crumlin had his free hand clenched around Kate's arm. He'd got us both. We stared at one another mutely, and in her eyes I saw all that I myself felt: a terrible weariness, and self-reproach that I'd been foolish enough to be caught; and fear too, not yet at a full boil, but on the brink. I hoped they didn't have Bruce as well.

'Well, isn't this an unpleasant surprise,' Crumlin said. He reeked of fish soup. It seemed to be steaming from every pore of his great sweaty body. 'When the captain's done with you, you'll wish you were back in that pit.'

He blinked and took a breath as if to steady himself. For just a moment his grip around the pistol faltered, and then he came back on full alert. But the sleeping elixir must finally be starting to work. I glanced at Kate, but couldn't tell if she'd noticed.

'Walk,' Crumlin shouted, shoving me with his gun.

We turned on to the keel catwalk. Forward, near the door to the passenger quarters, waited another pirate. I could see that it was the one-handed fellow, Rhino Hand.

'I've got the both of them,' Crumlin called out to him. 'Rathgar's got himself locked in the starboard engine car. Go back and get him out. And make sure both those engines are fired up again.'

Rhino Hand started walking towards us. He kept tilting off balance against the railing, even though the ship was flying steady.

'What's wrong with you!' Crumlin barked. 'Too much juice?'

Rhino Hand said nothing, just waved his hand dismissively and muttered inaudibly to himself. He almost tripped again.

'Cripes, man, you're a disgrace!' Crumlin roared, but when I looked back at Crumlin I saw his own eyes flicker. He lifted his pistol hand to his temple and jerked his eyes wide, as if trying to clear his blurry vision. I wondered when we should make our break for it.

Rhino Hand was still about ten metres away when something dropped down on to the catwalk between him and us.

It was a sleek beautiful bundle of misty fur and teeth and claws. It was the cloud cat, nostrils flaring.

'You little monster!' hissed Crumlin, squinting and blinking as though he'd been confronted with a ghostly apparition. He stopped walking. Rhino Hand had stopped too. The cat was looking from one to another. I could see its shoulder muscles tense and its rump drop and I knew it was about to lunge.

'I'll have you on my wall!' Crumlin roared, and raised his pistol.

The cloud cat jumped, up into the rigging above the catwalk, the wires and alumiron struts enough like branches that I wondered if it felt at home here after all. It leapt nimbly to the other side of the corridor, then back again, coming at me and Kate and Crumlin, shrieking. Even then I thought: It's magnificent.

Crumlin shoved Kate hard to the floor and tried to take aim with his pistol as the cloud cat bounded for us. But the pirate was unsteady on his feet, his vision misted by drink and sleeping elixir, and the pistol trembled in his fist.

He fired.

He missed the cloud cat, but hit Rhino Hand down the corridor. The pirate clutched at his neck, and a dark stain of blood seeped between his fingers as he sagged to the floor, cursing his life away. Crumlin fired again and again missed. I threw my whole weight against him and he was dopey enough to stagger off balance. His gun clattered to the floor.

'Come on!' I yelled at Kate, grabbing her hand and hauling her up.

But it was Crumlin the cloud cat wanted. Glancing back over my shoulder, I saw the pirate sluggishly scrabbling about for his gun as the cloud cat leapt at him. Maybe it remembered Crumlin from the island, and was hungry for revenge. Maybe it just liked his fishy odour. The creature engulfed Crumlin's head and torso with its own body, a whirling bundle of fur and claws. Crumlin roared and threw up his arms to pound the creature off, but the cloud cat nimbly retreated into the wiring overhead, escaping the bludgeoning force of Crumlin's fists. He was bleeding badly from the shoulder and neck. Then the cloud cat lunged in again, quickly slashing with its claws and teeth, before again retreating beyond Crumlin's clumsy blows. He turned and lumbered off, but the cloud cat launched itself at his back and knocked him over. He scarcely tried to get up.

After that, I stopped turning back to look, and Kate and I just ran as hard as we could along the keel catwalk towards the ship's stern. I did not know what the cloud cat would do when it was finished with Crumlin. I couldn't imagine it still being hungry after feeding on him, but maybe this was not simply a matter of hunger. Maybe it was like those wild bears or lions who, after a taste of human blood, cannot forget it, and go on craving it madly their whole lives.

I wanted to get back to Bruce. I shouldn't have left him alone, not in his current state. He was supposed to meet us in the port cargo bay. In my head I counted pirates. Five were gone now, that left three; two probably in the starboard lounge keeping guard, but getting sleepier by the second, if Crumlin and Rhino Hand were any guide. I hoped it wouldn't be long until Captain Walken and the officers could make a move and overpower the guards.

But Szpirglas, who would not eat fish, would be in

the control car, and wide awake, and steering us back to the island. I could only hope that Bruce had managed to shut down both his engines.

But as we neared the aft-engine gangways, I heard the telltale vibration of the port propeller. The starboard one was silent at least. Maybe Bruce was just having trouble shutting down the port engine. I felt a queasy wave slosh through my guts. I stopped, suddenly afraid to turn down the gangway. I made Kate stand back and then carefully poked my head around the corner.

Bruce lay crumpled on the floor. Blood pooled stickily about his head. I rushed to him, bent down and felt for his pulse along his jaw, but just by the cold touch of him I knew he was already dead.

'Oh,' Kate gasped, kneeling beside me. 'Oh.'

At first I thought maybe the cloud cat had taken him, but then I saw the precise bullet hole in the side of his skull. He'd been shot at close range.

From the starboard engine car I heard the propeller suddenly kick back to life. Footsteps rang on the access ladder.

'Run!' I told Kate. 'Go to the cargo holds and hide!'

I heard her protest, but didn't wait. I ran down the gangway towards the starboard engine car. If I could get to the hatch in time, I could slam it shut and lock the pirate on the outside. It was Szpirglas himself, and he was nearly at the top of the ladder, about to come through into the ship. He saw me. I grabbed the hatch and swung it, but he caught it against his shoulder before I could close it. I heaved with all my weight, but it was no good, he was the heavier and stronger by far, and with a final powerful push he sent me sprawling backwards.

I scrambled up and ran before he could take proper aim, and heard the bullet whispering past through the rigging. I careened round the corner on to the keel catwalk and was relieved to see no sign of Kate.

I jumped on to the companion ladder and started crawling up towards the axial catwalk. Szpirglas stood below me. I was an easy target, straight overhead, so I jumped off the ladder and into the bracing wires where I was partially hidden behind cables and the edges of the great shimmering gas bags. Up I went like a spider, Szpirglas's bullets whizzing past me and slicing through the goldbeater's skin and releasing small mango-scented geysers of hydrium. I heard him cursing and then his boots on the ladder and knew he was coming up too, and just as fast as me, for the ladder was easier work than monkeying through the rigging. Cold hard thin wire bit at my raw feet.

Somehow I reached the axial catwalk first, grabbed a wrench from an open locker, and heaved it at Szpirglas' head as he came up the companionway. It struck him in the temple and he cursed, but it bought me a few seconds more to toss the rest of the contents of the locker at his head, including a pot of patching glue which splashed on to his face and blunderbuss. He clambered on to the catwalk. He was not sleepy. He had eaten none of Vlad's fish soup. His eyes blazed with a fury I'd never seen in any man before.

He raised his blunderbuss at me and fired, but the gun only gave a thick gluey clunk, for its snout was clogged with glue. Szpirglas cursed and lunged at me. The only way for me to go was up again to the aft crow's-nest. So up I went.

I reached the glass observation dome, flung it open, and hauled myself out on to the ship's back. I had to squint fiercely, for the sun was ablaze in the sky. Blue sea stretched all round, and dead ahead was the island. We'd reach her in less than ten minutes by my reckoning.

Crouching, I hurried forwards, one hand looped around the guide wire. At the mid-point I glanced back and there was still no sign of Szpirglas at the hatchway. I hesitated. Maybe he was coming up to the forward crow's-nest to lie in wait for me. I was scuppered, not knowing which way to go.

The forward observation hatch was already flung open, and as I stared in disbelief, a white shape sprang out from it.

The cloud cat was on the ship's back. It crouched there, fur matted against its body by the wind, looking all around. It had not been in the sky since the day of its birth. It was not interested in me at the moment, perhaps had not even spotted me, hunched down motionless against the ship's skin. But I dared not go closer. Its muzzle was stained red from feasting on

Crumlin. It was blocking my only escape route.

Hurriedly I turned back to the aft observation hatch. Perhaps Szpirglas had given up. He had the ship to fly after all. He needed to land her on the island.

When I was not twenty metres from the aft hatch, Szpirglas climbed out through it, on to the ship's back. In his hand was a knife. The sun winked off its serrated edge. His face was impassive, eyes focussed on me, intent on the job ahead of him.

It was over. There was nowhere left to run. I didn't know if Szpirglas saw the cloud cat behind me, for it was hunkered down flush against the ship's skin and my body was directly in line with it. I didn't know which would be worse, being savaged by the creature, or stabbed by Szpirglas. It shamed me, but I had to admit I was tired out. I was finished with running, especially when it was all futile. There were two paths and each took me to my death.

Szpirglas advanced towards me, his balance expert. I noticed the wind picking up some, and realized that he must have taken the *Aurora* lower in preparation for landing. The island was still a way off, but the *Aurora* would surely collide with the central mountain if left unchecked. Even now I didn't want to see my ship harmed, especially when all aboard might still be saved. It might be just me who was to perish. And Bruce already. Poor Bruce.

'Quite an escape artist, aren't you?' Szpirglas was only a few paces from me. 'You're an impressive lad. If you hadn't defied me so, I might have offered you a home on my ship.'

'This is my home,' I told him dully. And I'd never felt it more than now. How I'd bundled everything into this ship, all the good feeling I had, all my sense of belonging was beneath my feet, every hope of happiness. And I thought that at least I would die here at home.

'Just tell me, lad, for I've got a craving to know. How did you get out of the hydrium pit?'

'I flew,' I said savagely, hating him.

He chuckled darkly. 'Then fly again.'

Both his hands took hold of my shoulders and he gave me a mighty shove. My arms windmilled uselessly and my feet left the ship's back and I fell.

I fell backwards and instinctively opened my arms, spread my legs. I could feel the air pouring over me, felt how it parted for my head and over my shoulders and over my chest and down my torso to trail off my legs. I tucked an arm and rolled my shoulders so I was falling face first towards the ship's stern.

I was not frightened.

This was how my father fell.

It was the most natural thing in the world. I knew it would be like this. It was very smooth and slow. I had time to look down at the sea. I even looked back over my shoulder and saw Szpirglas watching me, and the cloud cat, still crouching further forward. I gazed ahead and saw the ship's great fins coming towards me. I would soar clear over the horizontal fin on the starboard side. Then I would be free of the ship and it would be just me and the air.

If my father could do it, I could do it. I was born in the air.

Some part of my brain, though, must have known I did not want to overshoot the ship. I needed to go down. I closed my legs, folded my arms back against my sides, tilted my head and shoulders, and plunged towards the fin. Everything was starting to speed up, and for the first time, I felt fear. I fanned my legs wide and pushed my arms forward to break my fall. I hit the great flat fin and felt the skin on the palms of my hands evaporate as I tried to slow myself. I was in a scalding skid. The fin's edge soared towards me. I kept my chin up so I could see. The elevator flaps were coming fast.

There was a narrow gap between the flaps and the fin itself, and I drove my hands and arms into it, grabbed hold of a metal strut and held on. My whole body jerked and buckled and my arms shrieked with pain as I came to a violent halt. I'd been spun around so I was now facing towards the ship's bow, my legs and torso flattened against the elevator flap, the wind smacking at my face.

I could not fly. I had crashed. I was not lighter than air after all.

I'd fallen and a great shame seeped through me.

I was heavy as stone.

All my life I'd told myself I was light and could soar

412

free of things. I was light and I could outrun sadness. I could fly away and keep flying for ever.

But I could never catch up with my father. He had fallen like Gilgamesh and I had not been there to save him with an all-powerful Enkidu hand. He was gone, well and truly gone, and now everything had caught up with me: all the years of sailing away from my family, and my sadness.

I knew I could not hold on for long, and there was no way to scramble back up the fin. My hands would lose strength, my fingers would let go and I would slide off for one last inglorious freefall to the waves.

Up above me on the ship's back I could see Szpirglas, standing tall, turned towards me. It would not be hard to see me in the full daylight, my dark shirt against the ship's silver skin. The cloud cat was there too. I wanted to look at this creature rather than Szpirglas.

Then an amazing thing happened. It didn't seem possible that the cloud cat could have slipped, so it must have jumped of its own free will. Its wings flared and it glided off the ship's back. But the crimped left wing did not open fully and the cloud cat slewed through the sky, falling too fast.

It was falling all over again, just as it had the moment it was born. Only this time there was no island beneath to break the fall.

Come on. Fly now.

Somehow, despite its crimped wing, the cloud cat levelled off. I saw its wings move up and then down in a power stroke, and it lifted a bit. Gradually it gained more altitude. It was still tilty in the air, hadn't quite worked out yet how to steer and stay level.

But it was flying.

It soared away from the *Aurora*, trying out its wings, playing with this new thing called flight. It did a couple of clumsy turns, but with every second was getting better. I was laughing and crying and I think I must've been a little mad with the pain and knowing my own death was close, and yet I no longer felt sad or afraid. It was so good to see the cloud cat fly, back in its own element. It was never meant to be landlocked. I kept my eyes fixed on the cat until I could see it no more.

I smiled and closed my eyes and put my face down on the ship's cool skin, soothing my fevered cheek. I wanted to sleep now. But through the ship's skin I could hear a thumping vibration, growing stronger.

Groggily, I opened my eyes. I looked up and with a shock saw Szpirglas, coming towards me. He'd found a safety line, had used it to rappel over the ship's side to the fin. He was crouched low, making his way back to the elevator flap where I lay.

Why bother, I wondered. I would fall soon.

He made his way carefully towards me, gripping his safety line in one hand.

'If I turn my back on you,' he shouted above the wind, 'you might appear again to vex me!'

He kicked at my fingers with his boot. They had so little feeling in them that I didn't even cry out in pain.

Somehow I kept them locked around the metal strut.

'Let go, boy! Do I have to break all of you?'

'You'll never break all of me,' I said.

With the last of my strength I rolled to one side and swung my legs hard against his feet. It took him by surprise and he staggered off balance and skidded on to his knees. The knife lurched from his free hand and was whipped away by the wind. The safety line jerked loose from his other hand. He started slipping off the fin, and in disbelief I thought I'd defeated him. But at the last moment he snatched the rope back into his fist. He stood tall. He came towards me, and the anger in his face was terrible to behold. His booted foot drew back.

Something flew past him, low over his head. A flash of pale fur, a huge span of wing. I blinked and squinted and looked up and saw a winged sky, dozens and dozens of cloud cats, streaming past the ship, heading for the island. They were flying low over the *Aurora*'s spine, wheeling around her flanks and skimming beneath her belly, as if curious about this huge airborne thing.

Szpirglas must have seen the shine of amazement in my eyes, for he too lifted his face to look. A huge group of them wheeled over the fins, and I could feel the wind from their mighty wings as they passed, and couldn't help laughing aloud in delight at this glorious turbulence. The sight of so many of them! It was what Kate's grandfather had seen from his balloon.

Not birds, he'd written. Amazing creatures.

One of the cloud cats dipped lower than the rest and its rear claws, maybe without meaning to, struck Szpirglas on the shoulder. His feet went out from under him and he skittered down along the elevator flap headfirst. The safety line was plucked from his fist and this time he did not regain it. He shouted out and tried to clutch at the fin's edge, but he was too late.

Down he went, spinning through the air.

And I thought: His boy. His poor boy.

The cloud cats saw him and dived for him all together, predators locking on to prey. One snatched him up in its claws, slowing him for a moment before dropping him again, while another took a bite from his neck. And so they volleyed Szpirglas amongst themselves, tearing at him and feeding off him as he fell.

Szpirglas' safety line danced before my face. I lifted my broken hand to it and tried to take it, but my grip was so weak I was afraid I would not be able to hold it. With a grunt I released my good hand and grabbed hold as well, and to this day I do not know exactly where I found the strength, but I hauled myself along the rope, hand over hand up to the ship's back. Maybe it was just my will to live, or maybe concern for the ship and all aboard her, or maybe it was my father's spirit, still free in the air, passing through me and shunting me along, guiding me back on course.

Before I lowered myself through the crow's-nest hatch, I looked once more at all the cloud cats wheeling high, and there, at the edge of the flock, was ours, Kate's and mine. The one with the crimped wing, the one that fell. She skirted along the outside of the group and then was absorbed into it and she was one of them finally.

But the island was coming up, and its mountain, and the *Aurora* was too low, and I was sure we would not clear the peak. The weight of both Szpirglas and me on the elevators must have tipped the ship even lower into its fatal course.

There was no one at the controls.

It all passed in a blur: I lurched down ladder after ladder, staggering forward along the catwalks to the control car. I ran into the great glass sweep of the bridge. As I'd feared, it was empty. Through the front windows I saw the island and her gaunt mountain, looming large. We would surely crash. The arrays of controls hummed and glowed expectantly around me. For a moment I froze, but then imagined the captain's voice in my head.

'Take her up five degrees, Mr Cruse.'

I did not think of anything else, not Bruce, not Kate.

I seized the elevator wheel and turned it gently, watching the inclinometer on the console before me, but also feeling the ship's floor beneath my feet, knowing instinctively how steep our climb needed to be. I wanted all her engines, but saw from the board we only had two, and no time to mess with starting up the others.

I increased our pitch a little more, and saw the island and her mountains slowly dropping away beyond the bridge's wraparound windows. But would it be fast enough?

'Mind the engines, Mr Cruse,' I imagined the captain saying. The climb was a steep one on only two engines, and I was careful to watch the gauges to make sure she did not overheat carrying such a load.

I rushed to the rudder wheel next and turned her so we began to swivel away from the mountain. I glanced over at the gas boards. We still had almost full lift, a little leakage from cells two and four, from the pirates' bullets no doubt, but that was not urgent business right now.

It would be a close call. I angled the ship as much as I dared, and turned her hard over, and then there was nothing more I could do. I watched out of the windows and saw the mountain coming, and we were close enough to see the texture and colour of the stone, and we were turning and climbing, turning and climbing, and at last the nose of the ship pulled clear.

'That's my girl,' I told the ship.

We would not crash.

'Put her on a heading of 165, Mr Cruse, please.'

'Very good, sir,' I muttered to myself before I realized I was no longer imagining the captain's voice.

I turned and saw him standing in the doorway with the first officers and Baz, and Kate was there too, hurrying towards me with the biggest, nicest smile I'd ever seen.

'Sir!' I said, giving him a salute. 'Sorry but she needed bringing up, sir. The mountain.'

'Very good, Mr Cruse.' The other crew came in and started taking up their positions and duties and I stood back from the rudder wheel, but the captain looked at me and said simply, 'Carry on, Mr Cruse. Take us to our new heading, please.'

'Yes, sir,' I said.

'Thank you, Mr Cruse. Miss de Vries has told us everything. We've trussed up three pirates, and I gather you've taken care of the others?'

'Yes, sir.'

'Very good, then.' He put his hand on my shoulder as I completed the turn. 'There we are. Straighten out. Excellent. You were born to it, Mr Cruse, no question. You're flying now.'

SIX MONTHS LATER

21

AT ANCHOR

It was difficult to get close to the skeleton, there was such a crowd of people around it, the men in their tall top hats and the women with an abundance of fruit and flowers and stuffed tropical birds sprouting from their wide-brimmed headgear. It was like being back in the jungle all over again, only smellier, with enough colognes and perfumes and toilet waters to choke an anaconda.

I had to wait quite a while for the crowds to thin before I could get near the display case. And there it was: the reassembled skeleton of the cloud cat. It seemed bigger than it had when Kate and I first discovered it in the tree. They'd built a wire frame for it, so it didn't look crumpled any more. It was poised and proud and alert.

'It's good to see you with your feet on the ground, Mr Cruse.'

I turned and saw her. I must say I was a bit in awe of her after sitting in on her lecture. She'd stood there before her Lumière projector and showed her photos of the skeleton and explained them, and then described our encounters with the cloud cat in the middle of the

Pacificus. When she answered questions from the audience, her voice never shook and she rarely stumbled on her words or hesitated. Quite apart from that, she looked wonderful in a fitted striped suit with dark lapels, and her hair chestnut and glowing.

'Hello,' I said. 'You're famous now.'

She laughed. 'No, not really.'

'That was quite a round of applause.'

'Well, I'm popular with the general public,' she said wryly. 'Most of the important scientists have stayed away. They think it's a freak show. I've heard there's one group already writing a paper claiming the whole thing's a hoax.'

'How could they?' I asked indignantly.

'No amount of proof is enough for some people.' She shrugged. She seemed to be taking it very well.

We stood looking at one another and I didn't know how best to greet her. Six months ago, when we'd parted in Sydney, she'd given me a tight hug and cried, but now we were all grown-up and composed. I would have liked another hug but there were so many people around I felt self-conscious.

'Where's Miss Simpkins?' I asked, for at the moment I could think of nothing better to say.

'Oh, she's here somewhere.'

'I'm amazed she stayed on with you.'

'Well, we've come to an understanding, Marjorie and I. I never told my parents how hopeless she was aboard the *Aurora*, and she gives me quite a bit of freedom now.

Like talking to young men, unsupervised,' she said with a mischievous smile.

'I hope you're not making a habit of that,' I said. 'Has she forgiven you for drugging her?'

'She does watch me quite carefully when I pour the tea,' Kate remarked. 'Speaking of tea, why don't we have some? We can go to the Senior Common Room.'

'Does that mean you're a senior someone now?' I asked, amazed.

'No, no, I just get a special pass during the exhibition. It's very nice.'

She led me out of the exhibition hall and through long, high-ceilinged galleries filled with dead animals in glass cases. I'd never seen so many dead animals all in one place. It seemed the museum had one of everything that had ever walked, crawled, flown or slithered across the planet. Then Kate turned down a dark, wood-panelled corridor and led me to the very end. There was an enormous door with a knob in the middle and a small brass button to one side. Kate pressed the button and almost at once the door was opened by a steward.

'Good afternoon, Miss de Vries,' he said, opening the door wide. 'Some tea?'

'Thank you very much, Roberts.'

It was a grand room, as Kate had promised, and filled with light from an entire wall of floor-to-ceiling windows. Polished wood and leather and brass gleamed everywhere. Old important moustached gentlemen sat in armchairs reading the newspapers and sipping port and exhaling yellow cigar fumes up to the high ceiling fans. Several of the gentlemen looked up at Kate as she entered, but none of them acknowledged her, except to give a low grumble of distaste.

'Smoky old farts,' I muttered.

'As you can see, I'm wildly popular with the scientific community,' Kate whispered to me. 'They don't know it yet but I'm going to have their jobs and offices before long.'

'I hope you do,' I said.

A warm spring breeze blew through the open French doors.

'Let's sit outside,' I said.

We went out on to the terrace and sat down at a table and looked over the river. On the other side was the Champ de Mars and the Eiffel Tower.

'How are you enjoying Paris?' she asked me.

This was the way grown-ups talked, I thought, and felt sad. We seemed uncomfortable with one another, now that we were in civilized clothes in a civilized room in a great city, ready to drink tea out of fine china.

'Paris is grand,' I said, 'as grand a place as I've ever seen on earth.'

'On earth.'

'That's right.'

'But aloft is still best?'

'Of course.'

She smiled. 'Tell me about the Air Academy.'

There'd been a hefty reward, it turned out, for

information leading to the capture of Szpirglas and his pirates. Once we reached harbour, we were able to give the co-ordinates of their island to the Sky Guard. They'd sent a large detachment to the pirates' base and captured the lot of them. I'd asked about Szpirglas' son, and all they would tell me was that he'd been placed in an orphanage, and was being taken care of. I hoped he was all right, that he still had someone to tell him wonderful stories.

My share of the reward was more than enough for tuition to the Academy, and with letters of reference from Captain Walken, I was offered a place starting in the spring term. The remainder of the reward money took care of my mother and sisters, while I was a student and sending back no salary from the *Aurora*. And there was even some money set aside, in a big brick bank in Lionsgate City. I'd never thought I'd have my own bank account.

'I'm learning a lot here,' I said, 'though I kind of wish there was more flying and less sitting in the classroom.'

'Well, I hope you're paying attention,' she told me, rather severely.

'Of course I'm paying attention!'

'This is not an opportunity you want to squander.'

'You sound like a blinking teacher!'

She smiled, rather pleased about that. 'I'm just practising being stern. I think you need to be stern for people to take you seriously. Especially in public debate.'

'I'm sure you'll be terrifying,' I said.

Our tea arrived with a three-tiered platter of little sandwiches and scones and patisseries.

'On the island,' Kate said, pouring me a cup of tea, 'you worried you'd never be able to be happy on the ground.'

I blushed to think of that moment in the cave when I'd panicked, and all my fears had spilled out. But I was also surprised and pleased that she'd remembered a conversation we'd had so long ago.

'But you're happy here,' Kate said, looking at me.

'As happy as I can be, at anchor.' I took a deep breath. 'I'm getting better at standing still.'

It had not been easy. When I'd first started at the Academy there'd been many bad, sleepless nights. I missed my bunk on the *Aurora*, and Baz and Captain Walken and all the crew. I missed being in motion. And I missed my father, more acutely than I ever had before. There'd been plenty of times I'd been so lonely and miserable I'd wanted to quit and return to the *Aurora*. But then, unexpectedly one night, I'd dreamed of my father, even though I was landlocked. I was flying alongside the *Aurora*, and he'd come and joined me, and when I woke up that morning, everything was different. As long as I could still dream about him, I knew everything would be all right. I didn't need to be aloft to find happiness. It could find me wherever I was: on the *Aurora*, or here in Paris, or back home with Mom and Isabel and Sylvia.

'I'm glad,' Kate said. She didn't need to say it. Her eyes said it all for her: she really was happy for me.

'What about you?' I asked.

'Oh, I'm having a grand old time,' she said. 'For now I get to be toasted and toured. I've got three more museums who want the skeleton this year.'

'You'll be insufferable by then,' I said.

'Probably. Really, I need you to come along and smarten me up regularly.'

'And what do your parents think of all this?'

'I think they're' – she paused and seemed a little bewildered – 'I think they're proud of me, you know.'

I smiled. 'Very good then.'

'Makes a nice change, doesn't it? They've agreed to let me go to university next year.'

'That's fantastic!'

'Well, I think they were rather forced into it after all this. Think how bad the press would be if it slipped out that all my dazzling promise was to be squished by brutish parents. It would embarrass my mother no end.'

'It looks like you're to get everything you set your sights on,' I said.

'And you too,' she replied.

We clinked teacups.

'To us,' Kate said. 'We're fabulous.'

'Look,' I said, pointing at the sky. 'She's coming in now.'

'That's not the *Aurora*, is it?' Kate asked.

'It is. She's doing a transcontinental. All the way to the

Siberian Sea, and then across to San Francisco. She's been completely refitted since the autumn. New engines and outer skin.'

We watched as the ship turned slowly and came in to dock at the top of the Eiffel Tower. The summit had been equipped with a special mooring mast, and now, from the upper observation deck, a long, articulated gangway swung up and locked with the *Aurora*'s underbelly. I could see passengers coming on and off.

I gave a sigh. 'I just hope there's a position on her when I finish here.'

'I'm sure Captain Walken will do everything he can.'

We fell silent for a moment, and I felt awkward again. On the island or the ship I'd never felt tongue-tied like this, and I hated it.

'I'm sorry I've had this so long,' Kate said suddenly. She reached into her purse and brought out my father's compass.

'You didn't wrap it up in your knickers?' I asked.

She flushed a little.

'Thank you,' I said, taking it back. Holding it again, I realized how much I'd missed it. But I was also sorry it would no longer be in her hands. I'd liked to think of her holding it, watching the needle spin north.

'Don't want you veering off course,' Kate said.

And then suddenly we could talk again as we used to. We were just Matt and Kate again, walking through the forest and whacking away ferns and watching out for devilish little red snakes. We talked about the *Aurora*, and the pirates and the island. Neither of us mentioned the kiss in the forest, though I had thought about it often, and sitting across from her, there was nothing I wanted to do more. But there she was in her suit and hat, so prim and newly famous and much more ladylike than I remembered her, and I just could not imagine it. I liked her better in her torn harem pants, her face streaked with dirt.

'He was really brave,' I said. 'Bruce.'

She nodded gravely. 'He was in a lot of pain, and he still kept going. I don't like thinking about it.'

I remembered him often. We couldn't have escaped without Bruce to help us. What made it worse was that I'd always resented him. And what made me saddest of all was that he died before he figured out what his dream was, what he most loved and wanted to do with his life.

'I'm going back, you know,' Kate said. 'To the island.'

I wasn't surprised. 'When?'

'As soon as I can raise money for a proper expedition. The pirates are all cleared off now, they say. We'll need to charter a ship. Will you come?'

'Of course,' I said. 'I'll fly you there myself if you can wait two years.'

'I'd like that,' she said. 'Tell me again how you saw all of them.'

She leaned against the table on her folded arms

and listened attentively as I told her about all the cloud cats flying around the ship, dozens and dozens of them.

'She rejoined her flock,' she said.

'Yes.'

'Do you think her mother was still there?'

'I don't know. I suppose she would be, wouldn't she? Unless she died in the meantime.'

'That's very satisfying, isn't it? A family reunion.'

'Heartwarming. Just remember,' I warned her, 'our pretty cloud cat would have no qualms about lunching on you.'

'Oh, I know.'

'They are beautiful, though,' I said.

'Beautiful creatures,' she agreed. 'I wish I'd seen the whole flock.'

'You will.'

We both looked out over the river in silence.

'Baz is getting married this summer,' I told her. 'I promised to sail down for the wedding. He's asked me to be best man.'

'That's quite an honour.'

'I feel too young to be a best man,' I admitted.

'He's lucky to have a friend like you,' she said.

'Have you decided where you'll study?'

'Not yet. There's Lionsgate City, London, Constantinople, and of course here in Paris.'

'Really?' I said.

'Yes, the university here is very well regarded.'

432

'Look, she's about to cast off,' I said, leaning against the balustrade and pointing to the *Aurora*.

I thought of Captain Walken aboard, all the crew I'd lived with, my bunk and little porthole through which I could see the passing clouds and stars.

'She really does look sensational, doesn't she?'

Kate rolled her eyes.

'You and your airships,' she said. 'I honestly wonder if there's room in your head for anything else.'

'I think Paris would be a grand place to study,' I told her.

'Do you?' she asked.

'I do. The university's just on the other side of the river from the Air Academy. I've walked past it many times.'

She smiled. 'Well, I'll certainly consider it very carefully then.'

Just then, the *Aurora* cast off from the Eiffel Tower and was free again, gracefully rising and turning in the wind to begin a new journey.

'That's my girl,' I said, and took her hand.

SKYBREAKER

Kenneth Oppel

Another thrilling adventure story set high in the sky – at altitudes never before explored.

Matt Cruse has been accepted at the Airship Academy, his days as cabin boy over for the moment. He has difficulty settling down to life on land, but is helped by the fact that Kate is in Paris too.

During a training flight aboard the freighter *Flotsam*, Matt helps save the ship when it is caught in a deadly storm over the Indian Ocean, and thrust to dangerously high altitudes. There, Matt spies a frozen airship, drifting aimlessly at 20,000 feet – it's the legendary ghost ship *Hyperion*. Rumoured to be carrying great wealth, the *Hyperion* left harbour fifty years ago, but never reached her destination. No wreckage was ever found . . . until now.

And it is not just gold the *Hyperion* is reputed to carry, but a collection of strange zoological specimens. Kate is desperate to recover them, and she and Matt embark on the most dangerous of treasure hunts . . .

SILVERWING

Kenneth Oppel

Shade – the runt of the bat colony – is determined to prove himself on the long and dangerous migration south to Hibernaculum. But he is bolder than he is strong, and when he strays from his mother and is lost in a storm, he is on his own.

He knows he must rejoin his colony, and so begins an epic journey – from the pigeon stronghold in the city's spires to the rat kingdom in the caverns of the ground. He meets Marina, a Brightwing; Zephyr, a mysterious albino who can see into the future and the past; and Goth, a formidable giant jungle bat. But who can he trust – and where will his journey end?

'*Silverwing* is top-notch fantasy adventure writing. Go for it.' *The Daily Telegraph*

Also from Hodder Children's Books

SUNWING

Kenneth Oppel

Shade, a young Silverwing bat, discovers a
mysterious human building which houses a huge
forest. Home to thousands of bats, the indoor forest
is as warm as a summer night, teeming with insect
food, and free from the deadly owls. Paradise? Then
why are bats disappearing without trace?

Soon, Shade and his friend, Marina, are swept up in
a perilous adventure that takes them far south to
the jungle home of Goth, the diabolical king of the
cannibal bats. Shade must use all his cunning to
rescue his long-lost father – and prevent Goth from
creating eternal night . . .

'Cracking stories, brimming with adventure . . .
never faltering when it comes to thrills and page-
turning power.' *Carousel*

Also from Hodder Children's Books

FIREWING

Kenneth Oppel

The forest splits and heaves in a terrible quake, and Griffin – a Silverwing newborn – is sucked down a fissure deep into the earth. Shade, Griffin's father, soon realizes that his son has been drawn into the Underworld, and embarks on the most dangerous of journeys to rescue him . . .

But something else is hunting Griffin – a deadly foe Shade hoped he would never see again. Who will find Griffin first? And who will survive to embark on the perilous journey back to the land of the living?

'The third book in a riveting saga . . . capable of enthralling both 9–11s, as well as an older audience.'
Achuka website